Rough
Exposure

SCEPTRE

Rough Exposure

KATE SHARAM

SCEPTRE

First published in 1998 by Hodder and Stoughton
A division of Hodder Headline PLC
A Sceptre book

A CIP catalogue record is available from the British Library.

ISBN 0 340 69510 2

Typeset by Palimpsest Book Production Limited,
Polmont, Stirlingshire
Printed and bound in Great Britain by
Clays Ltd, St Ives PLC

Hodder and Stoughton
A division of Hodder Headline PLC
338 Euston Road
London NW1 3BH

With love to my son, Richard

ACKNOWLEDGEMENTS

I would like to thank David Williams for his advice about photography and the Torbay *Herald Express* for an insight into the world of regional journalism.

1

The scream died before it was born. Its life strangled by the hand that seized the girl's hair.

Other hands came at her.

They tore off her school bag and her coat, her new coat, her birthday coat, her costly coat, and trampled it under their feet until it lay dead and unrecognisable in the dirt. Her grief was unbearable, unthinkable. Then the scissors came out, great green kitchen shears with teeth like a shark's. They threatened her hair but knew what hurt, so they ate off the sleeves of her coat. The two lifeless tubes, detached and discarded as dross, and she wished they had cut off her own arms instead.

All the time, the voices. The loud cutting voices that tore her apart as easily as the coat. A sudden thump in her back sent her sprawling to her knees, pain fierce and raw down her spine.

'Lick it.'

A foot thrust under her chin. The black trainer she had yearned for. Its Nike flash obscured by mud.

She licked it.

But it wasn't enough. Not even that was enough.

A knee in the nape of her neck knocked her face to the floor, but she twisted and turned before they could trample her like a bug underfoot. She pushed up to her knees, and then to her feet, seeking a path of escape. She put the wall at her back to prevent rear-attack and faced them and their foul and filthy words. They insulted her hair and her breasts, her clothes and her breasts, her parents and her breasts. Her breasts. Too big and too soft, a betrayal of the body inside her head and she hated them with the hatred of the young.

A hand snaked out and clutched one, squeezed and squished it as if it were Play-Doh and she thought she would be sick. To vomit up her life and have it over with.

'No,' she screamed. 'Leave me alone.'

And then they hit her.

2

The camera flashed and Anthea Courtney fell off the stool.

The movement was a silent surrender of control that took Jodie Buxton by surprise. She knew she should have seen it coming, but she hadn't. She had been too intent herself. Too preoccupied. Totally seduced by the shadows that draped their pliant greys in the curves of each angle of flesh and bone. Behind her the large room loomed in a semi-darkness that seemed content to sit and watch the fierce pool of light that encircled her sister on the floor. Jodie laughed, a soft regretful sound in the high-ceilinged flat, and decided that maybe that last vodka of Anthea's had been a mistake.

'For heaven's sake, get a grip. You're useless. If I were paying you, I'd demand my money back.'

'But you're not paying me, you cheapskate.' Anthea lay in a comfortable, loose-limbed heap on the goatskin rug, showing no inclination to regain the vertical.

The skin of her bare arms was as pale as candle-wax and still had that translucent unused look of a teenager's, despite the years of high living in London. Jodie had wanted to capture that vulnerability on camera, that tantalising newness that was quite distinct from the knowing, smoky grey eyes, but it was as illusive as it was unexpected in a woman of nearly thirty. The soft swathe of extra padding round the hips and stomach of her older sister was equally new to Jodie's gaze. Too many business lunches and boozy evenings. Like this one.

Not that there could have been too many like this one, Jodie thought and giggled like a two-year-old. It was the fault of that vintage port, of course, that had settled heavily on her stomach, as dangerous as a primed landmine.

'Anthea,' she said in the exact cadences of her father, 'you're drunk.'

'True.' Anthea smiled at her sister sweetly from the floor.

'You're useless.'

'And alone.'

Anthea's smile remained pinned in place on her immaculately made-up lips, but, as if from a different time and place, two huge tears formed in her eyes and dribbled down her cheeks, carrying spidery tracks of mascara with them.

Jodie abandoned any thought of taking more photographs and flopped down on the floor beside her sister. The rug felt silky under her hand, like a sleeping animal, and she almost expected it to purr. Or growl. She patted it to soothe its feelings; just in case. The feeling of life in it was irresistible and she understood for the first time why her sister had them scattered in every room.

'Oh God, Jodie, we're a mess,' Anthea moaned and let her eyes fall shut to blank out the world. Her lips moved as if to say something more, but before any sound came out, she was asleep.

'Speak for yourself,' Jodie murmured gently and stroked the delicate head of long tresses that were the mirror image of her own, so that they fanned out black as a crow's wing on the rug.

It wasn't meant to turn out like this. Anthea had invited her up to London to come and inspect her new flat overlooking the river and Jodie had disentangled the strings that held her in Westonport and come. It was not often she got the chance to snatch, however briefly, a piece of her older sister's luxury lifestyle. And it had been fun. No doubt of that. Anthea had not treated her like some dumb hick from the backwoods and had introduced her to the other dinner guests as 'My sister, the photographer.' That had been fine until they asked what magazine she worked for and whether she had done the Paris shows.

'One day, sis. One day. Just wait.' Waiting was not something either of them was good at.

She smoothed out a tiny wrinkle that had tightened above Anthea's nose, somewhat shorter and broader than her own, and felt the skin twitch under her finger. Her gaze shifted, seeking something neutral to mop up the overspill of emotion, and travelled round the room, corner by corner. It was one of those flats high up in a converted warehouse with windows so big you could play ice-hockey on them and a vast main room that was designed to remain half empty. She stared with admiration at the spiky Italian furniture and paintings, all bought out of Anthea's hard-earned income as a dealer in the City.

No husband to feather the nest. Not any more, anyway. Instead there was a new and desirable hunk for her bed, who irritated Jodie with his crisp, authoritative way of delivering his words so that they sounded impressive, until you thought about them. He was the one who had caused all the trouble this evening. Feeling ignored, he had started an almighty row in the middle of dinner, so that everyone had sloped off home early.

Goodbye hunk.

'You're better off without the rat,' Jodie had comforted Anthea and that was when they had started in on the vodka and the port.

Inevitably, Jodie had turned to her camera; it was always that way. She needed to look at people through its lens. At scenes, situations, objects, it didn't matter what. Her camera lens provided the framework and gave them a meaning that her own eyes seemed to miss. It had been years since she had photographed her sister; and the fashion session, with Anthea wearing clothes as if they were part of her body and striking elegant poses on one of her chrome stools placed in front of the velvet drapes, had been a revelation. Jodie had livened up the mood by singing, repeatedly, their old school song, while Anthea had cursed the hunk loudly, thoroughly and from the heart. The vodka had helped, of course. And through the lens, Jodie had been able to see what she had not realised before: that her sister was desperate to be loved by somebody, even if it was only the camera.

Struggling with a wave of affection, Jodie patted Anthea's arm and found defenceless goosebumps there the size of grapefruit, so she went and pulled a duvet off one of the beds and spread

it over the sleeping figure. Whether it was because the air in
the flat was clogged with the mingled scent of perfume and
lingering cigarette smoke, or just that she needed to fill the
hole of loneliness that had opened up capriciously inside her,
she didn't know. But she unlatched the glass door that led on
to a frail-looking balcony and stepped out into the welcome
darkness.

The night was very still and the river as black as molten tar.
She breathed deeply to quieten her head and felt her lungs object
at first, but then pop open, sucking greedily at the cool damp air.
The sounds of traffic drifted up to her like heart murmurs from
the city below. Beside her on the wall the glow of a lamp tempted
moths each evening to batter their wings against it, unwilling
to learn from their mistakes. She stood without moving. Being
motionless was her way of pretending she wasn't there at all.
Not there, not anywhere. But this time it didn't work. High
up like this, she could feel, with a clarity that confused her,
the unbearable strain of the humanity below, and realised she
must be drunker than she thought.

She extinguished the lamp and returned indoors. Her sister
had not stirred, so she dumped her own dress on the floor and
collapsed on to the sofa where, instantly, her stomach started
to growl and threaten revenge. She closed her eyes and tried
to remember where the bathroom was. Whatever dreams were
due to needle her sleep that night, she had to be at work in
Westonport next morning.

3

Jodie prodded the bell of the small bungalow. The door sprang open. A young girl of around fifteen stood before her, hair as variegated as a tabby cat's, mouth wide and laughing. From somewhere behind her came the sound of ferocious snarling.

'Come in. Quickly, come in. I rang the *Gazette*. He's in here.' The girl turned and scurried into a room that opened off the hall.

Jodie followed, her Nikon ready in her hand. It turned out to be the dining-room and it was total bedlam. Chairs lay on their backs with legs in the air like dead animals, smashed ornaments had spread a confetti of china over the carpet and a standard lamp had nose-dived on to the floor.

In the middle of the chaos towered a massive dog.

An Irish wolfhound or maybe a Russian one. She was not well up on canine subtleties but the cause of the animal's fury was obvious. The poor creature had his head wedged tight inside a tin and was throwing himself around the room in a frenzy of rage, frantic to tear himself free. Jodie ran off a bunch of film from various angles. She worked quickly, acutely aware of the animal's suffering, and had just captured a good shot of the wolfhound rearing up blindly on his hind legs, when the dog zapped the tin against the table and came to a standstill. She pitied the poor brute's brains. For a brief moment, his encased head hung wretchedly and the grey slabs of his sides heaved with exhaustion; but when she began to edge towards him, the frantic snarling and crashing round the room started up again.

The teenager giggled nervously. 'He's really freaked out.'

'Have you tried removing the tin from him?'

'No, the stupid dope won't let me near. He stuck his greedy head in the biscuit tin and got it jammed. But it wasn't my fault, honestly it wasn't,' she insisted.

Jodie ignored the girl's bleating and made another determined attempt to approach the frightened animal. This time she managed to tighten her fingers in his rough fur before he jerked it out of her grip and whirled away snarling piteously to the other end of the room. Jodie noticed he had cut his pad on the scattering of china that littered the floor and had left a trail of strawberry smears across the carpet. She bent and picked up the worst offending pieces.

'Are your parents anywhere around?' she asked, already certain what the answer would be.

'No, they are out at work.' The girl frowned uneasily. 'But it's not as if it's really hurting him, is it?'

'Try it yourself some time.'

'No way.'

'Have you telephoned for help?'

'Not yet. I wanted his picture in the *Gazette*.'

Jodie gave her a long look and left the room. The telephone was in the hall and it was the work of a moment to dial the fire-brigade and to summon a vet. If she didn't leave now, she would miss the arrival of the cruise ship *Isis* she was meant to be covering at Westonport docks, and she had heard a rumour that Nick Nolte might be on board. An almighty crash erupted behind the door, followed by a howl of misery. Jodie replaced the receiver and headed back into the dining-room.

The drive back to the office gave her time to calm down. It was the beginning of the evening rush-hour and the roads of Westonport had become as sluggish and unhealthy as blocked arteries. While she crawled bumper to bumper behind a wheezing Metro that was puffing blue smoke into her lungs with every change of gear, Jodie noticed that her own hands were wrapped round the steering wheel, far too tightly. Like they wanted to throttle it. She coaxed them into easing their grip. It was always like this. The tail-end of the adrenalin still pumping.

She accelerated into a gap in the traffic and concentrated her thoughts on Roy Dunmore. As the Gazette's news-editor, he could be a real pain in the arse when he didn't get what he wanted. His last words to her had been quite explicit: 'Don't miss the *Isis*', and she had just chosen to do precisely that. By the time she did eventually get down to the docks, it had been too late; the ship had docked and passengers disembarked. No Nick Nolte in sight. She was only too aware that a static shot of the liner at the quayside did not compare with the pomp of it cruising in from the open sea. Roy would comment colourfully on that fact. So the sooner she got this film into the *Gazette*'s developer, the better.

She sneaked her black Mini through a set of lights on amber and swung a right to head uphill towards the roundabout that marked the division in Westonport between town centre and industrial outskirts. Her own flat was in the heart of town, right where she liked it. The nosy, cosy countryside was not for her. City Slicker was stamped in concrete on her soul the moment she realised that for every mile you moved nearer to the centre of a town, the number of people sticking their nose into your business and passing judgment on your life dropped by a satisfying number of thousands. In the city no one cared a damn what you wore down the street. Not a damn. Anyway, Jodie saw no point in living where you couldn't get a packet of Maltesers from the corner shop when the urge seized you at two in the morning. No point at all.

Her camera was contented with her choice and thrived on the urban subjects that were presented to its lens each day. But even now, after working for nearly two years on the *Westonport Gazette*, Jodie did not always find that the image of herself slotted easily into her head. 'My sister, the photographer', Anthea had said. Jodie Grace Buxton, photographer, was printed on her passport; so it must be true.

And Roy Dunmore trusted her.

Her blue, almond-shaped eyes relaxed into a smile. And why the hell shouldn't he?

The office car park was full. It was always the same. Didn't they ever go home? Jodie spotted a minuscule gap in the corner, accepted the challenge and reversed neatly into it. As she walked over to the main building, a light aimless drizzle was making the offices look glossier than they deserved. The newspaper had transferred its premises out here four years ago from elegant but cramped quarters in the centre of town, and though its squat new home would never win any prizes for architectural enlightenment, it certainly won the approval of the hacks inside.

Jodie pushed open the door. The reception hall was small and busy, and always hit her with a sense of nerve-end energy bouncing off the walls. Too many deadlines to meet. One wall carried a display of *Gazette* posters and on another sat a row of folders packed with recent editions of the paper for public reference. Opposite them was an array of faces. These were pictures of the thirty-two journalists and seven photographers on staff, herself included, frozen in a reader-friendly cheerfulness that made Jodie grimace. It was hard to decide which of them was the worst.

Clutching her heavy camera case, she hurried across the carpet-squares, hoping to avoid getting hooked on any of the comings and goings around her. She thought she had made it, but at the last moment was stopped by the voice of Lisa Fellows. Lisa was the *Gazette*'s chief receptionist. She was around thirty and possessed a mane of blonde curls, today pinned into submission on top of her head, and very pale eyes that missed nothing.

'Jodie.'

Jodie was tempted to continue on her way as if she had not heard, but knew that Lisa was not likely to leave it at that.

'Yes, Lisa?'

The receptionist waved a professionally manicured hand towards the corridor behind her. 'Roy wants you.'

'I'm in a rush.'

'He said, as soon as you came in.'

Jodie took two steps nearer the swing-door. 'I'll just dump this in photography first.' She indicated her case.

'He means now, Jodie.'

Jodie thought, not for the first time, that Lisa would have made the perfect schoolteacher. The frown, the expression, the intonation, everything honed to perfection, and exactly designed to crawl under Jodie's skin.

She tried a conspiratorial smile but it floated right over the blonde curls. 'I really have to get these films started in the developer. Roy doesn't know I'm back yet. I won't be more than a few minutes.'

Lisa wavered.

'Honestly,' Jodie assured her.

'All right. But be quick.'

Jodie flashed a smile that she hoped looked grateful and left, her dislike of Lisa stubbornly intact.

The photographic department was where she was happiest. It was a stark and uninspiring room, with grey metallic machines that did the work and emphasised the speed at which they functioned by a low-pitched hum, like a postman whistling to himself. But it was here, to this high-tech haven, that Jodie loved to come. To see the magic happen before her eyes. To capture a moment of time inside a camera and transform it from a moment in the past to being a part of the present. And even of the future. Every time, the extraordinary impossibility of the deed never failed to send a visceral shudder of excitement through Jodie. Each photograph was a creation of her own that depended on her for its very existence. With a camera she could reshape her world.

'I've finished with the developer, if you want to use it.' It was Kerry Dainton, the technician. She was black, and as slender as a pea-stick, with hair cut in a geometric bob and small round glasses that made her look intelligent.

'Thanks,' Jodie smiled. 'I've got Roy on my tail and I want these as glossies to wave at him, in case he bites.'

'Jack was in here earlier looking for you.'

'Oh yes? What was he after? As if I need ask.'

Jack James was one of the *Gazette*'s reporters always on the scrounge for a photographer to cover his latest piece.

'I don't know exactly. He didn't say. But he was in a rush.'

Kerry slid a group of colour prints into a folder and breathed a lengthy sigh of relief. 'That's me done for today.'

'Time for a coffee?' It would taste of stale plastic but it would be wet, warm and, at this stage of the day, welcome.

'My shout,' Kerry offered and headed out into the corridor, just as Jack James walked in.

'And one for me, sweetheart,' he called after her. 'Plenty of sugar.'

Jodie said quickly, 'Push off, I'm busy.'

'You certainly know how to sweet-talk a guy,' Jack smiled at her. 'Anyway, I'm on my way out. I vaguely recall that somewhere in this town, if I think hard enough, I do have a home to go to.'

Jodie laughed. 'Okay, but don't interrupt. I'm rushing to get these prints finished before Dunmore finds out I'm here.'

'You'll be lucky. He's got eyes that see through walls.'

He drifted closer and peered over her shoulder. His breath was warm and intimate on her neck. Too damn intimate. Jodie twitched her curtain of dark hair to cover the spot and turned to face him. He wasn't attractive. Everything about him was long and angular and only loosely tied together. He moved as if his limbs found it all too much of an effort, so that people who didn't know better thought he must be lazy. Under a shock of unruly brown hair, his face was narrow and bony but his eyes were as bright and watchful as a ferret's. It was the humour in them that made Jodie excuse his tendency to hang around the photographic department rather more often than she might otherwise have wished.

'I hear you were looking for me earlier today. What was that for?' She picked up her Nikon and started to load in a new film.

He leaned his bones against the colour-copier. 'I was covering some story about a trampolining marathon to raise money for a new jock-strap or ping-pong bat or something and wanted you along for a picture. It would have been good, especially as the coach who was organising the whole caboodle dropped dead at my feet. Nearly gave me a heart attack.'

'Horrific!'

'He had been bouncing up and down like a turquoise yoyo for too long, I guess. He jumped off the trampoline to do the interview and that was it. Down he went. Everyone ran

around doing mouth-to-mouth and so forth, but it was no use.
A doornail had more life in it.'

'Jack, that's gruesome.'

He shrugged his paper-thin shoulders and grimaced. 'Worse
for the guy in the peacock tracksuit. Shame you weren't there to
immortalise his final moment.' He said it casually, a professional
slickness effectively cloaking the reality in the eyes. As if he saw
dead bodies every day.

Jodie snapped shut the Nikon in her hand and put it down on
the desk. 'Front page?'

'Yep.'

'Lead story?'

'Certainly is.'

'Shit.'

'Found something better?'

'Maybe.'

'What have you got? You were at the docks covering that
ship's arrival, weren't you? Anything interesting? Did Nick Nolte
turn up?'

'No, it's not the ship. And those Hollywood stars already have
egos too big to photograph.'

'What then?'

'A dog.'

'You've got to be joking.' Jack burst out laughing, a quick
animated sound that stung her pride.

She gave him a smile that did not quite succeed in keeping
her irritation under wraps. 'Joking is not the word, Jack. Barking
mad is more like it.'

'That's the one.' Roy Dunmore picked up a print from the array
of photographs spread out on his desk and held it up for closer
inspection. 'It's good.'

That was all. No argument. It was the one of the dog on its
hind legs. Every bit as dramatic as she had hoped.

His shrewd grey eyes were satisfied. He was a large man in his
mid fifties with heavy jowls and a paunch that ruined the cut
of his suits. He ate, slept, dreamed and breathed the newspaper
business. It had seen him through two divorces already and word

had it that he was on the brink of a third. A persistent rumour
also whispered that his chin leaked pure black printer's ink when
he cut himself shaving. But then newspapers lived, and died, on
rumours. Dunmore had been brought in as news-editor to turn
around the paper's fortunes and he had done just that, halting
its decline and kicking its staff out of their complacency.

'I'll hold it over till Wednesday and run it on the front page.
Tomorrow will be taken up with the trampolining death. Did
you hear about that?'

'Yes.' She changed the subject. 'That picture of the vet will
have to go in as well.'

Dunmore chuckled deep in his chest and picked up the photograph she had referred to. 'Chattington won't like that much.'

It was a shot of the town's most eminent veterinary surgeon
flat on his back with the dog standing over him, its metal head
only inches from his own. Eventually the firemen had managed
to restrain the animal long enough for him to insert a needle
into its swollen neck, and once quiet, it took a fireman only a
few seconds to tin-open it out of its helmet.

'And the *Isis*?' Jodie asked, aware that her editor had passed
no comment on those pictures.

Dunmore waved a hand dismissively. 'We'll stick it on page
four. Alongside entertainments.'

Not a good position but not quite graveyard. Could have
been worse.

'Get Matt to do the dog story.' Matt Reynolds was one of the
Gazette's reporters. 'Tell him I want it first thing tomorrow.'

'Sure, I'll brief him. But I don't know if he's in at the moment.
What's he been working on today?'

Dunmore sat down at the desk, a frown folding his face into
habitual grooves. 'Matt has been over at Wyndame School.'

'Anything serious?'

It might be nothing. Schools were always calling journalists
and photographers over to record the achievements of their star
pupils. No need to think this was a heavy story. No need at all.

It was just the way Dunmore had said it.

'Could be,' he replied, sharp eyes keeping their knowledge tan-
talisingly out of reach. 'Check with Matt, if you're interested.'

'I will. When I see him.'

Dunmore produced one of his rare smiles. 'Or ask the head-master.'

'No thanks,' she said. 'I'll just stick to getting this dog story sorted out.'

'It was a punch-up at the school.'

'Again?'

'Again. Another kid received a mauling. So I'll need you to yank the usual photograph of the headmaster out of the files. Matt will have got a decent quote out of him, I'm certain.'

'Right. No problem.'

Jodie turned to leave, but before she reached the door Dunmore caught her off-guard with, 'And Jodie. When I say come and see me as soon as you get in, I don't mean half an hour later. Clear?'

Jodie muttered a grudging 'Yes', and escaped. How the hell did the old devil always know precisely what you least wanted him to?

4

Jodie had intended to drive straight home. The persistent ache at the nape of her neck told her that it had been a long day and the last thing in her mind was to make it even longer by going over to the school.

So why was she driving through its gates?

It was seven-thirty and the sun had at last penetrated the heavy white cloud-layer that had hung around since early morning. It had set her teeth on edge and she had wondered why, until she realised it put her in mind of the smooth unpleasant underbelly of a shark. A stiff breeze licked up from the sea, carrying with it the chilly reminder that September had ousted the warm breath of summer and was preparing to steal the leaves from the trees.

Wyndame Comprehensive School was perched like a white concrete fortress on the brow of a hill and surrounded by a moat of green playing fields over which a handful of boys were, even at this late hour, chasing after a ball. A crop of gulls was cruising the area, on the sharp look-out for anything worth a final scavenge before settling down for the night in a sheltered corner of the rugby pitch.

Jodie shot up the drive well above the speed limit and parked in the visitors' car park. Hers was the only car. She grabbed her camera and hurried over to the main entrance. The school looked all wrong to her like this, empty and lifeless, with just an occasional figure idling along a path. A school needed armies of kids clogging its corridors with their boisterous laughter and the odour of their over-active young bodies. That's how it had been when she was here and that's how she liked to remember it. She pushed open the door and went inside.

It smelled just the same. A mingling of floor polish and bleach, with an odd salty overlay that she assumed was left behind by the legion of crisps consumed there each day. Somewhere in the distance an electric-polisher whirred efficiently, wiping out any trace of the children, and nearer at hand footsteps approached along a corridor. Jodie crossed the empty reception area and even now, after all these years, still felt a tingle of the old dread whisper through her brain as she passed the staffroom door. The footsteps materialised into a female teacher who did no more than give her a polite nod as their paths crossed.

Jodie knew exactly where to go for information. That was the sixth-form common-room. It was the hub of gossip and though the school bell had long since granted freedom, there was usually some activity going on in the school that warranted a few sixth-formers still hanging around. In the corridor outside, she could hear the sound of voices but when she opened the door, the room was empty. The voices were issuing from a cassette player on a low table in the centre of the room.

'Are you looking for someone?'

A tall boy with hair way below the acceptable collar-length had walked in behind her, a cup of coffee in his hand. A girl joined him, plump and pretty and wearing a prefect's badge.

'We've got permission,' the girl said quickly, indicating the cassette. 'It's for the play.'

Jodie smiled, remembering what it was like, and raised her camera to indicate where her interests lay. 'I'm from the *Gazette*. Here to take a few pictures.'

'What of?' the boy asked defensively. 'Not the rehearsal, is it? We're still crap at the moment.'

'No, not the rehearsal. I heard there was a fight here today that got a bit out of hand.'

Instantly she had their attention. The girl switched off the cassette player.

'Yeah,' the boy grimaced. 'A massacre it was.'

'Do you know where it happened?'

That was what she was after, a picture of the scene of the struggle. She wanted to show it lonely and deserted. Pain was a lonely experience.

'Yeah, behind the old changing-rooms.' He waved an arm off to his left.

Jodie knew the place. Even in her day, that was where boys went to settle their differences, but this recent spate of attacks at Wyndame Comprehensive was more vicious, some serious enough to put one or more of the participants in hospital. No wonder the headmaster would issue no names of those involved, just carefully worded comments, protective of the school's reputation.

'Do you have any idea what the fight was about?' Jodie asked.

'It was some sad little third-former, I was told,' the girl said without concern, secure in her sixth-form superiority. 'Too lippy, I guess.'

'Okay. Thanks for your help.'

The sixth-formers watched her turn and head for the door, and were disappointed at losing the attention of the Press.

'A reporter was hanging round school earlier, sussing it out,' the girl added quickly. 'Until Miss Helman chucked him out.'

Poor Matt. Helman, the Deputy Head, was adept at making herself objectionable. As Jodie well recalled.

'I'll watch my step,' she said.

The boy went further. 'I heard there was a whole heap of sexual insults being thrown around.'

Jodie's interest plummeted. Two more males who kept their brains in their trousers.

'So some guys were arguing over a girl. Tell me something new.'

'No, of course not. The stupid bints *were* girls.'

That got through. Jodie stared, aware that now she had a story.

'Are you telling me it was two girls who were fighting?'

'That's right. Except the word around school is that there were more than two of them. But no one knows for sure. The victim is keeping dead quiet. Wise move, if she doesn't want it to happen again.'

'Do you know her name?'

'No. Just that it was a third-year kid.'

'Is she in hospital?'

'I don't know.'
'Do they know who did it?'
'No way. No one is grassing.'
'Are the police involved at all?'
He shrugged. 'No idea.'
Nothing more.

Jodie gave him a smile wide enough to deepen the colour on his young cheeks. 'You've been a great help. Thanks again,' she said and left.

As she nipped out of a side door, she wondered if Matt had got hold of this.

The wall had been recently painted. The old changing-rooms were not often used now that the new ones had been built out of the slush fund the school had been given to coax it to opt for grant-maintained status. But the old concrete block had received a quick lick and a promise. The building was near the edge of the school grounds and had been constructed in an L-shape, with the sheltered corner of the right-angle situated at the back. Only an ancient laurel hedge overlooked its secrets.

Private.

No one to see. No one to hear.

But the freshly painted white wall was no longer as fresh or as white as it had been. At shoulder height there was a smear of brown that narrowed into a thin spear pointed at the ground. Dried blood. Someone had obviously made an attempt to wash it off but had only managed to spread it over a wider area. To Jodie it looked like a smudged crucifix.

She flipped her camera into action, fingers adjusting the dials. The light was dying fast. The back of the building fell in the shade, so she gave the film as much exposure as possible. She concentrated on what she was doing and kept her mind off the images that lurked behind the stain on the wall. She was a photographer. Not a social worker.

On her way she had made a detour via the games-hall and, unobserved, had borrowed a blazer from the boys' changing room, which she now arranged on the ground. She was careful to place the school badge in clear view and while doing so, came across a book in its pocket. *Lord of the Flies*. Truly apt. She added it to the arrangement but without revealing its title. There was such a thing as gilding the lily.

It only took a moment or two and the job was finished. She varied the angle of shot a couple of times, but there was no need for any fancy stuff. Anyway, she was eager to be gone. A hot bath beckoned and if she remembered correctly, there was one packet of Maltesers lurking unmolested in the kitchen cupboard. She would eat them in the bath. Though last time she tried that, she had dropped one and all the chocolate melted off it in the hot water. Undeterred, she had fished it out and eaten the bald mothball that was left.

Jodie packed away her camera. All she wanted now was to get away. This corner hid its secrets in the shadows. It sent edgy shivers crawling over her skin. She knew why, and it wasn't just the stain on the wall. No. It was the sharp, jagged piece of her personal history that lay in this same spot. She made an effort to shut the memory out of her thoughts but it seeped around the edges and trickled into her head against her will, until there was nowhere else she could look. The shadows deepened in the lee of the building and she turned away from them, directing her footsteps and the blazer back towards the games-hall. But it was too late to turn away from what was going on inside her head.

It had been only a minor incident. Stupid, really. Not worth remembering. It happened when she was in the fifth form and had taken up smoking. Behind the changing-rooms was where she and Dana Simpson sauntered at break times to have a quick drag and compare lustful daydreams about James Frobisher, who looked a bit like Kevin Kline but with Jeff Goldblum's mouth. They had fantasised about that mouth. Endlessly. Then one afternoon, a Friday that had already turned sour because Dana had been caught snogging Randy Andy in the boys' toilets and been sent home, a strutting little second-year kid had come and stuck her nose in. Jodie could still see her face, sharp and clear, ginger curls and matching freckles. Plus a smirk that got right up Jodie's nose. The girl threatened to report her for smoking. Report her to the headmaster unless she handed over whatever worldly wealth was currently in her purse, all three pound fifty of it.

Jodie had refused. No way was she going to let a lippy thirteen-year-old walk over her. The kid had leant against the wall, just near where the blood smear now marked it, and demonstrated her irritating smirk.

'Okay, dumb-arse, if that's how you want to play it, I'm off to the head's study. And he won't be exactly pleased, will he?'

That was when Jodie had hit her. Just an open-handed slap across the face. Not even hard. Just enough to get rid of that smirk.

'You open your mouth to him and there'll be more where that came from,' Jodie threatened.

'Oh yeah?' the young voice jeered, all bravado. 'It'll take more than that to shut my mouth.'

Jodie was taller than the second-former by at least six inches and she stepped up to her, real close. But still the kid kept the smirk in place.

'What would it take?' Jodie asked softly. 'This?' And she hit the girl in the mouth.

The teeth hurt her knuckles. When she withdrew her stinging hand, they were covered in blood. The sight gave her a sickening jolt, like she'd just jumped off a cliff, because she knew it was not her own. The girl was leaning forward, sobbing, clutching her face, blood and tears dripping from her chin on to the grass. Suddenly she seemed smaller; younger.

Jodie hated herself at that moment. And had hated ginger-haired people ever since. She did not want to be reminded when she looked into their freckled faces of the vengeful girl that lived inside herself. That girl had been locked up with her shame and the key thrown away. Thrown into the sewers where nasty, stinking things went to die.

Jodie reached the games-hall. The boys were still running their legs off on the playing field, so she replaced the blazer unseen, glad to be rid of it.

It was her grandfather who had shown her a different way to communicate. One afternoon when she was just mooning round his nettle-patch of a garden, a refugee from the pressure at home to revise for exams, he had thrust his ancient Instamatic into her idle hands. He wanted some snaps of himself holding his new litter of pups, and that had been the start.

It had been a revelation to find she actually had a talent for something. From that moment on, it was cameras. And more cameras. First had come a cheap Kodak, but she soon had a Cannon with a crazy wide fish-eye and eventually a first-rate Pentax with all the functions. Every penny she earned in holiday jobs had been hoarded for the latest lens or light-meter; the dwarf-size cupboard under the stairs became her dark-room and she lost count of the number of solitary, breath-holding hours she spent waiting for the perfect shot or the right light. Her mother had stopped calling her a wastrel and started filling her Christmas stockings with reels of film, while her father had approved of the results of her creativity, but never did believe her when she claimed to have been out half the night because she was lying in wait outside a badger's sett.

Jodie smiled to herself. He wasn't that dumb.

She was hurrying round the corner of the science labs with the car park just coming into sight, when she walked slap bang into the headmaster. Oh Christ. Two more minutes and she'd have been out of there.

'Good heavens, Jodie, what on earth are you doing here?'

He was a tall grey man, grey hair, grey suit and straggly grey eyebrows which he declined to trim. Very headmasterish. He walked unnaturally upright, spine poker-straight and shoulders pulled back, as a perpetual example to his pupils and a deliberate assault on the slouching gait of modern youth.

Jodie took a step backward, away from him, and smiled innocently. 'Hi, Dad.'

She slipped her jacket over the camera. With the headmaster for a father, she had spent much of her school life performing similar secretive gestures.

'What are you doing here?' he repeated. 'If it's Matt you're looking for, he's long gone.'

It was as good an excuse as any. She nodded. 'I was told he was covering an incident here.'

He frowned for a moment, the eyebrows entwining over his nose, and changed the subject. 'Anyway, it's nice to see you. You haven't been round to the house for a while.'

'I know. Sorry about that, but I've been so busy, I honestly haven't had a second to scratch myself.'

She saw him wince at her choice of phrase and asked herself why she always felt the need to irritate him like that. Repentant, she suggested, 'I'll drop by tomorrow morning, if that's okay. I've got a job to do around ten o'clock at the Catholic church, so I'll come along afterwards.'

'Your mother would like that.'

'How is she?'

'Bored.'

'Poor old crock.' Her mother had broken her leg a month ago and was finding the plaster and confinement hard to bear with any display of patience. 'I'll bring some of the *Gazette*'s crosswords over for her to do.'

Pleased by the gesture, Alan Buxton smiled, and she wished he would do it more often.

'She will appreciate the crosswords, I'm sure, but if you could telephone her more frequently, Jodie, it would help. You know how she likes to hear from you.'

The guilt again. With parents, there was always guilt.

'Okay, Dad. I'll try, I promise.'

'Good. As you're here, there is something else I want to . . .'

A boy came hurtling round the corner, skidded to a startled halt and continued on his way at the sedate, approved pace for movement about school.

'Tuck your shirt in, Hawkins. How many times have I told you?'

'Yes, sir.'

Muddy hands shoved the flap of cloth that hung behind like a flattened tail into his trousers, but the moment he turned the next corner, both Jodie and her father could hear his footsteps break into a gallop once more. Alan Buxton shook his head, but the slight twitch of amusement on his lips surprised Jodie and for a ghastly moment she felt sorry for him, always having to play the disciplinarian. But where did the playing stop and the being start? Sure as hell, she couldn't tell, and maybe neither could he any more.

She was just feeling a sort of mushy, confused sympathy for him, when he came out with, 'Jodie, I want you to instruct that newspaper of yours to keep its nose out of what is not its business. Your tribe just love to make trouble. It sells more copies, so you think it's good business. But it's irresponsible. That tabloid reporting does harm to my school and I won't stand for it.'

Jodie's loyalties nailed themselves firmly to her profession. 'Come on, Dad, get real. This is a school. Every one of its parents has a right to know what goes on here and if there's any trouble, then it's our paper's job to inform them of it.'

'No, Jodie, don't hide behind that old flannel. Your paper operates on self-interest and nothing else.'

They had been through this before far too often. It was such well-worn ground between them that Jodie sometimes wondered whether they would one day both fall into the deep trenches they had dug and only then realise that maybe they should have built a bridge. But neither was ever willing to concede that the other might have some kind of point, so they just kept on at it, hitting their heads against their respective brick walls. And getting annoyed when it hurt.

Jodie side-stepped a fraction. 'I gather it was a couple of girls gouging chunks out of each other this time.'

Her father made no reply, but looked at her with wary eyes and suddenly she saw the disappointment in them, a disappointment that was so familiar that she couldn't stand seeing it yet again. She glanced down at her watch. 'Got to go, I'm afraid.'

'Yes, so must I.'

What was this? Some kind of competition?

'Give my love to the invalid,' she offered, to placate him.

'I will. And can I say you will definitely be over to see her tomorrow?'

'That's right.'

'You will come, won't you? I don't want your mother getting her hopes up for nothing.'

Jodie gave a reassuring smile and edged away. 'Of course I will. You can rely on me.'

Her father made an odd sound, a kind of wuffling snort, like a dog with an irritating fly up its nose. 'That'll be the day.'

As Jodie hurried to her Mini, she kept telling herself, he was joking. For heaven's sake, don't get so heavy. He was only joking.

*　　*　　*

The moment the door shut behind her, Jodie felt a sigh escape from where it had been hiding somewhere down in her boots. It was always like that. Coming home. As if out there, she could work her butt off, even if it was only to come up with a picture of a screwy seagull that raps on a pensioner's patio door for its breakfast of cheese and muesli each day, or of the biggest pumpkin in the allotments, both of which she had done this morning. But as soon as she was inside these four walls, it was as though the outer crust-grubbing skin sloughed off and beneath it she was once again shiny and fresh. Without meaning to, she put a hand to her face as if to check that the itchy ill-fitting skin had gone, then, satisfied, she set off up the stairs.

Her flat was up on the first floor of a large three-storey house built at the turn of the century, with a wide staircase that wound up through the centre of the building. In recent years it had slid down the social scale and was now rented out as separate flats, but half a century ago in Westonport's heyday, it had been a desirable residence. Westonport had spent its infancy as a fishing village, but at the end of the eighteenth century its natural harbour was employed to shelter the English fleet during the Napoleonic Wars, and the town developed to house and entertain the officers' wives. Though the port still remained at the heart of the town, its future was now being developed in the high-tech industrial parks that arched around Westonport's outskirts like bands of a rainbow with the promise of a pot of gold.

Jodie could not help smiling as she entered her flat. It had nothing of the glossy stylishness of Anthea's, but nevertheless it always pleased her because it was her own. She kicked off her shoes and walked through to the bedroom where she slid her camera case into its usual place under the dressing-table. The carpet carried its imprint like a sleeping memory even when it was not there.

She slipped out of her skirt and blouse, did a few stretches to un-crick her spine, then removed bra and panties. Instantly she felt lighter. The last of that troublesome outer skin lay on the floor along with her underwear. Her naked body relished its free-dom, smooth and weightless as she headed for the bathroom, her long hair caressing her bare shoulders like the breath of a lover.

The bathroom was white and warm. Too warm. She looked quickly to her left, at the bath itself. Through a haze of steam, eyes the colour of wood-smoke gazed back at her.

'Matt,' Jodie said with a smile that took over her whole face, and she felt an involuntary pulse thump into life at the base of her throat. 'I didn't know you were home.'

'The harbour development meeting ended early because so few people turned up, so I reckoned my duty was done.' He grinned up at her from under a thatch of fair hair that the water had streaked to a darker brown in places, like fingers of wet sand. 'How about you? Good day?'

It took her by surprise. Every time. Even though it had been over a year now. The way her need for him kicked in, somewhere deep and desperate inside, each time she laid eyes on Matt Reynolds. When she was away from him during the day busting a gut to chase pictures for the paper, she sometimes forgot. Forgot the need. Until she saw him again. It was as if somehow he possessed the power to remove a grey filter from her eyes, so that even the most banal objects suddenly leapt out at her, bright and intense. She looked away, to adjust her mental focus, and picked up a hairbrush from the windowsill.

'Not too bad actually. Two scary stunts. One with a dog that had its head stuck in a tin and was petrifying the neighbours. That was bad enough, but the other was running into Dad at the school just now.' She bent over, hanging her head between her knees and started to brush the straight dark hair with slow strokes that set it crackling down its length to the floor.

'Did he give you a hard time?' Matt asked. 'I was over there today.'

'So I was told.'

'He wasn't exactly welcoming.'

'A reporter's life is a tough one,' she said, smiling behind her upside-down curtain.

'Your father is trying to pretend there is no trouble at the school, so as I was sniffing around, I'm not exactly his favourite person at the moment.' He flicked a fine spray of soapy water at her. 'What were you doing over there?'

'Dunmore told me about the fight, so I went over to see if I could get a shot of where it took place. To make a more interesting picture for your piece than just Dad's head again. It's frustrating that we can't show the victims.'

'No chance.' After a pause, he murmured, 'This bath was intended as relaxation, so would you mind not doing that in here?'

'Doing what?'

'That.'

'I'm only brushing the dirt out of my hair. Did you find out who the poor kid was this time?' She heard the water slooshing but paid no attention.

'Not the name. But it was a girl.'

'Oh, you know already. I was hoping I would surprise you with that.'

'I'm an investigative journalist and don't you forget it.' He said it with a self-mocking laugh that came from right behind her and she felt his hand touch her buttock. She let it linger there a moment before she stood upright, tumbled her dark mane to one side and moulded her naked back against his warm soapy skin.

Just the touch of him started the ache.

'Did you get the shot you wanted?' he murmured into her neck.

'Yes. It should be good. I can feel it.'

'I can feel it too,' he whispered, and ran a damp hand up over her breast to the erect nipple.

'Matt . . .' Jodie breathed, her fingers circling in the rivulets that trickled down his thighs. 'Do you think a headmaster has the right to keep the names of the victims of bullying a secret?'

'No, I don't. How about you?'

'I'm not sure. I can see his point. They're just kids. Maybe they've been through enough already, without all the publicity as well. But on the other hand . . .'

'The publicity might stimulate the school to do more about it.'

'Exactly.' She was breathing heavily as his fingers started stroking her mound, teasing the hair into tingling antennae.

'It's our job.'

'Exactly.' Her tongue had stuck on the word. It felt heavy and moist in her mouth.

'Our job is to investigate.' He was licking her neck.

'Exactly.' Her flesh shuddered. 'But there's something else I need to investigate first,' she said, and led him back to the bath.

It was gone midnight, and though Jodie remained in bed she could not sleep. Her energy seemed at its peak and swirled in fierce spurts through her body, so much so that her legs escaped her control and flicked and fluttered like disturbed bats in the cave under the duvet. Beside her, Matt slept with enviable persistence, now and then snoring an irregular soft grinding sound that she found pleasant company.

Her mind felt ice-clear. It was an illusion, of course. She was well aware of that. A tired brain was adept at playing tricks, and night-time musings too often melted to mush when exposed to the light of morning.

Her father was the problem.

How many times had she lain awake with that thought grating in her head?

Where to draw the line?

She shook her head on the pillow, but it did not dislodge the question. She was remembering things at different levels. Not just today, but a history of todays. His quickly summoned smiles when she had pleased him, but more often the barely suppressed anxiety on his face when it was directed at her. Her mother tutting irritably and pointing out yet again that her father had enough on his plate at the school.

The school.

His school.

It had never been *her* school. Not even after seven long years there.

She reminded herself that the school meant to him what the *Gazette* meant to her. Maybe more.

So who was right?

The question gnawed at her like a piranha fish and her legs kicked out to flick it away, but its teeth had sunk too deep. She knew her father regarded her as being intentionally troublesome, whereas she argued that it was part of being a professional. She was a photographer, for Christ's sake. It was her job. But at this lonely hour of the night she was willing to recognise that each person's connection with reality was inevitably subjective. Reality was in the head, and therefore, by definition, her father's reality could never be hers, nor hers be his. So all you could do was live your own reality. Whatever that was.

'You'll tie those legs of yours in knots soon. Can't you sleep?' It was Matt; he rolled towards her, wrapping an arm around her restless body.

'No, I can't. Sorry if I woke you.'

He stroked her hair with soft somnolent movements, as if he could stroke the unsettled thoughts inside back to sleep. His face touched her own and she could feel his breath warm and comforting on her cheek, as already he started to slip back into his dreams. She turned her head, brushed her lips on his arm and inhaled the familiar scent of his skin, musty from sleep.

'Matt,' she whispered, softly enough not to wake him, 'you get trapped between us, my poor love.'

He stirred in his sleep, his arm tightening around her, locking her body against his own as if to draw her into his dreams. As she lay there, almost a part of him, she wondered if maybe she had got it wrong about which one of them was trapped.

5

Anthea Courtney was drunk.

Again.

She didn't like to admit it to herself, so she practised walking up and down an imaginary line along the centre of the room but kept wobbling off it.

To hell with sobriety. Who needed it?

She flopped down on to the long white sofa and its leather skin felt cold and unloving against the heat of her body, so she rolled off it on to the rug on the floor.

Poor goat. Poor dead goat. She stroked its long silky hair and thanked it for being her companion, then reached up to a nearby table and lifted a glass of vodka off it. It was already three-quarters empty and the ice had melted to the size of a lemon pip which Anthea's tongue scooped out and swallowed.

She had put together some sharp deals on the market today.

No complaints there.

That smart-arse Julian Maynard had eaten her dust. She took a large mouthful of her drink and felt it gouge its way down her throat.

No, no complaints.

Except in her head. There were complaints in her head.

She did not want to listen to them, so she drained the last of the vodka into her mouth until the glass was tipped upside down on her nose and she felt better. She stumbled to her feet with an effort, refilled her glass and picked up the telephone. It took her three attempts to get the number right but then it just rang and rang.

Pick up the damn phone, you bastard.

Nothing.

She let it ring, but felt her eyes slowly close and her head droop on to her chest as the repetitive chirping crooned monotonously in her ear.

It stopped abruptly, waking her up. It had run out of time.

'Bastard,' she murmured without venom now and pressed the buttons again, in a different order this time.

After only three rings it was picked up and a sleepy voice said, 'Hello?'

'Wakey, wakey, Jodie. It's me.'

'Anthea, what on earth's the matter? Is something wrong?'

Anthea laughed. 'No, of course not. I just felt like speaking to my little sister, that's all. Nothing wrong with that.'

'Except that it's the middle of the night.'

'Is it?' Anthea looked at the swaying darkness outside the expanse of window and wondered how long it had been there. 'What time is it?'

'One forty-five.'

'Oh! Are you in bed?'

'Of course I am in bed. In bed and asleep. So if it's nothing important, goodnight.'

'No, Jodie, don't go. Please don't go. I just felt like a chat.'

There was a pause, so long that it crossed Anthea's mind that her sister had fallen asleep, but then Jodie said, 'Anthea, you're drunk.'

Anthea heard the gentle affection in the voice and smiled back, as though Jodie could see her.

'Not very,' she chuckled.

'Are you alone?'

'Yes. Utterly and miserably.'

'Poor old you. Or do I mean rich old you? Either way, my dear drunken sibling, you should be tucked up in bed and snoring your head off prior to sharpening your knife ready for a day in the City tomorrow.'

Anthea moaned, a sound like a wounded cow. 'That's the trouble. I don't want to go in tomorrow.'

'But why not?' Jodie asked with surprise. 'You love your job. You're always telling me how much . . .'

'That was then,' Anthea interrupted. 'Now is now.'

'What has happened?'

'Nothing. Nothing much. I'm just tired of it all.'

Another pause. 'Anthea, what you need is a good night's rest. Everything will look better in the morning.'

'Promise?'

Jodie gave a soft laugh that reminded Anthea of when they used to make up jokes to amuse each other. Jodie's were always the best. The best and the dirtiest.

'Promise?' she repeated.

'I promise.'

'Okay, I'll believe you.'

'Can I go back to sleep now?'

'Is Matt in your bed?'

'Of course he is. He lives here.'

'Lucky you.'

'No sign of Julian?'

'No, he's dead and buried.'

'Then go out and find yourself another man, Anthea, if that's what is making you miserable. And this time look for more than just a bunch of muscles with a bloody great prick.'

Anthea giggled. 'There aren't many unattached ones out there.'

'Don't be a defeatist. You don't need a guy anyway. You've got everything going for you. Brains, looks, money, the lot. But if you're that desperate, rush out there and pick yourself one. And in the meantime, go and get yourself some beauty sleep.'

'Okay, I can take a hint.'

Jodie laughed again and Anthea wanted to give her a hug, but instead added, ''Night.'

'Goodnight. Sweet dreams.'

'And you. Give Matt a kiss from me.'

'I will.'

'Let me hear it.'

'Hear what?'

'You giving him my kiss.'

'God, Anthea, you really must be drunk,' Jodie said, but she must have obliged because the next thing Anthea heard was the unmistakable moist sound of a kiss, followed by a faint masculine rumble. Then the line went dead.

Anthea returned to her goatskin and curled up on it, feeling even lonelier.

6

Jodie was showing a party of complete strangers round her parents' house. She was just wondering why she was wearing only a bikini, when a police siren went off sending them all into a panic stampede and their cries of alarm dragged her up and out of her dream. With an uneasy stab into the drowsy intestines of her mind, it occurred to her that it was the telephone.

Not again. She opened her eyes and peered at the luminous red numerals watching her from beside the bed, but they still said the middle of the night. Three twenty-seven.

'If that's Anthea again,' Matt sighed from somewhere under the duvet, 'tell her we've moved.'

Jodie picked up the receiver, listened in silence for a moment, then said quickly, 'Ten minutes', and hung up. Immediately she was out of bed and pulling on a pair of jeans.

'What was that about?' Matt asked, instantly alert. Night calls invariably meant a disaster.

'It's a fire.'

He flung off the duvet and reached for his clothes. 'A good one?'

'Matt, you're turning into a ghoul.'

'Well, we haven't had a decent fire for ages. Where is it?'

'At the school.'

'Which school?'

'Dad's.'

'Christ!'

'Jack didn't know how big it is, but he said the fire-engines are out there in force.' She stopped, one arm thrust into a thick sweater. 'You don't have to go. Jack is covering it.'

'I'm coming,' he said.

'Good.' Camera already around her neck, she grabbed her car keys. 'Let's go.'

The flames reached up savagely into the night sky, whipped up into a furious frenzy of destruction by the south-westerly that blew in from the sea. Showers of sparks and ash swirled and struggled in its grip and threatened to carry the fire to nearby buildings, as they escaped above the reach of the firemen's hoses.

It was the science block. The moment Jodie fought her way through to the front of the crowd of onlookers who circled like vultures, she knew it was the death of the new laboratories, her father's pride and passion. Opened only nine months ago, they were to be the school's flagship in its attempts to claw its way up the league tables. She felt a sickening wrench as some emotion she thought was long since buried inside her pulled loose and she searched among the faces for that of her father, but it was nowhere to be seen.

Matt was at her side. 'My God, that's one hell of an inferno.' Even from this distance they could feel the heat.

'It must be the chemicals. It's the science labs.'

'I'll start asking questions and see what I can find out.'

She nodded, the shutter in her head already at work. 'I need to get closer.' The bulk of the main building was blocking out too much of her view of the fire behind it.

'Flash your Press pass and they should let you through. But don't go getting your nose burnt.' He was about to move away, but turned and looked at Jodie more closely. He touched her shoulder. 'It can be rebuilt.'

'I know.'

She began to edge along the police tape that had been strung up to cordon off the danger area. Everything was clearly well under control, the police cars and fire-engines were surely proof of that, and yet it felt like chaos. As if something wild and raw had escaped, something that stung sharp and acrid in her nostrils and shrieked exultantly as it consumed her father's school. The fire was a disaster for him, she knew that, and yet she could feel the excitement kicking deep down in her gut and see it reflected on the faces of those who crowded in at the kill.

It was her first fire. She knew she had to watch her exposures because the intense illumination from the flames could distort the reality on film, and she did not want to lose the deep contrasts. She needed to catch some detail in the shadows. The auto-exposure would, like the people around her, look only at the flames. Quickly and efficiently she sought out vantage points from where she took shot after shot. The fascinated shock on faces, the patient professionalism of the police, the blood-red fire-engines like waggons circled in a defensive corral, the casual courage of the firemen at work. She strove hard to capture them all. But it was the fire itself that drew her ever closer.

Time and again she was turned back. Her path blocked by men bristling with uniformed authority. The Press pass won her an occasional inch or two, but nothing like the mile she wanted. Frustrated, she was resorting to more crowd reactions, when a hand on her back made her jump. At times like this, she was in the zone. A zone where she became as much a part of her camera as its spool or lens, so intent on observing that she forgot she was still a person who was expected to communicate with the world in a way that her camera did not have to. It took her mind a moment to catch up with her body.

'Fiona. I thought you would be around here somewhere.'

Fiona Bowles was a photographer on another paper, the *Westonport Weekly News*, and despite occasional professional rivalry, they enjoyed a cheerful friendship that enlivened some of the more dour civic functions they were obliged to attend.

'Quite a bonfire, isn't it?' Fiona enthused. 'Have you got anything decent yet?'

'Still working on it. What about you?' Jodie asked.

'I need a tight action shot of the firemen.'

'I know, it's that bloody building in front. Right in the way. Half the fire is hidden behind it, and the cordon the police have strung out is far too wide.'

'Tell me about it! By the way, I saw Matt a few minutes ago talking to the headmaster.' She looked across at Jodie, curiously. 'Hey, he's your father, isn't he?'

'Yes.'

'Lucky you. An inside track.'

'He doesn't see it like that.'

'Useful though, I bet.'

Jodie shrugged. 'Not really.'

A sudden and furious fusillade of flame and smoke drew attention as a section of the roof caved in. All eyes turned to it. Jodie did not hesitate. She was under the cordon and racing into the shadows in the lee of the main building, before the eyes had done more than blink.

The abrupt darkness around her came as a relief after the scorching glare of the flames, but as she moved closer, the heat became more intense. She could feel it like something alive on her skin. When she rounded a corner, the full extent of the fire leapt into view and for the first time it was obvious that the whole of the new block had been lost, as well as the smaller art building beside it. The firemen were able to do no more than fight to prevent the flames engulfing the rest of the school.

Jodie dropped to a crouch and started taking more photographs. She was totally engrossed inside her camera's eye when a running figure flicked across her line of vision. Slight and female, and hunched as it ran. She could not see what it was bent over, but there was something large and bulky in its arms. A heartbeat later, five more black figures streamed out of the back of the main school building, totally unaware that from Jodie's position, they were silhouetted as clear as ducks in a shooting gallery against the fierce light of the fire behind them Each one of them was clutching something. Something heavy, judging by the way they moved.

Jodie's fingers worked automatically, independent of her head. Her heart kicked inside her chest, the way it did when she knew she had something good. At the far extent of her range of vision, the figures merged into the darkness that became the black outskirts of the school grounds, and disappeared.

Jodie waited.

The heat was vicious. Squalls of gritty smoke crept into her eyes, making them sting and blur. She blinked to keep their focus clear. With her back pressed against a shadowed section of the wall, she was all but invisible and her patience was rewarded when the six figures reappeared and raced across the open ground back towards the main building. Anyone glancing over from the fire would not have noticed them, black shapes against a black background, and they headed confidently in through the entrance from which they had originally emerged.

Jodie crept closer.

The heat increased, making her skin tighten, and she was aware that the shadows around her were fewer and greyer. She felt more exposed. A determined eye could spot her now. Her throat was dry as sand, and it was not just because of the fire.

Before she expected it, the figures were back. This time, at closer range, she could see them better. Six girls, with blackened faces behind black scarves, black clothes and black woollen hats. Again each carried a bulky object which Jodie at first identified as a television and video machine, but then realised it must be a monitor. A monitor and computer. They were stripping the computer suite.

The thieving bastards.

She pressed the Nikon's button over and over.

Though all looked in her direction, their eyes must have been dazzled by the flames, because none of them registered that she was there in the smoky shadows. She did not wait for them to disappear again, but turned and ran back the way she had come, hurling herself under the cordon belt. She pushed through the throng of people and rushed over to the nearest police car. Inside sat PC Flannigan, a good-natured young officer with whom she had come into contact before.

'Greg, hurry. Kids are looting the school at the back of the main building. There's a group of . . .'

He reacted instantly. A few words into his police radio and then he was out of the car and off in the direction she had indicated. He picked up another constable at the cordon, but turned to face Jodie who was following in their wake.

'Sorry, Jodie. No further for you, I'm afraid.'

'But I was the one who told . . .'

'No. It's not safe. Stay behind the barrier tape.'

A policewoman emerged from nowhere and laid a hand on Jodie's arm. 'You can remain here with me,' she said with a firm smile.

'No thanks,' Jodie retorted, shook off the hand and moved

away into the crowd. Maybe she could find Matt, or even Jack James, and get them primed.

But Matt and Jack were nowhere to be seen. The person she found was her father. He was standing well back from the crush of the crowd, deeper in the shadows, but even there the glow of the flames managed to paint his grey hair a lurid gold. He looked sick. As if someone had kicked him in the stomach. The stoop of his ramrod back made Jodie want to look away. She had the sense to keep her fingers off the Nikon. But what could she say to him? What was there to be said? She knew no words of hers could stop the haemorrhage inside him, so she went over and just stood at his side. Close enough to hear the faintest of groans, like a whisper of pain, each time he breathed out.

It took several minutes for him to realise it was her.

'Jodie,' he said and though he turned his head briefly in her direction, his eyes remained on the fire. 'It's gone.'

The rawness in his voice made rage thud into her skull. 'The police will catch them,' she assured him.

'Maybe.' He spoke quietly, staring at the fire's frantic attempts to side-step the firemen's efforts. 'But they can't bring it back.'

A shout and a surge of movement somewhere off to their left drew Jodie's attention. 'If it was arson,' she said, 'they will throw the book at the culprits.'

'No, I think not. They will probably never even catch them. But my laboratories are gone.'

'It might not have been deliberate arson. Perhaps it was an accident with a cigarette end.'

She said it to comfort him. To remove the sting from the pain. And because she vividly recalled her own careless behaviour with cigarette butts when she was that age. Not because she believed it.

A sudden wayward eddy of wind brought a billow of smoke and sparks in their direction, sending people near them into paroxysms of coughing, but her father took no notice of it. Just shut his eyes. Jodie choked on a lungful of the suffocating air but her interest in the commotion to their left overcame her discomfort, as she tried to make out what was going on over there. She glanced back at her father and found him watching her.

'Go and take your pictures,' he said in a voice that chilled the heat from her skin. 'It's what you're here for, isn't it?'

Jodie reached out and touched his arm. It felt stiff and hard under the ancient tweed of his jacket. 'Dad, I'm sorry. I . . .'

'Just go, Jodie. Go. Or you'll miss the action.'

Her hand was not enough to bridge the gulf, so she let it drop to her side, and after an empty pause, turned away. She left him standing alone in the shadows.

The commotion was around a police car. Jodie forged a path through the crush of bodies until she was close enough to spot Matt's blond head at the front. She elbowed her way to his side.

He turned to her. 'Where have you been hiding?'

'Inside a cloud of smoke fumes.'

He smiled at her and she could see that his whole face was bright and excited, his pupils immense, and she wondered if hers was the same. Is that what her father had seen? She looked around at the other faces. All were hungry for adrenalin.

'What's going on here?' she asked, raising her camera.

'The police have caught somebody.'

'Is it a girl?'

'Yes.' Matt looked at her curiously. 'How did you know?'

'I'll tell you when we've finished with this. It'll make a good story. A scoop.'

'Tell me what . . .'

But Jodie had ducked her head and was snapping pictures of the inside of the police car where a young figure in black cowered with her hands over part of her face. Beside her sat the policewoman. PC Flannigan was standing by the driver's door and at that moment spotted Jodie. 'As you see, we've caught one of them. Thanks for tipping us the word. We'd have missed them completely without it.'

'So you owe me one,' Jodie reminded him.

The constable gave a nod. 'I'm glad I've seen you, because I'll need you to come down to the station to give a statement about what you saw.'

'Okay, but I'll just finish off here first.'

Matt was impatient. He drew her away from the attentive ears that surrounded them. 'Okay, let's hear it.'

So she told him. About the dash through the cordon, the girls looting the school, the wait for their return and the search for police assistance. She told it all. Even the policewoman's restraining hand on her arm. Only the bit about her father was left out.

'That's fantastic,' Matt congratulated her. 'I can't believe you've got photographs of them. A real shot in the dark.'

She laughed, but not much.

He bent his head. 'Are you all right?'

She nodded. 'It just makes me so mad.'

Matt put an arm round her shoulders and gave her a little shake. 'Don't get caught up in it, Jodie. I know this fire strikes close to home, but you mustn't become so involved.'

'I know, I know. I've heard it a thousand times.'

'You have to maintain a professional distance. For your own sake. You mustn't let the job get to you.'

'I know that, but this time it's different.' She looked at him bleakly. 'I can't.'

7

Elizabeth Buxton was well aware of her younger daughter's tendency to be obsessive. It was a characteristic she was all too familiar with, as her own father possessed it in irritating abundance. Neither of them knew when to stop.

Like the fire.

It had not known when to stop.

Not until it had reduced her husband's pride and joy to blackened stench and grotesque rubble. Ashes to ashes, dust to dust. Oh Alan, my poor Alan, it's a bunch of science laboratories, bricks and mortar, not breath and mind. This morning when he returned home briefly for a shower and shave, he had looked terrible, as though grey ash had settled on his soul as well as on his skin. She had offered him breakfast and sympathy, but he had been able to swallow neither. And now Jodie was here, bristling with her theories and voicing her disdain for the police's chances of catching the rest of the thieves.

'The girl is saying it was an act of impulse,' Jodie was explaining. 'Claims she saw the fire and made the most of the confusion to get into the school. She is one of Dad's pupils, so she knows her way around. Others were doing the same, but she claims she has no idea who they were.'

'Maybe it's true.'

'And maybe snakes have balls.'

Elizabeth passed no comment, but her eyebrows puckered in a frown.

'There's no proof,' Jodie added, 'that those girls started the fire. Not yet anyway. But I believe they must have been in on it. It's all too convenient otherwise.'

'Jodie, just leave it to the police and concentrate on your photography. That's your job. It's what you're good at.'

'Just wait until you see today's front page. It's one of my best. The black figures are in tiny silhouette against the burning glow of flames and on one side of it a fireman and his hose are wrapped in a snarl of smoke. It's really great.'

Her mother smiled at the irony. What had devastated her husband, had inspired her daughter.

'It sounds wonderful. Are any of the figures of the girls identifiable?'

'No. But it wouldn't be too difficult to track down these computers. The thieves are bound to try to shift them right away. They won't want to be caught with the evidence at home, so if I scour the "For Sale" adverts in our paper and trek round a few car-boot sales, I might . . .'

'Leave it to the police,' Elizabeth repeated. 'Investigating is something you know nothing about. It's bad enough having your father talking of questioning every pupil at the school himself.'

Jodie gave the sideways twitch of her lips that Elizabeth recognised as her Oh-God-what's-he-up-to-now? expression.

'For heaven's sake, tell him not to. Dad doesn't have any idea. All he'll do is make things worse by accusing kids of something they didn't do.'

'No, of course he won't accuse anybody. Only ask a few questions. Trust him. And trust the police. They're both experienced and know what they're doing.'

'And I don't?'

Elizabeth smiled at her daughter. 'Jodie, you're a good photographer. Stick to that.'

Jodie leaned forward in her seat. 'But Mum, I can help.'

She looked at her daughter's animated face, the passionate blue eyes with their fringe of dark lashes, so committed, so single-minded that it sent a shiver of alarm skittering through her nervous system and set her leg aching. Damn the blasted leg. She rubbed the plaster, as if she could send comfort through its hard shell. Elizabeth had seen Jodie like this before when she got so fired up over something that she lost interest in all else. Like the summer she went in for that photography competition.

She was sixteen at the time and had decided to make it a study of birth and death. Of animals, not people, thank God for small mercies. She had spent every waking hour at farms and vets and even at her grandfather's house, because one of his ancient old dogs – the really evil-smelling one – was dying of kidney failure. But at the same time one of his horde of cats was about to give birth. Jodie hadn't slept at all then. And now there was that same look about her. Maybe it would be worth having a word with Matt.

'Feel like a cup of coffee?' Jodie asked suddenly, standing up. 'I expect you got hardly any sleep either last night. Is your leg no better?'

Elizabeth grimaced. 'Old bones. They take their time about everything.'

Jodie bent down and gave her a hug. 'Rubbish, you're not old,' she said. 'Grandad is the one who's old. Like Methuselah, he is. You're still at your peak.'

Elizabeth laughed, pleased by her daughter's attempt to cheer her up. 'That's what I like to hear. Flattery.' She kissed the smooth young cheek. 'Better than any medicine.'

Jodie tapped the plaster. 'That'll teach you to go climbing trees at your age. You can buy plums from a supermarket instead of skydiving off a branch for them, you know.'

'I thought you said I was at my peak.'

Jodie laughed. 'I'll make the coffee.'

While her daughter was in the kitchen, Elizabeth shut her eyes and found herself immediately drifting into a mental no-man's-land where thoughts bobbed past in disconnected bursts. She was glad Jodie had come. Had kept her promise. Today of all days, knowing what was going on at the school, she needed company. Even those silly crosswords would be a mild distraction for later, when she was alone. Elizabeth prided herself on the speed with which she could dispose of the *Telegraph*'s crossword, so the *Gazette*'s efforts were a bit like a trip back to kindergarten, but she appreciated the fact that Jodie had remembered to bring them.

Her mind was just jostling with the reminder that her father's clean bed-linen was still stacked neatly on her tumble-drier instead of on his bed, when her coffee arrived. Perhaps she could ask Jodie to take them over to him. She scratched a patch of dry skin above the plaster and groaned inwardly at this wretched dependence on others.

'Coffee for the walking-wounded,' Jodie announced, and placed it with a plate of chocolate biscuits on a table within reach.

The biscuits were a nuisance. Since giving up her job as a chemist a year ago, Elizabeth had put on weight. It had annoyed her at first, until she had stopped weighing and stopped worrying, but now she found herself indulging in some serious eating out of boredom and frustration. With Jodie here, she reminded herself, she wasn't bored, and so could manage to ignore the plate.

'My visit to Anthea's new flat was fun. She's got it looking brilliant, of course, and it has a great view over the river. Have you spoken to her recently?' Jodie enquired, her hands cupped round the coffee.

'Yes, I rang her this morning to tell her about the fire. She sounded really down in the dumps, but she wouldn't tell me anything.'

'It's man-trouble.'

'Oh, my foolish Anthea. She seems to go from one unsuitable fellow to another. Is that Julian out of the picture now?'

'Yes. A waste of breath, he was. She's better off alone.'

Elizabeth felt an irresistible and overwhelming urge to gather her two girls into her arms and make everything better, but instead she made do with a sigh and a sip of coffee. It was a long time, a very long time, since she had been able to perform that miracle. 'Maybe I'll invite Anthea to come home for a few days,' she suggested. 'I'd like to see her, and a weekend away from London will do her good.'

She could tell by Jodie's face that it was a bad idea.

'I don't think Dad will be in the mood, Mum. Nor Anthea, for that matter.'

She was right, of course. Alan would at the moment not have the patience for other people's needs, not even those of his elder daughter. Elizabeth shelved the idea for now, and in doing so experienced a swan-dive of disappointment that sent her hand reaching for the chocolate biscuits.

Damn the leg. And damn all fire-raisers.

*   *   *

'Take the blasted things back and tell her I don't want them.'

'Grandad, behave yourself.'

'Get away with you or I'll set Tess on you.'

Joe Bond was standing on the doorstep, holding the dog by the collar to restrain her frantic efforts to throw herself at Jodie and cover her with ecstatic affection. Tess was a black-and-white sheepdog-cross whose manners were no better than her master's.

'You don't scare me, you bunch of wussies,' Jodie said and squeezed past them.

It was a small terraced house with a narrow hallway that smelt of cat's pee and had wallpaper that carried a grey grease-mark along its length at knee height, the result of countless contacts with canine backs. Jodie was surprised that there was any wallpaper left there at all after the number of times she had seen her grandfather's pack of mongrels in full cry.

'If I don't scare you, Goliath damn well will,' her grandfather muttered with obvious relish, as he shuffled after her into his front room.

Her heart plunged. Goliath always did scare her. Rigid. No matter how often she went through the routine, her blood froze in her veins every single time. She had learned to paste a tolerant smile on her face, but it didn't fool Goliath. Nor her grandfather.

The snarling started the moment she stepped through the door. The Dobermann stood stiff-legged in the centre of the room, a sleek slender killing-machine, and showed her the white fangs that were about to tear her throat out. Jodie did not move. Not a muscle, nor an eyelash. She waited for her grandfather to amble past her and it seemed to her that he was ambling even more slowly than usual, to make her pay for the arrival of the clean sheets.

'Shut up, you brute. Or our dainty visitor here may think she's not welcome. God forbid that!' he said with a wicked cackle and wrapped a hand round the snarling muzzle to hold it shut.

It was a frail mottled hand, with a thumb swollen into arthritic revolt, that the animal could have snapped off as easily as a dried-out twig, yet at his touch its hackles instantly subsided, its fury was replaced with moist devotion and a soft wet tongue crept out to apologise. Jodie was always impressed. Her grandfather had once been a man of average height and build, but now, at eighty-three, it was as if the years were leaching his body as well as his life, so that he had become as thin and brittle as one of the shrivelled leaves she had stepped on in the street. Yet he could silence this animal with a touch.

'One day that dog will take your hand off.'

He chuckled and stroked the smooth black head pressed against his scrawny thigh. 'No chance of that. He's a fussy eater. I'm all gristle and bone. But young flesh, now that's a different story. Moist, tender meat with hot blood coursing through it,' he smacked his lips with satisfaction, 'that's what you have a fancy for, isn't it, Goliath? Am I right?' They both eyed Jodie speculatively and she felt like knocking their heads together.

'Behave yourselves, the pair of you. I'm here bearing gifts.' She walked over and held a hand out to Goliath. He sniffed at it with interest, wolfed down the Malteser it contained and wagged his stump of a tail at her. She patted his head. 'We go through this foolishness every time, Goliath. When are you going to grow up?'

But she knew what it was about. His previous owners had abused him brutally. Grandad had found him in a gutter and nursed him back from the dead.

'And these are for you.' She dumped the fresh bed-linen into her grandfather's arms. 'With strict instructions to put them on the bed. Right now. I am to take the dirty lot back to her.'

He scowled, his skin seeming to rustle. 'The trouble with your mother is that she won't give up.'

Jodie laughed. 'I can't imagine where she gets that from.'

He dropped the armful of sheets with distaste on to a chair and a cat promptly materialised on top of them. 'I like my bed just the way it is, thank you, and that's how it's staying.'

He eased his bones down on to a hard chair and Jodie heard them both creak. Another cat instantly jumped on to his shoulder and started to rub its great black head against his stubble. Two other cats watched with mild interest from the cushion of dust on the windowsill, and Jodie lifted a fifth from an armchair which looked as if it had peeling sunburn, it was shredded so badly by sharp claws. She sat down and replaced the sleeping bundle on her lap. It was elderly, with bones that nudged into her legs. Somewhere around the house lurked another three or four felines and Jodie suspected they were probably on the bed that was not to be disturbed. Along with three more mongrels.

'Grandad, did you hear about the fire?'

'At the school last night, you mean?'

'Yes. It was appalling. Dad is gutted.'

'I heard your father interviewed on local radio this morning. Nearly spoiled my porridge, he did. He sounded bloody mad.' His watery colourless eyes brightened at the memory. 'Not often I've heard him like that. As if the cork had been pulled out of his arse. I thought headmasters were supposed to stay calm and in control at all times.'

Jodie leaned forward, disturbing the cat. 'What did he say?'

'Oh, I don't rightly remember. But he was mad all right. Went on and on about the terrible damage to the school. You'd think it was a person who had died, the way he was carrying on. Not just a bloody building.'

'You know what he's like. The school means so much to him. Losing the science labs is like . . .' she uncurled a sleepy limb from the cat on her lap 'old Minnalouche here losing a paw. That's how much it hurts.'

'He was going on about the girl they caught. Said she was letting down the school and all that kind of claptrap.'

'Yes, I know. I've heard it before.'

Joe Bond laughed, a high whinnying sound that startled Tess who had settled into a doze under his chair. 'I bet you have, girl. I bet you have. More than once.'

Their eyes snagged on each other and Jodie shifted the conversation to a subject out of harm's way. 'Did he know how long the rest of the school would have to be closed?'

He stared at her for a long moment, as if studying a chess move, then said with a sudden loss of interest, 'Just until the firemen say it's safe. He reckons that will be soon.'

'Well, that's something anyway. It could have been much

worse. The labs have gone but the main body of the school is untouched.'

'Saw it, did you?'

'Yes.'

'Photograph it?'

'Yes.'

He gave her a slow smile. 'Good, was it?'

She gave him back the smile with the added bonus of an incredulous shake of her head. 'Yes. It was something else!'

'Missed a treat, did I?'

'Oh Grandad, you should have been there, you would have loved it. All flames and smoke and chaos. And I took a great shot for the front page. You'll see it in the paper this afternoon. A sensation, I reckon. But don't tell Dad I said so, or he might think I started it.'

Her grandfather grunted his approval. 'It's bound to be insured, so he'll get it all back. He just likes making a fuss.'

'No, you've got it wrong. The money's not the point. It's the fact that there are kids at the school who would do such a thing. That's what gets to him most. I've tried in the past asking about the gangs there, the bullies and the trouble-makers, but he doesn't want to admit there's a problem. It smells too much of failure.'

'Yes, well, just 'cause he can spout the bloody *Encyclopaedia Britannica* doesn't mean he's got a scrap of sense in that pompous head of his. Ask your mum who built his bonfire too close to the fence last week.'

Jodie's eyes popped open wide with surprise. 'Dad?'

'Got it in one. Bloody arsonist himself, he is.'

Jodie burst out laughing. 'They certainly kept that quiet.'

Joe Bond was chuckling contentedly to himself, a wheezing sound that whistled in and out of his bony ribs like a punctured balloon. 'Ken Norris told me. His son works in the nursery garden over at Diphay that sold your father the new fencing.'

Ken Norris was her grandfather's companion in crime. He drove over in his ancient Bedford van twice a week to bundle the pack of dogs in the back and whisk them all off to the woods. The two old vandals took a saw with them and gradually they were stripping the woods and building up a huge mountain of logs in her grandfather's back garden. They sold it off for beer money throughout the winter.

Jodie stroked the comatose bundle of bones on her lap and was glad she had come.

'Fancy a beer?' she asked suddenly.

The old face cracked into a broad smile. 'Don't take after your parents much, do you?'

'I try not to.'

They both laughed and Jodie went into the kitchen. A crate of bottles was sitting on the floor and she picked up one, dusting it on her black jeans. She liked hers cold, so she went in search of one in the fridge, giving a wide berth to the sink which was overflowing with encrusted mugs and plates. She averted her eyes in case anything crawled among them. If he could chop down forests, sure as hell he could wash up dishes. The fridge was sprinkled with food, but it smelt musty and she could not help wondering about the date-stamps on the packets. But there was no doubt in her mind that Grandad would rather suffer a dose of the runs than a dose of her fussing, so she rooted out a beer next to a tube of toothpaste and returned to the front room.

'Why do you keep your toothpaste in the fridge?' she asked as she handed his beer to him. She sat down with her own, unwilling to risk one of his murky drinking glasses. Goliath wandered over and lay across her feet. She was tempted to kick him off, but thought better of it.

'Toothpaste tastes better out of the fridge, and anyway, my teeth like it cold. They're in great shape.' Proudly he raised his thin lips and displayed a wolfish set of yellow teeth. At least they were his own. 'I do them in the kitchen sink.'

Jodie thought about the dishes and her stomach squirmed. Young people weren't the only delinquents round here. She decided to forget about the sheets and opened her beer.

It was during the afternoon that the reaction began to set in. Jodie went through the motions, but nothing more. Her limbs felt heavy and disobedient and several times when she looked through her camera lens, it misted over as though someone had put too many filters across it. Her eyes seemed reluctant to focus on the realities in front of them. Her mind kept flicking away from whatever subject she was photographing – a bunch of schoolchildren, a pub sign that was causing aggro, the new landscaping around the harbour – and chasing back to the images of the early hours.

Flames that burnt away part of your life.

A headmaster's face, ash-grey and crumbling.

Six figures, hunched and running.

A smoke-saturated fireman throwing up over his hose.

Frightened young eyes cowering in the back of a police car.

The images twisted and struggled in her head and somehow mixed themselves up with the smudged crucifix on the wall behind the old changing-rooms.

It was a relief when she returned to the office. It hummed with activity; people walked faster, spoke louder, the way it always was when a big story broke. As if quicksilver had been injected into their veins.

Community.

That was Roy Dunmore's constant clarion call. The paper had to be involved in the community and to keep the community involved in the paper. Well, sure as hell her camera was involved in both. A good night's sleep was what she needed. Her eyes were stinging as if the smoke of last night still clouded them, so she went to find herself a black coffee. It wouldn't make them better but it might wash away some of the images in her head.

At the drinks machine she bumped into Jack James. He looked even worse than she felt. His thin face was the colour of her grandfather's stubble and his eyes had settled into slits.

He greeted her with, 'You can take that fat smirk off your face.'

Jodie grinned at him. 'Don't get touchy just because my picture ousted your moribund trampolinist off the front page. And before you say it, no, I didn't set fire to the school for that precise purpose.'

Jack pushed more coins into the machine. 'I wouldn't put it past you. But it's a good thing they've caught one of the culprits, isn't it?' He turned and handed her the coffee.

'Thanks.' She sipped the grey liquid and winced at its sweetness. 'She is denying the arson charge, don't forget.'

'I can't imagine her sticking to that story for long. Not now she's all alone without her mates to back her up.'

'Just because she denies starting the fire, that doesn't make it true.'

'Of course not. But she's probably well aware of the consequences. If she's got any sense, she'll keep her mouth shut.'

'At fourteen, they're not going to give her a custodial sentence for pinching a computer. But if they can prove she's a fire-raiser, then she becomes a menace to the community. A whole different ball-game.'

'Bloody stupid kid.'

Jodie recalled the cornered eyes in the car. 'She's far worse than stupid, Jack. She's dangerous.'

'Don't exaggerate. These kids just do it to show off. It's part of their rites of passage. They think it makes them look big to be seen flouting the law. I would guess that they had no intention of lighting such a bonfire and it scared the shit out of them, just as much as it did us.'

'You mean a scam that got out of hand?'

'Most likely. Children have always loved to play with matches. We all went through it at some stage.'

Jodie placed the coffee cup on top of the machine and slipped a few coins into the slot. 'I think you're being naive, Jack. These are not children messing around. It was obvious the girls knew exactly what they were after.' She pressed the hot chocolate button.

Jack yawned, displaying a mouthful of uneven ivory. 'I'd better get back to the keyboard before I die on my feet. Dunmore's put me on a burglary over at Plainmoor. Apparently a couple of eye-witnesses say they saw a girl climbing over the back fence.'

'Interesting.'

'That's what I thought until I went over there this afternoon and found they are a couple in their eighties and as blind as geriatric bats. Both have cataracts and wouldn't know a girl from a goat, if it bit them on the nose.'

Jodie smiled. 'You can't win them all. Word gets round and it becomes contagious. Teenage girls will now be sprouting up all over the place and get every local crime from highway robbery to date rape dumped on them.'

Jack picked up his own coffee. 'Got to go. People to phone, words to write.'

'Stones to crawl under?'

'Bastard,' he laughed and loped off down the corridor.

Matt looked up when Jodie perched herself on the corner of his desk.

'How come you look so bright and breezy, while I'm like something the cat spewed up last night?' she asked.

He smiled and studied her face long enough to make her feel self-conscious.

'Because I don't stuff myself with Maltesers all day?' he suggested.

Jodie laughed. 'That might have something to do with it.' She leaned over and scanned what was on his screen. It was for tomorrow's paper. A further piece that speculated about what emergency measures were being considered to cover the school's lack of science facilities. A few solid quotes from her father were included.

'You spoke to Dad?'

'Yes. This morning.'

That surprised her.

'How did he sound?'

'Very subdued. As if he's still in shock and functioning on auto-pilot.'

'Did you see him at the school?'

Matt shook his head and altered a word on the screen. Jodie knew she was interrupting him but couldn't let it go.

'At home?'

'No.'

'Where then?'

Matt abandoned the screen and sat back in his chair. 'Do you really need this now?'

Jodie nodded. 'Yes.'

'Okay.' He ruffled a hand through his hair, as if to readjust his brain, and swung his chair round to face her. His leg touched hers. She felt the warmth of it through the denim and wondered if he even noticed. 'Okay, I had a talk with him. But it was only on the telephone, so I have no idea whether he looked dead or alive. Nearer dead, I would guess from his voice. As if he was not involved.'

'Or could not bear to be involved any more? Reached saturation point?'

'Could be. The strange thing is that he was the one who rang me.'

'Dad rang you! I don't believe it.'

'It's true.'

'He was on the radio as well, Grandad says. So he's at last discovered enough sense to try to manipulate the media, instead of putting up the barricades.'

'Yes, that's exactly the impression I got. And he did actually say that he was telephoning because he wanted the paper to get the facts straight. That this was too important an occurrence for him to risk any scare-mongering on our part. He wasn't exactly endearing, but I got his drift. His message came across loud and clear.'

'What was it?'

'To reassure parents and children. Business as usual, starting next week.'

Too often in the past Jodie had sworn that her father was infuriating, but now he was in trouble. So who did he contact at the *Gazette*? Matt. She kicked her heel against his desk.

Matt put a hand on her knee. 'Ring him, Jodie. Talk to him.'

'He'll think I'm just after more copy for the paper.'

'So what? Let him think what he likes. But do it, if that's what you want.'

It was always the same. Just when she was veering way off-line and making herself miserable, Matt would straighten the rails and get her back on track. It was an extraordinary knack he had for knowing precisely the moment when she would listen.

'Okay,' she agreed, 'you're right. I'll go round to see him this evening.'

'Sense at last.' He returned his hand to the keyboard. 'Now will you clear off and let me get back to work?'

She jumped off the desk and gave him a quick kiss, rare in the office. 'You may.'

At that moment, Roy Dunmore approached and placed a broad

hand on the shoulder of each of them. 'You did a good job last night, the pair of you. Got us talked about. It's obvious you make an effective team.'

'I'm just finishing a follow-up for tomorrow,' Matt said. 'I've spoken to the local education department for their comments, but the police are not giving out anything more yet.'

'Right, keep at them and get some background on the girl.' His eyes fixed Jodie with a grey stare. 'Maybe your father could help us there.'

So that was it. Inside info. Jodie shook her head. 'I doubt it.'

Dunmore nodded, and she was surprised when he did not ask her to push it. Instead he said, 'The girl is a minor, so we can't name her. But what I want you two to do is find out more. Drop anything else and work on this. This is a story worth building. Get hold of her friends, her family, boyfriends, whatever. Plenty of pictures. I don't want this story to die yet.'

'That's great, Roy,' Jodie said. 'If we can connect her to the fire . . .'

'That's a big "if",' Dunmore commented. 'That picture of yours, the one of the thieves in front of the flames, has got everyone fired up, if you'll excuse the pun, and I want to give them more. If we can keep their interest up, they will want the latest developments each day. This could be a real boost to the *Gazette*'s circulation.'

'Wherever I went today,' Jodie said, 'people were talking about it and asking me for more details.'

Roy Dunmore glanced at his watch. 'It's late now, almost eight o'clock, so there's not much more you can do now. Make an early start tomorrow. I'll get Jack to pick up whatever else you're working on, Matt.'

'Right.'

Matt and Jodie exchanged looks. Jack was going to love them.

The news-editor turned to leave but stopped to add, 'Jodie, that was a brilliant picture. Real heroine stuff. I'm putting it out to the nationals. They may well pick it up.' He set off back to the news-desk, his suit more crumpled than usual, as if it had had a restless day.

'Oh God,' Matt groaned. 'Now she's going to be unbearable to live with.'

'You bet I am,' Jodie promised. 'Especially if I make it into a national paper.'

'Go home quickly, while I finish up here. Soak your head in a bucket of ice and maybe it will shrink.'

Jodie patted his cheek before she left. 'Count yourself lucky, Matt Reynolds. Heroines are few and far between.'

8

As Jodie walked to the car park, she did not even notice the unpleasant autumn drizzle, dense as mist and dark as ditchwater. Her thoughts were running haywire in other directions, already planning where to start. She would find out from Matt this evening how far he had gone with the police and the school, and tomorrow, armed with the name and address of the girl who was caught, they would go hunting for information about the crowd she ran with. They needed to find those other girls.

Dad *could* help. But would he?

Unlikely.

But maybe if she explained to him what this meant. How important it was to her. Her first real assignment in investigative journalism, instead of the usual snapshots to fill the community's photo-album.

And then there were the nationals.

The word chimed inside her head like a striking clock that has been overwound and won't shut up. The sound sent reverbera-tions rippling through her limbs, so that the soles of her feet tingled as they hurried over the wet ground. If she and Matt could put together a really effective piece on this . . . If one of the national papers would pick up her picture and maybe the whole story with it . . .

If.

For a brief moment as she approached her car, she let her head be distracted by the dream. It was the one that kept her going when she was on her tenth photo-call of the day and felt that if she had to take yet another shot of a big cheesy grin straight at camera, she would weep. But that was what the locals wanted, pretty pictures of themselves in their moment of glory. They rushed out and bought four copies each. So no arty stuff, please. But on a national, well, it was a different story. The complete reverse. A telling shot of a politician yawning at an inopportune moment, the back of a crumpled dress or the twist of a head, intimate and revealing, and capable of stopping you in your tracks.

That was what she wanted. So bad it made her teeth ache.

'You're Jodie Buxton, aren't you?'

The voice came out of the darkness. Jodie was standing with one hand on her Mini's door, car keys an inch from business, but she turned and peered with curiosity through the curtain of drizzle.

'Yes, I'm Jodie.'

From behind a silver Mondeo that belonged to Jeff Blakey, one of the subs, a figure had emerged, small and feminine, and hardly discernible among the surrounding shadows. It was wearing black. All black. A black scarf wrapped round the lower half of the face.

Jodie's heart kicked viciously in recognition.

'Yes, I am Jodie Buxton. Who are you?' She stepped forward quickly, hand outstretched to snatch at the scarf, but the figure danced nimbly to one side and laughed. It was a soft, low sound and infinitely galling.

'Don't try that kind of rough stuff,' the voice warned. 'You're out of your league.'

'I think not,' Jodie retorted, making another grab at the girl and this time her fingers touched a damp sweater, but nothing more. It melted away into the rain.

The mocking laugh came again and seemed to multiply. Jodie swung round, her eyes seeking the elusive figure, her hands determined not to let it escape a third time. But with chilling clarity, suddenly through the darkness Jodie saw why the girl could afford to jeer with such confidence and she felt a grinding spasm of unease clutch at her stomach.

There were more of them.

Five.

A pack of five girls. Five wolves. Garbed in identical black that transformed them into one, not five. They were pressed together, touching at hip and shoulder, like Siamese twins that shared one heart. But these, Jodie knew, shared one purpose.

She faced them. 'What is it you want here?'

'You're the one who took that fucking picture.' It was a different girl who spoke, taller, her voice angry and harsh.

'Yes, I am. And you are the girls in it.'

'We don't like that picture.'

'I bet you don't.' Jodie took a step towards them. 'But the police do.' She focused on the shorter girl at the front. Not the nimble dancer who had escaped her grasp before, but a heavier member of the pack who would be slower when she reached for the scarf.

Casually, as if part of a familiar routine, the tall girl brought forward one hand and showed Jodie what it held between its long fingers. It was half a brick. Ragged at the edges and cement-covered on one side.

Jodie stopped thinking about the scarf.

'You put our mate in the nick,' accused another of the black figures. 'She heard the frigging cop thank you for it, so don't say you didn't.'

'Fucking grasser.'

'Get your nose out of our business.'

'Cocksucker.'

'Big-mouthed bitch.'

Jodie could feel the temperature around her rising, blistering her skin. She edged a step backwards.

'I did report it to the police,' she said and was not sure how much her voice betrayed her. 'But they are more interested in the fire than in the stolen computers. So if what your friend says is true, that the fire had already started and you just made the most of the opportunity, then you should speak to . . .'

'We're speaking to you, bitch. That's what we're here for,' the tall one hissed at her and raised the fist that brandished the brick.

The others instantly spread out, stretching the Siamese bonds to the limit, and took up positions circling Jodie. She could sense their excitement like a solid wall around her. If she reached out, it would be there, hot and hard to the touch.

She could fight.

Or she could run.

She made a dash for the widest gap and thought she had made it, but a hand seized her long hair and yanked her back into their midst.

She screamed.

The dancing girl laughed, delighted, and leant over and spat in Jodie's face. It slithered wet and warmer than the rain down her cheek. Jodie kicked out at the girl's shin and connected. The laugh became a shriek.

The sound of it was broken by male voices. 'What's going on over there?'

'Who the hell is making all that row?'

Heavy footsteps were running across the car park. Jodie felt her hair released and turned to see the sports editor and his deputy pounding towards her, shouting and gesticulating. The girls had evaporated into the dark blur that seemed to wrap itself round the edges of her vision, leaving a narrow central tunnel through which she could see with any clarity. For a moment she thought it was a camera lens.

But it was shock.

She blinked it away and as it retreated, she caught sight of the tall girl standing alongside the stubby bonnet of her Mini. The girl waited until their eyes met, hot-tempered eyes, dark above the mask of the scarf, and then very deliberately she hurled the brick through the windscreen. It shattered into a hailstorm of glass, just as the two men reached it.

'You bloody vandal,' one shouted and the other made a grab for the girl, but she was up and running before he even came close.

Jodie snatched a deep breath and took off after her.

Her lungs hurt.

But nowhere near as much as her head hurt. Anger pounded inside it with a brute force that threatened to split it open as she ran. Jodie concentrated on keeping her feet moving and her eyes focused on the dark figure ahead. She had lost it twice already as it twisted and ducked through the back streets of the town, but by a bit of frantic second-guessing, each time had regained sight of it and renewed the chase.

The rain was falling harder. It had stripped the pavements of any occupants but made them slick and greasy underfoot. Jodie had seen her quarry slip and almost stumble to the ground at one corner, so that she had gained a few precious metres, but the girl had picked herself up and lengthened her stride. She was fit. Fitter than Jodie. Maybe she was used to running. But every time the tearing pain in her lungs threatened to persuade her to stop, she saw again the windscreen exploding like ice under a hammer blow and the picture poured fresh adrenalin into her exhausted muscles.

Run.

Just run.

Don't think.

She had no idea where she was. In the darkness, she had lost all sense of direction. The streets were growing noticeably sleazier, the roads narrow and ill-lit and empty of cars, and she assumed she was heading into the dockland area. The running figure ahead now seemed to be coming gradually nearer, as if slowly being reeled in, and the realisation sent greater strength into Jodie's limbs. The gap was narrowing. She felt her over-worked heart give a feeble whoop of triumph and heard the thud of her feet quicken on the pavement.

Run.

Think Mini, and run.

And when you catch her, what then?

I'll tear off that mask of hers, that scarf, and get a good look at her face.

The gap was down to less than twenty metres, when the fleeing figure leapt over a long wall and disappeared from sight. Jodie raced up to the wall, clambered over it and dropped down the other side. The drop was twice the height of the wall and took her by surprise. She stumbled, knocking the breath from her lungs and taking the skin off her knee.

It was very dark. A narrow alleyway with no lights, sunk down between two high walls. She crouched where she was, letting her eyes adjust, and listened for footfalls, to judge whether to go left or right, but the drumbeat in her ears drowned out all else.

The girl could be hiding nearby right now. The thought made her jumpy and she glanced quickly over her shoulder into the gloom.

No one. Just more dark, rain-sodden night.

It was as she turned her head that she picked up the sound again. Footsteps, still running, but not so fast now. The girl was slowing. Perhaps thought she was safe. Quietly, Jodie set off in the same direction, taking care to avoid barging into the walls or slipping on the debris that littered the ground. Every now and again she stopped to listen, but the footfalls had ceased, so she approached more warily. Abruptly the alley turned a left-hand corner and opened up into a wide yard over which a dim lamp shed a feeble arc of light. In the centre of the arc stood the girl, chest heaving, hands raising the scarf from where it had fallen away from her face. Her eyes were furious.

'You fucking witch,' she screamed at Jodie. 'Don't you ever stop?'

Jodie had no breath to speak but her legs kept her moving forward. The yard was at the back of what looked like an abandoned factory or warehouse, and a ten-foot gate of rusting iron blocked any further progress. It was a dead end. The girl could run no further.

Jodie managed a satisfied smile. The only way out was the alleyway behind Jodie. But to her surprise the girl just stood there in the centre of the yard and let her approach, and suddenly there was a smile on her face.

'You stupid bitch,' the tall girl laughed.

Jodie heard the movement behind her right shoulder too late. She swung round in time to see the four other girls fanned out, blocking her retreat, but not in time to avoid the blow between her shoulder-blades or the kick in the back of her knee that sent her sprawling. She tried to scramble to her feet but a hand seized a hank of her drenched hair and forced her face on to the wet ground, while other hands held her down. A Nike shoe was thrust in front of her mouth.

'Kiss it.'

She tried to twist her face to one side, but earned a vicious yank on her hair.

'Kiss it.'

'Go to hell,' Jodie spat out.

The foot thumped into her lips and she tasted blood.

'Kiss it.'

She opened her mouth and sank her teeth into the leather shoe with all the fear and anger she possessed.

The owner of the Nike trainer screamed and then the feet started to kick her. It felt like an army of them, lashing out at her, thudding into her bones and trampling on her flesh until she was unbearably grateful when one caught the side of her head and sent her toppling down into the heart of an explosion that blew her into a thousand pieces, just like the windscreen.

9

A thin slit of light crept under Jodie's eyelids. She shut them tight against it because sunlight made her brain hurt. The hospital had too many windows, too much sunshine. If she kept very still, possum-still, corpse-still, and breathed only the shallow breaths of a child, it became bearable.

An octopus of pain had taken over her head. Its tentacles squirmed and touched and probed, wrapping themselves around her eyeballs and sliding along the channels of her ears. They left her nowhere to hide and no ledge above their reach where she could escape and wait for the tide to ebb.

Dimly, she heard voices. They came and went and came again, but her ears were blocked by the tentacles, so she could not hear what they said. There was no room for sound in her head.

No room for thoughts.

At times she sensed the octopus growing inside her skull, growing and expanding, pushing out all else. She could feel it soft and slimy, pulsing in time with her heartbeat, and every once in a while she heard its groan escape out of her own mouth.

10

Anthea Courtney sat and stared. She felt sick. Really sick. She made an effort to drag her eyes away from the battered face that lay so still on the hospital pillow, but it was pointless. They clung there, wilful witnesses to the unthinkable. They traced the shape and colour of each bruise and swelling, each twist of the bandage, over and over again. As if trying to convince themselves that this stranger could possibly be her sister. Ever since the telephone call came from her mother last night, the horror of it had tangled her thoughts and knotted her stomach. She perched uneasily on the NHS chair, holding the limp fingers in her own.

The hand did not move. It felt dead. Every now and again she gave it a gentle squeeze, but it did not even flicker. Only the certainty that it was still warm gave her any relief.

Oh hell, she needed a drink to settle her stomach. And to drown out the murderous imprecations in her head. What deformed kind of mind could do something like this? And don't tell her that it was some poor maltreated victim of abuse who could find no other way to express his pain. Bullshit.

'She'll live.'

It was her grandfather who spoke. He was sitting opposite her across the bed, restless and uncomfortable, and she had the feeling he would soon be off.

'Of course she'll live,' Anthea asserted confidently and caught Grandad watching her. He was looking older than she remembered. 'She's tough enough to survive a scratch like this.'

Her grandfather grunted and shifted his gaze back to Jodie. 'It's this place that'll kill her. Gives me the willies it does.' He shuddered, his thin body rustling inside his jacket and reminding

Anthea of crumpled tissue-paper. 'Like a bloody morgue it is.'

She looked around. The ward was small and silent, six beds with six supine occupants, each one asleep, though it was already ten-thirty in the morning, and other visitors were murmuring in undertones across the taut counterpanes.

'How's your mother taking it?' he asked abruptly.

'Badly.'

'She always was one to fuss.'

'Grandad, her daughter has just been beaten to a pulp. She has a right to fuss.'

Joe Bond gave a growl, as though talking to one of his dogs. 'Women love making a palaver about everything. Give them a good illness to chew on and they think it's bloody Christmas. Yak, yak, yak, over every ache and pain.' He rested his forefinger, ancient and crooked, on the smooth skin of Jodie's arm and stared at it. 'I'm not fussing.'

Anthea reached over and patted the desiccated flesh of his hand. 'I know, Grandad. I know.'

There was a long silence that mopped up the overspill in their heads, while Anthea's eyes crept back to the bruises. 'The bastards. The bastards. The sodding bastards,' she muttered without realising she was speaking aloud.

'Hanging's too good for whoever did this.'

'Bastards,' Anthea said again.

'What do the police say?'

'They are making enquiries. The usual meaningless noises. But as they haven't been able to speak to Jodie yet, they haven't got very far. They seem to think the injuries are too bad to be just the girl she chased out of the car park. More like some man, or men, who attacked her when she was alone in the dark.' She glanced up at his stricken eyes and added quickly, 'But she wasn't touched. Not sexually, that is. Thank God.'

'I wouldn't bother thanking Him. A fat lot of good He was to her.'

Anthea kneaded her sister's hand but it was no more responsive than dough. 'The stupid, stupid girl. What did she think she was doing?'

'They broke her windscreen. She wasn't about to stand for that. Not Jodie. Am I right?'

'Yes, Grandad, you're right.'

He lifted his head and it looked too heavy for the chicken-thin neck, but his eyes had come to life again. 'So, how is the headmaster reacting?'

'Quietly.'

Joe Bond sniffed, and Anthea felt obliged to add, 'But of course he's upset.'

'Upset? Upset about his sodding school, more like.'

'Don't be such an old sourbrain. He spent all last night here with Mum, and they'll be back again any minute now. You underrate him.'

He crinkled his face with distaste. 'You haven't known him as long as I have.'

'Just because you two have never hit it off, that's no reason to bad-mouth him over this. For Christ's sake, can you imagine what it's like having to put up with you as an in-law?'

That made him cackle, then cough. 'I need a fag,' he announced and stood up, his spine clicking audibly into the vertical. 'And to check on Tess. She's outside in the van with Ken.'

'I'll join you,' Anthea said and tried to remember if there was a pub nearby.

'What in heaven's name is the matter with you girl? You're knocking back that stuff like a drowning fish.'

Grandad's comment in the bar had stuck in Anthea's head. That's exactly what she felt like. A drowning fish. Slipping and slithering to the bottom of the pond where she would lie in the mud and slowly rot, or maybe, be chewed up in painful chunks by her cannibalistic colleagues.

She sat down on her single bed in her parents' house and drew her knees up under her chin, where she reverted to picking at her toenails. Oh God, she thought that habit was long since sloughed off. That was the trouble with returning to your childhood habitat, you tended to fall into your childhood habits as well. She had enough adult bad habits to deal with, never mind re-acquiring any of her old ones. She breathed out heavily, managed to stop her teeth clamping down on to a fingernail and shivered slightly. It was not cold in her room but the images of her sister's battered face kept rising to the surface and flowing through her blood as sharp as broken ice. Out there, somewhere, was a brutal bastard who must be brain-dead.

Brain-dead.

The thought flipped her stomach. That's how Jodie could have ended up, the stupid kid. Though who was she to accuse anybody of being stupid? Not when she could lay such claim to it herself. Anthea Stupid Courtney, the stupid cow who had got herself into a stupid financial mess.

Oh shit.

But heaven knows why Jodie was so nuts about that black cube of a car of hers, and nuts enough to try to protect it the way she did. It just wasn't worth that kind of hassle. The hell-hole Jodie was in now was her own dumb fault, but nobody was saying it. Not even Dad. But Anthea was certain he was thinking it. No wonder he was so quiet.

She lay back on the pillows and pondered that fact. Her father had always been the first to apportion blame where deserved, yet here he was biting his tongue and hovering at the bedside like a mother hen, all recriminations swallowed. Abruptly she rolled off the bed. She opened the bedroom window and leaned out over the sill, taking in great gulps of rain-soaked air and feeling it sweep away the constriction that had been gripping her throat for the past three weeks and which no amount of vodka had been able to flush out.

Her mother's phone call in the middle of the night had been a godsend. Not even her manic boss, David Carson, could dispute that a call to the sickbed of a comatose sister was a valid reason for being absent from one's desk. God knows, she hadn't missed a day for well over a year. She had deposited a brief message on his answerphone and fled down the motorway with gratitude gripping her heart. Jodie had got her off the hook. Maybe only for a few days, a week if she was lucky, but it gave her time to think. The rain had slowed her progress and she had been careful to drive with meticulous attention, uncertain about the alcohol levels in her blood. A bastard in blue clutching his blasted balloon was all she needed right now.

Then at the hospital everything got worse. Jodie had looked like a dead thing and her parents like dumb-struck zombies. No words. Just tears. Her own predicament became immediately so mundane that she had felt ashamed of her concerns, so had hugged her sister tight and was pleased when an answering groan of pain meant Jodie felt it.

She lit a cigarette and exhaled a lungful of smoke out into the evening air, aiming it towards a herbaceous clump of something pink and bedraggled. Damn it, Jodie, but your pain is my gain.

It was half an hour later, after she had made a call to London, that she heard her parents return home from the hospital, and the sound of plates clattering in the kitchen beneath her made her realise she should have prepared something for them to eat.

To hell with should-haves. There was no altering the past.

But as soon as she went downstairs and saw her mother at the sink, leaning lop-sidedly on her crutch while trying to rinse out a lettuce, she regretted it. Her father was nowhere to be seen.

'Mum, you look dead on your feet. Or do I mean on your foot? Let me do that.'

Her mother hesitated, but exhaustion got the better of her and she collapsed into a chair, put her arms on the table and buried her face in them. Her shoulders started to shake uncontrollably.

It was a shock.

Never before had Anthea seen her mother give up like that. Even at the hospital, when the tears had flowed, it had been without abandon. But now at the old kitchen table, her sobs seemed to act with the force of a drill on the foundations of the family and frightened Anthea.

'Mum, Jodie's not worse, is she?'

A shake of the head was the only response.

Anthea breathed again and hated herself for wanting to creep off back upstairs. She dumped the lettuce in the sink, pulled a chair up next to her mother's and wrapped an arm around her. The navy cardigan leaned heavily against her and made Anthea realise that except for the standard hugs at hellos and goodbyes and present-givings, she had not touched her mother for years.

The navy cardigan was solid and reassuring, and Anthea felt her fear receding. She stroked the well-padded back and the greying hair.

'Poor old Mum. First your leg, then Dad and his school, now Jodie. It's just too much, isn't it?'

Her mother gave a gutteral moan, but the shoulders were settling into a slower rhythm.

'A stiff drink is what you need,' Anthea declared and moved with alacrity over to the corner cupboard where the alcohol was kept. A can of cider, an unopened Bristol Cream and a bottle of German hock was the only choice it offered, so she opted for the sherry and filled two good-sized wine glasses to the brim.

'Here, you'll feel better with this inside you,' she said and pushed it in front of her mother, before resuming her seat and taking a mouthful of her own drink. God, it was years since she'd had sweet sherry; it tasted like medicine.

Her parents had never been drinkers. A social sherry, a glass of wine or a very occasional beer was about their limit, so it took Anthea by surprise when her mother suddenly sat up and downed half the glass in two gulps. Her mouth screwed up in a fierce grimace, but as the alcohol found its way down, her whole face relaxed and Anthea recognised that loosening of tight-fisted tension that comes when the first drink hits the spot.

'That's it, Mum. Drown the devil and send his demons back to hell!'

They both laughed. It amazed Anthea that they could, but they did.

'She spoke to me,' her mother said in a watery voice, and lifted her glass again. This time she took no more than a couple of sips.

'Jodie?'

'Yes.'

'She's awake?'

'Yes.'

'Oh God, that's fantastic. I knew she was too tough to take it lying down for long.'

Her mother smiled.

'What did she say? Something along the lines of go get the bastard and hang him up by his hamstrings?'

'No, just a hello. Whispery and weak. But she's conscious. And she knew me.' Another sip of sherry. 'The doctor has given her something to make her sleep now, so your father and I felt she was safe enough to leave for a few hours.' She dug out a shrivelled tissue from her sleeve and blew her nose.

'That's great. Really great. Let's celebrate.' Anthea refilled their glasses, raised hers and said brightly, 'To Jodie.'

'To Jodie,' her mother echoed. Her eyes threatened to fill again with tears, so she banished them with a good strong gulp of her drink and added, 'And to you, Anthea. Thanks for coming so quickly. I know how busy you are.'

'No sweat. God help the mister who comes between me and my sister, remember?'

'Like the time that Merritt boy snatched your skipping-rope and gave it to Jodie as a present.'

Anthea gave a noisy hoot of laughter. 'Stupid twerp. Got himself sat on, he did.'

'By Jodie?'

'Of course.'

Her mother banged her glass down on the table. 'Always so hot-headed. Why has that girl never learned to listen to sense? Just does the first thing that comes into her head.'

'Aw, Mum, come on. Don't be hard on her. She's grown up a lot in the last couple of years, since she's been working on the *Gazette*. You said so yourself. And since she's been hanging round with Matt.'

'Matt,' her mother said harshly and retrieved her sherry.

'I thought you liked him.'

'I do.' She knocked back the rest of the glass.

Anthea copied her. 'So what's the problem?'

'He's no good for her.'

'Why on earth not? He's gorgeous.'

Her mother flapped a hand at the air as if waving him away. 'Too good for her.'

'For heaven's sake, Mum, that's a dreadful thing to say about your own daughter. You don't mean it.'

Her mother's eyelids were slowly descending. 'I do.'

'You don't.'

'Do.'

'Why?'

A sigh escaped her, along with a word that sounded like 'besotted'. Her forehead hit the table with a bang but she did not even wince. She was fast asleep.

Anthea smiled at the inert figure of her mother and lifted her own glass to her lips. 'Sweet dreams.' When it was empty, she refilled it again, and then again, and was rolling around the thought of remaining a week or so down in Westonport, playing Nurse Nightingale to the two invalids, when the door opened and her father walked in.

'I thought supper would be ready by now,' he said, studying his wife and daughter with an uneasy frown.

'Lettuce,' Anthea said.

'Pardon?'

'Lettuce.'

He passed no comment for a moment, then asked, 'Is she as drunk as you are?'

'No, Dad, she was tired. Asleep.'

'Asleep or drunk?'

'Does it make any difference?'

She could see his jaw twitching as he clenched and unclenched his teeth. 'I don't think you are a good influence on your mother.'

Anthea knew she should take offence at that, but felt no real inclination to. She gave him a wobbly smile instead.

He walked stiffly over to the fridge from which he removed a slab of cheese. He cut several slices off it, found himself a tomato and a bread roll in total silence, then carried his plate to the door.

'Great news about Jodie,' Anthea said as he reached it. 'I can see you are overjoyed.'

His critical grey eyes rested heavily on her and his lips tightened as if biting hard on something that tasted bad.

'We are all overjoyed,' he said and left.

Anthea raised her glass. 'I'll drink to that.'

The house was quiet. A familiar grey fog shrouded Anthea's brain and she could not recall where she was. But by the time she had finished swearing at every product of the grape, and cursing all money-markets, both national and international, she had regained an awareness of what bed it was that she had woken in. She risked raising her eyelids a millimetre. Big mistake. The interfering shafts of morning sunshine that slid past her curtains speared her eyeballs like javelins and she groaned in wretched anticipation of what her head would say when she sat up. Her eyelids collapsed again and she decided to delay the moment.

It was two hours later that she floated up to consciousness once more and this time she woke hungry. Taking care to cradle her head as if it were newborn, she wrapped herself in the towelling robe she had slopped around in as a sixteen-year-old and guided herself gently along the wall and down the stairs. It did not take her long to discover she had the house to herself. She assumed her parents had already left to go to the hospital and was struck by a mild twinge of guilt that she had not accompanied them.

To hell with guilt.

She put the kettle on and dialled the hospital. Yes, Jodie Buxton was making good progress; yes, her parents were at her bedside and yes, the nurse would pass on Anthea's good wishes and promise to visit after lunch. Anthea thanked her and hung up. It occurred to her briefly to wonder how her mother's head was feeling but she didn't dwell on it. She made herself a slice of toast and drank a mug of black coffee, whereupon she promptly threw up in the downstairs loo and felt better. Armed with another slice of toast, she wandered into her father's study.

Matt was looking the worse for wear. His hair was rumpled, his shirt looked as if it had not been off his back for at least twenty-four hours and he had not shaved. He had agreed to meet her at three o'clock in the hospital snack bar, but was making no secret of the fact that he was in a rush. Anthea knew that feeling only too well, so did not resent it.

He sat down heavily in the seat opposite. 'Hello, Anthea. Five minutes is all I've got.'

'Hello, Matt. You look tired.'

'No, I'm fine. I'm on my way to cover the unveiling of the plans for the new library extension.'

'Don't they ever give you time off on that paper of yours? In the circumstances, I would have thought that . . .'

'I'm fine,' he interrupted, plainly not interested in what she thought. 'What is it you wanted to see me about?'

Anthea had never made a habit of coming back to Westonport any more than she had to, so had met Matt only a few times before, but on those previous occasions she had been struck by his good humour. Good humour and good looks. Neither was much in evidence today.

'Have you seen Jodie this afternoon?' she asked.

'Yes, I've just left the ward. Your father arrived.'

There was no need to say more.

With a well-painted nail, Anthea tapped the cup of tea that sat growing cold on the Formica table between them, but did not pick it up. 'Would you like some tea?'

'No. No time.' As an afterthought he added, 'Thanks any-way.'

'I'm going up to visit Jodie in a minute. How is she?'

'Better. But not good. One of the drips has been removed, but it hurts her to breathe.'

'With ribs broken front and back, it's not surprising.'

'No,' he said and rubbed a hand across his eyes. 'No, I suppose not. It's just that . . . oh, I don't know. She looks so . . . invaded. By tubes and doctors and needles and bruises.'

He shrugged, and Anthea felt a soft swirl of sympathy for him. She would have reached out to touch his hand but sensed it would not be welcome. It was bad enough having your sister beaten up. What must it be like if the victim was your lover? To see the body you had kissed and caressed so tenderly now torn and brutalised and helpless. Anthea had examined her own reactions while the sherry was liberating her thought processes the previous evening, and came up with all the old clichés – anger, sorrow, revulsion, vengefulness. And fear. Fear that it could one day happen to herself.

Christ Almighty, not that. Never that.

'Anthea, will you please get to the point?'

She unclogged her brain. 'Yes, of course. It's about the police.

I thought you would have a good idea what they're doing. How much they know and whether there is any hope of them catching the bastard who did this. As you're a journalist and in the know, I mean.'

Matt glanced at his watch and spoke fast. 'The police interviewed Jodie this morning and she told them it was a gang of girls.'

'Girls!'

'That's right.'

'I don't believe it. No way. Look at the mess they've made of her. Girls wouldn't do such . . .'

'Yes, they would. They did.'

'Oh God, poor Jodie.'

'She believes it was the same pack of girls who stole the computers from your father's school, even though their faces were covered.'

There was a long silence.

'Is that what she told the police?'

'Yes.'

Anthea leant forward. 'And do they believe her?'

'Of course. Why shouldn't they?'

'Well, she is prone to being a bit over-dramatic at times, you must admit.'

'What are you saying?'

She shrugged, pulled out a cigarette and lit it. 'Just that maybe it makes a better slant on the story that way. For the *Gazette*.'

He stared at her, too exhausted to be annoyed. 'Bullshit.'

Anthea exhaled a long trail of smoke. 'If the police already have the name of one of the computer thieves, it shouldn't take them long to find the rest of them. Should it?'

'We'll see.'

Anthea concentrated on her cigarette. 'In my father's study this morning, I found a letter from a Sergeant Dawson requesting the names of all the girls who are her known associates at the school.'

'That should get things moving.'

'Let me know if you hear of any progress, won't you?' She slid her business card across the table to him.

He gave her a ghost of a smile and pocketed the card. 'Of course I will.' He stood up. 'I have to go. But I'll contact you when I learn any more.'

'Thanks.'

He nodded a brief goodbye and walked quickly away from the noisy little snack bar, as if glad to be clear of it.

'Would you mind putting that cigarette out?' A woman with rigid grey curls and broad hips had placed herself beside Anthea's table. 'Smoking is not allowed anywhere in this hospital.'

Anthea took one more drag to pacify her lungs, then stubbed the cigarette out in her saucer.

'Thank you,' the woman said with a satisfied smile.

Anthea decided that maybe even a week in Westonport would be too long.

Upstairs was even worse. It felt like the valley of death. The bed nearest the door had its curtains drawn and Anthea's imagination supplied the rest. She hurried past.

For someone who was supposed to be getting better, Jodie looked terrible. The bruises on her face were, if anything, more livid than yesterday, the stitches marching like barbed-wire across her cheekbone. But today the eyes were open; bloodshot but open.

'How you doing, kid?' Anthea asked.

'I'll live.'

'I'll remind you of that.' She dumped the bunch of supermarket flowers she was carrying on the table.

'Christ Almighty, Jodie, you look like a Halloween mask, all purple and black to spook the neighbours.'

The right side of Jodie's mouth twitched into half a smile. 'Thanks. You always knew how to make me feel better.'

Anthea sat down on the bed and held her sister's hand. 'Hey, would you prefer I laughed or cried?'

Jodie repeated the attempt at a smile. 'Cried.'

'That would make my mascara run. God forbid.'

She leant over and popped a kiss on the bandage that obscured part of Jodie's forehead. 'Poor old dope. Who did you think you were? The cavalry?'

'Something like that.'

'But this is the real world, Jodie. It kicks back. No good you hiding behind that camera of yours and thinking you're safe. No one is ever safe in this shitty old world.'

'Not even you?'

'Not even me, my sweet. Not even your big bold sister,' Anthea said with a big bold smile. 'But I tell you what, we don't half give it a good run for its money.'

Jodie attempted a laugh, but winced as she did so.

'Bad, huh?'

'Mmm.'

'Giving you something for the pain, are they?'

'Mmm.'

'Where is it worst? That thick skull of yours?'

'Ribs.'

'Grim.'

'Mmm.'

'Talkative little sod, aren't you?'

Again the half-smile.

'No more bull-at-a-gate stuff,' Anthea told her. 'Okay?'

'Okay.'

'Good. Behave yourself in future.'

Jodie looked tired. With both her parents and Matt visiting today, and now Anthea herself, it was no wonder. A bit of chatter to amuse her and then she would leave her to sleep. Anthea stretched the kinks out of her back. 'It's good for me to get out of London for a while. And I like to leave them to sort out their own crises every now and again.'

Jodie's hand squeezed Anthea's. 'Are you in a crisis?'

'Heavens, no. No more than usual, anyway. You find me a City dealer who says he's not in a crisis, and I'll show you a liar.' She pushed back a wing of glossy dark hair in a gesture of dismissal. 'Anyway, I've turned off my mobile, so no one can get hold of me to start moaning.'

The bruised eyes stared at her disconcertingly. 'Is that safe?'

Anthea laughed. 'Safer than houses. It'll prove to them I'm completely indispensable. Anyway I didn't want that numb-nuts Julian pestering me on the phone.'

Jodie did not look convinced.

'Really. I'm over him and already cultivating a replacement. No one you know. But you shall be the first to meet him when I reel him in. Name of Henry Mackintosh.'

'Nice?'

'Quite tasty, especially in the wallet department. Not as young and hunky as your Matt, of course.'

The half-smile came again. 'Matt was here. Nearly every time I opened my eyes.'

'Truly, a man among men.'

The smile widened. 'Piss off.'

'In a minute.'

'And Mum and Dad. They've been in a lot too.'

'They're supposed to, you silly; they're parents. Though I'm a bit surprised about Dad, to be honest. Not really his scene, is it, a bedside vigil?'

Jodie frowned. 'No.'

'Especially when his school's just gone up in smoke.'

'I know.'

'Well, it just shows how much he really cares about you, doesn't it?'

'Mmm.'

'Come on, Jodie, I know you two have had your differences in the past, but that's over now. Parents are, by definition, ancient old crocks only fit for the scrapheap, but it's patently obvious he wants you to know before he gets there that he loves you.' She gave her sister a cheerful grin. 'You must have given him a nasty fright.'

Jodie sighed, and Anthea winced in sympathy when she saw how it hurt. She quickly shifted the conversation into painless areas like hospital meals, the pros and cons of BUPA, the phenomenon of nurses looking more appealing in uniform than out, and the outrageous charges that florists exact. Jodie gradually relaxed until her blackened eyelids would occasionally drop shut for a couple of minutes at a time. Even when Anthea mentioned Grandad's visit yesterday and Tess waiting outside for him in the van, Jodie showed no real animation.

At that moment, a nurse bustled up to the bedside with a bright professional expression on her neat face. 'Jodie, I've got a telephone message for you. From someone called Fiona Bowles.

She sends her love and says she will be in to see you tomorrow.'
She bustled away again.

'Who's Fiona Bowles?' Anthea asked.

'A photographer. On another paper.'

'Oh, right.' She studied Jodie's face. 'Are you sure you want
all these visitors?'

Jodie closed her eyes. For a long moment she said nothing, as
though the place inside her head was enough for her.

'Want?' she whispered eventually, eyes still firmly shut. 'Who
gets what they want?'

'Jodie. Don't.'

'Did I want the police going over it all again and again? Did
I want Jack Jones asking for extra details for the *Gazette*? Did I
want Matt dumping his anger on me? Or Dad with his lectures or
Mum and her tears? No, I didn't. I didn't want any of them.'

Anthea groaned.

'Nor you, Anthea, with your talk of bull-at-a-gate stuff.'

'Look, Jodie, I'm sorry if . . .'

Jodie's eyes opened. 'I know what it is I want.'

Anthea had no idea how the conversation had so abruptly
slipped out of her grasp but decided it had definitely gone too
far. 'Jodie, sweetheart, you've been through a rough time. It
must have been hideous for you, but give yourself space. Time
to heal.'

'To heal my head, you mean.'

'Yes.'

'Inside?'

'Yes.'

'But what if it doesn't, Anthea? What do I do if it doesn't?'

'It will. If you want it to.'

'Promise?'

'I promise.'

Anthea was again relieved to see the half-smile reappear on
Jodie's face and she bent over and gave it a reassuring kiss. 'You
need some rest.'

'Mmm.'

'I'll go now, but make sure you concentrate on nothing but
getting well quickly. Just chill out. No black thoughts, okay?'

'Okay.'

'Good.' Anthea gave Jodie's hand a squeeze and stood up. Christ, she hated hospitals. 'Get some sleep now,' she said, blew her sister a kiss and headed for the door.

'Bye, Anthea.' Jodie's voice hardly reached her across the ward.

As Anthea pushed open the swing door, she could not help wondering what door Jodie had pushed open inside her mind and into what dark room she had crept.

It was only two days later that she was pushing her Lexus hard up the motorway, one eye on her rear-view mirror on the look-out for police cars and the other on the clock.

Three o'clock she had told Henry. In the bar of the National Gallery. He was well into art and had been delighted at the suggestion. If she kept her foot down and the traffic was feeling benevolent, she would have time to get home and change first. Something short and sexy. Men take one look at a hemline and their brains sink into their trousers. And sure as hell, it wasn't Henry's brains she was after.

She pushed the speed up to ninety. She didn't feel guilty about leaving Westonport early. She had done her bit. Jodie was on the mend and would be out of that morgue next week. Anthea had not told her office she was returning to London prematurely.

That gave her three days.

More than enough.

Surely.

Elizabeth Buxton was enjoying life. She kept glancing down at her leg, newly released from its incarceration, and smiling at it, as if it were a long-lost friend. She stuck an extra peg on Jodie's blouse to make sure the wind did not whip it off the line, and heard herself humming a snatch of a Streisand tune. She even beamed at a bad-tempered robin that was stamping its spiky feet on the fence, waiting for her to vacate its territory, and returned indoors.

The kitchen smelt of freshly baked sponge. Jodie might be ready for a bite to eat now, so she put the kettle on. She chose the tray with the picture of the Arc de Triomphe and memories of a holiday in Paris, and added a plate of butterfly cakes. As she stood waiting for the water to boil, she reminded herself not to mention the visit from the police. Let Jodie enjoy her tea in peace. No need to spoil it.

She pushed open the sitting-room door with her shoulder, careful not to limp, and was disappointed to see Jodie stretched out on the sofa, eyes closed. Asleep again. Feeling mildly thwarted, she told herself she might as well leave the tea anyway and placed the tray on a small table beside her, but not even the deliberate clinking of china disturbed the resolutely dormant lashes. Thick dark eyelashes that skirted the two-inch scar on her cheek. Thank God the stitches were out, but the flesh underneath was still red and alien. Elizabeth kept her eyes averted.

She stroked the dark head, knowing it was not allowed when Jodie was awake, picked up a cake and sat herself down in the arm-chair opposite. She peeled off the paper case and began to eat.

*   *   *

'Aren't you bored?'

'No.' Elizabeth smiled at Jodie. 'Did you have a nice sleep?'

'Not really. I'm stiff now.' Jodie eased herself into a sitting position and performed a few deep breathing exercises to loosen the knots in her ribs.

She looked pale. Much of the bruising had healed in the two weeks she had been at home but had left her skin with an unhealthy yellowish tinge that made Elizabeth think of her father's grubby cat-saucers. She wished she could tempt her outside. The October sunshine was treating them to a fairly convincing imitation of summer and her rosebushes were having their final fling, so an hour in the garden would do her good. But no, no dice.

'Let me make you some fresh tea. That one must be cold.'

'No, don't bother.'

'It's no bother, dear. I wouldn't mind a cup myself.'

She picked up the tray, conscious of the fact that only one butterfly-cake sat in solitary state on the plate, and headed for the kitchen. Without the plaster, her leg was moving faster every day. Admittedly, it ached more but that was to be expected with all this extra running around. She replenished the mugs and plate and returned to the sitting-room, but Jodie was no longer on the sofa. She was standing by the window, staring out across the garden at the road beyond. Elizabeth felt a little shuffle of unease in her stomach.

'Here you are, darling, come and sit down. I thought we could have a bash at the *Times* crossword together, as Dorothy from next door remembered to pop it over for us. How about it?'

'No thanks.' She remained by the window.

'Come on, Jodie, you enjoy it. A bit of a challenge. And it keeps the cogs turning.'

'My cogs are turning okay, Mum.'

'Then come and help me with it.'

'You don't need help.'

'I do.'

There was a short silence that Elizabeth filled with a hopeful glance at the paper. Jodie abandoned the window and returned to the sofa, and it took a real effort for Elizabeth not to help her into her seat. It was obvious every movement hurt.

'What is this about, Mum?'

'What do you mean? What is what about?'

'This. Are you trying to check out whether I've got brain damage or something?'

'Don't be ridiculous!'

'What then?'

'It's a crossword, Jodie, that's all.'

Jodie's blue eyes looked at her and there was something in them that hadn't been there before. Before the attack, that is. A smoothness. It took Elizabeth several moments to realise it was a wall.

'I just want to help, Jodie, that's all. For heaven's sake, you're my daughter and I just want to help you.'

'You have already. You've nursed me. Matt could not have done that properly because of his job. So I am grateful. You know I am.' She gave a smile to prove it.

The smile annoyed Elizabeth. She could feel the wall behind it. She reached out and seized another cake, tore off the paper and took a big bite. To keep the words inside her mouth.

'It's just that I worry about you, darling.'

'I know, but don't. I'm getting better every day.'

'It's not healthy the way you just sit there. With that blasted photograph of yours on your lap.'

'I'm not just sitting, I'm thinking.'

'I know. That's what worries me. The crossword is to make you think of other things and to make you talk. Oh darling, you must talk.'

'I do.' She gave a stiff shrug. 'When you corner me.'

'Exactly.'

'I'm talking all the time. There always seems to be someone coming over and trying to scramble round inside my head. Yesterday it was Grandad, this morning it was Fiona again and the rest of the time there's always you or Matt or Dad. It's like a motorway in here.'

'I admit it has been quite busy.'

'No more visitors today, please. Okay?'

'Ah.'

'What?'

'That could be a problem.'

'Why?'

'It's Sergeant Dawson. He rang earlier when you were asleep.'

'What did he want?'

'A word or two. Not long, he said.'

'Do I have any choice?'

'Not really.'

'That's what I thought,' Jodie said and looked at the picture that was propped up on the arm of the sofa. It was her photograph of the fire.

Sergeant Grant Dawson was an exceedingly polite and well-mannered young man, and Elizabeth was delighted to invite him in. She offered him tea, which he declined, but made up for it by enquiring after her leg and complimenting her on her roses. It was therefore extremely galling to her to watch her daughter give a display of bad manners that befitted a six-year-old.

'Don't tell me you can't take it any further,' Jodie snapped. 'You're the police, aren't you? So go and do some policing.'

'Miss Buxton,' Sergeant Dawson asked with well-trained patience, 'has anything else occurred to you about the attack? Something that you had not recalled before? I mean, now that you are recovering from the initial shock, maybe there's some new information you can give us.'

'No, of course not. I have already told you everything that happened.'

'Then I'm afraid there's nothing more we can do.'

Jodie snatched a cushion from beside her on the sofa and for one ghastly moment Elizabeth thought that she was going to throw it at him, but she jammed it behind her back instead.

'Too busy out chasing motorists, I suppose.'

'Jodie!' Elizabeth exclaimed.

'No, Miss Buxton. It's just that there were no witnesses and you did not see their faces. So we have no leads to go on.'

'What about that girl you caught taking the computers? She's a lead. What was her name?'

'I'm sorry, she is a juvenile, so we cannot release her name. I know you believe it was the same gang, but we cannot prove a connection.'

'Have you even tried?'

Dawson's eyes flickered with annoyance but none of it showed in his voice as he explained, 'Yes. We have interviewed all her known associates, but they all have an alibi for the night of the attack on you. And on the school, for that matter.'

'I bet they have.'

'The girl denies any knowledge of the attack on you. She says it had nothing to do with her. Or any of her friends.'

'And you believe her?'

'There is no proof that ties her to the gang that attacked you, so we cannot proceed further. I'm sorry, Miss Buxton, I do understand how upset you must be.'

'I doubt that.'

'Without identification . . .'

'So you're just going to do nothing?'

'There's nothing more we *can* do.'

Elizabeth watched her daughter glare at the policeman and she was grateful when the doorbell rang.

'I'll get it,' she said and hurried from the room.

Elizabeth put the kettle on. 'Coffee or tea, Matt?' She had brought him into the kitchen to avoid the confrontation taking place in the other room.

'Coffee, please. So how's it going in there?'

Elizabeth grimaced. 'Don't ask.'

'That bad, is it?'

'Worse.'

'It was inevitable,' Matt said. 'She had her hopes too high.'

'I know. Poor Jodie.'

'I was thinking more along the lines of poor policeman.'

Elizabeth laughed and piled coffee into the cafetière. She liked Matt. He was intelligent, easy company and she was not yet too old to get a kick out of attention from an attractive young man. Admittedly, he did have a tendency to tease her at times, not something she was used to, but it made her laugh, so she didn't mind. His only drawback in her eyes was his effect on her daughter. Which was nuclear. Complete wipe-out. Not that Jodie made it obvious, of course, but Elizabeth knew her well enough to recognise the signs. There had been other relationships in the past, many of which Jodie had taken up just to make a point, but even those she had cared about had been nothing like this. This one was on a different planet. So what would happen if he left her? Jodie was not always the easiest of people to live with. Especially now.

'Sergeant Dawson is handling her very well,' Elizabeth said. 'He's good at being polite.'

Matt grinned. 'That's your criterion for a good police officer, is it?'

'Yes. Yes, I think it is.'

'But the police will have to drop it. There was never any realistic chance of them putting a case together. Not without positive identification.'

'So it seems.'

Matt took a mug from the cupboard. 'I think you've ladled enough coffee in there, don't you?'

Elizabeth stared at the mountain of grains inside the glass jug. 'Oh blast, I'm not concentrating.'

'Mental hiccups. I think we've all got them at the moment.'

'So it seems.'

'It's allowed.'

'Matt,' she said uneasily, 'do you think I repeat myself a lot?'

His eyes registered surprise at her turn of thought. 'Not particularly.'

'It's just that occasionally I hear myself saying the same thing twice. Sometimes just a phrase, like I did just then, but it can be a whole sentence. And I wondered . . .'

'Yes?'

'Whether you had noticed it.'

He looked at her oddly.

'You see, Matt, it's just that . . . you know. Since my mind . . . well, since a year ago . . . I worry that my mind . . . well I . . .'

Matt was staring at her.

'Come on, Matt, you know what I mean. Help me out here.'

'No, no chance. I'm enjoying watching a grown woman blush.' But he smiled and held out his mug.

'You are a pest, Matt Reynolds.'

She took the mug from him. A year ago Elizabeth Buxton had suffered a stroke. Nothing major. Within forty-eight hours she had recovered completely. But it had shaken her. That was why she had given up her job as a pharmacist. She had told everyone she wanted to spend her remaining years enjoying life instead of slaving over bottles of pills and potions, but that was not the real reason. The reality was that she didn't want the responsibility any more. Not now she couldn't trust her mind. That's why she made it do endless crosswords each day. She was always on the look-out to see if it was slipping.

'It's the stress,' Matt told her kindly. 'You're worrying about Jodie, that's all it is.'

'Yes, you're right. Jodie and Alan, the pair of them. And Anthea as well, actually. I can't help it.'

'Well, no need to worry about Jodie much longer. She'll be off your hands soon.'

Elizabeth fiddled with the coffee and kettle. 'What do you mean?'

'What do you think I mean? She'll be coming home to the flat as soon as . . .'

'No, Matt, no. She's not ready. You can't leave her on her own all day while you're out at work, not the way she is now. It wouldn't be right. Surely you can see that Jodie still needs to be looked after properly.'

'Of course she needs to be looked after properly. And between us, we will do that. But at the flat. Not here.'

'There's no point in . . .'

'Jodie is the one who will decide.'

'Exactly. And she hasn't expressed any desire to step out of the front door yet, never mind half-way across town. She's too frail, Matt. Don't rush her.'

He accepted the coffee she proffered. 'I miss her,' he said simply.

'I know you must. I would suggest you move in here yourself for a few weeks, but it's Alan. You know how he feels about that.'

'Yes, I do know. He made it quite clear when Jodie came out of hospital.'

'Don't rush her, Matt. Please don't rush her.'

'Now you *are* repeating yourself.'

'I know,' she smiled. 'I know. But she's not right yet. Don't take her away.'

Elizabeth poured herself a mug of coffee and stirred in two sugars. Without thinking, she added a third. Tomorrow she would bake Jodie a cake, a big marble one with chocolate icing. Jodie would like that.

Elizabeth lay in bed reading. She liked crime novels because they made her think. She knew all the clues were there, she just had to sift through the facts and assemble them in the right order. She could feel her grey matter hard at it, and was reassured.

'Can you stop wriggling, please, Elizabeth? I can't concentrate on these figures.'

Beside her, Alan was going over a sheaf of papers and as she glanced across at him, she noticed that though he was still as slim and upright as when she married him thirty years earlier, a small fold of skin had formed into a jowl on his jawline as he bent his head over his work. It took her by surprise. How long had that been there? And why hadn't she seen it before? Or had she? She looked away quickly, afraid for her short-term memory.

'Sorry, Alan, it's my leg. It won't stay still.'

She had overdone it today, and was therefore forced to endure what felt like an army of mice in steel-capped boots marching up and down her shin-bone.

'Sore is it?'

'A bit.'

'Bad luck.' He returned to his figures.

'Shouldn't the board of governors or the accountants be doing that?'

He nodded. 'I just like to check them. You can't trust builders.'

Elizabeth's father had been a builder.

'Anthea rang this evening.' She had forgotten to tell him earlier.

'Oh yes.'

'Sounded on top of the world.'

'Oh yes.'

'Said she might come down to see us again soon.'

'Oh yes.'

He was not really listening.

'I thought it would be nice to go out for a meal tomorrow evening, as it's Saturday. Just the two of us. Now that my leg is mobile.'

She had been hoping for another 'Oh yes' and would have booked a table at the Castle Inn first thing in the morning. But it was not to be so easy.

Her husband glanced across at her. 'Do we have to?'

'It would be nice.'

He shrugged. 'If you really want to.'

'Good. It would be nice for Jodie and Matt as well. To have some time alone together, I mean. They miss each other.'

Alan put down his papers and stared at her with the look she was sure he used on pupils who had disappointed him. 'I see,' was all he said.

'Alan, don't be difficult. They're young.'

'Every time I turn round these days, that boy is under my feet.'

'His name is Matt.'

'Hasn't he got his own home to go to?'

'Of course he has. But he comes here to be with Jodie because he's concerned about her. We all are.'

Her husband returned to his columns of figures.

'Alan, don't pretend you're not concerned. She's your daughter and you're every bit as worried as I am. Admit it.'

He nodded jerkily, as if it hurt to make the simple gesture of agreement.

'So will you talk to her?' Elizabeth pressed her point. 'Make her see that she must put all this behind her and get on with her life. And not keep badgering the police to do more. It's over now.'

Alan Buxton placed his papers neatly on the bedside table and switched off his lamp, making the room lop-sided. 'I'll have a word with her, Elizabeth, if you think it might help. But Jodie has made a particular point of never paying any attention to whatever I've said in the past, so why should she start now?'

12 ∫

Jodie drew the curtains shut. The glare of the midday sun was like a blowtorch in her brain and the heavy drapes brought relief. With the room wrapped in a dusky twilight, everything settled into soothing soft-focus and she felt better. She began her exercises: deep breathing, arm raising and lowering, chest twisting and more deep breathing. At the end of twenty minutes, her ribs felt as if someone had rattled them with a red-hot poker and her head was throbbing. She drank a tall glass of water and lay down flat on her back on the rug in front of the electric fire.

It was good to be home, back in the flat.

Shame about the row with Dad though. She heaved a ragged sigh and closed her eyes.

She was still lying there when Matt opened the door several hours later.

'Jodie, you're home! It's great to have you back.' If he'd had a hard day, it didn't show, and his broad smile of welcome made the flat feel lived-in again. 'You should have let me know and I would have collected you. How long have you been here?'

'Not long.'

She tried to uncurl from the floor but her bones had stiffened into rigid scaffolding and it was a struggle. She had only got as far as her knees, when Matt lifted her to her feet and put his arms around her.

'Welcome home,' he said and kissed her mouth.

It felt so good, she wanted to tell him never to stop. 'Matt,' she breathed against his lips.

'What is it?' He drew his head back. 'Are you okay?'

'Yes, I'm fine. Just fine.' She nodded over and over. 'Really fine,' and then she burst into tears.

She buried her face in his shoulder and he held her close.

It was two o'clock in the morning and Jodie was still awake. But she did not mind. It wasn't as if she had a busy day ahead of her. She lay absolutely still, not wanting to grate any bone-ends nor disturb Matt in the bed beside her, though the number of celebratory beers he had drunk should ensure a blissful oblivion.

The warmth of his body radiated into hers, and she felt a frisson of pleasure tiptoe across her bare skin. It had taken a mammoth effort to walk out of her parents' house into the taxi, so great it had left her exhausted and shaking, but it had been worth it. Worth it just to be here. It was strange the way any attempt to go back was a mistake. It had been like that at her parents' house. That was her past. This was her present. And her future?

Maybe.

Her mother's fussing had driven her nuts, and the way she ensnared her to sit and drink tea or coffee with everyone who called. Even the friends from the bridge club. Jodie smiled into the darkness at the obviousness of her mother's attempts to re-socialise her daughter; she could afford to smile now. Now that she was gone. Her mother had meant well, she knew that, and it must have been unnerving to have such a silent, battered creature dumped on her hearth. But Jodie had needed the silence. To fix her head.

She reached up with her hand and touched her own face, her hair, her ears, just checking. Sometimes she grew frightened that the outside of her head was still as messed up as the inside. But no, it felt okay now. She allowed the hand to rest on Matt's thigh and to stroke the firm muscle that she loved, the quadracep muscle, so long and lean and essentially male. Her own thigh, in comparison, felt soft and fleshy, despite its slim outline and the occasional grind in the gym.

She shut her eyes and wondered what on earth her mind was

doing. Thighs, for Christ's sake. A comparison of thighs. What kind of smoke-screen was that?

Okay. So what was behind the smoke?

An hour later, it felt suffocating. Hot and airless inside her head. At times so bad that she uttered a parched moan that only left her more confused, and bestirred Matt to turn on his side, away from her. But by early morning, when the first blink of dawn pushed brashly into the room and the pain of exhaustion reverberated in her head like the sound of a train inside a dark tunnel, she had found her way clear.

Her fear.

Her father.

Her anger.

She would have to deal with each of them. One at a time.

The wind was gusting through the window, though it was open only a few inches, and snatching at the curtains, but Jodie was able to stand in front of it without flinching now. Three weeks and that was all she had to show for her efforts. But at least her ribs were healing. Another five minutes and then she would allow herself to shut it. She made herself concentrate on the smells the wind carried and forget what else might be out there. But all she recognised were car fumes and a brief snatch of a bonfire. She was so absorbed that the slam of her own front door made her jump.

Matt walked in a moment later, Jack James in tow. Both looked windblown, cheeks tingling red and hands flapping to keep warm. They brought with them a whirlwind of cold air from outside that felt alien as it took over the flat. Jodie retreated to a distant chair. It was too much. Too much too soon.

Matt came across and gave her a kiss. 'Hi, gorgeous, feeling hungry? Jack and I thought we'd come over and take you out to lunch. A quick bite at the Black Horse. How about it?' Behind his easy smile, he was watching her.

'Sounds like fun,' she said.

The two journalists made an unconvincing pair; Jack's face so long and thin and his grin too keen, while Matt's laid-back manner did not fool her.

Jack loped across the room and took her by the hand. 'Great, I'm starving.' He pulled her to her feet. 'Let's go.'

Jodie extricated her hand from his. 'Sounds like fun, but some other time, guys,' she smiled at them. 'I don't feel like it today. I'm really not hungry.'

'Jodie, don't be such a spoilsport,' Jack complained. 'It's only for an hour or so. We've come especially to get you.'

'Thanks, I appreciate the thought.'

'Oh, come on,' Matt said, 'you've got to eat.' He grinned at her. 'So you might as well do it in the company of the *Gazette*'s two top reporters.'

'You wish!' she laughed.

He put an arm around her shoulders and started to walk towards the door. 'Just think of it. Benny's trout and chips. Your favourite. And tiramisu for pudding with . . .' He pulled a red packet from his pocket. '. . . Maltesers on top.'

She felt like a dog being tempted to perform a trick. And she wanted to say yes. She really did.

'No, Matt, honestly. Another time. Not today.'

'Why not?'

'I told you, I'm not hungry. Anyway, Grandad's coming round this afternoon.'

'Not until three o'clock, you said. Are you sure you won't come?'

'I'm sure.'

Matt said nothing more. He looked at her, then released his arm and opened the door. 'Come on, Jack, let's eat.' He walked out.

'Won't you change your mind?' Jack asked in a last-ditch effort.

'No. But thanks anyway.'

'Next week maybe?'

'Maybe.'

She listened to their footsteps descending the stairs and felt miserable. The wind was still rattling the window, so she hurried over to close it, to shut out the noise and the smells from outside. And the people. Especially the people. While she was pushing the sash-frame firmly back into place and resenting the stab of pain it brought to her ribs, she risked a glance down into the street and saw Matt and Jack charging along the front path to the gate. She didn't wave. Nor did they look up. As if they knew she would not be there. Matt's well-travelled Beetle convertible was waiting for them at the roadside, dead leaves chasing round its tyres. She watched him unlock it and saw Jack duck inside out of the wind, but Matt hesitated, said something, then ran back into the house.

Jodie felt her heart jump against her chest. She backed away from the window and almost drew the curtain shut, but managed to keep her hand off it. She turned and stared at the door. A second later, Matt walked in.

'That was a quick meal,' she said.

'Bugger the meal, Jodie.' He strode over to her and placed a hand on each of her shoulders, pinning her down like an insect when all she wanted to do was scurry under a stone. 'You can't go on like this.'

'Like what?' Wide-eyed and innocent.

'Like this. Hiding yourself away. Not going out at all.'

'Don't be silly. I'm just recuperating.'

'Jodie, stop it. You've been back in this flat for three weeks now and have never put a foot outside that door. Every time I suggest it, you find an excuse and deny that there is even any kind of problem. There is a problem. And it's time we talked about it.'

She shrugged off his grip on her. 'I don't want to talk about it, Matt. I am dealing with it. In my own way. There's no need for you to get upset about it.' She scraped a smile up from the bottom of the barrel. 'Honestly, Matt, everything is under control. So go and enjoy your lunch with Jack.'

He stood in front of her, breathing heavily. 'I think you should seek professional help, Jodie. A counsellor.'

'No way. Forget it. I tell you I'm fine, and sure as hell I'm not putting up with any busybodies sticking their beaks in.'

'Why do you always have to be so bloody-minded, Jodie? Just for once, trust someone. Trust me. I want to help you, but you've built such barricades around yourself since that bloody attack that I can't even get close.' She could hear the frustration in his voice. 'You won't talk about it.'

Jodie knew what she was doing to him. Driving him from her.

But it was as if her head was too full already, and she couldn't stop herself. She made an effort.

'Matt,' she said softly, 'I'm sorry. But I have talked about it. I've told you everything that happened.'

Matt shook his head. 'Everything that happened in the street. But not what happened to your mind. I know you're angry, that's understandable, but . . .'

From the street below came the sound of the VW's horn. Jack was getting bored.

'You'd better go, Matt.' She came forward and kissed him. 'Enjoy your lunch.'

'Come with us.'

'No, I can't.'

'Please.'

'No.'

'We would look after you, one each side to protect you. For your own sake, Jodie, face what's out there.'

'I'm sorry, Matt. It's still no.'

He left. No kiss.

Jodie walked over to the window and looked down at the Beetle. Behind it was parked her Mini.

'Look what I brought you.' Grandad chuckled, pleased with himself. He plonked his bony frame down on the sofa next to Jodie, unaware of the shockwaves he created, and put his hand in his pocket.

He had made a habit of walking across town once or twice a week to drink her beer. She had given up offering him tea or coffee whatever time of day it was, and as soon as he arrived at the flat, puffing like a scrawny fox in search of a bolt-hole, she put a bottle in his hand and a bowl of water on the floor. The bowl was for the dog. Or dogs. This afternoon it was just Goliath. The stupid animal made no pretence of ferocity today, as he rubbed his head against her thigh, but she gave him a Malteser anyway.

'What is it this time?'

Last time the present had been a bunch of rosemary that stank the flat out. For remembrance, he'd said. She had not asked him remembrance of what.

He chuckled again and held out his hand. In it lay a torch. A small pocket one with a pencil beam and red plastic casing. He switched it on, dumped it in her lap and said, 'That's for you.'

Jodie wondered whether her grandfather's last few brain cogs had finally slipped.

'Thank you.' She picked it up and pushed the switch to off. 'But why on earth would I want a torch?'

'To help you see in the dark.' His lungs were wheezing with the effort of laughing and speaking at the same time.

'I'll bear that in mind next time I'm out in the dark.'

'Don't talk rot. You're sitting in the dark right now.'

'What?'

'In the dark, that's where you are, and not doing a blind thing about it. Not a blind thing.'

'Grandad, you don't know what you're talking about.'

'I know that I never thought no grandchild of mine would take this lying down, would take a beating like you got and not lift a finger to help herself. Those kids must think you're some kind of marshmallow or something.'

'Grandad, shut up.'

'I'll shut up when you look at me straight and say you'll get up off your back and stop playing dead.' His eyes, tiny in their folds of loose skin, skin that now seemed too big for him, were intent on provoking her.

Jodie dug her heels in. 'It takes time for ribs to heal. I'm still recuperating.'

'Recuperating, my arse.'

'Grandad, I don't need this.'

'Sure as hell you need something, my girl. I think the doctors must have got it wrong and it was your spine that got kicked to pieces, not your ribs.'

'Lay off, Grandad, there's nothing wrong with my spine. Never has been.'

He reached out and wrapped his frail bird's-feet fingers round her hands. 'I know that, girl. That's what I can't understand. Not like you at all, this dormouse act. Your mother says it's because you're growing up at last, but I tell her that's a load of balls. Anyway, you've got all the rest of your life to grow up in. Growing up is just another way of saying growing old. That's why I try to avoid it like the plague.'

Jodie smiled affectionately at him. 'You seem to have succeeded.'

'Do you think so?'

'Definitely.'

He grinned, highly gratified, giving her a blast of his yellow teeth. 'Thank the Lord for that.' He drained the last of his beer and stood up. 'Fancy another?'

'No thanks. But help yourself.'

While he was gone, Goliath transferred his head on to her knee. She stroked the glossy fur, tracing the fine bones underneath and ignored the moist pleading in the eyes. The rest of the Maltesers were for herself.

Her grandfather returned from the kitchen, an open beer in his hand. 'The daft bugger. He's sulking because Madonna's had her kittens and he thinks they're getting too much attention. Big hulk like him jealous of a bunch of fluff that would be no more than a mouthful to him.' He tugged at the dog's ear. 'Daft bugger.' He sat down, careful not to spill his drink. 'And talking of daft buggers, your father is in the paper today.'

'Oh? What's he done now?'

'Just showing off the plans for the replacement labs at that school of his. Reassurance for parents, I suppose. It had a picture of him standing beside the row of new computers they've got now, but it was a shame you weren't the one to take the photograph.'

'Don't, Grandad.'

'So when are you going to get off your backside, Jodie? It's no good that boy of yours going on about agoraphobia, as if it were a bloody war-wound or something. Just look at you. Fit as a fiddle, you are.'

Jodie felt like grabbing his scraggy neck and shaking him till his bones rattled. 'I'm certainly fit enough to throw you out of my flat, if that's what you mean.'

Her grandfather chuckled. 'That's more like it.'

'I'm getting there, Grandad. That's all I'll say.'

He leant towards her, eager as a ferret. 'Oh yes?'

'Yes.'

'Taking your time about it, aren't you?'

'It's my time. I'll take as much of it as I like.'

'All right, I'll shut up. But I don't like to think of those girls laughing at you.'

After another beer, he and Goliath headed for home.

As Jodie shut the door behind him, she thought about what he had said. Agoraphobia. Is that what Matt was calling it?

It was two hours later that Jodie stood at the window again, staring down at the street below. Heavy grey clouds had robbed the day of the last of its life and cloaked it in the muted shroud of twilight. A cat was asleep on the bonnet of a car that had parked across the road and a couple of children were kicking a ball repetitively against a garden wall. Otherwise the street was motionless; no cars passing, no people walking. No danger to anyone.

Abruptly, Jodie abandoned the window and headed for the door. She did not stop to put on a coat. No more excuses. Keys were already in her pocket. As her fingers touched the door handle, she felt the sweat break out on her skin and her teeth started to ache because she had clenched them too hard.

She turned it.

Nothing. No disaster. Nobody lying in wait.

She opened the door. Still nothing. Her heart was frantic in her chest and her tongue so dry it was welded to the roof of her mouth, but she was not going to stop now. A rogue brain-cell suggested that this was far enough for today, the rest could wait until tomorrow, but she ignored it, shut the door behind her and started down the stairs. She kept close to the wall, its touch cold but reassuring on her shoulder. Once she reached the main hallway, she was trying to get the hang of deeper breathing, when she heard a noise to her left that sent her heart-rate back into overdrive.

'Hi, Jodie, are you better?'

Jodie almost melted with relief. It was Andrew Watson, the kid from downstairs. 'Hi, Andy,' she managed.

The small boy bounced right up to her, close enough to see her shaking. 'You don't look better to me.'

'I am.'

'Have you been running?'

'No.'

'You look hot. I'm going to the station with Mummy. To meet Aunty Carole. Why are you leaning on the wall?'

'I'm tired.'

'I'm not.'

The door to the ground-floor flat slammed and Andrew's mother, Charmain, made a dash for the front door. 'Hi, Jodie, glad to see you up and about. Come on, Andrew, must rush.' She grabbed his wrist and was gone. Jodie heard her car start up and rattle its way down the road.

She waited.

She waited a long time.

And just when she thought she was never going to move again, something seemed to click inside her brain and release the control mechanism of her legs. They walked to the front door, waited while she opened it, then took her outside and down the path before she had time to object. It was almost dark now and for a sickening moment Jodie thought the darkness had seeped out of her own head, shadows stealing away her safety, but when she saw the street-lights burning holes in them, she realised she must have spent longer in the hallway than she thought. She clung to the gate with one hand, found her keys with the other and made a run for the Mini. She was shaking. Not just a slight tremble but a gigantic quake that seemed fit to shake her eyeballs out. No one was in the street. No one. So stop it.

But her fingers did not listen. The key was jumping all over the place and it took numerous attempts and both hands to slot it into the lock. Then she tumbled into the seat and slammed the door behind her. She locked it. The glass of the replacement wind-screen looked incredibly fragile. So breakable she was frightened to breathe on it.

Her eyes were fixed on the hands of her watch. It was pitch-dark now but the luminous dial informed her she still had another eight minutes to go. Fifty-two minutes she had been sitting in the car and she was freezing. Her heartbeat had slowed to no more than a gallop and her breathing was now almost normal, so that she was able to look up without panic when the black shape of a car or pedestrian hurried past. The cat had long since gone, slinking along the gutter like an inky shadow, and one of the lamps at the far end of the street was flickering irritably, but there was nothing here to stoke up the fires in her head.

Jodie was pleased with herself. Every now and then she cast a homesick glance at the solid walls of her flat and had actually counted out loud the number of paces she reckoned it would take to reach the door – sixteen, if she made them big – but she was still here. In her seat. For the last seven minutes she had allowed her hand to rest on the door-handle.

Five more minutes.

Three hundred seconds.

She had just started counting them to herself when the sound of a car rounding the corner behind her made her turn her head. Its headlamps were like searchlights that sought her out and aimed straight for her. The car drew to a halt inches from her rear bumper and a figure jumped out. It was female. In dark jacket and jeans. A black scarf was wound round the lower half of her face. The figure ran past the Mini without a glance, unaware of Jodie's silent presence, up the path and rang the bell.

Jodie hung on. Hung on and kept her mouth shut. For ten seconds she watched the girl stamping her feet and pushing at the bell and then let herself out of the car. This time that girl was going nowhere. She raced up the path and threw herself on the dark figure.

There was a terrified screech and an agonising elbow in Jodie's ribs that took her breath away, but she held on tight. She yanked the scarf off and stared at the petrified face behind it.

'Oh no, I'm sorry, Fiona.'

It was Fiona Bowles, the photographer from the *Westonport Weekly News*. Fiona was small and slight and could easily pass for a teenager. Her dark eyes registered shock.

'What the bloody hell are you doing, Jodie? You scared the life out of me.'

'I'm sorry. It was a mistake. I thought you were someone else.'

'Is this how you greet all your visitors now?'

'No, only those I like.'

Fiona laughed. 'You're out of your mind, do you know that?'

'That's quite possible,' Jodie said and wrapped her arms round her chest.

'Come on, let me in, it's freezing out here.'

Jodie dug the keys from her pocket, remembered to lock the Mini, and led her visitor upstairs, ribs objecting every step of the way. Her own stupid fault. In the flat, she opened a bottle of red wine, poured out two glasses and collapsed into a chair. She sipped her drink.

'Recovered?' she asked.

'Just about. So what were you up to?'

'I was in my car outside and . . .'

'I thought you didn't go out at all. Not any more.'

'Don't be silly. Whatever gave you that idea? I've been waiting till these blasted ribs healed, that's all. Your elbow has crunched them into bonemeal again by the way.'

'Oops, sorry. But if you will insist on sumo-wrestling everyone who touches your doorbell, what do you expect?'

'I had a good reason.'

'Did you think I was a burglar?'

'No. I mistook you for one of the girls who almost kicked me to death.'

Fiona's eyes popped wide. 'Really?'

'Yes, really. You were dressed the same. Dark clothes, the scarf round the face.'

Fiona leant back in her chair and shook her head at Jodie. 'But that just goes to show that you could be wrong.'

'Wrong about what?'

'Wrong about it being the same gang that stole the computers. It's damn cold out there, Jodie. Everyone is wearing scarves. Maybe you were mistaken about them.'

'No.'

'Not even a ripple of doubt?'

'No.'

'Okay, I'll take your word for it,' Fiona said, unwilling to push her point. 'So what was it you wanted me over here for? On my answerphone you said to get my arse over here a.s.a.p., but you didn't say why.' She sipped her wine, put her feet on the coffee table and smiled at Jodie. 'So here I am.'

'Thanks, Fiona, I appreciate it. It's just that I need a bit of help and you're the one to give it to me.'

'Sounds ominous.'

'No, it's a breeze. It'll only take you a minute.'

'I've heard that one before.'

Jodie laughed and refilled their glasses while Fiona eyed her suspiciously. 'Well, maybe two. But not long, I promise. I just want a few pictures.'

'That reminds me, doesn't Dunmore want you back at the *Gazette* yet?'

'He can want as much as he likes. I've got a doctor's certificate giving me sick-leave until Christmas. They've taken on an extra freelance to cover for me.' In fact Jodie did miss the work, not so much the paper itself as her lens-view on the world. Sometimes she took pictures inside the flat, just to fill the gap.

'If they've got a freelance, why do you need me?' Fiona asked with a confused shrug.

'It's not for the *Gazette*. It's for me. I need a few pictures of some school-kids. Straight in, straight out. Simple.' Jodie smiled encouragement.

'What are you up to, Jodie Buxton?'

'It's not complicated. All I want to do is talk to the girl the police caught the night of the fire. I have a photograph of her but I don't know her name, so I can't find her.' The *Gazette* had got nowhere with its enquiries, so had abandoned the story.

'Go on.' Fiona was intrigued.

'The police have dropped my case.'

'The bastards.'

'Exactly. But this girl might provide some help. I took a picture of her in the police car, not very clear because half her face is covered, but it gives me an idea of what she looks like. I should be able to pick her out of a group photograph, and hopefully she might even be standing with her friends.' She took a quick breath. 'So I need you to sneak into Wyndame School and take pictures of the fourth-formers. She's fifteen, so that should be the right year.'

'What! I can't be hearing right. Why don't you just ask your father straight out for her name?'

Jodie picked up her wine. 'I have.'

'And?'

'Nothing. No help at all. We had a row fit to blow the roof. That's why I left my parents' house.'

Fiona looked at her friend and asked gently, 'Oh Jodie, why won't the old bugger tell you? Surely he would want to help his daughter.'

Jodie shrugged and downed more wine. 'You'd think so, wouldn't you? But no, he said he had a professional loyalty to pupils at his school and could under no circumstances reveal her name. Anyway, he wants me to stay clear of them and says I'll only get myself into more trouble.'

'He could be right, you know.'

'Fiona, don't be such a wimp.'

'Hey, save the insults for him, not me.'

'Sorry. I get jumpy when he enters the conversation.' She smiled and went for a straight answer. 'So will you do this favour for me? I'd do it myself, but they would recognise me.'

Fiona groaned. 'I know I should say no.'

'I'll take that as a yes then.'

13

The fear was going. Jodie could feel it seeping out of her veins like blood from a graze, droplet by droplet. After that initial dash to the car, she had taken it more slowly because in bed that night she had suffered a fit of the shakes and knew she had pushed too hard. Matt had assumed it was his fault, the result of the pressure he had put on her that day, so had backed off and had not chivied her any more. That made life easier, even if she did catch him looking at her sometimes like a dentist looks at a decaying tooth.

She took it a step at a time. First, the door to the flat. On the hour every hour, she opened it. At times it felt as if it was made of dead-weight lead and it took all her gut strength to move it, but during the first few days she did not attempt to go through it. That had come next. A whole week of it. The stairs had proved easier than she expected, maybe it was that wall at her shoulder that helped, but the front door had been a nightmare. After one attempt, she spent the whole of the next day in bed wrapped in her duvet. But was back at it once more the following morning. Again she made no effort to go through, until she could open it without buckling at the knees.

But now she had made it. She was in the Mini and felt safe. Safe-ish, anyway. The rain helped. She had waited till a wet evening when the darkness and the curtain of rain cut visibility to almost nothing and wrapped her in a cocoon that kept her untouchable. The windscreen and windows had misted over and she knew she was completely unseen by any eye, secure in her metal cube and in her separation from humanity. She sat there, damp and isolated, feeling her breathing settle to a comfortable rhythm, and experienced a sense of real achievement.

One down, two to go.

While still waiting for Fiona to come up with anything, Jodie telephoned Kerry Dainton at the *Gazette*, and asked her to dig out certain pictures from their library. Then when Matt was out on a job and she was sure her mother was at her bridge evening, she rang her father. The warmth of his greeting took her by surprise.

'Hello, Jodie, it's good to hear from you. I've been thinking of you a great deal. How are you doing?'

'Not too bad.'

'Are your ribs any better?'

'Yes. The Araldite seems to be working.'

He even laughed at that. 'What can I do for you?'

Do for her? Since when!

Despite the row over his refusal to give her the name of the one girl the police had caught, he had insisted on coming at intervals along with her mother to visit the flat and made a point of remaining on speaking terms. Maybe Anthea was right. Maybe he really did care.

Care, my arse. If he cared, he would give her the name.

'Dad, I wondered whether you were busy at the moment.' At seven o'clock on a Friday evening he was usually buried in his study. 'I could do with a chat.'

This time it was his turn to be surprised.

'What about?'

'Can you come over here? Just for half an hour or so. There's something I want to show you.'

She could almost hear the alarm bells ringing in his head. 'Look, Jodie, if it's to do with the gang of girls who . . .'

'Dad, please come.'

He thought about it. 'Give me ten minutes and I'll be there.'

It was nine minutes. Punctuality was another of his irritating habits. By the time he arrived, she had a glass of wine waiting and a dish of Pringles and cheddar cubes on the table. He smiled when he saw them.

'You know my weakness,' he said and she almost choked on her wine. Weakness was not a word she had ever heard him apply to himself.

'Help yourself.'

He sat down, shoulders looser than usual, and counted out a precise number of crackers and chunks of cheese into his hand. Four of each. And proceeded to eat them alternately, as if they were numbered. It was to this desire for order that she intended to appeal. But sometimes she wondered what kind of chaos lay in his soul that needed to be so strictly boxed in. But first, a little soft soap wouldn't go amiss.

'You're looking tired, Dad.'

He straightened his back. 'No, not at all. Just a bit sick of all this rain. The amount of mud that is walked into school on a day like today is enough to build us another rugby pitch.'

'Talking of building, how are the temporary classrooms working out?' While the charred remains of the science block were being cleared preparatory to rebuilding, her father had managed to install prefabs to fill the gap.

He grimaced, uncomfortable with the enforced lowering of standards at his school. 'Not ideal, but we're doing the best we can. David Harris, you know he's our new head of science, has got them pretty well equipped now, but how can you expect pupils to feel enthused or committed when they're working in something not much better than a cardboard box?'

She hated it when he asked questions like that.

'They'll manage.'

'I hope you're right,' he said and took another Pringle.

'Just tell them that Pythagoras and Einstein produced their best work out of damp cellars, and that today's kids ought to count themselves lucky. That should go down well.'

Alan Buxton looked at his daughter, uncertain whether she was teasing him, and decided to get to the point.

'All right, Jodie, we've done the small-talk. Now what is it you want to show me?'

She lifted up a dark blue file that was lying on the table between them and held it out to him. 'This.'

He took it, eyes fixed on hers, searching for enlightenment. 'Any comment?' he asked.

She shook her head. 'Just look at what's in it.'

As he opened the file and started to flick through the pile of photographs it contained, she found herself twisting a long strand of her dark hair round her finger while she waited, as if trying to strangle it, a habit that irritated her in others. She searched for a reaction on his face, but other than a slight frown of concentration, he gave none. When he reached the last of the photographs, he did not even raise his gaze but went through them again from the beginning, more slowly this time. The only sign of agitation he displayed was that his breathing was now audible. To distract herself, she studied the greyness of his hair, robbed of all trace of pigment at the temples, and realised with a ripple of shock that he must be coming up to retirement age soon. A time when you could no longer ignore what you had done with your life. Or not done. She wondered if that frightened him.

'Where did you get these?' he asked, raising his head and looking already as if he regretted coming.

'From the *Gazette*'s files. Kerry brought them over for me.'

'Not exactly pleasant viewing.'

'No, they're not meant to be.'

They were photographs of damage. Damage inflicted on the community. There were pictures of foul-mouthed graffiti sprayed on walls and bus shelters, litter bins displaced and defaced, shop windows shattered, floral displays torn up and awnings torn down. There was one of the pier on fire and of the theatre's box-office after petrol had been poured through its letterbox and a cigarette thrown in, and a particularly sick one of a cat after a live firework was tied to its tail. Then came the people. Faces, both young and old, with cuts and bruises, noses broken, eyes swollen shut, limbs twisted till they snapped.

'All were taken in the last twelve months,' Jodie informed him. Most had appeared in the paper, but only one or two at a time. It was only when gathered together like this that their full impact could be felt, like an avalanche that knocks the breath out of you. 'And all were committed by teenagers.'

He shut the file and looked at her. 'Is that meant as an accusation?'

'Teenagers attend schools, and as a headmaster you are therefore to some extent responsible for them, yes.'

'Jodie, I am only too aware of that responsibility, as you
already know. So what is the point of this parade of photographs?'

'It's shocking, isn't it? When you see it like that.'

'Yes.' He gave a sigh that spoke of a level of depression that
Jodie had not suspected. 'Yes, it is.'

'Shocking enough for you to want to do something about it?
To control such deliberate flouting of law and order? You know
as well as I do that these acts of violence are not normally
committed by one or two kids on their own. It's the mob
mentality that takes over when there's a gang of them. They
get their kicks from being a threat to society. If you could break
up even one of those gangs, it would help.'

He stood up. 'Jodie, I have no intention of going over all this
again. I thought we had finished with it. I don't want another
argument with you. It will serve no purpose.'

'No purpose!' Jodie felt a valve pop open inside her head to
release the pent-up steam. She could feel it surging, hot and
moist, coming out of her ears, her mouth, her nose. 'Look at
me, Dad, look at my face.' She touched the scar on her cheek.
'Anybody who deliberately does this with their feet to another
human being is wrong in the head. They were girls, Dad. Girls.
A pack of vicious, sadistic girls. You can help. So why don't
you?' She was on her feet now, facing him, blue eyes wide and
challenging.

He turned away from them and resumed his seat. Very controlled. Quietly he said, 'I will explain it to you once more. You
are my daughter and I do not want to see you hurt again. If I
give any names to you, which I remind you I *have* given to the
police, you will go at them like an avenging valkyrie and only
end up in trouble. Or worse. So as far as I am concerned, society
will have to continue to suffer the onslaught of this particular
gang, because I am not, I repeat *not*, giving you the names of
that girl's associates at school. That is final.' He looked up at her
expectantly, braced for a further outburst.

But Jodie just nodded. 'So your silence is for my own sake?'

'Of course.'

'Why is it I don't believe you?'

'You think I'm just protecting my school.'

'Yes. And your own reputation. But what about the other kids out there being bullied and beaten up by them. Don't you care? If you people in authority won't protect them, who will?'

Her father rose abruptly to his feet. 'There is no point my staying.' He handed her the file. 'Goodbye, Jodie.'

She waited until he had gone and then threw the file across the room.

She reached her car in six minutes this time. Faster than yesterday, but not fast enough. Her palms were sweating. The adrenalin punching through her system after her father left had carried her easily as far as the street-door, but there she had stuck. Feet in concrete and head struggling with tunnel vision. The darkness outside seemed to be watching her through the central glass panel in the door, watching and waiting; until she switched off the hall light and then it couldn't see her any more. She had opened the door, swapping one darkness for another, and almost sauntered the last few yards to the Mini.

Once inside, door locked and seatbelt on, she felt positively safe. This was as far as she had got previously. Ready to go, but not quite ready. She put the key in the ignition and switched on the headlamps. It was like the flash of her camera, bringing illumination to her eyes at the touch of a button, but at the same time turning her invisible to whatever was caught in its beam. She sat there, savouring the sensation.

Time to make a move.

She checked that her Nikon was on the seat beside her, Grandad's torch in her pocket for luck, and started the engine.

The roads were busy. It was nearly eight o'clock but the High Street was open late for Christmas shoppers, so that the bright lights and garish decorations were on full blast. Oddly, Jodie liked them. They created a kind of fantasy world in which reality was just a dirty word.

It was Friday night. Alongside the harassed women with

the plastic carriers chipping at their calves and the pushchairs and the husbands subdued into reluctant docility, paraded the teenagers. Free, unfettered and flashing their wares as brightly as the shops. For them the hour was early yet, so they were cruising in twos and threes along the pavements, wasting time, gazing at fashion displays or pub menus, and grabbing window seats at McDonalds so that they could watch and ridicule the passersby.

Jodie drove round the one-way system three times until her nerves had settled, then headed to the end of the High Street and turned left onto the long slow hill that dropped down to the marina. This was where the nightclubs were clustered. Though it was far too early for any action in them, the teenagers were drifting in that direction, gathering in noisy huddles on the walkways and in the bars, mixing and matching, and only just beginning the night's drinking. Already the police were out in force, making their presence felt, and Jodie spotted a few faces she knew. She found them reassuring.

At the bottom of the hill, she made a U-turn and parked facing back up it. It was darker here, a black oasis between the frenetic activity at the top of the town and the lights of the marina behind her. Along the waterfront stood a colourful row of shop fronts selling watersports equipment, marine and fishing supplies, and a range of seafood and tourist tat. In the distance, the pier glittered like an elongated Christmas tree above the darkness of the sea. It was so solid. So black. It threatened to creep into her mind. Jodie turned her back on it and concentrated on the street ahead.

She remained seated in the car. Checked that the doors were locked, then very slowly wound down both windows six inches. She felt her breathing accelerate and for no reason her ribs kicked in with a grinding ache, but she ignored both. A group of three lanky youths was heading down the hill on the other side of the road, but they caused her no real concern. They were not what she was after, so when they stopped under a lamppost to light their cigarettes, she watched them with only half-hearted interest. They couldn't be more than sixteen at most. They pushed and shoved each other for fun, like young bucks jostling for dominance. One boy with a narrow face and the rudiments of designer stubble was carrying a four-pack under his arm and making enough noise to indicate it wasn't his first. The shortest of the three, a black youth wearing very expensive looking trainers, suddenly pointed back up the hill, then leaned with exaggerated cool against the lamppost. He shouted something Jodie did not catch.

A moment later, into the circle of light that surrounded them sauntered two blonde girls, like palomino ponies, tossing their manes and prancing on long slender legs.

Jodie raised her camera.

She only just made it to the flat in time. The Nikon was back in its case under the dressing-table, the reels of film safely stowed in the spare bedroom which also did service as her darkroom, and she had folded herself into a stiff, chilled heap in front of the fire, when Matt walked in. His hair was windblown off his face, accentuating the angular lines of his forehead and cheekbones, and his smoky eyes were roused to a darker grey that Jodie knew from experience meant acute frustration. He carried the outside world with him, like an overcoat he had forgotten to take off. He had been to a meeting of the town's Small Businesses Association, who were in dispute about the pedestrianisation of the upper section of the High Street around the town hall. Judging by his expression, he had not enjoyed the heated discussion.

'I thought those mealy-minded morons were never going to stop arguing,' he said and threw himself down beside Jodie on the rug, holding a hand out to the fire. 'No one was listening to anybody else, so it was a completely pointless exercise.'

'Poor old you.' She rubbed her shoulder against his. 'Stir it up by writing a really shitty article on them tomorrow. That would certainly make them think twice about boring you to death next time.'

He flicked a glance across at her. 'You're very perky this evening.' She could see him mentally discarding the overcoat. 'What have you been up to today?' he asked.

'Oh, exciting stuff like boiling an egg, waxing my legs and

finishing that godawful jigsaw Mum gave. Oh yes, and Dad came over earlier this evening.'

'No wonder you've got colour in your cheeks.'

Jodie touched a finger to her face and felt the heat. She brushed a hand across one cheek as if she could wipe it away. 'That's from the fire.'

'So what did he want?'

'Nothing constructive. He just trotted out the usual. About protecting me from myself by not giving me any of the names involved. Trash like that.'

Matt stared silently at the fire for a moment, as if seeking the right words inside its electric glow. 'Do you think you need protecting from yourself?' He turned and looked at her, his full attention denying her any place to run.

But she didn't want to play that game. She wrapped an arm around his waist and snuggled her head into the crook of his neck. 'I rather hoped you would be the one I need protection from.'

He said nothing, but she could feel the pulse in his neck like a spin-cycle against her ear. She tried to distract him. 'Did you bring today's *Gazette* home? I want to see how the freelance guy is getting on. What's his name again?'

'Dan Acheson.' But Matt was not listening to himself. His fingers were running down the silky tumble of her dark hair in long, slow movements that left her in no doubt that his mind was still on the subject of protection. She knew what he was going to say and knew equally well that she did not want to hear it.

'Jodie,' the stroking did not break rhythm, 'let's talk about the fact that you are frightened to go outside this flat.'

Oh no. Let's not.

'Do we have to?'

'I think we should.'

'Well, it's not true.'

She felt him take a deep, controlled breath.

'You won't admit that you're frightened, but that doesn't mean it's not true. You're a stubborn little mule, I know, but we've tried it your way, the pretending-everything-is-normal way. It doesn't work. So let's try mine.'

117 •

'And what's your way, Matt?'

'For you to open up and let others help you. Let *me* help you, even if you won't seek professional . . .'

She lifted her head and placed a kiss, warm and appealing, on his mouth to silence his words. But he pulled away.

'Not this time, Jodie. Sex is not enough between us. There has to be more.' The words came out roughly and caught Jodie with a sideswipe she had not been expecting.

'Matt, I don't . . .'

'Listen to me, Jodie.' His hands took hold of her by the arms and sat her up straight, facing him. 'I love you, but there's more to love than just sex. However much we enjoy jumping on each other's bones, we have to be able to jump into each other's heads as well. At the moment, you have yanked up the drawbridge, dropped the portcullis and are repelling all comers.' His hands gripped hard. 'Admit it.'

'No, I don't admit it.'

He dropped his hands. His whole face seemed to slacken, as if for one catastrophic moment he wanted to give up on her, but then it tightened again and he gave her a smile. 'I always said you were a mule.'

'Coming from a donkey like you, that's a compliment.'

'Don't kid yourself!'

She laughed to hide her anxiety and leapt across the moat that divided them while she could still make it. 'I'm not kidding myself or you, Matt. Honestly. If you think I'm too frightened to go outside, I'll prove to you you're wrong.'

He looked unconvinced. 'Right now?'

'Right now.' She stood up, her ribs reminding her she had overdone it today, and stretched out her hand to him. 'Come on.'

He got to his feet and, still clutching her hand, walked to the door, where he stepped to one side and said, 'Feel free.' Doubt was written in letters three feet high on his forehead.

Jodie could feel her teeth clenched tight, and she prised them apart.

'Easy,' she said and opened the door.

She stepped through it. With one hand in his and a smile stitched firmly in place, she got her legs all the way down the stairs and as far as the front door without stopping. The hand helped, she had to admit. But even so, to her ears the drumming of her heart sounded as deafening as a two-year-old with a wooden spoon and six saucepans. Maybe she could stop here.

One look at Matt's grey eyes and she felt that hope trickle away. With a movement that should have won her an Oscar, she casually turned the doorknob and pulled it towards her, letting a rectangle of darkness usurp its position. She held her breath, and stepped out into it. The wind that evening felt as if it had slipped into town straight from the Russian tundra, so after a couple of metres up the path, Matt shivered, turned her round and said, 'Let's get back into the warm. It's freezing out here.'

She had not even noticed the temperature.

With the front door and then their flat door once more back in place behind them, a sense of refuge closed about her. The wind and the darkness were locked outside. Matt looked closely into her eyes but if he saw anything untoward, he gave no sign.

'I'm impressed,' he said and tightened his arm around her.

The warmth of his body next to hers sent the usual shockwave through it and she curled her hands up round his neck. His hair felt soft and silky, and the back of his neck was a satisfying curve of muscle and firm skin. Their bodies fitted so perfectly together, like interlocking jigsaw pieces, so why did he not leave her mind alone?

'I apologise for doubting you,' he said and kissed her. 'But that's not the end of it,' he breathed against her lips.

She pretended she had not heard. Her mouth held on to his.

He pulled away. 'Jodie, we haven't finished.'

'You bet we haven't.'

He laughed, but she knew he was just humouring her. That she could only push him so far.

'Okay, okay,' she said and sat down in front of the fire once more, but on a chair this time. If he wanted straight, she could do straight. 'What now?'

He remained standing. The crease across his high forehead made him appear depressed and she wanted to put her fingers on it and smooth it away, to iron out any intrusive sign of the reality underneath.

'I want to know what you intend to do about the girls who attacked you.'

This one was easy.

'Matt, what on earth *can* I do? Look, my darling, they've disappeared. The fact that they put me in hospital and I hate their guts is irrelevant.' A tiny piece of the anger broke off inside her and floated away. As if admitting its existence stole a part of it. She shut her mouth.

Matt wasn't fooled.

He came over and knelt on the rug in front of her. The fire painted his skin with a rosy glow that was at odds with the grey unhappiness in his eyes. 'Of course you're angry. And of course you're frightened. Those girls are dangerous. But I know you. That's why I'm telling you to leave them alone. Your father is right to keep any names from you. I don't want you hurt, Jodie.' He lifted a hand and rested it on her knee. 'Please. Forget about them. And prove it by giving me the photograph of the girl in the police car. The negative as well.'

His hand felt like a shackle on her leg. Gently, she picked it up and held it cradled between her two hands. 'I can't, Matt. I can't give it to you. And I can't forget about them. I don't *want* to forget about them. I want to know what's in the head of the leader of that gang out there, what makes her take such infinite pleasure in kicking my head in. To know what kind of monster has taken up residence inside her head. That's what I want.'

Jodie knew she had said more than she meant to.

The telephone rang and saved them both. Matt stared at the fire, ignoring the abrasive chirp, and Jodie felt an urge to throw him to the floor and tear off his clothes, or her clothes, it didn't matter which. Anything to replace that frown with one of his big hell-raising smiles. Instead, she rose to her feet and answered the telephone. It was Fiona.

'At last,' Jodie said. 'I thought perhaps you'd emigrated.'

'Have you any idea of the trouble I had? It'll only take a minute, my arse!'

Jodie was aware of Matt listening.

'It went well, did it?' she asked casually.

'No, you nitwit, it did not go well. I got thrown out twice.

That school is getting more like Fort Knox every day. And the bloody kids, well, they all need drowning in a vat of oil.'

Jodie smiled sweetly. 'I'm glad you had a good time. I'll see you here tomorrow then. Come and share a boiled egg for lunch. Bye.' She hung up. 'That was Fiona.'

Matt nodded. 'When she comes, maybe you can get her to talk some sense into you.'

Jodie returned to the rug and curled up against him in a docile, clinging gesture she recognised as worthy of Goliath. That same desire for uncritical warmth.

'I promise I'll listen to whatever she says.'

Matt kissed her cheek, the one with the scar on it. Not for a minute did Jodie suppose he was deceived by her performance.

The lunch ended up as a pizza. Fiona had arrived wet from the rain sheeting down outside and demanded hot food a damn sight more enticing than a boiled egg. Once it was on a tray in the oven, Jodie herded Fiona into the sitting-room.

'Come on, then, hand them over. Let's see what you've got.'

'Don't I even get a drink first?' Fiona moaned. Her short well-cut fair hair had been towelled enough to take off the worst of the rain, but was still damp round her face, giving her the look of a helpless waif. It was a look she found useful on occasions, but not this time.

'No. Hand over.'

Fiona pulled a large manila envelope out of her shoulder bag. 'Here. Some of them aren't up to much, but I reckon I deserve a medal for bravery. Some of those school kids need a damn good hiding.'

Jodie took the envelope. Inside were twelve large colour prints. She had drawn a map of the school for Fiona, indicating where the fourth-year classrooms were situated and had suggested her best chance would be on a wet day at break-time, when they would be crammed into their forms, rowdy and restless as caged polecats, but at least en masse. Any excuse would do. Like her paper wanted to illustrate an article on the number of pupils in classes, or that they were doing a comparison of school uniforms throughout the region. Just use your imagination, she had told Fiona.

She pulled out the photographs and felt a kick of excitement. At last, she was getting somewhere. Fiona had had enough sense to exclude the boys. The pictures were of groups of girls, seated on desks, lolling with impudent grins on chairs and windowsills, faces young and self-conscious, eager to be immortalised on film. It never failed to fascinate Jodie the way even the shyest of people were so easily bewitched by the camera's eye.

'I told them the paper was running a series of articles on women commenting on their environment,' Fiona said smugly. 'The trouble was, I then had to listen to their crappy comments.' She shook her head in disgust. 'I swear to God we had more sense when we were that age.'

Jodie was not listening. She was flicking through the photographs. No face jumped out at her, but then school uniforms always disguised a person, emphasising the child in them, rather than the maverick adolescent. She was going to have to study them more closely. She replaced the photographs in the envelope.

Fiona looked disappointed. 'No luck?'

'There are several possibles, but I'm not absolutely certain. I'll have to go over them with my magnifying glass to be sure. But thanks, Fiona, I do appreciate it.'

'I'll expect some inside info, if you get a story out of this. The negatives are at the bottom of the envelope, by the way.'

'Thanks. I'll have a good look at them later.' She did not want to conduct the search in front of Fiona. It was too private.

'When I'm gone, you mean?'

'Yes. I'll need to concentrate.'

'You're infuriating, do you know that?'

'I think I may have heard that fact mentioned before,' Jodie smiled.

'How about a drink instead, then?'

'There's a beer in the fridge,' Jodie said and took the envelope into the dark room for safe-keeping.

14

The small circle of light crawled slowly from one face to another. Jodie sat at her cluttered desk in the spare bedroom and peered intently as the pencil beam from her grandfather's torch illuminated each girl's head like a halo. As if they were angels. Every now and again she glanced across at the photograph on her left, a blow-up of the girl in the back of the police car the night of the fire. She was wearing a woolly cap that effectively concealed her hair and one hand obscured half her face, so the image was unclear. But the one eye that showed so sullen and frightened was unmistakably blue, and the cheek slender.

Jodie had already eliminated the obvious ones. Big black satisfying crosses blocked out any face that was dark-eyed, black or Asian, or carried too much weight. Out of just over fifty girls in the twelve photographs, that left nineteen possibles. Not counting those who might have been absent from school that day. She placed a question-mark on the three who wore spectacles. Contact lenses were of course a possibility.

Down to sixteen.

Jodie pulled a magnifying glass out of her desk drawer and started again on the first of them.

By three-forty, she was outside the school. It was the first time she had taken the Mini out in the daytime and her chest felt hot and tight. She had brought along with her a can of Coke from the fridge at home, but instead of drinking it to ease her dry throat, she held the cold metal against her forehead. It helped. But not much.

She had tucked her car in the entrance to the car park nearest the main buildings. The fact that it was already full and was the staff car park did not concern her. Its position meant that all the pupils would have to walk past her, whether they journeyed by car, by coach or on foot. She was well aware that a few took short-cuts across the school fields and out through the hedges, but she had to rely on the amount of rain that had fallen recently and the mud it had churned up to act as a deterrent.

Churned up. It wasn't only the mud that was churned up.

A thin trickle of navy-blue teenagers started to drift past her, a variety of shapes and sizes, the smaller ones lopsided from the weight of the school bag on one shoulder. She was pleased to see so many of the boys wearing their ties askew and their shirts hanging loose, a public declaration of their own personal battle against authority. A daily battle she remembered well. The girls were less obvious about it, strutting and pouting and flouncing their long hair.

Jodie concentrated on the three faces on her lap. Not that she needed to. She knew each one of them intimately. The sixteen had been whittled down to three. Three possibles. Blue eyes and slender features that were almost interchangeable. Only the hair was different. Short and blonde, mousy curls or long and straight. In her dark room she had enlarged the photographs to produce stronger impressions of each face. The girl in the police car was too blurred for a positive comparison.

She sat and waited, studying every girl who passed. The trickle had thickened to a steady flow, and then to a sudden tidal wave as four o'clock arrived, so that Jodie had to have eyes everywhere. And suddenly she saw one. The mousy curls were easy to spot. The adrenalin rush hit hard and made Jodie want to leap out of the car and accost the girl. But that was not an option. Any questioning, asking for names or touting of photographs among the pupils would be round the school like wildfire, and her prey would either retreat into hiding or go for a second attack on her.

Just the thought of it made her feel as if someone was sticking pins in her brain.

Nerves. That's all. Nervous reaction.

She kept her eyes fixed on the mousy curls. Pretty, childish curls, but what kind of mind did they conceal? The girl was part of a group of three and Jodie scoured each of them for any resemblance in shape or movement to the black figures at the fire. And at the attack. But it was hopeless. Nevertheless, she raised her camera and sneaked off several shots. When it was clear that they were not heading for the row of school buses but for the parents' car park, she was just about to reach for the ignition, when a knuckle rapped on her window. Impatiently, she rolled it down. She did not recognise the female face that bent down to peer at her but she recognised the expression of disapproval. It had to be a teacher.

'This car park is for staff only. And parking at the entrance like this is particularly dangerous.' The woman was only in her early thirties, but already talked and dressed like a headmistress. Her mouth had settled into a firm line.

'I'm sorry. I'm just leaving,' Jodie said, but the woman was not prepared to let it go at that.

'The demand for parking spaces is a perennial source of difficulty for us and we have to be quite strict about it. I'm sure you must understand that if everyone behaved like you, we would have real problems.'

'And if everyone behaved like you, we would have even worse problems.' She started the engine and drove away.

But she had lost the girl.

The curls had disappeared, along with the two friends. Cars were streaming on to the narrow slip-road out of the other car park, as parents manoeuvred round each other in the familiar routine of the school-run. But getting off the school grounds and back on the main road always took time because of the queue, so Jodie abandoned her Mini on the pavement and took to her feet.

A quick chase round the car park yielded nothing. She hurried further down the slip-road, cursing all women teachers. She struck lucky. One of the sixth-form boys was driving his mother's Fiesta. The car displayed a big set of L-plates and judging by his performance, he was very new to the game. He had stalled its engine at the junction with the main road and was so flustered that he was making a botch of any kind of recovery. Directly behind it purred an electric-blue small Rover. The woman driver was patiently watching the boy's efforts, but the three girls in the back were in hoots of laughter. The mop of curls in the middle was unmistakable.

Jodie beat a rapid retreat to the Mini and pushed its squat nose into the queue in front of an elderly Saab. A quick count told her she was seven cars behind the Rover.

It was much easier than she expected. Following a car in heavy traffic all headed in the same direction was not nearly as difficult as they made it look in films. At one junction, she lost two of the intervening cars and at the next set of lights the Golf immediately in front of her took a right filter. Four cars left. They provided an effective screen without causing her any trouble in keeping the bright blue hatchback in sight.

Half of Westonport's population seemed to be out on the roads ferrying its children around, which meant the traffic was slow. But that helped. No sudden movements to take her by surprise. Nevertheless, her heart did stop briefly when the Rover went through a set of lights on amber and she was left to sit and fume behind the remaining cars on red. But no real harm was done. There was a straight stretch of road ahead, so she caught up, but was now nine cars behind. Her palms had started sweating.

She almost missed it.

She had been reduced to only occasional glimpses of blue whenever the road curved left or right, and was just pulling out in the hope of hopping past the van in front of her, when she glanced up an innocuous turning on her left and saw the Rover disappearing round a corner.

Oh shit, oh shit, no.

She swerved abruptly left and just made the turning, but not without an angry blast of the horn from the car behind as it hit its brakes. It was a quiet street of terraced houses, each with a tiny front garden that looked miserable in its barren winter greyness. The Mini reached the corner and took it fast, but there was no need. Right in front of her the Rover was waiting for a builder's lorry to park. She almost ran into its bumper. The girls in the back glanced round, but with no real interest.

By the time they set off again, Jodie had herself under control. She let the Rover pull well ahead, so that after a number of twists and turns during which the two other girls were dropped off at a street corner, she had plenty of time to find a parking space nearby when it indicated that it was going to pull into a driveway on the right. She sat in her car and watched over the low front hedge, as the woman backed the car into a garage that adjoined the house. The big double door closed and swallowed the girl from Jodie's sight.

It took her ten minutes to get out of the car. She knew she had to, but her whole body rebelled. Enough was enough. For one day, enough. Please. This was the part she had not rehearsed. Walking out in the open, in broad daylight, talking and smiling as if there were nothing to fear. Her panic-stricken search at the school car park did not count. And what if it was the wrong girl? All that effort for nothing. You've done enough for today. Just drive home now.

She opened the door. The skin round her mouth was numb and tingly. As if it had suddenly developed frostbite. She was tempted to look in the rearview mirror to see if it showed on her face, like a mask of ice. But she didn't. She was nervous of what she might see there. The photographs lay on the seat beside her. She picked up the enlargements of the other two girls, leaving the curly-haired one behind, took two deep, slow breaths and climbed out of the car before she could think of any more excuses.

The street was quiet. As if it had settled down in front of the television ready for *Neighbours*. The houses were semi-detached and painted white, built in the thirties with big bay windows and stained glass round the front doors. Jodie opened the gate and walked up the path. A hydrangea bush at one end of the square of lawn had transformed its flowers into puffball skeletons of lace that made Jodie think of the bones of her own skull. Delicate, pale and fragile. She could crush the hydrangea skeletons between her fingers.

She rang the doorbell.

While she waited, she cast glances up and down the street, but the pavements were empty except for the skittering of dead leaves in the gutters, refugees from a chill wind. When the door at last swung open, she had to stop herself pushing inside, into the safety of the four walls.

'Can I help you?'

Jodie had been expecting the mother. Or maybe the girl herself. But she was faced by a man in his forties, tall and broad-shouldered, filling the doorway with his bulk. His expression was helpful, as if he welcomed the interruption of her visit. She wondered if he was unemployed.

'Hello,' she smiled at him and held up an identity card she had created on Matt's computer only an hour earlier. 'I'm from social services.' She was wearing the boring black suit she kept for formal occasions and funerals.

He glanced at the card without seeing it and she tucked it back in her pocket.

'I'm here to make a few enquiries. You are Mr . . . ?'

'Stephens. Michael Stephens.'

'You have a daughter at Wyndame School, I believe.'

'That's right.' He was looking interested but not uneasy.

'Her name is . . . ?'

'Louise.'

'Louise Stephens.'

'That's right,' he repeated. 'What is this about?'

If you had a daughter who had not long ago been caught stealing, you would not be asking a representative of social services what it was about. Disappointment added itself to the lead weight already sitting in her stomach.

'It's about the theft of the computers from the school.'

'Oh no, not that again. I thought it was over and done with. Though why you people can't do something to keep girls like that Richards kid under control, I don't know.'

'The Richards kid?'

'Yes. Your lot must know her. The one who got caught.'

'For stealing the computers?'

'That's right.' He took a couple of paces back.

'Just two more questions, Mr Stephens. I am new on this case and obviously there has been a mix-up somewhere. I was given your address instead of the Richards'. I do apologise, but you wouldn't believe how much paperwork we have to fight our way through.' She smiled. It came easily now.

'I used to work in local government, so I know what it's like.'

Jodie held out the two photographs for him to see. 'Is she one of these?'

He looked at the young girls smiling up at him and pointed immediately to the one on the left, the one with short hair. 'Yes, that's Emma Richards. She and my Louise used to be friendly when they were at primary school. Not any more though,' he added emphatically. 'Thank God.'

'And do you know Emma's address?'

He shook his head. 'No, I don't. It used to be somewhere up at the top of Stanwell Road, but I have no idea whether they're still there. I don't want to know, either.'

'I see. Well, thank you for your time. I appreciate your assistance.' She rewarded him with another smile.

He nodded. 'Glad to help. But it does seem a bit odd to me that you come to the wrong address, not even knowing what the girl looks like, and . . .'

Jodie cut short that line of speculation. 'As I told you, I'm new. Still getting to know the ropes. Thank you again.' She left quickly, before he could come up with any more objections.

There were two hundred and forty-eight Richards in the phone book. She made the mistake of starting from the beginning. It was not until she reached two hundred and ten, a Mrs S.A. Richards, that she found Stanwell Road. She wrote down the number.

She replaced the phone book in its slot, slipped smartly out of the telephone kiosk and into her car. It was almost dark now. Lights were glowing warm and tempting from windows each side of the street and she felt an overwhelming need to be on the inside. It was so strong it seemed to squeeze her lungs, as if a gigantic fist had taken hold of them.

She started the engine.

Number twelve Stanwell Road proved to be one of an identical row of terraced houses, the kind with front doors that opened straight on to the pavement. Even in the gloom, it was obvious that its paintwork was reasonably recent, unlike its neighbour which drooped with neglect. A satellite dish graced its upstairs wall.

Jodie parked a few yards down from it on the opposite side of the road close to a small rectangle of grassland that boasted a few sad swings and a roundabout, all deserted now. She contemplated her next move. Apprehension made her throat dry and she remembered the Coke. She pulled its tab and sipped the sickly sweet liquid, grateful for the moment's respite it gave her. She felt the need for a Malteser. Her fingers rummaged in the door pocket among the maps and the jumble of used pay-and-display tickets, more to prolong the delay than with any real expectation of finding chocolate.

A shadow passed her.

She looked up quickly. In front of her car stood the girl. About to cross the road. Her shoulders were hunched against the cold and her face turned first one way, then the other, checking for traffic. The pretty mouth was pulled down in an expression of discontent. Jodie recognised her immediately as the girl who had cowered on the back seat of the police car. Without waiting to give any inner voice of caution a chance to get going, she opened the door and leapt out. The cold air was so chill, it was like jumping into a freezer.

'Emma.'

The girl turned. Her blue eyes stared blankly at Jodie for a moment and then widened with recognition.

'You.'

'Yes, me.' Jodie approached her, but slowly, as she would an untethered animal. She was wearing a long padded jacket over her school uniform and touting a bag on one shoulder.

'What do you want?' Though only fifteen, her face had already lost the open freshness of youth and replaced it with an adult's guarded frown that took nothing for granted.

'I want to talk to you.'

'What about?'

'About your friends. The ones that wear Nike footwear.'

'Nearly everyone I know has Nike. Nike or Reebok.'

She edged away, as if to put a more comfortable gap between

herself and Jodie, but Jodie did not let her get away with it. She moved closer. The light from a nearby streetlamp cast their elongated shadows on to the road where a car ran over them. The girl turned to face her, as if squaring up to any threat, and Jodie caught a movement off to one side out of the corner of her eye. Her heart rocketed to her throat.

Not again, no, not again.

She spun round quickly, arm already coming up as protection. But this time it was only a dog out with its owner for an evening saunter, sniffing at a vehicle's wheel and cocking its leg. Her eyes retreated to her own car, its interior offering a refuge that would waft her back to warmth and safety at the turn of a key.

She turned to the girl. 'Emma, let's go and have a quiet talk in that park over there.' Her feet headed off towards the patch of grassland but the girl's did not follow. Jodie stopped and looked back at her. 'Or would you prefer that I went and knocked on your door and we conducted our conversation in your house?'

'No,' the girl said quickly. 'No, I wouldn't.'

Jodie said no more. She walked along the pavement to the grass rectangle and up the path to the swings. She sat down on one and waited for the girl to join her.

When Matt came home, she was in bed. It was not yet seven o'clock but Jodie was wrapped up tight inside the duvet with the light off. She was not asleep. She heard the front door close and his voice call her name. She burrowed deeper into her nest of down. Tried to blank out her mind. It felt red and raw, exhausted by going round and round in circles that took her nowhere.

'Jodie, are you all right?' Matt switched the light on. 'What are you doing lying here in the dark?' He sat on the edge of the bed and pulled the folds away from her face. 'Are you feeling ill?'

'No, I'm not ill. Just tired.'

'Tired? But you've done nothing all day. How can you be tired?'

She could hear the implication. The voice of one who has been working all day and doesn't need the self-indulgent flutterings of an idle girlfriend. Maybe he was right. Maybe she was ill.

'I went out today. Overdid it.'

'What did you do?'

'Oh, just drove around. Chatted to a few people.'

He stroked her hair into a fan of rippling shadows on the pillow, but she wished he would stop. Her skull felt ready to shatter. 'Jodie, it's almost Christmas, and you're supposed to be back at work when it's over. How are you going to cope if you can't even manage to drive around and chat to a few people?'

'It was just a bad day, that's all. I'll be better tomorrow.'

He took her hand in his and held on to it. 'Tell me why it was a bad day.'

'Because I missed you,' she smiled and lifted up half of the duvet, destroying her nest. To include him. 'Come and show me how much you missed me as well.'

She saw a flash of real impatience darken his grey eyes and then it was controlled. He kicked off his shoes, bent his head down and started to kiss her lips, her throat, her breasts. As if he was trying to find her hidden behind them somewhere. She wrapped her hands in his hair and hung on.

But it didn't work.

She did try. Her flesh responded to his touch as if it belonged to a completely different body from her head. It writhed and groaned and grew heated with the need he knew so well how to create in her, but her head just sat there and watched. No red mist of passion. No loss of sense of time and place while plunging into nothing but the now. No existence but this moment.

No, none of that.

While his body panted and heaved on top of hers, and her fingers dug hungrily into the taut damp muscles of his back, her mind was sitting in the dark in a shabby patch of grassland on a swing.

Emma Richards had not been exactly helpful. She had slouched on the narrow plastic seat, clinging to the chains, and given resentful little kicks at the ground to set it in motion. Neither of them had commented on the deepening dusk or the icy wind that turned the metal so cold it burned their fingers. The hinges creaked above their heads for want of oil. A smear of orange light from the streetlamp reached only as far as their feet, like a pool for them to dip their toes in. Jodie had explained quite calmly what she wanted.

She wanted the name of the leader of the gang who attacked her.

'You have to be joking!' the girl had jeered in scornful astonishment. 'I don't know the names of that gang, but if I did, why should I tell you? You're the one who got me into trouble in the first place.'

'I know. But it was because of you that I'm in trouble now.'

The girl turned her head and stared at Jodie. At this close range, the spark of interest was clearly visible. The sullen downturn of her mouth was replaced by the flicker of a smile. 'What kind of trouble?'

Jodie let the swing rock her back and forth several times, let the winter darkness wrap her in a chill cloak of secrecy before replying, 'No trouble that I would tell you.'

The girl kicked out at the ground. 'That makes us quits then. Neither of us tells anything.'

'And both in trouble.'

'Not me. They let me off with an official caution, the pigs did. The school got its frigging computer back and they couldn't lay the fire or the other computers on me. I grovelled like a baby in court and got off.'

'So I heard.'

'It was the first time they'd ever been sharp enough to catch me. And that was only because of you. So you can stick your trouble where it hurts.'

Jodie leant back and pushed the swing higher. 'Tell your friend I want a word with her. She can contact me at the *Gazette*.'

'No chance.'

'Just tell your friend what I said.'

The girl burst out laughing. 'My friend! I don't know her name, I tell you, and she's not my friend. But if she was, she wouldn't want to talk to you. There's nothing in it for her.'

'Maybe not. But there's something in it for you.'

'Oh yeah? What's that?'

Abruptly, Jodie jumped off the swing and it jangled noisily, disturbing a cat that was stalking in the shadows. She leant over Emma Richards' startled face and placed her hands on the chain either side of the blonde head that in the darkness looked grey. 'Peace of mind.'

'What?' The eyes were uneasy now.

'Because if you don't pass on my message, you are the one *I* will be coming after.'

'Get stuffed!' But the words were as empty as her brain. Her nerves were rattled. Alone, in the dark and under threat. She glanced anxiously in the direction of her house. The hall light shone out like an invitation through the skylight above the door.

'Just make sure you pass on my message, that's all,' Jodie said and gave the chains a jerk that sent the girl lurching backwards. Only her clutching fingers saved her from a fall.

She nodded.

That nod had stayed in Jodie's mind. Stuck there like a thorn, sharp and irritating under the skin. The gesture had been so eager to please. So packed full of . . .

Matt murmured something about tasting like ice-cream and began kissing the inside of her thighs. They responded with tingles that shot up into her groin and brought a moan to her lips.

But her head would not be distracted.

Full of what? Go on, say it. Admit it. Of fear. The nod had been packed full of fear. Fear that Jodie herself had inflicted. She shuddered, and this time it had nothing to do with sexual need.

She stayed under the duvet. Matt dressed and heated up a chicken Kiev for each of them but she did not want hers, so he ate them both. He sat on the end of the bed and chatted to her, telling her of Roy Dunmore's decision to include a quarter-page slot for a photograph of random interest or amusement in the paper every Saturday. Maybe sometimes a moody nature picture. Jodie would bet her chicken Kiev that the idea had originated from Matt. His attempt to entice her back to work. She was grateful to him but wished he would not interfere. She was dealing with it.

When the telephone rang in the sitting-room and Matt went to answer it, Jodie yanked the duvet over her head again. She had frightened herself out there in the park. On the drive home her hands had been shaking. Was that how it happened? Such a small step to transform the bullied into bullies, the abused into abusers. Because it was the only currency of communication they understood.

It felt as if a stranger had set up home inside her, a squatter who did not belong. She wanted to put her hand down her throat and tear this person out, but she had a sickening feeling that she would be ripping herself out with it and would bleed to death inside.

'Jodie.'

Matt's voice came from next to the bed. How long had he been standing there?

'Jodie, it's Anthea on the telephone. She wants to talk to you.'

'Tell her I'm not in the mood.'

'For Christ's sake, just put yourself in the mood. If you don't want to talk to her, tell her yourself.' He walked out of the room.

Oddly, Matt's outburst was easier to handle than his kindness. With the duvet still wrapped round her naked body, she slid off the bed and padded into the sitting-room. It was empty, but the telephone receiver lay waiting.

'Hello, Anthea. How's life in the big bad city?'

'Bigger and badder than ever. You'd love it.'

Jodie smiled. 'We've got our fair share of that here in Westonport.'

There was a moment's awkwardness, as if Anthea realised she had allowed the conversation to stray into unpleasant territory. 'I was ringing to sort out about Christmas.'

'Are you still intending to spend it down here?'

'Of course. I wouldn't miss Mum's turkey stuffing and brandy sauce for all the world. Anyway, I wouldn't dare. Can you imagine what she'd say if I did?'

They both laughed. Even when Anthea had been married, she and her husband, Jonathan, had dutifully attended the ritual at her parents' house on Christmas Day each year. His parents had lived in South Africa, so there was never any tussle over who went where. But it was the one event that Matt declined to be a part of. He had already arranged to visit his own parents in Bournemouth and would not be back until

New Year's Eve. It had been the same last year and the loss of him had been like having a tooth pulled with each breath. But Anthea had just received her decree nisi, so she and Jodie had amused themselves playing Trivial Pursuit all day and taking a mouthful of vodka every time they got the answer wrong. By the time it came to the Queen's Speech, they were laughing like hyenas. Their father had hidden himself away in his study until Christmas was over.

'I'm glad you're coming,' Jodie said. 'We can make it Block-busters this year.'

Anthea chuckled. 'God, my head ached for a week. But this year I'll have to behave myself.'

'Since when!'

'Since I'm bringing a friend with me.' She announced it proudly.

'Is it . . .' She sought for the name Anthea had mentioned on her last visit. '. . . Henry?'

'It is. My one and only Henry.'

'It must be serious if you're risking exposing him to the parents. What's he like?'

'Adorable.'

'So when do we get to meet him?'

'We'll be driving down on Christmas Eve. We're going to try to avoid the worst of the traffic, so it will probably be latish by the time we get there. You'll meet him when you come over on Christmas morning.'

'I look forward to it, Anthea. I really do.'

'You'll love him.'

'I'm sure I will,' Jodie reassured her.

'And what about you? Looking forward to going back to work in the New Year?'

'Can't wait.'

A pause. 'Do I detect a note of sarcasm there?'

'I don't need you to start pushing and prodding at me as well. I get enough of that already.'

'Sorry. It's just that . . .'

'I know, Anthea. You're worried about me. But if you'd all just leave me alone, I might stand some chance of sorting myself out.' She said it gently, unwilling to hurt her sister.

'All right, I'm receiving you loud and clear. No more fussing.'
'Good.'
'We can have a chat when I'm down for Christmas. I'll lend you my shoulder.'
'I don't need a shoulder.'
'Just wait until I get a couple of vodkas into you. Last year you were so plastered, you told me all about how you like to make love with Matt in the bathroom and have him . . .'
'Okay, okay, I was out of my mind, I admit it. Remind me to be more discreet this time,' she laughed. 'But where's the fun in that?'
'Exactly.' In the distance came the sound of Anthea's doorbell. 'Oh hell, that's Henry and I'm still in my bra and pants. Oh well, I dare say he won't mind that. I must go.'
'Bye, Anthea. See you soon.'
Jodie hung up and wondered about Henry.
'Jodie, come here.'
Matt was calling her from the hallway of the flat. Tightening her grip on the duvet, she shuffled out to him. He was standing by the door of the spare bedroom, holding it open and his eyes were blank grey screens, denying her access to whatever was behind them.
'What is this about?'
There was no need to ask what he meant by 'this'. Normally he did not go into the spare bedroom. He left it to her and her clutter. Other than the unused divan in there, it was where she had her desk, kept her chemical baths and did her developing or enlarging. He pushed the door fully open. She knew what she was going to see.
'Tell me what this is all about,' he said again.
All four of the walls were covered with faces. Literally hundreds of them. All girls' faces, all young. Blow-ups of faces laughing and talking, some animated, others still and thoughtful or frowning in sullen silences. Girls walking in the street, leaning against shop windows, smoking cigarettes, drinking in doorways and driving in cars, and even one crying into a torn tissue. All colours, all shapes, all ages between ten and twenty.
'What is this about?' Matt asked for the third time.

'I've been taking photographs. When you've been working late.'

'So I see. Why?'

Jodie walked calmly over to the door and pulled it shut. 'Matt, I do not want the third degree, thank you. It's obvious why I took them. To see if I can recognise in them any of the girls who attacked me. It's not so strange that I should want to find them and this seemed a sensible way to try.'

Matt's face was rigid. She could see the struggle between frustration and understanding. Frustration won.

'Sensible!' he exploded. 'This isn't sensible. This is insane. It's obsession.'

'I know that, Matt,' she said quietly. 'But at the moment, that's the way I am.'

She headed back to bed and was relieved when several hours later her thoughts finally chased themselves into oblivion and she fell asleep. But that was when the first of the nightmares began.

15

Elizabeth Buxton adored Christmas. She took no notice of Alan saying she made it into a rod for her own back every year. She loved all the doing and the planning and the preparing. For weeks beforehand she was making advent calendars, buying and wrapping, creating new ornaments for the tree. The mountains of mince pies, chocolate Christmas trees, coconut snowballs, chestnut stuffing and hazelnut meringue were always eaten up, despite everyone saying she had overdone it yet again. And she could tuck in greedily without being the only one.

So what was going wrong this year? As she arranged slices of Christmas cake on a plate in the kitchen, she felt like crying. Everyone was trying very hard, making conversation and laughing in that over-eager way people do when they don't mean it, so that on the surface it seemed to be going very nicely. But they were pretending. Elizabeth knew that. Pretending for her sake. But the strain showed. When one of the balloons popped as it drifted down on to one of the candles, everyone jumped a foot in the air.

She slipped a stray chunk of marzipan into her mouth without noticing. It had started with Henry Mackintosh. Anthea had arrived about ten o'clock the previous evening and introduced him as if he were God. All right, Elizabeth was willing to admit he was obviously intelligent and not bad-looking, as well as rich because he drove a flash car that Alan had told her was a Jaguar XK8. And courteous. Courtesy went a long way in her book. But he was too *old*. Nearly as old as Alan, for heaven's sake. Knocking on fifty anyway. Elizabeth shook her head and bit the heart out of a mince pie. It burnt her tongue. Silly, silly Anthea. What did she think she was up to? She was young. Sophisticated and self-financing. So why on earth did she need *him*? Maybe the fact that he couldn't keep his hands off her had something to do with it. Always touching her, he was; trailing a finger along her leg, wrapping an arm around her waist, popping a chocolate in her mouth. Elizabeth hated it.

She drowned her sorrows and her burnt tongue in a glass of wine, then carried the tray through to the others. They were sitting round the coffee table playing Blockbusters. Grandad was revelling in his role of question-master and insisted on everyone calling him Bob. It was Alan and Henry against Anthea and Jodie. Alan and Henry were winning hands down. The old ones against the young ones. She plonked the tray down on the coffee table and got moaned at, but at least it ended the game. She handed round the cups.

'Tea, Jodie?'

'Thanks. No cake for me.' Elizabeth thought Jodie was looking miserable. Maybe she was missing Matt.

'I'll have some.' Anthea took both the cake and a coconut snowball and gave her mother a beaming smile in return. 'So will Henry. He loves your cooking.'

She was trying too hard. And Elizabeth did not like the way that she was hiding herself in a long skirt and big shaggy sweater which, Elizabeth presumed, were more to Henry's taste than her usual skimpy dresses. Don't change for him, she wanted to shout at her daughter.

She handed the cakes round and was proud of herself for passing no comment when her own father sneaked half of his to Tess, who was sitting so close, she was almost inside his skin with him. She had told him a thousand times not to feed his dogs anywhere except in the kitchen, but he still did it. Parents, like children, were uncontrollable. At least Alan was pulling his weight. He and Henry were deep in conversation about the brilliance of William Lyons' designs for Jaguar. Elizabeth had not realised Alan knew so much about cars.

Grandad smiled his toothy smirk, as if he knew exactly what was going on in her head. 'Sit down and stop fussing, girl,' he said. 'Have another piece of that cake. Might as well enjoy the fruits of all your labour. It's too rich for me.' He turned his head, still in its ridiculous paper hat, to Henry. 'Constipation is the bane of my existence,' he explained.

'Dad, not now. Please.'

But Henry smiled. 'Not something I'm troubled with, I'm glad to say.'

He didn't look to Elizabeth as if he'd be troubled by anything. His hair was thinning and streaked with grey, but he had a strong, confident mouth, and eyes that were alert. As though he was used to watching his back. For his age he was in reasonable shape, though a little overweight. But it was the way he moved that said it all: at ease with himself and possessing that quiet authority that meant he was accustomed to power-play. Anthea had told her he was chairman of a company that did something or other in high-tech software. She had added that he had been divorced. Twice. Maybe that's where the deep furrows round his eyes had come from.

Anthea carried the tea tray out to the kitchen and asked as she clattered her mother's best china in the sink, 'What's up with you? It's going really well. Everyone is enjoying themselves.'

Everyone, meaning Henry and herself, of course.

'I'm glad, dear.'

'Not worrying about Jodie, are you?'

'Not so much now. I think what she needs is a few weeks back at work to take her mind off all this attack business. Your father thinks it's a case of idle hands make idle mind.'

'He would,' Anthea laughed and gave her mother a peck on the cheek. 'So what is it that is spoiling your Christmas? I can see you're a bit edgy.'

Elizabeth put down the tea towel and came right out with it. 'It's Henry.'

'Henry? But he's being gorgeous. Twisting Dad round his little toe, haven't you noticed?'

'I know. He is charming. Don't get me wrong. It's not that I don't like him. I do. It's just that . . .'

'He's too old?'

'Yes.'

She felt better now she'd said it. Oddly, Anthea did not seem to mind. And somehow, that reassured Elizabeth. As if her daughter was well aware of what she was doing. In fact, now that Elizabeth came to look at her, she was positively glowing. It made her realise by contrast how tense and miserable she had been when she had last come to stay, though at the time she had put it down to a sisterly concern over Jodie's injuries. But she was not so sure now.

'Mum, there's something I'm bursting to tell you.' Anthea abandoned the soapy water and faced her mother. Her dark hair was tied back off her face, emphasising the excitement in her eyes. They were so big and boastful that Elizabeth knew with dreadful certainty what was coming next.

'What's that?'

'Henry has asked me to marry him.' She announced it triumphantly. 'He proposed in the car on the drive down here. We planned to tell you all tomorrow, but I just had to let you know. Isn't it wonderful?'

Divorced not once, but twice, and now he was having a third go at it. Oh my child.

Elizabeth stepped forward and hugged her daughter. 'Congratulations, darling. I'm so happy for you.'

In the evening, Grandad went home. He had spent the last hour asleep in his chair, mouth open and snores merging with those of Tess. Alan and Henry became engrossed in a game of chess in the dining-room, leaving Jodie and Anthea to sit on the rug in front of the log fire, toasting marshmallows and reminiscing about childhood Christmases. Elizabeth waved aside their offers of a dripping marshmallow and stretched out on the sofa, leg begging for a rest and mind limp with exhaustion. Her eyes soon closed. She was on the very edge of sleep when she heard Jodie say in an undertone, 'Henry's not your type. You know that. So why are you with him?'

There was a long silence. Elizabeth was tempted to open her eyes, but restrained herself.

'The same reason you're with Matt. He gives me what I need right now.'

'A damn good shag, you mean?'

'No, that's what I give him. He's never had it so good. He's like a dog with six tails at the moment and wagging them all.'

'It's obvious he adores you and makes no secret of it. He must be round the bend, of course.'

Anthea laughed. 'Of course.'

'But it's also obvious you are up to something.'

'How obvious is obvious?'

'Don't worry, he won't notice. He's too busy being the perfect future son-in-law.'

'Yes, he's surprisingly good at that, isn't he? Dad hasn't enjoyed Christmas so much for years.'

'So, what's going on?'

Elizabeth heard Anthea release a huge sigh that must have been bottled up inside for a long time. 'I'm happy, Jodie. Don't underrate that. He has asked me to marry him and I've said yes. He and I have struck a deal, just the way I do every day in business, but this deal is the most important one of my life.'

'A deal? You've struck a deal? What happened to emotions, Anthea? Where is love? Real involvement?'

Anthea sounded serious now. 'Who are you to preach about love and involvement? You hide behind that camera of yours because being an observer keeps you at a safe distance.'

'That's bullshit.'

'No, it isn't. You and I both, Jodie, we are using our mates. You for sex, and me for . . . well, let's say more practical purposes and leave it at that.'

'What could possibly be more practical than sex?' Jodie said it teasingly, and Elizabeth was grateful to her for not taking offence at Anthea's earlier comment. She risked a glimpse through her lashes. The picture was blurred, but she could make out that Anthea was holding out a melting marshmallow on the end of a fork as a peace-offering. Jodie accepted it and popped it in her mouth. 'Okay, let's hear it,' she continued. 'You say it's a deal. You get a shiny gold band on your finger in exchange for . . . what?'

Anthea chose not to fill in the gap, but shook her head dismissively.

'Don't tell me it's in exchange for money,' Jodie pushed. 'Surely you're not that cheap.'

Anthea looked away into the red caves of the fire.

'Anthea, tell me I'm wrong.'

'Shut up, Jodie, you don't know the half of it.'
'So tell me.'
Anthea helped herself to another marshmallow from the packet, chewed on it steadily, as if chewing on her thoughts, and then she did something that Elizabeth had not seen her older daughter do for many years. She blushed bright scarlet. It made her look eighteen instead of twenty-eight.
'All right,' she said snappily. 'But you won't like me.'
'I don't like you anyway,' Jodie said and it brought a smile to Anthea's lips.
Elizabeth held her breath.
'Henry was my client,' Anthea explained. The words came out quickly, in a tumble, as if they had been stacked right on the edge and ready to fall off. 'I over-invested. The old story. So sure I could recover, but it got worse and worse. I tried to recoup my losses. I'm a dealer, for Christ's sake. A respected dealer with a respected City firm. I should have known better. But I got desperate, Jodie. I poured good money after bad.' She shrugged. 'Except that it wasn't my money. It was Henry's. I swindled him out of forty thousand pounds.'
A moan escaped from Elizabeth but she managed to turn it into a snore. Both daughters glanced in her direction and lowered their voices.
'My God,' Jodie gasped. 'You don't do things by halves, do you?'
'No.'
'What did Henry say?'
'We're getting married. It's what he wants.'
'You mean he doesn't know about the forty thousand?'
'Not yet.'
'He'll divorce you on the spot.'
'No, you're wrong, he won't.'
'What makes you so certain?'
Anthea smiled. 'Firstly, because I've worked bloody hard to make sure that he really is madly in love with me. Or in lust with me, anyway.'
'Poor misguided fool that he is.'
'And secondly, because I'm pregnant and he thinks it's his.'
Jodie stared at her sister for a long time. 'You've got it down

to a razor-fine art,' she said finally and hugged her. Two dark heads locked tight together, as if thoughts were seeping from one to the other. When they separated, both faces, so similar in structure and yet so different in detail, were wearing huge grins that seemed to Elizabeth to be the first genuine ones she had seen all day.

'And what about you, Anthea? Do you really *want* to marry him?'

'Oh God, yes. Yes. I'm tired of the self-obsessed egos of the young guys I've been going round with. They think they want a relationship, but there's no room in their lives for anyone but themselves.'

'But do you love Henry?'

'Maybe not. Not yet anyway. But we get on well together. No heat of passion to blind you to the realities. And the reality right now is that this way I will not end up in prison.'

'You stupid idiot, Anthea. You had better marry him as fast as you can. And I hope you'll be very happy.'

'What, no moral high ground?'

'No. That's what Dad is for.'

Anthea laughed. 'Talking of Dad, and because I want you to be happy too, but I know you won't be until you've got this girl attack business out of your skull, I'm going to give you a piece of information that might help.'

'What information?'

'The name of the girl who was beaten up at school just before the attack on you. I found it in Dad's study at the time. In a letter he sent to the police. I'm telling you only because you look so miserable and I want you to go and talk to her. It might help you to share with her whatever it is you won't share with us.'

'Her name, Anthea? I don't need the lecture. Just her name.'

'Holly Dickinson. She lives in Albert Road, number twenty-three I think it was.'

'Why didn't you tell me before?'

'Because I didn't want to encourage you. But now I can see you need to get it out of your system.'

'I wish Matt would see the same.'

But Elizabeth was no longer listening.

Her mind was shell-shocked. All that money. How could a

daughter of hers do such a thing? Thank God, thank God for Henry. She took back everything she had thought about him earlier. And a baby. Anthea was having a baby. She would be a grandmother at last. *A grandmother*. Instantly her thoughts started ticking off a mental list. She would redecorate Jodie's old bedroom and turn it into a nursery; dig out the sewing machine for new curtains and get Alan to bring down the old cot from the attic. Or maybe a new one would be better. Certainly a new mattress anyway. She wanted to laugh out loud. And cry. A baby. It was exactly what she needed. The perfect Christmas present.

16

Jodie was restless, not ready to pack it in for the night. Without Matt the flat would feel like an empty freezer and she didn't want to attempt sleep yet. She was too keyed up. After what Anthea had told her, her head was buzzing. Christmas Day was always exhausting but this one had been particularly so. As she drove away from her parents' house through the dark streets, rain was falling monotonously and occasional gusts of wind tore at the slates on the roofs, seeking a chink in their armour. It was only ten-thirty but the roads were almost empty, as behind bright smiles and closed curtains people made a last-ditch effort to make Christmas Day a success.

Jodie headed for the harbour. Some of the pubs would be open and maybe a few bored teenagers would have escaped the parental net. In her heart she knew it was pointless, but it made her feel better. She parked the car by the waterfront where it was well-lit with festive decorations, and after counting to sixty, opened the door. The rain had increased in tempo, so she ducked into the first bar she came to. It was smoky, drab and depressing, despite someone's efforts with a few strands of tinsel. She ordered herself a grapefruit juice and sat on a stool at the bar. Then surveyed its customers.

There weren't many. Older drinkers mainly, with a few women sitting at the tables, noisier than their men. Jodie could see only one group of teenagers and they were all male, so she downed half her drink and thought about leaving. It was stuffy in the bar where a pall of cigarette smoke hovered over their heads like the angel of death. She was just about to vacate her stool, when a young man in his early twenties pushed open the door and shook himself like a dog after a swim. He had long fair hair that hung to his shoulders in corkscrew curls and a clean, cheerful face that grinned at Jodie when he noticed her watching him. He walked over to the bar and ordered a pint of ale.

'Bloody weather,' he grumbled but with no real animosity.

Jodie smiled and climbed down off her stool, but had only taken a couple of steps towards the door, when he said, 'I recognise you.'

She stopped and turned to face him. He was staring at her oddly. As if she had two heads.

'Well, I don't recognise you. Have we met?'

'No, but I've seen you all right. In your car outside the cinema. A black Mini, it is. With a camera.'

A shudder rippled up Jodie's spine but did not dislodge her smile. 'Yes, that's possible. I'm a photographer and I'm doing a study of young people for an exhibition. I find their faces intriguing. Still in the process of moulding.' She heard her voice. It sounded very confident, very sure.

He sipped his pint and wiped a hand across his mouth. 'Looked like voyeurism to me.'

'Professional interest is what it is called.'

'In their faces?' He grinned at her again. 'Or their bodies?' Suddenly his voice was softer and more intimate, as if whispering in her ear. 'Like the girls, do you? Young and tender.'

'Get stuffed,' she said, and walked to the door.

'Better watch yourself,' he called after her. 'Word gets around fast in a place like this.'

Jodie stepped out into the rain.

Number twenty-three Albert Road was the middle one in a row of five Victorian houses. Strips of long narrow gardens set them well back from the road and were fronted by stubby stone gateposts that had stone globes perched on top of each pillar, like petrified footballs. Jodie had checked the Dickinsons' address in the phone book. Anthea had made no mistake. She pushed open the gate and walked up the path. The garden was overgrown with a free-for-all of shrubs and bushes struggling for space, their bare stems giving the place a forlorn and bedraggled appearance that was echoed in the rectangle of lawn which looked as if it had seen too many games of football. Bald patches spread over it like mange.

Jodie rang the doorbell.

No response. Boxing Day was not the ideal day for visiting. Maybe the family was away for Christmas. She rang again and stamped her feet against the cold. More rain clouds lay hunched on the horizon, as if resting before another tactical advance. It was midday, so Jodie had hoped to catch the family slumped in a post-Christmas stupor in front of *Mary Poppins* or *Clash of the Titans* or whatever was being given its annual outing this year. She rang again and kept her finger on the bell.

It brought results. A scrabbling on the other side of the door ended in it suddenly swinging open, and a surprisingly big voice from a very small boy announced, 'Mum's out.' He was around six years old and in Spiderman pyjamas.

'Hello, I'm Jodie.'

'I'm Jason.' He grinned at her as if that made them even, brown eyes bright as a chipmunk's. 'Mum's gone to the sales. She wants a new coat.'

'That's okay because it's not your mother I've come to see.'

'I got a PlayStation for Christmas.'

'That's fun for you.'

'And a kitten.'

'Lovely.'

'And some trainers and a watch and a . . .'

Jodie had a feeling she would be here forever. 'Is Holly in?'

'Dad's in bed.'

'What about Holly?'

'Yeah. She's in.' He abruptly lost interest in the conversation and scuttled up the stairs.

Jodie was not going to waste the opportunity. She walked straight into the hall, thankful to have four walls around her, and contemplated her next move. From a room to her right came a trickle of gentle laughter. The door was ajar, so Jodie stuck her head round. It was a pleasant sitting-room, airy, with high ceiling and square bay window. In a plump arm-chair was sitting a slight young girl, looking no more than twelve or thirteen, legs tucked under her and a Siamese kitten sprawled on her lap, all spindly legs and triangular ears. The girl's head was bent over it and she was tickling its creamy stomach, laughing each time it sank its miniature fangs into her finger.

Jodie tapped on the door.

The girl looked up, startled. The laughter drained from her eyes like rain off a roof. They were as large and brown as her brother's but bore an expression that was instantly defensive. After the initial contact, they darted away.

'Hello, I'm Jodie.' She omitted her surname and its connection with the headmaster. 'Are you Holly Dickinson?'

'Yes.'

Jodie walked into the room. 'What a gorgeous kitten. What's its name?'

'Dipsy.'

'He's beautiful. Is he a chocolate-point?'

Holly nodded and stroked his fudge coloured ears. But the laughter was gone.

'May I sit down?' Jodie asked. 'There's something I want to talk to you about.'

The girl nodded miserably.

'Don't worry,' Jodie said, 'I'm not from the police. Nor the school authorities. And I'm not a social worker, if that's what you're thinking.'

The girl spent a split-second studying her as if searching for the right pigeon-hole, but turned away without asking. Her shoulder-length hair swung across her face as a shield.

'I'm a photographer. With the *Gazette*. But that's not why I'm here.'

Still the girl asked nothing. As if questions could put her at risk.

'Would you like to know why I'm here?'

The brown eyes flitted up, seeking the catch.

Jodie knew she had found someone in a worse state than herself.

'Holly, I want to help you. And I want you to help me. I was the one who got kicked to a pulp a few weeks ago. It was a gang of girls.' She indicated the scar on her cheekbone. 'This was one of their efforts.'

The girl's pupils widened with interest. Some of the wariness edged away, but still she kept her mouth shut.

'It was after the fire at the school. I reported the girl stealing the computer to the police. As a result, her friends paid me a visit.' Just talking about it made Jodie's hands start shaking and she tucked them between her knees.

The girl stared at her. 'I know the girl who was caught. She's at my school,' she admitted quietly.

'Emma Richards?'

'Yes.'

'And do you know her friends as well?'

But it was a question too far. Her cheeks flushed and she murmured, 'No.' Her attention returned to the kitten.

'Holly, I know what it's like to be scared. So shit-scared you feel sick as a dog, day and night. But I can't leave it at that. This gang could be the same one that had a go at you. Maybe is still getting at you. Help me, Holly. Help me and help yourself.'

Jodie let a couple of minutes tick by in silence. All she could see was the curtain of hair as the girl kept her head bent and her shoulders hunched.

'Bullying can be controlled, Holly. But if the authorities won't do anything to help us, then it's up to us to sort it out ourselves.' She could hear the shake transfer from her hands to her voice.

The girl said nothing. Just hid behind the bars of her hair.

Jodie rose from her seat and went over to the teenager. She touched her shoulder and to her dismay felt the girl cringe, as if her fingers were a branding iron. She withdrew them.

'If you can't face them, Holly, let *me* do it. Tell me their names.'

Suddenly the girl raised her head. Silent tears were sliding down her cheeks. 'Leave me alone,' she cried. 'You'll make everything worse. I don't know who they were because I had never seen them before. That's what I told the police. That's the truth. Just leave me alone.' Her voice choked and she buried her face in the kitten's protective fur.

'If that's the truth,' Jodie said quietly, 'why are you still so frightened? Is it because they're still bothering you?'

'Go away.' Holly's voice was muffled. 'Please, please, go away.'

Jodie crouched down in front of her but did not touch the

girl. 'You need help, Holly. If the school doesn't give it, and the social workers can't, I . . .'

Suddenly Holly Dickinson was on her feet. 'You!' she shouted, clutching the kitten to her throat. 'What can you do? You've seen what they do to squealers. Stay away from them. And stay away from me. It's my Christmas holidays. Can't you leave me in peace?'

Jodie rose to her feet and left.

She was mad at herself. For expecting too much, and for letting it get to her. For allowing Holly Dickinson's pain to enter her mind and add itself to her own. It made her head feel heavy and blocked, slowing her thoughts.

After an hour under her duvet, she rang Matt and wished him a happy Boxing Day. He sounded positively cheerful and it made her wonder if it was a relief for him to get away from her. She returned to the duvet. Sometime during the afternoon the telephone rang, but Jodie did not answer it. It would be her mother inviting her to tea. Surprisingly, she slept. When she awoke it was dark. The bedside clock said seven-fifteen. She got up, showered and then studied herself in the bathroom mirror. From a cabinet she took out a pair of scissors.

Ten minutes later, she dialled Fiona Bowles' number.

The silver Nissan Micra sat unobtrusively in a row of parked cars. Jodie had taken care to avoid the brightly lit stretch of streets around the clubs and had tucked it well into the shadows. Behind her in the marina dozens of skiffs and sailboats rocked in gloomy rhythm on the ebbing tide and the forest of bare masts tinkled continuously in the wind. Ahead of her lay an open area of wide walkways, flowerbeds and benches, designed as an attraction to strollers and boaters alike. An army of Victorian streetlamps added charm and safety, both of which were meant to deter the hordes of youths who clustered there. Every Friday night the council prayed that for once it might survive intact, but the onslaught of boots, spray cans and broken bottles always managed to leave its mark. It was rumoured that closed-circuit television was on its way.

Already several groups of teenagers had gathered in huddles around some of the benches, their young bodies seemingly oblivious to the wind-chill that was slinking in off the oily black sea. Inside the Micra, Jodie was some distance away from them and her fingers itched to pick up her camera and zoom lens to gain a closer view. But she left it alone. She could not afford another incident like the one in the pub last night. One warning was enough. A couple wandered hand-in-hand towards her and stopped to kiss and fondle each other's bodies in the shadows, unaware of her silent presence in the car beside them. The girl looked hardly any older than Holly Dickinson. Jodie was relieved when they drew breath and ambled on past.

It was only nine-thirty. She had driven over to Fiona's flat, swapped cars and settled into this space over an hour ago. She was cold now, but barely noticed it. She ran a hand through her cropped hair to remind herself that no one would recognise her, wound up the window and made herself abandon the safety of the car. The moment she was out on the broad pavement, she felt exposed. But no one stared. Two girls in minuscule skirts walked past her, heading for the benches, but did no more than flick a glance in her direction. Jodie took a few icy breaths, thrust her hands into her jacket pockets and followed them at a slower pace. She was wearing jeans and a sweater and carried no handbag. No identification. With short hair and no make-up, she knew she could pass for a teenager, especially as she had no trouble adopting the watchful self-awareness of the young.

She selected the left-hand path that threaded along the road edge of the wide promenade, skirting a raised flowerbed that was laid out in a horseshoe shape and surrounded by a low stone wall. Inside the horseshoe a group of four girls was seated on the wall, and Jodie listened carefully to their voices as she passed behind them. But none of them set her teeth on edge.

'Going somewhere?'

Two lanky young men had stopped in front of her, blocking her path. 'You're much too pretty to be out on your own. Fancy a drink to warm you up?'

Jodie did not even bother to break her stride. She veered round them and kept walking, relieved when they moved off to try their luck elsewhere. She did not need that kind of hassle right now. With head down and avoiding eye contact, she worked her way close to every girl hanging around the promenade, up to the far end and back again, as if cruising while waiting to meet somebody. No one else accosted her. Despite wearing dark clothes and keeping as much as possible to the shadows, she felt conspicuous. Her ribs were hurting, but she put it down to the cold air. The fact that she was breathing so rapidly that she was in danger of hyperventilating escaped her notice.

By the time she was back at the horseshoe, the noise of the rattling masts and the drag of the waves carried in on the wind was grating on her nerves. In the darkness, she did not know what might be whispering behind it. The group of four girls had increased to five and there seemed to be some sort of argument in progress. Jodie rested on the wall at the foot of the flowerbed, more to ease her ribs than to eavesdrop.

'I don't give a flying fuck what you say. Me and Tamsin had nothing to do with it.'

The angry voice was from a small, slender girl with blonde hair as spiky as her words and a temper clearly as short and fragile as her elfin frame. Out of the corner of her eye, Jodie watched her strut aggressively up to a black girl twice her size. 'So get off my back.'

'You were the only one in there,' the black girl insisted, 'so don't hand me that crap.'

'I'll hand you more than that if you don't . . .'

One of the others intervened, a tall girl with long frizzy hair and large breasts, emphasised by a skin-tight jacket. 'Pix, just shut up, will you? You've got such a mouth on you. All of us know you were the one who took it.'

The blonde Pix reacted like a little firework going off. She jumped up and down on the spot, gave vent to a stream of obscenities, and then rocketed off at high speed in the direction of the beach. The laughter of the girls followed her. When it had died down, Jodie slipped off the wall and set off in her wake.

She found her among the pebbles under the pier. Jodie had

watched her bob down the steps on to the beach, her fair hair metamorphosed into green straw by the lurid overhead lights that picked out the outline of the pier. She attempted to follow her, but when she saw the total darkness of the shingle below her, it was like staring again into the black alleyway down which she had chased the fleeing figure. Like looking into a pit of tar. Dark and suffocating. What was waiting down there?

It was the sound of stones clanging off one of the metal pillars of the pier's substructure that alerted Jodie to the girl's position. Where the wooden walkway above was joined at right angles to the promenade, it formed a V-shaped cave underneath, as the shingle sloped high against the sea wall. It reminded Jodie of childhood summers when she and Anthea had played in its shade to relieve the tingle of sunburnt backs. It wasn't her back that was tingling now. She brushed a hand against her cheeks and despite the icy breath of the wind, found them hot and humid.

She got herself down the steps and across the pebbles to the water's edge. She ignored the pier. The moment her feet started to crunch over the shingle, the sounds from the cave ceased. Once away from the promenade lights, Jodie's eyes adjusted to the gloom, so that she could make out the lacy fringe of the sea, and she tossed a few stones into its hungry black mouth. The growl of the waves sounded like a warning. To her left stretched the strip of beach, a silent and invisible threat; behind her glowed civilisation and safety, while to her right loomed the pier with its secretive cave. She turned her footsteps to the right.

Jodie spoke first.

'What are you doing here?' She said it as if this sheltered spot was her own personal territory.

The girl bristled instantly. 'It's a free world. Why shouldn't I be?'

'Because I was going to strip naked and practise my Irish dancing, why the hell do you think?'

'Don't let me stop you.' The voice was sulky.

'I won't.'

In the darkness of the pier's overhang, Jodie could not see much but there was just enough reflected light to make out that the girl was reclining in a cradle of stones, half lying, half sitting, the tip of her cigarette glowing like a solitary firefly in the night air. She watched as Jodie wandered back and forth along the high-water line, rummaging among the seaweed and debris for driftwood. When she had collected an armful, she returned to the pier.

'What are you doing?' the girl asked.

'Building a house.'

The girl laughed, and it was a pleasant lilting sound that rippled through the darkness, opening it up.

Jodie gathered the smallest of the sticks into a loose pile, propped up some large stones round it to form a windbreak and squatted down. She searched her pockets for a lighter. As if she expected to find one.

'Shit,' she muttered and glanced up at the girl. 'Got a light?'

'Sure.' The sulkiness had gone, and she scurried over the pebbles, Zippo in outstretched hand.

It took them ten minutes to get it going. The wood was damp and the wind unhelpful, but after cursing and struggling and refusing to quit, they were rewarded when a wisp of smoke finally uncurled and the sticks began to spit and crackle.

'Brilliant!' the girl shrieked and dumped a load more wood on the fire, nearly knocking the life out of it.

Eventually, the flames took hold convincingly and breathed feeling back into their frozen hands and knees, as they hunched like cavemen around it. They examined each other's faces surreptitiously in the flickering firelight.

'I'm Jodie.'

'Hi, Jodie. I'm called Pix. Short for Pixie.'

'I can see why.'

She did indeed resemble a pixie. Her features were elfin fine, small and delicate, with an upturned nose, a dusting of freckles and green eyes the colour of peppermint cream. Her teeth were tiny and very even, and she had an odd habit of chattering them together when excited, like one of Grandad's cats watching a bird.

The light of the fire robbed them of their night vision, making them feel isolated together in the lonely circle of its warm glow, and Jodie took the opportunity to ask, 'What are you doing down here on the beach on your own? It could be dangerous.'

Pix shrugged. 'I ain't scared of no danger. I'm stronger than I look. Feel that.'

She held out her hand, as if to shake hands. Jodie took it. It was gloveless but warm from the fire, and felt soft and small in her own. But only for a second. With a delighted grin, Pix squeezed. It felt like one of the metal girders had detached itself from the pier and landed on her hand.

She allowed Pix the pleasure of hearing her squeal. It obviously satisfied her because she released the grip.

'See? Strong, huh?'

Jodie shook life back into her fingers. 'Strongest pixie I've ever met.'

'I work out,' Pix confided. 'On a punch bag. It's funny because people take one look and think they can walk all over me. Just 'cause I'm small.' She grinned. 'So I have to show them they're wrong.'

'I get your point. How old are you, Pix?'

'What you want to know for?'

'Just curious.'

'Sixteen. I really am, so don't go telling me I look twelve. I get sick of hearing that. What about you?'

'Eighteen.'

Pix accepted it without question. 'And what you doing down here?'

'Looking for some space.'

'Oh yeah?'

'Too much hassle at home. Christmas and families and all that hypocritical stuff.'

'Yeah, it's crap.' She scrubbed a hand through her blonde spikes and took Jodie by surprise with the comment, 'You need a decent haircut. At the back it looks as if a mouse has been chewing it.'

Jodie laughed. 'You can talk. Who cut yours? A hedgehog on hard times?'

'Get lost,' Pix giggled and shuffled closer to the fire.

Jodie chucked a couple of heavier sticks into the flames, and watched them turn black, sending smoke swirling above their heads. Every now and again a backdraft of wind sent a ghostly spiral of ash and grit into their faces, making them cough and squint their eyes. For a while neither said anything more. From above they could hear the occasional rumble of traffic and somewhere out there in the darkness the sea never let up as it ground the pebbles into sand.

Jodie was acutely aware of how lightly she had to tread. One wrong move and this will-o'-the-wisp would be off into the night. The bond they were sharing over the fire was gossamer-fine. She let the conversation meander at will down easy paths, sometimes drifting into a comfortable silence. It was after one of these that she asked, with no more emphasis than when she had enquired whether Pix preferred Chinese or Indian takeaway, 'What made you come down on to the beach? Not meeting anyone, are you?'

'No.' Pix kicked at a stone and it shot into the fire, sending up a spray of sparks. 'No, I was getting away from some mates. They were really pissing me off.'

'Yeah, I know what you mean. I've got a boyfriend who does that to me sometimes.'

Pix shook her head. 'This wasn't no shitty boyfriend. I can handle that. But it does my head in when girls who are supposed to be your mates start accusing you of stealing from them. That's not on. No way.'

'What made them think you did it?'

'I was in the wrong place at the wrong time.'

'That's what half of the inmates of Holloway bang on about.'

'Right.'

'So did you steal what they say you did?'

Pix giggled. 'Well, maybe a purse did happen to fall into my pocket accidentally.'

'Your mate's purse?'

'She's a new girl. I don't like her hanging around with our crowd. She's a real mare. In your face the whole time, she is.'

'Not like you, of course.'

'Hey, get off my case.'

Jodie soothed her hackles. 'Just trawling, Pix. No need to lose your cool.'

'Trawling, huh?' She slid her green eyes from the fire up to Jodie's face. 'Trawling for what?'

Here it was. Crunch time.

'Information.'

'What does that mean?'

'It means what it says, Pix. Just finding out what makes you tick. Me, I'm just a straight-down-the-line girl, who is hung up on Maltesers. A bit of a loner, maybe, but I don't go round grinding people's hands to mincemeat. But you, you're an oddball. Right off the wall. Interesting to be around.'

'You don't half know how to talk, Jodie. Real classy. I like that.'

'Words are easy, Pix. It's finding out what's behind them that is the hard part.'

'Dead right there. People duck and dive behind their words. Scumbags the lot of them.'

It was said with such vehemence that Jodie wondered where the scars were. She shivered. The night seemed to be closing in on her. She'd had enough of the cold and the dark, and just to add to everything, it had started to rain. She stood up.

'Come on, Pix, I'm starving. Let's get something to eat.'

'I can't. I'm skint.'

'I'll shout you a kebab. In return, you can introduce me to the new girl who does your head in.'

'You're the one who is crazy,' Pix laughed. 'Not me. But you've got yourself a deal.'

Jodie kicked a shower of pebbles on top of the fire. She didn't want it getting out of control.

17

It was like laying down a trail of sugar. Kebabs the first night, a bottle of vodka the next, a handful of teen magazines the next. There was never any doubt that the group of girls knew what she was doing, but they accepted it as her membership fee. Dues paid, no questions asked. No queries about where the money came from, what she did or where she lived. Initially they were wary, but Pix backed her so freely that they had let down their guard. They took to her.

For that, Jodie was grateful.

And she liked the outspokenness among them. There was no underhand criticism. None of the mealy-mouthed whisperings behind your back that so irritated her about middle-class minds riddled with insecurities. If these kids had something to say, they said it to your face. But they were touchy. God, were they touchy! As if a good brawl strengthened the bonds, underlined their need of each other and kept the lines of communication open. Lines that were blocked and tangled in other directions. As yet she had seen no sign of physical aggression, but it was early days. Or maybe not their scene.

The black girl was the one they deferred to most. Chloe was her name and she was the nearest to being their leader. Jodie put her age around seventeen and took an instant liking to her. On the second evening, Chloe had arrived brandishing a pair of scissors with bright-eyed relish.

'If I have to stare at that disaster you got the cheek to call a haircut one moment more, I'll tear my teeth out.' She spread her thick lips into a broad grin and snapped the blades together like hungry crocodile jaws. 'Don't worry, honey, I work in a hairdresser's.'

'She sweeps the floor,' Danielle pointed out. She was the tall girl with the frizzy hair whom Jodie had noticed the first evening at the horseshoe flowerbed. Her manner was gentle and she was the one who displayed her affection most openly, with a hug or a word of comfort when someone was down. Jodie found it curious to watch them together. It was as if they each had found a role within the group. Pix played the clown in elfin's clothing, Tamsin was the slow straight-man and Kit was the kitten. Soft and small and eager to please. And then there was Marianne. The new girl. Disappointingly, not the girl Jodie was seeking. Like Pix, Jodie did not take to her. Her role seemed to be that of group hackle-raiser. She wondered what her own was to be.

In the end, she let Chloe loose on her hair. The result wasn't bad. Longer on top, but shorn like a boy's at the back, with a wispy fringe. It made her look like a different person. Altogether sharper. She liked it. What Matt would say when he saw it was another matter.

Matt.

The name seemed to belong in a separate compartment in her head now. As if its connection with her life had been cut off. She spoke to him on the telephone every day, but it wasn't the same. Bournemouth was not so many miles away and yet it felt like a vast ocean divided them. It shocked her. What was happening to her? Where the hell was she heading? It was as if this obsession left her no room for distractions. No room for irrelevant emotions. She remembered the octopus of pain that had taken over her head in the hospital and wondered how it had transformed itself without her even noticing into a long wriggling worm of aggression. She could feel it burrowing inside her brain.

Time was running out. Only another four days and she would have to return to work at the *Gazette*. Matt would be home in two. Anthea and Henry had returned to London and her mother had burst into tears at the sight of her hair. None of it touched her. Her indifference frightened her. A clammy cold fear that she thrust out of sight.

When her mother gave her a plastic carton full of uneaten

Christmas goodies, instead of keeping them to share with Matt she took them to the horseshoe flowerbed. When her father invited her to accompany them to the theatre, she declined in favour of sitting on a damp bench in the pedestrian precinct singing in chorus 'Don't They Know It's Christmas?'. Each time she met up with her new-made friends, she felt she was one step closer. Maybe this time, and if not this time, then next time. Her conviction that one evening she would hear the voice of the girl, who smashed her Mini and her peace of mind, never wavered.

She felt safe with them. Protected amid the laughter, the fooling and the bickering. She was at the same time able to keep a sharp eye open for any sight of Emma Richards as they cruised the streets, the parks and the few pubs that would let Pix and Kit through their doors. But neither she, nor her friends in their black scarves, crossed Jodie's path.

The day before New Year's Eve, the temperature dropped like a stone. The night sky was startlingly clear, the stars so brittle they looked as though they would shatter if they were touched. The moon was full, and bathed the buildings and promenade in a frail, frozen light that distorted reality. Shadows twisted and turned as the moon climbed higher and Westonport seemed on edge. But Jodie was not sure any more. Maybe it was just herself. Two of the girls, Danielle and Kit, had come out for the evening with black scarves wrapped round their faces against the piercing cold, and the sight of them had given Jodie the jitters.

She decided it was the moment to push things along. No time to be subtle about it.

'Do any of you know an Emma Richards?'

They were drifting along the streets heading towards the amusement arcades. Chloe had announced that she felt like some action tonight and the arcade was where she went looking for it.

'To Chloe,' Pix explained, 'action means sex. She gets the itch whenever she's had a few smokes.'

'Don't knock it, Pix,' Chloe had exclaimed. 'You got to work off your frustrations somewhere. I'm on probation and got to watch myself.'

That was the first Jodie had heard of it. The first mention of anything to do with breaking the law. When no one responded, she repeated, 'Emma Richards. She's a no-good kid who got me into some real shit and she's been keeping her head down ever since.'

'Oh yeah? Needs fixing, does she?' It was Marianne who asked, her long narrow face leaning forward.

'No, nothing like that,' Jodie said quickly. 'It's the crowd she hangs around with I need to talk to. To straighten them out.'

'I know an Emma,' Pix volunteered helpfully. She was skittering around in front of them, her feet constantly on the move with nervous energy. She turned to face Jodie, moving backwards, weaving in and out of people behind her as if by radar.

'What does your Emma look like?' Jodie asked.

'She's round.'

'Round?' Marianne jeered. 'What kind of description is that?'

Jodie ignored her. 'Do you mean she's a fat kid?'

'Yeah. Round face, round body, round arse. She would roll down hill if you kicked her.'

'No, that's not the Emma Richards I'm looking for. She's nice-looking with short hair and blue eyes.'

Pix missed her step. The process of racking her brains clouding her radar. She collided.

'Watch yourself, Tiny Tim.' Two large men towered over her. Rugby players on the look-out for a night's entertainment. 'Shouldn't you be tucked up with your dollies?' one of them chuckled. He made the mistake of patting her on top of her head.

Jodie saw Pix turn bright red and spin to face him. Without a second thought, she slammed her fist into his face. Then she was off and running.

Jodie stared in disbelief.

The man's nose had exploded in a torrent of blood. He bellowed more in anger than pain and went racing after her. His friend followed, and Jodie could see that he was faster.

'We must help her.'

'Nah, don't worry,' Chloe laughed. 'They won't even get close.'

Jodie realised she was right. Pix was already out of sight.

'She's got a fist like iron and the legs of a whippet. How come?'

'How come you ask so many questions?' Marianne reacted.

'Just naturally nosy, I guess.'

But the others weren't listening. Their eyes were following the two men, already slowing in the distance. Pupils huge with the thrill of it. Jodie could feel it too. Raw adrenalin. She turned away abruptly and headed up the road. The others came after her, everyone talking louder, walking faster. The excitement was like a ball that they tossed between themselves, growing heavier and hotter each time they touched it.

The arcade was crowded. Danielle and Kit joined Jodie in propping up a pillar, while the others browsed. The machines flashed and whirred, whined and blasted out their electronic seduction of the teenage mind. There were far more male players than female, but girls were drifting around, on the prowl. Despite the cold, many of them displayed bare limbs or midriffs, while their laughter and giggles competed with the noise of the machines.

Jodie watched Chloe at work. She was neither too choosy nor too subtle in her approach. She started by the door and worked her way round, rubbing shoulders, bumming cigarettes, and wrapping an arm around any unoccupied male waist. But her antennae were pin-sharp and when a girl flounced away from an overweight guy at the Mortal Kombat machine at the other end of the arcade, Chloe was in there like a shot. Within seconds her hand was resting on his plump bottom and his tongue was hanging out with anticipation.

Jodie laughed. 'Looks like she's scored.'

'She always does,' Danielle smiled, but there was a sadness to it that touched Jodie. As though Danielle was not comfortable about losing her friend.

Kit was harsher. 'That's because she's a slag. Got no taste.'

'Not like us,' Danielle said, and they both laughed.

'What about you, Jodie?' Kit asked. She flicked her long fair hair from side to side, eager to be always on the move. But there was something soft and pampered about her, hinting at a good home just round the corner. 'Got a boyfriend?'

'Yes. But he's away.'

'Best place for them.'

'Right now, that's true.'

Danielle touched Jodie's arm, fingers soft and supportive. 'Hey, don't look so down. Men can be a real grind if you let them get to you. Be like Chloe. Sex on tap when she wants it, and the rest of the time she's got us.'

'That way nobody gets screwed up,' Kit added.

Jodie smiled. 'Screwed, but not screwed up.' She had just allowed her thoughts to wander away to Matt in her bed, when Pix bobbed up at her elbow. Her eyes were like saucers, vivid green with excitement and her breath ragged from running.

'Guess what I've seen?' she asked and did not wait for a reply. '*Impressions*' window is smashed.'

Impressions was a clothes shop in a small road off the main shopping street. It sold sportswear, expensive and stylish.

Kit reacted faster than a rabbit. She was at Chloe's side, dismantling her grip on the man's jeans, and rounding up Tamsin and Marianne. Seconds later, they were all out of the arcade and running.

They were too late. The window was stripped bare by the time they reached it. A police siren was wailing in the distance. Their disappointment was as sharp as the shards of glass under their feet. Further up the street a handful of boys was disappearing at speed, their arms trailing articles of clothing, and in the opposite direction a lone girl was scurrying away round a corner.

'Fucking vultures,' Chole complained, catching her breath. 'Pix, go see what she's got.'

Pix whooped with delight and her legs sprang willingly into motion once again. All that pent-up energy had found a purpose.

'Tamsin,' Chloe added, 'you'd better give her a hand.'

Tamsin, less fit and less keen, gave a groan but did not argue. She took a deep breath and ran for the corner.

'See you at the marina,' Chloe called out after her.

She picked up a half-brick that had been left lying on the pavement and, to vent her frustration, hurled it at the glass of the next shop window. It was a betting shop. It shattered in a vicious explosion of shrapnel, triggering a shrill alarm. Satisfied, Chloe set off at a steady jog back down the hill, aware that the police would be putting in a token appearance in seconds. Token, because there was nothing they could do except inform the owners, question the neighbours and stand guard over the shops until a carpenter came to board them up.

Jodie had lost count of the number of times she had been sent out by the *Gazette* to photograph the scene of a similar crime and ended up with a dull picture of a boarded window. But now she was on the opposite side, running until her ribs were ready to crack open again. They wove down backstreets she did not even know existed, their feet padding rhythmically like long-distance athletes, and she understood the staying-power of the girl she had pursued through the alleyway all those weeks ago.

It felt like light-years ago.

The thought of the girl made her angry. Angry and frustrated. Where the hell was she hiding herself? Surely their paths must cross soon. The anger put speed in her legs and she overtook Chloe.

'Running's for dogs,' Jodie said. 'I've had enough. No one is after us.'

She slowed to a walk and the others did the same. Their breath came out like smoke from their mouths, to be swallowed by the night air. Ahead of them the lights of the marina flickered and beyond it, the pier.

'I bet my guy is still in the arcade,' Chloe moaned, 'with some other tart's arm round his waist.'

'Forget about him,' Danielle said. 'Let's have our own Christmas party. A girl party.'

'Yeah, cool,' Kit enthused.

'Where though?' Marianne asked. 'The marina is too visible.'

'On the Crazy Golf course,' Chloe laughed. 'Let's find a ball to play with.'

'No way,' Marianne objected. 'After we messed that place up last month, the police cruise by there all the time. We'd get done.'

'Okay, big mouth, where then?'

'How about under the pier?' Jodie suggested. 'It's private there.'

Privacy was not really what Jodie wanted. She wanted to be cruising the night-time pavements, listening to voices, scrutinising faces. But her friends had decided on a party, and no way was she going to risk it on her own.

'Brilliant.' Chloe pounced on the idea. 'Let's find Pix first.'

They wandered round the marina. Teenagers ebbed and flowed about them in an adult-free zone, the night-time pavements yielded to the young. Jodie listened to the voices. Occasionally she even purposely bumped her shoulder into someone who looked about the right size and build, just to hear their words when they objected. But none matched the ones in her mind.

'Watch yourself, will you?' one tall girl said sharply, temper ready to flare.

'Get lost,' Jodie muttered, disappointment making her curt.

'You're asking for trouble, Jode.' It was Pix. She had materialised beside them, a black QuikSilver cap on her head and a ski-jacket tucked under her arm. 'Not everyone is as friendly as me, you know.'

'Friendly? Is that what you were to the girl who stole that jacket?'

Pix giggled. 'I used friendly persuasion.'

'Oh yes?'

'Yeah. She was happy to give it to us, wasn't she, Tamsin? Insisted we take it in the end.'

Tamsin was grumpy. 'I wanted the hat.' She ran a hand through her dark unruly curls to emphasise her need.

'Tough tit, it's mine,' Pix retorted and pulled it further down over her face. 'But honestly, Jode, you don't want to go round shoving into people. A bit green sometimes, you are. Older than me, but sure as hell no wiser. What are you up to?'

Jodie shrugged. 'Just curious to hear their reactions.'

'Looking for a fight, were you?'

'No. Just a voice.'

'Christ, you're weird. You'll get yourself into trouble.'

'No, I'm aiming to get myself out of it.'

At that moment, Chloe turned round and noticed the jacket. 'What's that?'

'For you,' Pix said with one of her big grins and held it out. 'A Christmas present.'

'Mental!' Chloe crowed and slipped out of her own jacket. She thrust her arms into the stolen one and wrapped its newness round herself. It was a soft wine red with darker cuffs and collar. It suited her. Chloe gave Pix an affectionate thump on the back, yelled, 'Let's party,' and set off towards the pier.

A couple of girls Jodie did not know joined them, and Marianne picked up another friend who greeted her with much cheek-kissing and a French accent. The ten of them linked arms as they walked, blocking the wide pavement and revelling in forcing others on to the road. Jodie had never got involved in this kind of street-life when she was a teenager. It had not appealed to her. Only once, to annoy her father, had she taken up with a boy he had just expelled for smoking pot on school grounds, and who liked to roam with a pack at night. But not even to rattle her father could she put up with him for more than a couple of weeks. He had been too in love with the insane sounds that burbled out of his own mouth. She had dumped him and spent more time with her camera.

But now she could see the attraction of the street-life. Out here, there were no rules. No one to say 'No'. No parents to refuse a party, no voice of authority to impose conditions. No compromise. But in the end, compromise was what society was about. The moment you side-stepped that rule, you were rejected. You became an outcast, along with the lepers.

'Hey, Jode, hang about.' Jodie had not noticed that she was walking fast, striding ahead of the others in an effort to outrun her thoughts. She slowed.

'Where's the fire?' Danielle asked and linked her arm through Jodie's again.

'In my head.'

'No need for that. Buy us some beers and we'll put it out for you.'

Jodie nodded. She had found her role.

The fire was bigger this time. Chloe had set them all to work fetching driftwood, feeling for it with cold fingers in the dark scattering of seaweed and plastic bottles that lay like a monk's fringe in a strip along the beach. The full moon washed their faces with its pallid light as they scurried hunch-backed in search of fuel. Jodie was grateful that the sea had changed its mood. Instead of the oily suffocating blackness of the other night, it displayed a fretful, glittering charm that banished any thoughts of gloom. She found herself enjoying the bonfire. Its flames seemed to burn up the adrenalin that had been racing through her veins and the cans of beer left them all relaxed and drowsy. The fire was again tucked under the pier, close to the sea wall, where the eyes of authority could not penetrate.

Whether it was the alcohol or just the sense of safety that enveloped her, she did not know. But she found herself talking too much. The French girl, who turned out to be an exchange student, had been complaining about the strictness of the Westonport family with whom she was lodging, which meant she had to climb out of her bedroom window at night.

'The father, he is a *cochon*,' she said. 'I do not like him one bit.' Her dark exotic eyes rolled with exaggerated emotion. 'He is a teacher and he thinks I have come here to learn the English behaviour. But it is only to speak English that I want.'

'My father is a teacher,' Jodie said, surprising herself. They were passing round a bottle of wine and she had just taken a long swig from it. 'A teacher of history. He was always telling me to take the long view of life, so that I would have an aim. Always wanting me to live by his rules and standards. "Your word is your bond," he would drum into me. Frightened I would shame him.'

'And did you?' Kit asked.

'As often as possible.'

They all laughed and drank more of her beer.

But it wasn't true. She had not tried to shame him. She had just tried to protect herself, her individuality, from the weight of his shadow.

'I got lucky,' Pix said and draped a long, twisting piece of driftwood across the fire. The flames flared greedily. 'I've never had anybody breathing down my neck, 'cause my mum let's me do what I like.' She shrugged. 'Doesn't give a damn. Too busy whoring around.'

'What about your father?'

'Pissed off when I was a kid, sodding bastard. There's always been loads of mum's boyfriends around, but I won't let them play the heavy with me. Don't take no shit from any of them.'

'Any brothers or sisters?' Jodie asked.

'No. Just me.'

'I've got brothers,' Tamsin said. 'Four of them. Stupid buggers they are.' But it was said affectionately. 'It's my sister I can't stand. Spiteful bitch, she is. I have to thump her sometimes, just to show her.'

Jodie looked at the naked face in the firelight. The words were said so casually.

'Do you enjoy it?'

A ripple shimmered through the group round the fire, as if she had touched a nerve.

'Sure I do,' Tamsin answered in her slow manner. 'So would you if you had to put up with her lip. She's older than me, but I'm bigger. So when she starts on at me, I thump her.'

Chloe leaned forward, picked a stick out of the fire and lit her cigarette from it. 'What about you, Jodie? Like Danielle and Kit, are you? A squeamish rabbit-brain?' Her dark face studied Jodie's, probing behind the watchful gaze. 'I can see some real heat in those baby-blue eyes of yours. Maybe you ain't as cool as you like to seem.'

Jodie smiled. 'I'm cool, Chloe. Cool as your fat arse on these stones.'

Chloe laughed and accepted the brush-off. 'Throw me another pack of your Maltesers, girl, and let's hear if you can sing.'

'Sing?'

'Sure. Who's ever heard of a party without music?'

'I bet she only knows hymn tunes,' Marianne said sarcastically. 'With her father being a vicar and all.'

'A teacher is what I said.'

'Same thing. They both teach you junk. You look like a teacher's pet.'

'Do you work hard at these insults,' Jodie asked, 'or is it a natural talent?'

Everyone broke into laughter and Marianne scowled into her beer.

'Okay, you masochists,' Jodie smiled, 'let's make ourselves some music.' Clapping her hands in a strong rhythm, she launched herself into an alcohol-sweetened version of 'If I Had A Hammer'.

The irony of calling her new friends masochists was lost on them.

The waves rattled the pebbles gently, as if not wishing to disturb the conversation. Chloe had wandered unsteadily down to the water's edge for a call of nature and Jodie had taken the opportunity to join her, away from other ears. Chloe was struggling to pull her jeans back up over her broad buttocks and finding her balance precarious on the uneven pebbles.

'Let me get this straight. You want me to come over with you tomorrow. To some kid's house.'

'Yes.'

'But I mustn't say anything.'

'That's right. Just stand at my shoulder looking big and black and brooding. I'll do all the talking.'

Chloe chuckled, a loose easy sound that made Jodie smile. 'Hey, Jode, I'm real good at that. Sometimes I even frighten myself when I look in the mirror.'

She tugged out of her hair the band that held her black curls tied behind her head and shook them loose into a wild afro. Instantly she looked larger and more impressive, like a dog raising its hackles. Her big-toothed grin disappeared behind an aggressive frown and she jutted her head forward threateningly.

'How's that?' she growled.

'Scary as shit.'

'I told you.' The grin returned and Jodie tried to reconcile the two Chloes in her head.

'You can just turn it on?'

'Sure. Any time I want.'

'Do it again.'

'Now?'

'Yes.'

'What for?'

'Because I want to check it out.'

For a second time the grin vanished and in its place were the narrowed eyes, the uncompromising chin and the stiff strutting body language. The moonlight robbed her of colour, so that even her full red lips and the new jacket looked dark and menacing.

'See?' she snarled. 'Easy.'

Jodie studied this stranger closely. Was it just a mask? Or was it a part of Chloe that she did not yet know, as innate as the big grin? Or maybe, like a headmaster, when you've played a part for long enough, you no longer know where you end and the acting begins. Jodie allowed the image of the brutal girls who attacked her to flood her mind. She struggled to make herself look behind the mask of their leader. But it was welded too tightly.

'Can I smile now?' Chloe scowled. 'Or do you want me to show you how I threaten to break an arm as well?'

'No, I don't, if it's all the same to you. I prefer the smile.'

The black girl relaxed, visibly growing smaller, and tied her hair back once more. Chloe had returned.

'You sure are one mean bastard,' Jodie said.

Chloe took it as a compliment. 'What time tomorrow?'

'In the morning. She's more likely to be at home. Probably still in bed.'

It had to be before Matt arrived home.

'No sweat.'

'Meet me at ten-thirty at the corner of Stanwell Road. Do you know it?'

'I'll find it. But do you want Marianne to come along too? She can act real mean.'

'No. Not Marianne. It's not an act with her. I wouldn't be able to trust her.'

Chloe laughed. 'Yeah, she sure is one big, tough mare.'

Too big. Too tough. Too much of a kind with the girl Jodie was searching for.

18

New Year's Eve dawned mist-covered and sleepy, as if reluctant to part with the old year. Every night Jodie went to sleep on her own side of the bed, but every morning she found herself on Matt's empty half, her body seeming to know better than she did where it belonged. At least there had been no nightmare last night. The first one free of them for weeks. It felt as good as a cool drink of iced water to a parched mouth and she let herself hover in the blissful dream-world between sleep and waking, feeling refreshed and relaxed. Her undisturbed rest was probably just the result of all the alcohol she had consumed on the beach last night, numbing even the subconscious into submission.

She kept her mind in neutral. Kept her very existence in neutral. The shapelessness of neutral meant no ice-picks in her brain. But it was a finely fragile state of grace and the growl of an engine starting up somewhere down the road was too much for it to bear. The threads snapped. She slid out of bed and headed for the bathroom. Cleaning her teeth was her immediate priority. They felt as if they had grown fur overnight. But as she leant over the washbowl, she remembered Chloe's big white teeth that seemed to glow like road signs in the dark, and asked herself again whether she was doing the right thing.

She gargled water and spat it out.

It had to be right. It was not only the right option, it was the only option. She had tried the other ways: the appeal to the catatonic Holly clinging to her cat, the threat to Emma Richards, the search in the crowds for the voice she could not forget. Nothing had produced results. Nothing at all. The police would not or could not get involved. Matt had gone away. Not even the school and her own father would help her. So there was no other option. All she had to go on were her own photographs. And the pictures in her head. So indelible they would not even give up their imprint at night. She *had* to use Chloe.

Jodie dipped her head under the hot tap, as much to wash away the thoughts as to wash away the night-time kinks. Roughly she towelled it dry. Her cropped hair still caught her by surprise each time she looked in a mirror and she wondered why she had not done it years ago. Long hair was too soft and too distracting. She ran a comb through it, pulled on her black jeans and roll-neck sweater and then heavy boots. She had to look the part today.

She made herself a pot of coffee, black and strong, but instead of sitting down to drink it quietly, she found herself wandering round the flat, room by room, her body as restless as her thoughts. Her ribs and collarbone complained while she put them through the daily grind of physiotherapy. That annoyed her. They should be used to it by now. But they were definitely mending faster. Maybe all that running was good for them. More oxygen pounding through her system.

She downed a mug of coffee, poured out another, drank no more than half, peeled herself a satsuma and resumed her pacing round the flat. The restlessness was not only because of her meeting with Chloe this morning. Her mind kept leap-frogging forward to the evening ahead and then jumping away again, like a cat patting water with its paw. She could not leave it alone, and yet it frightened her. It frightened her because Matt was coming home.

He would be arriving around six o'clock, in time for Jack James' New Year party. He had told her on the phone yesterday that his family were having a final lunchtime knees-up before going their separate ways. She could hear the pleasure in his voice, a laugh already there in anticipation. He had two brothers, a sister and numerous nieces and nephews who gathered each year at his parents' home. They all lived in and around the Bournemouth area, a close family who did not seem to suffer the tensions of her own. But then, from the outside most families looked normal. It was only when you were on the inside that you saw the cracks, the cobwebs and just occasionally, the spiders.

Part of her was desperate to see him. Could not wait to see

his Hi-gorgeous smile, hear the warmth of his voice in the flat again, feel his touch. Oh God, she wanted his touch like she wanted to breathe. But that part was shut away. Squeezed into a tight corner. The brick wall dividing it from the rest of her was growing higher and higher each time she remembered to look at it, so that she had to scrabble hard to climb over.

She was scrabbling now.

It frightened her to see Matt's face disappearing behind the bricks. And when she made herself look at them closely, run her fingers over their rough surface, each one of them had the word 'obsession' carved into it.

The woman who opened the door had dead eyes. They were as grey as ash, as if the life had been burned out of them. She looked at Jodie and Chloe as though nothing they would say could touch her.

'Mrs Richards?'

'Yes.'

'We're here to see Emma.'

'She's in bed.'

'Could you ask her to come down to talk to us, please? I'm sorry to disturb you.' Jodie was being polite. She did not want the door slammed in her face.

The woman glanced behind her at the flight of stairs, and they could see her contemplating whether it was worth the effort. She must have decided it was, because she muttered, 'Wait here,' and set off up the stairs. She did not hurry. There was no hurry left in her. They watched her tall, gaunt figure disappear from sight.

Chloe was impatient, pacing the pavement. 'Do you want me to go up there and drag her out of bed?'

'No,' Jodie said. She tugged her woolly hat down against the cold. Her ears had not yet adjusted to the loss of warmth that went with the loss of her hair. 'We do it my way.'

'You're too soft is your trouble.'

'Just get your scowl ready.'

'Look at me, girl. It's ready and waiting.'

Jodie nodded approval.

'But what if she don't show?' Chloe asked

'She'll show.'

'How come you're so sure?'

'Because if I was told a black bastard like you was standing on the doorstep waiting for me, I'd show.'

Chloe chuckled, flashing her large pink tongue. 'Ain't that the truth!'

Emma Richards' legs came into view at the top of the stairs. She was pushing them into a very new-looking navy tracksuit and it occurred to Jodie that maybe she had had something to do with the *Impressions* window. Glossy white trainers on her bare feet deepened the suspicion. Emma hurried down to them. Her blue eyes were bristling with caution as she joined them on the pavement. She pulled the front door almost shut behind her, leaving herself a bolt-hole if things got tough.

Jodie got in first.

'I'm still waiting to hear from your friend.'

Emma Richards eyed Chloe uneasily and edged away towards the wall. 'She's not my friend.'

Chloe took one step forward.

'Honestly,' Emma said quickly.

'I'm not here to argue,' Jodie said. She kept it calm and controlled. 'I asked you pleasantly the first time. This time my friend here . . .'

Chloe took another step forward. Her mean mouth looked quite capable of swallowing the girl for breakfast.

'. . . has come along to help me remind you in case you had forgotten. Make it your number one New Year's resolution.' She smiled, but there was no humour in it. 'I just want to talk to her. That's all. Nothing nasty. And no police.'

'Even if I did know her – which I don't,' she added quickly, 'I told you before, she wouldn't want to talk to you. You work for a newspaper, you do. That makes you trouble.'

'She should have thought of that before she decided to play football with my head.'

'I don't know nothing about that.'

'But she does.'

'I don't know who you mean.'

'I say you're lying.'

'Just get off my fucking case,' the girl suddenly shouted and made a dash for the door.

For a big girl, Chloe was fast. Her hand grabbed the girl's wrist and swung her round.

'Where you off to, honey?' she growled. 'My friend ain't finished talking.' Her black eyes dared her to make a struggle of it.

The girl darted a venomous look in her direction, but she had more sense than to attempt to break free. She stared at the pavement, her jaw mutinous.

That was as far as Jodie was willing to go.

'Okay, Emma, I think we understand each other. You know a name and I want that name. Go back to your bed and spend the rest of this morning thinking about my friend here.'

Jodie nodded at Chloe, who tightened her grip. The girl squealed.

'Then when you have thought long and hard, go and persuade *your* friend to come and talk to me. Got that?'

The girl nodded.

'That will make it a happy New Year for all of us,' Jodie said pleasantly and walked away.

Chloe gave one more growl, one more squeeze, then strode after Jodie.

'That was mental.' Chloe was strutting. Her pupils and her smile were huge, the seduction of adrenalin at work.

Jodie walked at her side. It was as though her nerves had been scrambled. Her heart was pounding out an erratic, uncontrolled beat that made her skin tingle. She felt sick each time she thought of Emma Richards' face.

'Is it the power that turns you on, Chloe? Or the risks?'

Chloe turned her big grin on Jodie. 'Hey, I got a buzz so frigging fantastic, I'm flying.'

'I can see your wings.'

'How come you don't get no kick out of it, Jode?'

'Kicks like that aren't my scene. That's why I needed you.'

'You're a wuss, you are. So let me loose on the kid. I could yank that name out of her throat in no time. If you want it that bad, I'll get it for you.' Chloe was flying so high, nothing was out of reach.

'No. Thanks for the offer, but no.'

Chloe slowed her stride. 'So what are you going to do if you end up face to face with this bad-arse mare you're after? Lie down and get your head kicked in again?'

Jodie felt the shudder. 'No, of course not. I intend to talk to her.'

'Talk to her!'

'Yes, that's all.'

Chloe burst out laughing, a loud raucous sound, that somehow made Jodie feel worse. It was so full of warmth, so good-natured, that it was impossible to reconcile with the Chloe who had manacled the girl's wrist so aggressively. Jodie glanced at her companion's hands. They were strong hands, full and fleshy, the knuckles black and large, nails painted a deep magenta. Hands that Jodie had invited to inflict fear.

'Hey,' Chloe's round dark eyes were floating back down to earth, 'what's this crap about you being a frigging reporter?'

Jodie shrugged, underplaying it. 'No, not a reporter. Just a photographer on the *Gazette*. But I've been off sick for the last couple of months.'

'Sick? You don't look sick to me.'

'Sick inside.'

'After you got beat up, you mean?'

'Yes.'

'Yeah? Headaches and stuff?'

'Something like that.'

Jodie tucked her arm through Chloe's, drew her closer as they made their way back towards the High Street where the Mini was parked, and had to decline again when she repeated her offer to extract the name of the girl. Jodie was acutely aware of the protective warmth of the body next to hers. It seemed to seep into her own with its strength and power, swaying the voices in her head and reminding her how easy it would be to say yes.

She was pushing the vacuum-cleaner around the flat when the

doorbell rang. It twanged into her mind, making her jump. But any conversation had to be better than her own thoughts. She switched off the machine. It was too soon for Matt. It occurred to her with a jolt that Emma Richards might have passed on her message. The sour taste of fear kicked in at the back of her throat and her palms were clammy with sudden sweat. She wiped them on her jeans.

'Who is it?' she called.

It was her father.

She was so relieved, she took off the safety chain, opened the door and gave him a wide welcoming smile. 'Hi, Dad, I'm glad to see you.'

He looked fractionally taken aback by the warmth of her greeting, then turned to the man standing next to him. 'Let me introduce James Hurst. I've brought him over to have a word with you.'

James Hurst was in his mid-thirties with the outdoor complexion of a keen sailor. His brown eyes were clear and healthy, and he smiled a lot. He extended his hand, so she shook it. It was firm and confident and knew what it wanted. What it wanted right now was to come into her flat. She stood aside and let them in. Her visitor glanced with interest around her flat and her father nodded with approval at the sight of the vacuum-cleaner. She wanted to tell him she was only doing it to drown out the noises in her head.

They sat down. Her father did not waste time on small-talk. 'I met James at a seminar on youth behaviour and felt you might benefit from his expertise. So I invited him over to speak to you.'

Jodie turned her gaze from her father's face to his companion's. The smooth features were held in an easy half-smile, the body-language deliberately relaxed and unthreatening.

'What kind of expertise is that, Mr Hurst?' Jodie asked.

'I'm a psychologist. I specialise in . . .'

'Mr Hurst,' Jodie said patiently, 'I don't know what my father has told you, but I do not need or want the services of a psychologist.' She stood up. 'I don't mean to be rude and I'm sorry that you have made an unnecessary trip, but I would like you to leave.'

'Jodie . . .' her father started, but was waved to silence by
James Hurst.

'That's all right,' he said with the same half-smile, but did not
move out of his chair. 'I quite understand. It's a difficult situation
when you are taken by surprise like this.'

'No, Mr Hurst,' Jodie said, returning his imitation smile. 'It's
not difficult at all. I understand that you are here to help, but I
do not want a stranger to sort out my life.'

'That's a perfectly normal reaction, Jodie,' Hurst responded
with irritating calm. 'But sometimes it is only a stranger who
is able to be objective enough to help a person see their way
through any present problems. We all become so enmeshed in
the complexities of our own lives and in our struggle to make
sense of our conditioned responses, that sometimes we lose sight
of our real motives and objectives.'

'I am well aware of my motives. And of my objectives, thank
you, Mr Hurst.'

'Jodie, please,' her father interrupted. 'Listen to James. He is
trained to help in situations like this.'

'Situations like what?'

'Let's not get confrontational,' Hurst instantly stepped in.
'What your father is referring to is your recent experience of
being physically attacked in the street. That was a traumatic
event in your life and will have initiated a variety of stress
responses that . . .'

'My responses are my concern. I thought I had made that
clear.'

'No one is disputing that they are your concern, Jodie, but they
are also the concern of your family who care for you and want
to help. Post-traumatic stress can have severe and distressing
repercussions on a person's mental state, leaving an aftermath
of phobias, nightmares . . .'

Jodie turned to her father. 'Dad, it was kind of you to want
to bring a mind-mender here, to wave his magic wand over me.
But when I say I am dealing with what Mr Hurst chooses to call
post-traumatic stress, I mean it. So let me get on with my own
thing in my own way. I don't want this kind of interference.
Please, take him away back to his ivory tower.'

Her father closed his eyes for a brief moment, shutting her out of his life. When he opened them, the headmaster looked out at her through them.

'Jodie, you must make an effort.'

Why didn't he listen to her?

She walked over to the door and opened it. 'Goodbye, Mr Hurst.'

The psychologist exchanged a look with her father. It infuriated her. As if he had some God-given right to burrow into her life just because he had a string of letters after his name.

He came over and stood facing her. 'I would like you to ask yourself one question, before I leave.'

As he was only two steps from the door, Jodie could afford to be magnanimous. 'What question is that?'

'What is it that you are so frightened of revealing? What is this "own thing" that you are hiding? Or should I say, hiding from?'

'That was three questions, not one.'

'So it was.' He said it as if he had scored a point.

She held out her hand. 'Goodbye, Mr Hurst.'

For the last time, he gave her his smile, shook hands and left. Her father was standing beside her and could not contain his disappointment. 'Jodie, when will you learn that you are your own worst enemy? You need advice but refuse to take it.'

'Dad, don't.'

But his frustration was boiling over. 'If you had a burst pipe, you would call in a plumber. Wouldn't you?'

'Yes.'

'If you had a broken leg, you would call a doctor. Wouldn't you?'

She nodded.

'So why, when you have a damaged mind, do you throw out the person who is qualified to help repair it? Why, Jodie, why?'

She stared at him, and instead of her father, she was shocked to see the face of a person who was in despair. He looked tired and disillusioned and on the verge of losing control. How much had that fire at the school taken out of him? Yet behind the anger and the bafflement, she caught a glimmer of a father who wanted to help his daughter but did not have the first idea how to go about it. So find an expert and let *him* do it. God forbid that you should try yourself to mess around with female emotions.

She wanted to place a hand on his arm, to smile reassuringly up into his worried face and say, 'I'm just fine now. No troubles at all.' But she couldn't bring herself to do it. Instead she said quietly, 'My mind is not damaged.'

He said nothing.

'Have a happy New Year's Eve, Dad.'

He frowned, as if it was something he had forgotten. 'Yes. And you.' He turned to leave, then added, 'Make the New Year a new start, Jodie. A fresh beginning. Out with the old and in with the new.'

Nothing had changed. He would never stop telling her what to do.

'Thanks for the thought.'

He managed a smile. As she watched him walk down the stairs, his back was as rigid as ever.

The flat felt suffocating. As if the good intentions of her father and the psychologist had been left behind after their departure and knotted themselves into a hot, heavy blanket that was wrapping itself round her, cutting off her air. She opened the window. It was only four o'clock but the sky was already beginning to darken, settling in for another long winter night. The last one of the year.

She drew in a deep breath, relishing the chill air.

The telephone rang.

'Hi, it's Fiona. I'm calling about the party.'

For a split second Jodie thought she meant the party on the beach, but then shook the thought out of her head.

'Party?'

'Yes. You know, Jack's party tonight.'

'Oh yes, of course.'

'Are you awake?'

'I'm sorry, Fiona. My mind was elsewhere. What were you going to say about Jack's party?'

Jack James had the misfortune to be born on the thirty-first of December, so always threw a joint birthday and New Year's Eve party for himself.

'You and Matt are going, aren't you?'

'Yes.'

'You could sound keener.'

'Matt is away still. He's due back around six. And I'm not in the mood.'

'Don't be silly. It'll be good for you. Get you back into the swing of things with the old crowd. We've hardly seen you since . . .' Her voice petered out.

'Since I was attacked. It's okay, Fiona, you can say it.'

Fiona laughed. 'That's good because this party will shake your cage tonight, my friend. You need to get out more and forget about the scruffy old past. Ring a ding ding, a New Year is in.'

Jodie smiled. 'It sounds as if you've started your party already. Save a glass of vodka for me.'

'That's more like it.'

'So what were you ringing about?'

'Jack's party.'

'So you said.'

'I need a lift. The taxis are all booked up already, blast them, and sure as hell I'm not driving. Any chance?'

The same had happened last year, so it came as no surprise. 'I suppose we could squeeze you into the boot.'

'Terrific. See you later.'

'Fiona.'

'Mmm?'

'No mention of photographs in Wyndame School.'

'God, you are a spoilsport.'

'I want Matt to have a good time tonight.'

'And you?'

Jodie shook her head, but there was no one to see. 'I'll settle for a good drink,' she said and hung up.

She went for a walk. She was not sure why. Except that she needed to be out there. Opening the front door still had the power to send her heart pounding up into her throat, but not even that deterred her.

She walked hard. First time on the streets on her own and she had thought she was ready. But it was a knife-edge. Eyes darting over her shoulder. Sweat on her skin. When she reached the horseshoe flowerbed, it was empty. Even she was surprised at the depth of her disappointment. She made herself go over and sit on its wall, just to prove she could do it alone. She drummed her heels hard against the stones. A few teenagers were drifting aimlessly around the promenade, but no one she recognised. It was too early for the rest of them, she knew that. But she had hoped nevertheless.

The wind blew in off the choppy surf making her shiver. Her eyes followed the progress of a crazy windsurfer on the sea intent on making this year his last, but otherwise nothing moved out there except the waves. Behind her the town was winding itself up for the revels of the night to come, but she did not feel a part of it. It was as if everything was out of focus. Everything moving in indecipherable shades of grey. She could not touch them and they could not touch her.

A shadow loomed close and she jumped.

So much for them not touching her. It was a man circling nearby. He looked at her with interest, but she kept her gaze on the sea and, without eye-contact, he cruised on by. Eye-contact, she had learned, was crucial. On the street, it was what got you into, or out of, trouble. A challenging stare could earn you a bloody nose. But a deliberate avoidance of eye-contact might get you through a situation unscathed. The confusion occurred when a pack was on the prowl, out looking for an easy target to bully. They would take their pick of the submissive, down-turned eyes. Jodie had seen it happen. A girl sitting quietly on a bench could suddenly became the one tormented. For no reason at all. She had seen her grandfather's cats play much the same kind of war-game.

She found Pix in the amusement arcade. She was putting up a good fight as Orchid, thrashing Fulgore. When she came off the Killer Instinct machine, she swaggered and preened, pumped up with aggression. Jodie bought a couple of beers to calm her down and they sat drinking them in the doorway of a boarded-up shop,

out of reach of the chill wind. Dusk was descending rapidly. The
streetlamps were already lit. A woman was walking briskly past,
trailing an elderly dog on a lead. It looked at them curiously but
was not allowed to linger.

'Pix, do you have a boyfriend?'

'Nah, I never keep them for long. They always want to
put chains on me. Boys are a bunch of gits. Like my mum's
boyfriends. They're all dickheads.' She shuddered.

Jodie looked across at the tiny figure of her friend tucked into
the corner, blonde hair as spiky as her words, and it occurred
to her that maybe one of her mum's boyfriends had got too
friendly when Pix was young. If so, Pix would keep it buried
deep. Whatever pain was hurtling around under those hedgehog
spikes was private.

Just like Jodie's was private. Not up for grabs to well-wishers.
Like her father and his Mr Hurst. Like Matt.

'Oh shit.'

Pix stared at her. 'What's up with you?'

'My boyfriend is coming back tonight and I have to go to
a party.'

'Do you want to?'

'No.'

'Then don't.'

Jodie rested her head back against the door and tipped more
beer down her throat.

Pix watched. 'You should do like Chloe does. Don't get too
involved.'

'But then I'd lose him.'

'So what? You can always find yourself another.'

'Not like this one.'

'Don't kid yourself.'

'I don't want a shell as hard to crack as Chloe's.'

Pix laughed and as always it took Jodie by surprise. How could
such a gentle sound come from a person who was at her happiest
throwing her fists around?

'Chloe's shell is real thick. Like Tamsin's head.' Pix's green
eyes were full of admiration. 'Nobody, no-frigging-body can hurt
Chloe.'

'Except Chloe.'

Pix frowned. 'What's that supposed to mean?'

'Work it out.'

'Hey, Jode, I said from the start you're smart. I like that. I wish I was.'

Jodie took the opportunity to ask, 'Do you go to school?'

'Yeah, worse luck. When I have to. That shit-heap Sheldon Comp. My last year and then I'm out.'

'What then?'

Pix shrugged. 'I might do like Chloe. In a hairdresser's.'

'You think Chloe is cool, don't you?'

'Yeah, too right. No one messes with her. She takes no crap from anybody. I've seen her drag a girl right across the road by the hair. Ended up with a fistful of it in her hand.'

Jodie shook her head.

'She did,' Pix insisted. 'She's well hard.'

Jodie did not want to hear more. What right did she have to judge, when she had just that morning made use of her?

'Pix, have you ever thought about what it feels like? To be the victim. How it can mess up your mind.'

Pix drained the last of her beer and threw the can out on to the road where a passing car swerved to avoid it.

'Sure I have.' She huddled her knees up under her chin and wrapped her arms around her shins. 'I was bullied plenty at school when I was a kid. Because I was so small. That's why I work out. And every time I wallop someone, I see it landing in the frigging face of the girls who gave me such a hard time.'

'But it doesn't, Pix. It hurts someone else. Someone who perhaps doesn't deserve it.'

'Tough.'

There was silence. Dusk was deepening into solid darkness and their doorway was sinking into shadows.

'I was bullied,' Jodie said. 'When I was at school.'

The words had slipped out of her mouth before she could stop them. Never before had she let them loose from their cage.

Pix waited for more.

Jodie could not put the words back in. It was like undoing a tourniquet. They flowed easily.

'When I started at secondary school. My father was the

headmaster. So I was fair game. Anything he did that they didn't like, they took it out on me.'

Her throat felt tight.

'And?'

'And so I became a dosser. I gave teachers lip and broke every rule I could find. Anything to show I was his daughter in name only.'

'Did it work?'

'Oh yes. Eventually. But not before I had taken my fair share of beatings.'

'Yeah?'

Jodie could hear the hunger in Pix's voice. The hunger for violence. Even second-hand.

'Yes. One day when I wore a new coat to school, they cut off its arms.'

Shark's teeth eating off the birthday sleeves. Feet trampling it to the ground.

'No shit!'

Jodie shrugged. 'Then they knocked me about. I told my parents I had lost the coat and that I'd banged my face falling down some steps.'

And they believed her. They had been so blind, they had believed her.

'Did you get back at the girls who mashed you up?' Pix wanted more.

'No.'

'Tough luck. You should have . . .'

Jodie stood up abruptly. 'I have to go.'

'Okay, Jode.' Pix did not get to her feet, but stretched out a hand and rubbed it lightly in a comforting gesture on Jodie's calf. 'Hey, I know what you're saying. It burns you up. But don't take it so bad.'

Jodie could not look down at Pix.

She walked away and when she reached the corner, she started to run. It took several minutes before she realised the moisture on her cheeks was not rain, but tears.

19

'What in God's name have you done to your hair?'

Matt was staring at her with horrified eyes.

Jodie ran a hand through it and smiled. 'I like it. It's . . .'

'Awful.'

She stopped smiling. 'It's different, is what I was going to say.'

He lifted a hand and touched the wispy fringe as though he thought it might bite. 'It's so short.'

'That's the whole point. I've had long hair since I was ten. Now I've grown out of it.'

He stroked her head and his smoky eyes looked mournful, as if he had lost a beloved friend. 'It was so beautiful.'

She touched his cheek. 'I should have told you on the phone. But I wanted to surprise you.'

'Surprise or shock?'

She kissed his mouth and murmured, 'Poor you.'

He smiled and pulled her close. 'I've missed you.'

'Good.'

They made themselves something to eat, just garlic bread, pâté and salad, but the act of functioning together in the small kitchen, brushing shoulders, making small-talk, bridged the gap with its familiarity. He did not mention her hair again, but she kept catching him giving it surreptitious glances when he thought she was not looking.

They ended up in bed of course. They both knew they would, party or no party. Their bodies eager to make contact, even if their heads were finding it hard. Their limbs entwined, touching, caressing, needing each other, and Jodie could feel the wall inside her start to crumble, brick by brick. She had missed him. Far more than she knew. Missed the smell of his skin, the warmth of his breath on her body, the feel of him deep inside her, a part of her. It had only been a week. Yet it felt like forever. Maybe she had gone further away than she realised.

She lay with her head on his chest, feeling content. Something that had been running very fast inside her had stopped for the moment. She could hear a heart pounding and thought it was Matt's, but was not sure that it was not the sound of her own in her ears. She turned and softly kissed his skin. It was hot and damp and tasted deliciously of salt. He was stroking her hair, slowly slipping his fingers through it, getting used to the new feel.

'Did you keep the hair?' he asked. 'That was cut off, I mean.'

She laughed. 'No, of course not. What would I want it for?'

'I thought you might have kept it as a memory.'

'No chance. I'm working on cleaning out the memories, not adding more to the clutter.'

His fingers kept stroking. 'I see your point.'

'Good.' She curled her legs loosely round his, closed her eyes and felt herself start to drift off in search of the sleep that had been eluding her all week.

'Jodie.'

'Mmm?'

'Talk to me. Tell me what's going on.'

Sleep shot out of reach.

'What do you mean?'

He laughed softly and ruffled her hair. 'Did you really think I wouldn't notice?'

'Notice what?'

'That I go away leaving in this flat someone who is miserable and jumpy as hell, a candidate for the Beachy Head brigade, and I come back to find her not only with hair cut like an urchin, but with a Cheshire cat smirk on her face fit to light up the whole town.'

Jodie lifted her head. 'Is it that obvious?'

'It is. So what have you been up to?' He touched her lips with his fingers, as if searching for the answer on them, and there was something more intimate about the gesture than anything they had just done during their lovemaking.

She lay back against her pillows. She started to tell him. Not an elaborate version, but the bare bones. At one point, when she mentioned Chloe's effect on Emma Richards, she looked across at him to gauge his reaction, but his expression was giving nothing away, as he stared, silent and attentive, at one of her photographs on the bedroom wall. It was a big close-up of a badger's face emerging from its sett, sniffing the air, in grainy black-and-white, but she did not think his eyes were seeing it. Like the badger, he was sensing danger. She could feel it in his stillness.

When she finished her account, there was a long silence. It lay like a fog in the room. Hiding them from each other. She rolled over on her side, facing him, watching the rise and fall of his bare chest, and waiting for the outburst of warnings that she knew was inevitable.

But she was wrong.

In a calm voice, he finally said, 'You don't need me to tell you that what you're doing is risky, Jodie.'

'No.' She stretched an arm across him and pulled herself close. 'I don't.'

'You are setting yourself up as bait.'

'Not bait exactly. More like an irritating gnat that she will have to deal with eventually.'

'And what if she tries to swat you?'

'I'll be like a boy-scout.'

'In short trousers and toggle?'

She laughed and kissed his shoulder, grateful for the joke. 'No, silly. Prepared. I'll be prepared.'

'I see.'

For a while there was nothing more. She thought he had finished. But again she was wrong.

'It doesn't have to be this way, Jodie. You can make it easier on yourself.'

'What do you mean?'

He turned and looked at her. 'By doing what I suggested before Christmas. Go and see someone who is trained to deal with this kind of stuff.'

Jodie pulled away from him. 'Oh no, don't start on that again, please. You're as bad as Dad. He brought one of those psychologists over here this afternoon. Smug and smooth he was, so full of himself. But I don't want to just hand my head over to someone else. It's my head, Matt, mine. And I'm the one who is going to sort it out. Can't you see that?'

Matt did not answer.

'I know it's hard on you, Matt. But . . .'

'But what?' he interrupted suddenly. 'But I don't understand? It that what you were going to say? Because I do understand, Jodie, I do. I understand that you have become obsessed with these girls and your obsession is a deep well down which you are willing to throw anything that gets in your way.' He leaned over and kissed her head. 'Even your beautiful hair.'

'The hair isn't important, Matt.'

'No. But our relationship is.'

'Of course it is. But please try to accept that right now I have to sort out what's in my head.'

For a moment he said nothing. Then quietly asked, 'What is it this gang of girls gives you, Jodie? By your own account, they are thieving thugs who are going nowhere in life. And don't tell me you are out there trying to help them.'

'No. Quite the reverse. They are helping me.'

'How? By teaching you to be prepared? That's what you said. That you would be prepared for this girl when you find her. With knuckle-dusters? Is that the kind of help you get from your gang of thugs?'

This was not what she wanted. Not how she intended it to be. They were supposed to be enjoying his first evening home. Not this. She did not have space for this. She realised that her eyes were shut. She opened them and stared at the ceiling. Its blank face was preferable to Matt's eyes.

'No, Matt. It's just that they make me feel safe.'

'Is that a backhanded way of telling me I don't?'

'No, of course not. But you don't know what it's like to have every movement make you jump, to dread what's round the next corner and pray the doorbell won't ring. Even this flat is not secure. That's why I fixed the safety-chain and bolts on the door. But with these girls I feel safe.'

'Oh my poor Jodie, that is exactly why you need help.' He rolled on his side and wrapped an arm round her. 'You can't fight violence with violence or you end up dead. If not dead outside, then dead inside.'

She turned her head to him. 'It's rage that creates violence, Matt. That's what those kids on the street are fighting. Rage against the way they were brought up, against the cruelties inflicted on them. It fills them up inside. I don't excuse their behaviour. I know it's wrong. But I do understand it.'

Matt took a deep, patient breath. 'Then why go after this girl who attacked you? Just put it down to her universal rage, don't take it personally, and walk away.'

For a split second, the temptation to do as Matt asked was enormous. To let it go and walk away. But she couldn't live like this, looking over her shoulder at every step. Rage and fear go hand in hand. Until she had faced the fear, the rage could not be cut free. It sat next to her heart like a sack of poison.

'Matt, I can't.'

Abruptly he sat up. His face was turned away from her and all she could see was his naked back. She ran a finger down the vertebrae of his spine but there was nowhere soft or flexible in its straight line.

'What will you do, if you do smoke this girl out of her hole?'

'Say when, not if.'

'Okay, *when* you smoke this girl out of her hole.'

'Thank you.' She kissed a particularly bony lower vertebra, one he had damaged playing rugby. The scent of his skin was strong in her nostrils and she wished her mind was as eager to open up to him as her body. 'When I come face to face with her, Matt, all I want to do is talk.'

He turned his head and looked at her with disbelief. 'Talk?'

'Yes. That's all.'

'What about, for Christ's sake? It's like wanting to talk to Hannibal Lector.'

She smiled up at him. 'Exactly.'

'Jodie, why on earth do you want to talk to her? What would you discuss? The weather? Your gang-bang rate?'

'Anything. It wouldn't matter what. I just need to see her as a human being.'

He stared at her for a disconcertingly long time. 'Instead of what?'

That was when the words stuck in her throat. She shut her eyes.

'Instead of what, Jodie?'

She said nothing.

'You say you want to see her as a human being. So what is it you are seeing her as now?' Suddenly his face was close to hers, she could feel his breath warm on her cheek. 'Tell me, Jodie.'

She opened her eyes and looked up into his intent grey gaze. 'A monster. She's a monster and she lives in my head.'

His arms were around her, pulling her close, his lips kissing her shorn hair. 'No, Jodie, my darling. No, she's just a teenage kid. A nasty, malicious, cruel kid who takes pleasure in hurting others. But I promise you she's human. As human as you or me.'

Jodie did not argue. She tasted the soft hollow of his throat with her tongue and heard him give a low moan. She had known he wouldn't believe her.

By the time they arrived at the party with Fiona Bowles in tow, it was already going at full speed. Only for Matt's sake did Jodie force herself to make the effort. The walls were vibrating to the sound of a heavy metal band that was a regular at the local pub on Friday nights and the noise level was rising, as voices and alcohol competed for attention. The house was a modern semi-detached on a new estate and bodies occupied every inch of space. Some were leaning against walls and furniture, others seated in loose-limbed groups on the floor or arguing on the stairs, and above them all hovered a foggy cocktail of cigarette smoke, alcohol fumes and sexual pheromones. The dining-room had been transformed into a dance floor where even more figures were swaying, disco lights flashing, and the heat rising. Every now and again a couple would sneak off to cool down upstairs. Fiona spotted a trio of unattended men and dived straight in.

'Jodie!' Jack shouted, kissed her warmly on both cheeks and took advantage of it being his birthday to land one on her mouth. 'You look gorgeous.' But she could tell he had already consumed sufficient alcohol to make even sackcloth and ashes seem appealing. She was wearing a tiny burgundy silk dress and her Nikon on her shoulder.

'Happy birthday,' Matt said, neatly swapping a bottle of scotch for Jodie.

Jack beamed. 'Come and get yourselves a drink.'

To Jodie's relief, he led them away from the crush of people and into the kitchen. Every surface had disappeared under a mountain of bottles and cans and a huge dustbin in the corner was already overflowing with empties. He waved a hand expansively. 'Help yourself. Food is in the other room. Bloody great it is, though I say it myself. It's a cauldron of chilli that'll blast your tonsils out.'

'Thanks for the warning,' Jodie laughed.

'Talking of warnings,' Jack began, swayed alarmingly, propped his unsteady frame against a cupboard and started again. 'Talking of warnings, Roy Dunmore, our esteemed news-editor, will be unbearable from now on.'

'Why is that?' Matt asked, sipping a Boddingtons.

'It's his New Year's resolution. To give up smoking.'

Matt groaned. 'Another obsessive! He'll make us suffer along with him.'

'What do you mean by "another obsessive"?' Jodie enquired softly.

But just then the door opened and a couple danced in, grabbed a bottle of wine and danced out again.

Jack grinned. 'Good crowd.' He unscrewed the cap of his birthday scotch, took a swig and steered Matt and Jodie out into the throng. Jodie left her question behind in the kitchen.

The noise and the music hit her like a wall. She fixed a smile in place and tried not to let it drop when people jostled her. A couple of mouthfuls from Jack's bottle helped contain her edginess, but she noticed Matt's eyes lingering on her face. Perhaps her nerves were more apparent than she supposed. If so, he passed no comment. She widened her smile, determined that he should enjoy his first night home.

'Looking forward to coming back?'

This time it was Kerry Dainton, the technician from the

photographic department. She was shouting in Jodie's ear to make herself heard. Jodie had lost count of the number of people who had asked her that same question in the last hour.

'I can't wait.'

'No need for sarcasm.' Kerry picked up a bowl of peanuts and took a handful. They were sitting on the floor in the dining-room, holding their conversation against fierce competition from the music. Jodie was watching Matt swaying on the dance-floor with a small, slender blonde who was drilling his chest with her nipples. Jodie had never seen her before but when she came over and asked Matt to dance, he had introduced her as a new recruit in the Accounts department. Good with figures. Especially her own.

'Don't you mind?' Kerry asked, nodding in their direction.

How could she mind? It was just a dance. She hadn't exactly given him an easy time recently, and was the first to object when he tried to interfere with her own choice of friends.

'Of course I bloody mind,' she said and went off in search of some of Jack's chilli.

Shut away behind the camera, she felt safer. For the first time since she had stepped through Jack's canary-yellow front door, the familiar headache that had spread up from the back of her eyes began to recede. It was as if the camera made her invisible, and therefore untouchable. Its rectangular view of the world was like a two-way mirror; she could see them but they could not see her. The fact that her face was hidden behind a piece of electronic gadgetry made her into a non-person, whom they could ignore without insult. It was the flash that upset them. Like some ancient reminder of God's wrath.

She moved from room to room. She had spent so many hours in the last few weeks taking pictures of young faces on the streets that the difference jumped out at her as soon as she looked at this crowd through the lens. The eyes all around her were well-guarded. Self-protective. Not like the teenage eyes that had not yet learned to hide the deadweight of emotional baggage they drag round with them. Most people laughed and struck foolish poses. That's if they noticed her at all.

She spotted Matt sitting on the floor, talking intently to a young couple. Jodie had been introduced to them earlier, but couldn't remember anything about them except that the man had a handshake that took chunks out of your bones. It was when her camera's eye pointed out to her his other companion that she felt a sharp pain like acid in her head. It was the blonde from Accounts again. His dancing partner. The flash caught his attention. He signalled for her to come and join them but she did not want to be a part of his cosy foursome. Her tongue felt too dry in her mouth. All she wanted was to go home, where there were locks on the windows and a safety-chain on the door. She took a couple more shots with the Nikon, then fought her way through to the kitchen where she headed straight for a bottle of vodka. She had opened a can of Coke, poured half of it down the sink and was topping it up with the vodka, when a flash of lightning made her jump.

It was not lightning, of course. It was Fiona Bowles.

'Caught in the act,' Fiona giggled. She was standing by the table, loose and relaxed, like a cat in the sun. Jodie wondered briefly who had been warming her. The Nikon was in her hand. She had come in to replenish her glass and to find a light for her cigarette, but the sight of Jodie's camera lying abandoned on the table had been too tempting for her to resist. 'Can I borrow it?'

'Yes, if you want. But it's your life on the line if you harm a hair of its head.'

'As if I would! Give me credit for being a good mother.' She stroked the Nikon's black case soothingly. 'Don't worry, baby, I'll take good care of you.' She grinned at Jodie. 'Happy now?'

'Ecstatic.' Jodie tossed her a box of matches that lay next to the stove. 'What picture are you after?'

'I saw Dave and Hazel slinking off upstairs. So I want to creep up on them.'

'There are names for people like you, you know, Fiona.'

Fiona laughed, lit her cigarette, dragging hot blue smoke down into her lungs and set off on her mission.

Jodie dumped her drink in the bin. She had suddenly lost her appetite for it. Without her camera, she felt acutely vulnerable.

And Matt.

Had she made him vulnerable too? Easy prey to sweet-sounding words from someone who was willing to throw a few smiles his way.

She turned on the tap, bent down and took a long, chilling drink into her mouth from the flow of water. She felt an urge to climb into the sink and be washed away down the drain. Out to sea. The thought made her straighten up and stare at the blackness on the other side of the window. Somewhere out there Pix and Chloe were having a good time.

A whistle. An explosion. A shower of phosphorescent light.

'Look at that!'

'Wow!'

The firework display had started. Jack's party-goers had moved en masse down to the marina for the ritual celebrations. The cold air worked like a new broom in Jodie's head, sweeping away the alcohol fumes and the dull throb that was back behind her eyes. By the time they reached the waterfront, the promenade was crowded with revellers, so that to rub shoulders with a cyborg or a spotted dalmatian was no surprise.

She noticed that Matt kept looking at her, checking that she was having a good time, willing her to enjoy herself out in the open, so she hung a smile on her face and kept it there. When the midnight hour struck and the first of the fireworks blossomed in the sky, the hugging and singing and kissing got underway in earnest. Matt was the first to kiss Jodie. He held her very tight, so that the high spirits of the jostling crowd could not snatch her away from him.

'Happy New Year, Jodie.'

She kissed him just as a rocket screamed up towards the black blanket of cloud and the strains of 'Auld Lang Syne' broke out around them. In her ears the sounds seemed magnified, the crowd pulsating and swelling, filling up her head and pressing in on her thoughts.

'Happy New Year, Matt.'

She wanted to stay where she was, wrapped safe in his arms. To tell him that if he would just give her time, time and space without surplus blondes, to finish what she had

started, everything would go back to the way it was. But the
words stayed where they were because she knew in reality there
was no such thing as going back. Like the rockets hurtling up
into the night sky, life can only go forward. So she folded her
arms around his neck, kissed him again, long and possessively,
and said, 'We'll make it a good new year, won't we, Matt?'

But instead of agreeing, he was gazing at her, his grey eyes
questioning hers. 'It's not as easy as that, Jodie. Don't kid
yourself. How can it even begin to be good or new, if you are
still stuck in the bad old one?'

She felt as though the floor had dropped out from under her.
Her stomach was somewhere round her throat. She wanted to
shake him. To shake that look of despair out of his eyes.

'Don't give up, Matt. Not yet. Not yet.'

Immediately he brought back the laughter to his face and
hugged her close. As she breathed in with relief, a faint musky
smell of a perfume that was not her own crept off his collar and
tormented the fine hairs of her nostrils.

'Jode, Jode!' a voice screeched from somewhere off to her
right. 'Get your tongue out of that guy's stomach.'

She turned. Across the partying crowd, she saw them. Silhouetted against the black backdrop of the sea, Chloe was leading a
wild conga along the top of the harbour wall. She was blowing
a plastic trumpet and kicking her legs in the air. Behind her, Pix
was wearing a crown of tinsel that made her look even more
like Titania, Danielle and Kit were both transformed into clowns
by red plastic noses and elaborate face-paint, while Tamsin and
Marianne brought up a very unstable rear that threatened to
plunge them into the icy water below at every kick. Jodie waved
and received a lewd gesture in reply.

'Friends of yours?' Matt asked.

'Yes.'

'Your gang of thugs, I assume.'

Jodie disliked his choice of epithets, however well deserved.
It seemed to her that suddenly their hold on each other felt
weaker, as though one of the cold black waves in the harbour
had washed up between them. Then arms came and snatched
them apart, as Jack scooped her up and whisked her round in a
drunken polka. To avoid his kisses, she turned her back on him

but hung on to his hands and started her own conga along the promenade. It gave her a solid feeling of protection to have her rear so well covered. Others joined in and soon she was weaving her own snake of revellers round the flowerbeds, laughing and shouting to show Matt she was fine, just fine, in and out of the clapping spectators, accelerating all the time. She saw the other conga's tail coming close on its parallel but elevated track, and Marianne turn and shriek a warning to Chloe. The trumpet blasted out but the harbour wall stayed firm. Jodie's snake of dancers on the promenade easily overtook them and she waved again. This time in triumph. Then doubled back.

She wanted to thread through the crowd again while she had the security of the conga around her. Eyes sharp. Ears alert for a voice. *The* voice. She was convinced the girl would be out celebrating on New Year's Eve.

For over half an hour her eye hardly left the view-finder of her camera. She hid there, invisible. There was no need to be secretive, as everyone knew the *Gazette* always ran a double-page on the festivities. With Matt and Jack on either side of her, she felt secure enough to seek out with her zoom lens the faces that lurked in hidden corners. If Matt thought her enthusiasm was anything other than professional interest on behalf of the *Gazette*, he passed no comment. In fact, he seemed relieved that she was mixing among strangers so willingly and concentrating on producing good pictures. Maybe he had begun to fear that she would never have the nerve to return to work.

Jodie stopped to reload.

'I'm off home,' Jack announced with a distinct slur. 'Coming?'

'Give us a couple of minutes and we'll follow,' Matt said, his breath spiralling like woodsmoke in the chill night air. 'You've got more than enough pictures, haven't you, Jodie?'

She slipped the film into her coat pocket. 'I thought I'd take one more reel.' She was disappointed. Despite all her efforts, she had seen no sign of the girl. But one look at Matt's face told her she was pushing her luck, and she was not yet ready to take on the crowds on her own. 'You're freezing,' she said, 'and so am I. Let's go and pour a steaming hot brandy into our bloodstreams at Jack's and then maybe we can come back down later to see whether anything more is going on.'

Perhaps the girl would have emerged by then. Out of her rat-hole.

They had left the noise and laughter behind on the promenade. Matt's arm was wrapped round Jodie's waist and because they could not find anything to say to each other, they were singing 'Happy Days Are Here Again' instead, as they walked back to the party. The sudden sound of running footsteps behind made them turn. A figure was flying up the hill towards them. It was small and slight and fast.

'It's Pix,' Jodie exclaimed and hurried down to her.

Matt followed at a slower, reluctant pace.

'Jode,' Pix gasped, her small frame quivering with excitement. 'I saw you leave. There's going to be a rumble. Mental action! Come on, we've got to watch.' She seized Jodie's wrist and started to tug her back down the hill.

'Wait a minute, Pix.' She put a stop to the momentum. 'What are you on about?'

'A rumble. Quick. Or we'll miss seeing it.'

'You mean a fight?'

'Yeah. A ruck. Two gangs have been getting up each other's noses and tonight is payback. Come on, let's move. Now, Jode, now.' Her strong grip pulled at Jodie more urgently.

A fight. A rumble, as Pix called it. A spectator sport. No way would the rat-hole girl miss out on that.

She turned quickly to Matt. 'I've got to go with her. This will be my chance to . . .'

'No, Jodie. No. Don't go.' He enclosed an arm around her waist, anchoring her and stared angrily at Pix. 'Get lost. Go to your ridiculous rumble. But Jodie is not going to be a part of it. Leave her alone. She does not need trouble like you in her life.'

Jodie looked at his face, so intense in its certainty of what was right for her. Leave it, Matt. Leave it. Please.

'I have to go. I have to. You know why.'

'For God's sake, don't be so bloody reckless, Jodie. This time, use your sense. A fight means trouble. You've been hurt once, isn't that enough? Stay out of it.'

'Jode, come on. Quick.'

'No, Jodie.'

'Let's get moving, Jode. Where does he get off telling you what to do?'

'Jodie, please don't. I'm asking you not to. This is *our* time together. It's a new year. Let's make it start with us together. Not torn apart. Don't do this.'

'Tell him to piss off, Jode.'

Jodie pulled herself free of both of them. 'Shut up, the pair of you. Matt, I'm not going over it again. You know already why I need to go with Pix.'

Pix gave a victorious smirk but Matt was not looking at her. His eyes were on Jodie's. Once more he said fiercely, 'Please, Jodie. Don't go. Give this up.'

His eyes tore at her resolve even more than his words. But he had been right when he called her obsession a bottomless well. She turned away and ran.

20 ∫

They were in the school yard. Voices, loud and raucous, all around her. But the game was not child's play.

It was a small primary school with a stone wall that was easily climbed. The yard was hidden from the road by the bulk of the classrooms under their steeply pitched roof, so that not even the streetlamps could penetrate its black secrecy. A few torches flickered around the arena, turning faces into hollow-eyed ghouls, but the darkness was lifting. The heavy clouds of earlier had gone, as if dragged away by the dying year, to allow the new one to start with a clean sheet. The moon was still hidden but now behind only a thin tissue of cloud through which its pale light filtered cautiously.

Jodie could feel the excitement. It was as tangible as the sweat on her back. All around her was the noise of hot, hungry mouths, the murmuring of eager expectation. And every now and then a boisterous shout of impatience because one of the gangs had not yet turned up. Not so very different from the sights and sounds of the Coliseum. So how had man progressed in two thousand years?

She shuddered. Uneasy. Nerves tight. Too many people. Too many shadows. And Matt's face embedded in her mind. *Give this up*, he had said. But how could she? Give up her own sanity? Not even for him.

'Can you see okay?'

It was Pix. Keen for Jodie to miss nothing. A broad circle taking up most of the yard was edged with the wide eyes of the spectators. They were crammed against the walls and jammed up on every available ledge. Already clamouring for action.

Chanting and jeering, male and female mouths, all baying for blood. In the centre of the circle strutted four girls. Tall and dark, they swaggered together, their bravado bright as a shield. All had cropped hair. No hand-hold there. They wore dark green fatigues and had stripped down to sleeveless singlets, indifferent to the cold. The waiting was winding up the tension.

'It's a no-show,' someone shouted.

Whistles and catcalls.

'The Reds are chicken.'

Someone started up with the noise of a hen and all around it was taken up, a jeering, clucking mindless sound that rattled in Jodie's head and set off a dull anger in the twisting folds of her brain. Beside her, Pix crowed like Peter Pan and perched on a ledge. Chloe and Marianne had pushed their way to the front of the crowd. She could not see Danielle and Kit, or Tamsin, but had no doubt that they were here somewhere. Loving every minute.

This was what they got off on. A release of aggression that sent the New Year on its way with a bang. But behind the aggression she could smell the fear. The tangy adrenalin of fear.

She'd had a gutful of fear.

A shoe thrust against her lips.

The arms of a coat dead on the ground.

The attack at the end of the alleyway did more than wreck her ribs and her face. It kicked down a door she had thought was locked.

It was open now. Wide open.

A shout came from one end of the schoolyard and suddenly the atmosphere was high voltage. The Reds had shown.

Red because of their hair. Five girls, five flaming heads, gleaming manes worn long and defiant. In your face to ginner-baiters.

The abuse started instantly.

'Ginner chicken-shit.'

'Scumbags.'

The moment all eyes were focused on the posturing of the rival gangs in the circle, Jodie started to move. She glanced at Pix, but her gaze was fixed unswervingly on the action in the centre, green eyes high and bright as stars. Jodie slid away through the crowd. Slowly and methodically, she worked her way past each group, avoiding elbows and shoulders, careful to spark no flare-ups.

'Go get 'em, Reds.'

'Tear the bastards to pieces.'

Jodie shut out the words. Only the voices mattered. The sound of the voice she had heard a thousand times in her head. When sleep wouldn't come. When shadows crept into a corner of the room. When the wind rattled the window, threatening to break in.

You fucking witch, the voice had screamed at her, *don't you ever stop?*

No.

I don't ever stop.

A sudden roar and an intake of breath. The fight had started. She caught a glimpse of a snarl of bodies, fists jabbing, feet flailing, a cry of pain.

She turned away.

Beside her a boy, no more than fourteen, full of pimples and Benzedrine, was yelling himself hoarse. Beyond him a girl, tall and clad in black, but when Jodie moved closer, the eyes were wrong, not the dark hot-tempered ones she was seeking.

Shouts and screams, laughter and abuse swelled around her, a bedlam of hysterics and madness. And everywhere the spice of violence. Like scorched pepper in the air, catching at the back of the nostrils and burning into the brain. For a second, it touched a memory, elusive at first and then she found it. The faces at the one and only football match Matt had taken her to. An organised expression of ritual aggression, where the chosen favourite can be urged to murder and mayhem. A fever of emotion, whipped to the very edge of control.

Torches cutting tunnels in the darkness, a red-haired skull head-butting a face, open mouths, cries and shouts, all pushing and stamping, crowded their way into Jodie's head. Like black-and-white images on a screen that flickered and flashed. The faint light of the moon struggled through the clouds, picking out a frozen face, a streak of blood that shone black and sticky as tar, young bodies craning forward unwilling to miss a moment of the show. A girl in front of her suddenly burst into tears and pushed her way out; a friend ran after her, soft and comforting.

Still Jodie searched.

She was half way round the circle when a voice behind her shrieked, 'You fucking bitch!'

You fucking witch.

Her heart kicked a hole in her chest and she felt cold air pour in. Blood turn to ice. Slowly, inch by inch, she turned her head.

The girl was on a windowsill. Standing and shouting and screaming. Towering above Jodie. Her dark eyes black as a shark's in a moon-bleached face. A long determined jaw and hair chopped into a sharp bob. All her attention was on the fight, but her voice was unmistakable.

All other sights and sounds went dead. As if someone had turned a switch in her head.

This was the monster.

Haunting her nightmares and darkening her life. Its shadow robbing her lungs of clean air, her mind of clean thoughts. This monster. This mutant.

This girl.

She stared, unwilling to let go.

Then smoothly, without shifting her gaze, she raised the camera that hung on her shoulder. Fingers adjusted exposure. No tremble. They knew what they were doing. The risk they were taking. A flash. A shout. But Jodie was again in the crowd, her back turned to the girl, feeling naked and assailable.

'Keep your fucking torches out of my face,' the voice shouted angrily to no one in particular.

Jodie waited a long minute, then moved off to one side. The girl's pack of wolves would be circling somewhere close. She slid with relief into the deeper shadow of the schoolyard's wall and leaned her back against it. The cold seeped from the stones, sharp and frosty, penetrating her coat and bringing a welcome chill to her skin.

On the windowledge, the girl still watched the fight. From where Jodie was now standing, she could no longer hear her, her shouts merging with the general uproar, but she could see the movement of her mouth, opening and closing, her fists pummelling the air in front of her. The image heightened the sick fear in her chest and she glanced away, eyes skimming the shifting crowd, her view of the fight thankfully blocked by the solid wall of backs. A face she recognised jumped out at her. It was Danielle, off to her right close to the wall, a protective arm around Kit. Not for the first time, Jodie wondered if they were lovers.

Suddenly, like a banshee from hell, a police siren wailed into the street outside, slicing through the night and splitting the drooling hydra of spectators into a stampede of panicked teenagers. Everyone moved at once. A dash for the walls, like woodlice from under a lifted stone, boys barging for survival to the front, girls hampered by skirts and heels but hoisting each other to freedom. At the first blare of the siren, the girl on the sill leapt to the ground and was running almost before anyone else had moved. Jodie recognised once again her feral speed.

She knew immediately there was no chance of catching her. The crowd between them might as well have been an ocean, so effectively did it divide them. The front wall was alive with surging bodies and the searchlights of police torches. She concentrated on her own escape. From her place in the shadows, she sped round two sides of the yard keeping close to the building until she reached a high narrow gate that led to a back service area of bins and sheds. Heart hammering in her mouth and dress up round her waist, she scrambled over it, leaving a slice of her calf on its metal spikes. She could hear others behind her, following her lead. It was too dark to see clearly here, but adrenalin sent her hurtling across the small gap, crashing into God knows what and eventually finding the far wall.

It was too high.

Behind her a clutch of black kids were panicking, like mice in a trap, and she wondered what they were carrying in their pockets that made them so jumpy. She made for one of the large waste-bins and started to drag it into place as a climbing block. The kids' muscle power added speed to her efforts and in seconds they were all over the wall. Her last glimpse before she let herself drop was of a policeman's face behind the metal gate, young and keen. The impact jarred her ribs into savage claws that raked her side, but the moment her feet hit the ground she started running.

She snatched a deep breath between strides. This was getting to be a habit.

The hit of adrenalin kept Jodie going. Even after her muscles were sick of it and the police nowhere in sight, her legs continued pumping. Fast through the dark and deserted back streets, uncertain in which direction she was heading. Her head felt airy and bright, lit up from within like a Halloween pumpkin. Her blood volatile and explosive in her veins.

It was addictive.

She forced herself to slow down to a walk and try to think straight, but immediately she became aware of how isolated she was. A solitary target. She walked faster. In her camera was the photograph of the girl. If the police had not turned up when they did, she might have discovered her name as well. Might have followed her. Spoken to her.

All might-haves.

So forget them.

She had seen her face. Taken her picture. It would not take her long to trace her, of that she was now certain.

'Nice camera you've got there, lady.'

Jodie had not noticed the man. He was in his fifties and drunk, but not so drunk he did not know what he wanted. He lurched out of a shop doorway and into her path. She glanced quickly around her. The street was dark and empty but not silent. It was two o'clock in the morning and a party was still in full swing in a flat above the small parade of shops that she was passing. The music blasted out with Freddie Mercury telling all those who would listen that he was the champion of the world. By the time she looked back at the man in front of her, he had been joined by another. This one was wearing a greedy smile on his face.

Jodie attempted to ignore them. She dodged to one side. Her intention was to cross the road but before she was even off the pavement, the second man, younger and more sober than the first, had swung her round and yanked at the camera strap on her shoulder.

She slapped his face hard.

Shocked, he released his grip. 'Now that's not nice, is it, lady?' He rubbed his cheek and in the light that spilled from the windows above, she saw his eyes shift from greed to aggression. Beside him, the drunk had bunched his fists in readiness. Violence begets violence.

'Okay,' she said in a voice that was meant to be calm. 'It's yours. But I'll keep the film.'

She pressed the rewind button and the electric motor whirred into action for a few seconds, then stopped. The men watched as her fingers extracted the film and held the camera out to them. The drunk snatched it eagerly. But the one she had slapped was not so easily appeased. He seized her wrist and had the tube of film twisted out of her hand before she was aware what he intended. In two seconds flat, he had her film open and exposed, tossed on the ground like a silky black snake. It wriggled for a moment and then died.

'You bastard,' she said quietly. 'You bastard.'

The man laughed, gratified.

A door banged.

'Trouble?'

Four young men had emerged from what was obviously the entrance to the flat above. They all wore paper hats and had some sort of green gunge dangling like noodles from their hair.

'Are these guys giving you a hard time?' one of them asked politely.

Jodie nodded, still staring at the snake of film. 'They've taken my camera.'

The drunks quickly made to leave, but the phalanx of young men blocked their path.

'Hand it over.'

They had more sense than to argue. The camera was passed to the party-goers and then to Jodie. She looked at their clean young faces and thanked them.

'Beat it,' one of them rapped out to the drunk. He did so. His friend deliberately scraped his foot along the length of the film, twisting it into the gutter and then shuffled after him.

The photograph was gone.

*   *   *

By the time Jodie reached home, she was furious with herself. She should have foreseen the risks. It would have been the work of a few seconds to pocket the precious film as soon as she was out of the schoolyard. How could she have been so careless?

Because she had been high as a kite on adrenalin. Her thought processes swamped. No longer kept safe by her fear.

The four young men had insisted on walking her most of the way home and it was strange that she had felt unthreatened by them. Maybe her system had reached overload. Or maybe all their signals had been decent. Whatever it was, they turned out to be neither sex attackers nor serial killers, but pleasant young men keen to start their year with a display of chivalry. They had wished her happy New Year at the end of her road and returned to their celebrations, but not before she had loaded a new film into her Nikon and taken a picture of them. Big teeth grinning at her, arms draped over each other. A photograph for her wall.

To remind her.

There was more than one world out there.

As she opened the gate, her mind registered that there was nothing parked in front of her Mini. Nothing but empty shadows. No VW.

Matt was not home.

Her heart kicked jealously and she told it to cut it out. He had probably squeezed himself into a passing taxi and was right now snoring like a bear upstairs in bed. She unlocked the door, took the stairs two at a time. The flat was in darkness. In silence. She knew the second she entered that it was empty, but she went through the motions. Checked each room. The bedroom last. Unwilling to face what she knew she would find.

An empty bed.

Its white cover lay smooth and unwrinkled, a blank face that told her nothing.

Matt was sleeping elsewhere.

He could still be at Jack's party, she reminded herself. He was angry. What more natural reaction than to get steaming drunk and sleep it off on Jack's floor? It had happened once before, last summer at a barbecue. A row over nothing, a night spent in separate flats. Almost worth it for the sheer exuberance of their remorse. But this time it was not over nothing. He was asking something of her she could not do.

Give this up.

No, Matt, I can't give it up.

Won't give it up.

It was the 'won't' that had hurt him. He must see himself ending up down that deep well of hers with all the other sacrificial lambs. But it was not true. She loved him. There was no way she could change that even if she wanted to. Her need for him was deeper than any well on earth. She would find him and explain.

Explain what?

There was nothing he did not already know.

She walked back into the sitting-room and circled the telephone for a long time. With an effort she moved over to the window. The curtains were not drawn and somewhere in the distant night sky a rocket exploded, streaking the clouds with a false silver lining. She could telephone the party. Or sit and wait. On the dark pane of glass in front of her, the face of the blonde from Accounts was smiling at her. A sweet beguiling smile that men had no idea how to resist.

Abruptly she picked up the phone. She was half-way through dialling Jack's number when she noticed Matt's computer. It was gone. Normally it sat with its mouse and its monitor in the corner of the room, looking expectant and efficient. Jodie liked to play on it sometimes to prove to it she was not phased by its antics. Now, the corner was empty. An ice-pick sank into her heart. She felt the pain of it so sharply that it robbed her of sight. A swirling sweltering rush of darkness swept into her head and then vanished.

'You're crazy,' she said dismissively. 'Crazy as a loon. Matt must have lent it to somebody and you didn't even notice it was missing.'

Not for a moment was she taken in.

Her eyes darted round the room. There was a gap on the mantelpiece where his hideous rugby trophy always stood, the stack of CDs was halved, his granite ashtray from Scotland was gone. This must be one of her nightmares. She would wake screaming in a minute to cling to the luxurious warmth of his body in her bed.

She screamed. Loud and harsh and shocking in the flat.

But she did not wake.

The bedroom. She walked there slowly, in no hurry for the truth, opened the wardrobe door and let out a sigh that tore its way up from deep inside her. His half was empty. Blank, dead space. No jackets or shirts or jeans, no sweaters pushed into her shelves or dirty socks thrown in a bundle among the shoes. Jodie inhaled deeply. The empty space still held a part of him. Invisible to the naked eye but hanging there as real and recognisable as his clothes had been. An intimate phantom in the aroma of his presence, in the feel of its breath on her skin.

She turned away.

'Matt, Matt, Matt,' she gasped out loud and began to tug at the innocent white bed-cover, harder and faster, pulling and pummelling at sheet and pillows, scrabbling and scratching until all the bedclothes lay in a tangled heap on the floor and the mattress stared up at her, naked and indifferent. Then she lay down on it and started to cry.

21

The sun was doing its best to put a gloss on the first day of the new year, lending a short-lived brightness to the uniform grey of winter. Elizabeth Buxton stared out of her kitchen window at the bony skeletons of the trees and watched a wood-pigeon drift down to land on her lawn. It looked too cumbersome for flight. She reminded herself to put something more out on the bird-table and check their water-dish for ice. A cat slid over the fence from next door. Elizabeth rapped at the window and its heartless eyes stared back at her blankly until she rapped again.

'Get out, you brute,' she shouted.

It turned and slunk off through a hole.

Every day of the year Elizabeth waged a vigilant war against the neighbourhood's cats. They had decimated the local wildlife and she did all in her power to keep her garden a cat-free zone where birds and mice could seek refuge. It was the reason the garden hose remained attached to the outdoor tap all year round, coiled for action like a sleeping cobra. Water and cats did not mix. How her father could give home and hearth to a whole horde of the marauding creatures, she did not know. Their dirty paws scuffled over everything regardless, but he didn't give a toss. She shuddered, and gave her sink another scrub, as if just the thought of the animals could pollute its germ-free cleanliness.

She switched on the dishwasher. Its grinding and rattling of her crockery reminded her of the previous evening. A couple of friends had come over to see in the New Year and she was glad to find that Alan had enjoyed it in the end, despite a quiet start. These days he was too often quiet. Ever since that blasted fire, nothing had been right. There had been the attack on Jodie, and then Anthea stealing all that money. That was really worrying Elizabeth, despite her daughter's assurances that Henry would take it no further. If only Anthea had not put herself so much in debt over her new flat, she could have borrowed it from the bank. That was the trouble now, no one was willing to wait for anything any more. Self-indulgence had become an art form.

Elizabeth sighed. She had tried to raise the money herself without Alan's knowledge. But forty thousand. It was too much. She shook her head to loosen the knot of worry between her eyes. How could she have brought into this world two daughters so totally unlike herself? Maybe Anthea's baby would be different. Just the thought of it made her feel better. The telephone rang. She was still smiling when she walked out of the kitchen and picked up the receiver in the hall. As she did so, she heard the click of the phone upstairs and Alan's voice say, 'Hello?'

Before Elizabeth could decide whether to speak or hang up, a girl's voice said curtly, 'The money is not enough, Mr Buxton. I want more.'

She heard Alan's sharp intake of breath. 'I told you never to ring me here.'

'Things have changed. Your . . .'

'Not here.' His voice was low. 'I'll be at the school tomorrow morning.'

'Fuck tomorrow. I'm talking now.'

'But I'm not listening. Tomorrow. At school. And don't you dare ever call me at home again.' He hung up.

Very quietly, Elizabeth replaced the receiver.

She parked her car in front of Jodie's Mini and walked up the path. She pushed the bell. The paintwork on the front door needed a good clean and she flicked away a few cobwebs in the corners while she waited for a response. The straggly girl from the flat downstairs opened it, her hair and her skirts floating around her, the little boy swinging on her hand. He always looked to Elizabeth as if he had rickets. Probably a vegan and slowly starving. But he was certainly lively enough, she had to admit, and possessed his mother's big warm smile.

'Hello, Mrs Buxton. Nice to see you. Have a good Christmas, did you?'

'Yes, thank you, Charmain. What about you and little Andy?' She smiled at the child. 'Did Father Christmas bring you . . . ?'

'I don't teach him those old lies,' Charmain said pleasantly. 'He knows Father Christmas is a commercial fairy story.' She stroked his head with a strange circular movement.

Probably massaging his brain, Elizabeth thought, and said quickly, 'I'll go up and see if Jodie is in.'

'Right ho. Come on, Andy, let's go back to our meditations.'

Meditations? Christ almighty!

Upstairs, Jodie opened the door to the flat very cautiously. It saddened Elizabeth to see her still so nervous. She looked awful. Her skin grey and washed out, dark smudges under her eyes that only heightened the whiteness of the scar on her cheekbone. And the hair. Elizabeth could not look at the hair. She hugged her daughter, wished her a happy New Year and glanced round for Matt.

'Out, is he?' It would be easier to talk to Jodie alone.

Jodie did not answer the question. 'I'm in the middle of doing some developing,' she said and headed for the spare bedroom.

Elizabeth followed her in and the red light overhead took her by surprise. 'Sorry, darling, I didn't mean to interrupt you in your darkroom. I should have rung first, I suppose, but . . .' She stopped.

All around her, faces stared out from the walls. It was unnerving. Like spying on a secret life. All young girls, laughing, talking, smoking, even crying.

'Good Lord, Jodie, what are you doing with these? Planning an exhibition?' Some of them were beautiful photographs, haunting in their intimacy.

'No. Not at the moment anyway. I'm just finishing a few from last night.'

Spread out on a long narrow table against the wall was a series of shallow trays containing various chemicals, while a black curtain blocked out all trace of daylight from the window, leaving the red bulb to spill its beam, like blood, over the trays. Jodie lifted a black-and-white print out of one of the chemical baths with plastic tongs and held it up for her mother to see. It was of a band of vicars and tarts, except the men were dressed up as tarts and the girls as vicars.

Elizabeth laughed. 'Looks like someone was enjoying themselves. I hope you did too.'

Jodie was preoccupied, eyes intent on the row of photographs spread out to dry on sheets of white blotting-paper. 'Oh yes,' she muttered, 'I had a riot.' She picked up a magnifying-glass and scanned them more closely, but, as far as Elizabeth could make out, it seemed to be the people in the background of the pictures she was studying.

Suddenly Elizabeth realised what was going on. 'Oh no, Jodie, this isn't about the girl who attacked you, is it?' She waved a hand at the walls of faces and the photographs on the table. 'You're not *still* after her, surely? Can't you just put it behind you and move on? Your father and I both think it's about time that . . .'

But Jodie was not listening. Her gaze was fixed on one particular photograph and her whole body was tense and alert.

Elizabeth sighed. There was no talking to Jodie when she was caught up in her photography. She just stopped hearing you, as if the rules of existence went into abeyance and she passed into some sort of parallel universe. Elizabeth had seen it too many times before to try to fight it now.

'All right, Jodie. I'll go and make myself a cup of tea. Come and talk to me when you've finished.'

She was not sure whether it was only the glow from the red light in the room, but as she walked out, she noticed that Jodie was already beginning to look better.

'It's a bit fuzzy, dear.' Elizabeth was studying the photograph Jodie had placed on the table.

'That's because it's an enlargement of a background detail and it was night-time. Despite all the lights on the prom, I had to open right up to 2.8. But if you knew her, you would recognise her from this.'

The girl in the picture looked normal enough. Dark-haired and long-jawed. Determined, certainly, but no sign of anything more. Yet Jodie claimed this was the person who attacked her.

'Are you really sure this is the girl?'

'Yes. There's no doubt.'

'But I thought she wore a scarf over her face that night. They all did, you said.'

'That's true, they did. But I came across her last night and recognised her voice. I assure you, Mum, there's no chance in hell of my forgetting it.'

Elizabeth felt a surge of sympathy for her daughter. She wanted to comfort her, to soothe away the misery in her eyes, but Jodie had always been so irritatingly private.

'Matt's not around,' Elizabeth commented to change the subject. 'Is he working?'

'No. He's not due back at the *Gazette* for a couple of days yet.'

'He hasn't gone over to Bournemouth again, has he?'

'No.'

There was something about the way she said it that made Elizabeth drop that subject as well. She wondered whether now was maybe not the right moment to bring up her own problem. She fiddled with the photograph. Something about it caught her eye.

'Good heavens, Jodie, look at that ring of hers.'

'Her ring?' Jodie picked up the photograph and scrutinised it again. 'What about it?'

The girl's hand was raised up to one side of her face and a large ring was visible to the camera's eye. It was a heavy band of silver coiled twice round in the form of a snake, its flat head rearing up towards the knuckle, revealing eyes of bright turquoise. It was a striking piece of jewellery.

'I think I've seen it before,' Elizabeth said thoughtfully. 'In fact, I'm sure I have.'

Jodie leant forward, eyes bright and intent on her mother's face, fists clenched tightly between her knees.

'Where?' she asked. 'Where did you see it?'

'It was ages ago, I'm afraid. I haven't seen it recently.'

'Okay. So when did you last see it?'

'It was when I was working as the pharmacist over at Hyde's Chemist, so that must make it about two years ago. Maybe a bit more. A woman used to come in regularly for Temazepam. In her forties she was, but looked much older. So dispirited. Mind you, I think she'd had a dreadful time of it.'

'What has that got to do with the ring?'

'It was always on her finger. You couldn't help noticing it because it was so incongruous on her.'

Jodie reached out and rested a hand very lightly on her mother's. Elizabeth could feel it shaking.

'Her name must have been on the prescription. Do you remember what it was?'

'Oh yes, I used to chat to her quite a bit. You know, to try to cheer her up. When I once remarked on the unusual ring, she told me that her husband had made it for her years before. Apparently he was a jeweller, but he was a really heavy drinker. It was the death of him. Quite literally, I gather. When he was drunk one night, he spilt whisky all over himself and over his chair, and set fire to it. Burnt part of the house down. They never knew for sure whether it was an accident or intentional. A hideous way to go though, don't you think? I can't imagine how people can bear to do such . . .'

'Mum, her name?'

'Yes, of course. It was Mrs Richards. Sheila Richards.'

Her daughter's hand was withdrawn. She looked disappointed.

'Does that help? Maybe if you could contact Mrs Richards, she could tell you how it came to be on this girl's finger.'

Jodie ran a tired hand through her tufty hair and shook her head. 'No need for that. I can guess.'

'Really? How?'

'Emma Richards was the one who got caught stealing the computer from Dad's school.'

'No!'

'I've seen her mother, your Mrs Richards. I agree that she looks half dead. She has obviously been overloading on Temazepam for years.'

'Foolish woman,' Elizabeth said, but with sympathy, remembering the despairing eyes that came to beg oblivion from a bottle. 'But what's the connection with this?' She tapped the photograph on the table.

'This girl is the leader of that gang. I'm sure Emma will have given her her mother's ring. Maybe as a kind of payment or just to keep her happy. For all I know she may demand regular symbols of allegiance.' For a brief second Jodie dropped her head in her hands and murmured something to herself, but the collapse was only momentary. She raised her head. 'Thanks anyway.'

Elizabeth felt uncomfortable and again shifted subject. 'Talking of rings, I telephoned Anthea this morning.'

'How is she?'

'Pregnancy suits her. She's like a dog with two tails because Henry has given her an engagement ring, the size of Wales she says. A sapphire with diamonds.'

Jodie smiled. 'I'm glad for her. She'll enjoy flashing that around.'

'You're right.' She sighed. 'Jodie dear, I'm sorry I haven't been of more use.'

Jodie shrugged, watching her intently. 'What's the problem, Mum?'

Elizabeth leant her head against the back of the sofa and knew she was going to have to let out the reason she had come. She couldn't keep it in. It was already gnawing its way through her stomach.

'It's your father.'

Instantly Jodie's eyes became guarded. 'If he is trying to get me to see his shrink again, tell him I'm not interested.'

'No, it's nothing to do with that.'

'What is it, then?' Her voice softened and Elizabeth was surprised to hear the concern in it. She must be looking more worried than she realised.

Embarrassment coloured her cheeks, but she did not let it stop her relating to her daughter the telephone conversation on which she had eavesdropped.

The sitting-room was empty. Elizabeth trailed unhappily behind Jodie as she headed for her father's study, pushed open the door without knocking and strode in.

'You're bribing that girl to stay away from me, aren't you?'

No preamble. No tiptoeing round the edges.

Alan was sitting with his back to the door, head bent over a sheaf of papers on his desk. He did not move. Elizabeth saw a tightening of the shoulders, but that was all. His self-control had always been impressive.

'I want to know what's going on, Dad.'

Her words were ice-calm and Elizabeth was relieved at the restraint. She hated it when they shouted. But she recognised the tone of determination and knew Jodie was not going to give up on this one.

Slowly Alan turned in his chair and looked at his daughter with an expression that was unreadable. It disturbed Elizabeth that even after all these years together, he could hide himself from her when he chose.

'Hello, Jodie.'

'You're paying her, aren't you? To leave me alone. That's why she won't come and talk to me. I've asked Emma Richards to pass on a message to her but she does not respond. Now I know why.'

They stared at each other in silence.

Alan was the first to look away. He rose to his feet, turned to Elizabeth and asked, 'What has brought this on?'

She opened her mouth reluctantly to explain about the telephone call, but Jodie forestalled her.

'Answer my question, Dad. Are you bribing her? Who is this girl?'

He frowned. 'No, Jodie, I am bribing nobody. How on earth you reached such an extraordinary conclusion, I cannot imagine, but I promise you, you are wrong.'

'You expect me to believe you.' It wasn't a question, but a statement of fact.

He took a long, patient breath and spoke slowly. 'That's up to you. It does not alter the fact that what I say is true. It's clear that you have been misinformed in some way, so I suggest we try to establish the truth. What do you base these wild accusations on?'

Elizabeth could not let her daughter take the blame. 'It was me, Alan. I told her. I overheard your telephone call. I didn't mean to, but I did. It was a girl and she was asking for more money.' Elizabeth could hear her voice growing agitated. 'What is it about, Alan? I need to know what's going on. It's not right that you should . . .'

He stretched out a hand, but let it drop before it touched her. 'Calm down, my dear. Getting upset won't help. Why didn't you just come and discuss it with me, rather than running off with all sorts of misinterpretations to our daughter?'

But Jodie was not so easily distracted. 'You had no right to interfere. None at all. You may think you are doing it for my own good, like you did with your tame shrink, but you're wrong. You are doing more harm than good, but you can't see it because you are always so sure you know best.'

'I am not interfering,' he said stiffly.

She shrugged dismissively. 'Just tell me the girl's name, that's all I'm asking. I'll find it out myself eventually, but you could make it easier for me.'

'As always, Jodie, you are not listening to me. I am telling you that I know nothing about this. That's the end of it.' He sat down and picked up the top sheet of paper on his desk.

Elizabeth was shocked to see it unsteady in his hand.

'I have work to do,' he said.

'But Alan, you haven't explained what the phone call was about.'

He spoke slowly again, as if to dimwitted children. 'The girl who rang here is one of my pupils. We are sponsoring her to enter a competition.'

'What kind of competition?'

'Chess. She's quite brilliant at it. The trouble is she always wants more travelling expenses than we can afford.'

'But she swore at you. I heard her.'

Alan sighed. 'Her language is sadly not as versatile as her brain.'

Elizabeth felt a warm surge of relief and smiled apologetically. 'I'm so sorry, Alan. I've blown this up out of all proportion, haven't I? You're right, I should have discussed it with you first and you could have explained everything straight away without my bothering Jodie about it.' She turned to her daughter. 'You see, that's why she was asking for more money. For her expenses. I got it all wrong.'

But Jodie was not smiling.

She was looking at her father with eyes that bore no trace of relief, and there was something in them that Elizabeth had never seen there before. After a silence that felt like a velvet curtain it hung so heavily in the room, Jodie walked over to his chair and looked down on him.

'You're lying,' she said quietly. Then turned and left the house.

22

Jodie drove straight from her parents' house to Stanwell Road. She parked right outside number twelve. She stared at her hands on the steering wheel. Still shaking. Was this ever going to stop? There was nothing out there that looked remotely threatening. Nothing. Absolutely nothing. Yet the sweat was gathering between her breasts.

She couldn't go on like this. It had to end. Whatever it took, it had to end.

The street looked fractionally less drab in the frail afternoon sunlight and a young child was rocking lethargically back and forth on one of the swings across the road. It was obviously the day for refuse collection because the pavement was guarded by a row of tall green plastic bins that looked ready to challenge any intruder. She ignored them and left the car's protective shell.

The doorbell was concealed behind a scribbled note declaring 'Out of Order', so she used the door knocker. It was warm from the sun's rays and felt alive in her hand. She wanted to hold on to it. But the response to her knock was immediate, as though someone was expected. The door opened a gap. It was Mrs Richards, wearing again the same grey cardigan and with the same dead eyes, but this time the sight of Jodie brought a flicker of distaste to them.

'What do you want?'

'Mrs Richards, I would like to talk to you about a friend of your daughter's.'

No response.

'May I please come in to discuss this in private?'

'No.'

'Very well, then I'll say what I have to say out here on the pavement.' She produced the photograph. 'This girl is a friend of Emma's. I need to find her. Do you know her?'

Still no response.

'Mrs Richards, she did considerable damage to me and it's quite possible that she is also harming your daughter. Maybe getting her to steal things. Have a look at the ring on her finger.'

The woman stared at the picture, but did not touch it. Her hand stayed on the door.

'Do you recognise it?'

She nodded.

'It used to be yours?'

Another nod.

'Did it disappear recently?'

Mrs Richards said nothing for a moment and Jodie was expecting another nod, but instead she snapped curtly, 'I gave it to my daughter. What she does with it after that is her own affair.' It was the gravel voice of a woman who has smoked too many cigarettes and for the first time Jodie noticed the nicotine stains on her fingers. Killing herself slowly.

'Mrs Richards, I don't intend to disturb your daughter in any way. It's this girl,' she held up the picture again, 'I am looking for. If you recognise her, please tell me who she is. She is a dangerous person, and will be a bad influence on Emma.'

The woman stared again at the face in the photograph and her lips tightened into a thin hard line. 'Go to hell,' she said and slammed the door.

In the flat, Jodie sat by the window and watched the patch of sky slowly darken, as inch by inch it gave up its brittle blue for a swarthy mask of shadows. Along the street the harsh gleam of streetlamps punctured its secrets at intervals. A wind had sprung up, tapping the glass pane with invisible fingers and the temperature had dropped to near freezing. She shivered. Her father was lying to her. Of that she was certain. And it brought her no relief to know he was doing so in the mistaken belief that he was helping her. How he had discovered the identity of the girl, she could only guess at. Most likely from the Richards girl.

But to pay her to stay away.

She replayed her conversation with him, going over his explanation, his defences, his patient sighs. Over and over, again and
again, filling her mind with her father's sombre grey eyes and
her mother's gullibility, anything to keep her thoughts away
from Matt. If she allowed them to stray there, she would crawl
under the duvet and might never come out. A car swept past
outside and its headlights chased across her ceiling, reminding
her that she was sitting in the dark. She stood up to turn on the
light, but first looked up and down the road again.

Empty.

How many times could you check a street in an hour?
Annoyed with herself, she headed for the light switch, but as
she passed the telephone, her hand reached out and picked it
up.

Matt.

She had to know.

She dialled Jack's number. It rang for a long time with no
answer, but she was determined to drag him out of bed. Finally,
a grumpy male voice answered it with the complaint, 'Who's
that? I hope you realise I was asleep.'

'Jack. It's Jodie.'

'Oh, cheers, Jodie. Wake me up, why don't you?'

'I'm sorry. I just want to know if Matt is with you.'

There was an uncomfortable silence. She waited.

'Sort of.'

'What does that mean, Jack? Surely he either is or he isn't?'

'Have you guys had a row or something?'

'Sort of.'

He laughed and it was immediately followed by a groan. 'Oh
God, my head hurts.'

'Serves you right. Wild orgies tend to have that effect.'

'Wild orgies? I wish! But it was a good party, wasn't it?'

'It was great, Jack. And happy New Year to you. Now tell me
about Matt.'

'Nothing much to tell. I'm not sure what time he got back
here but he can't have stayed long because I was searching for
him around two o'clock and he had gone again. But all his stuff
is in my spare bedroom.' He hesitated, then groaned miserably.

'This is all too heavy for my brain in its weakened state. So just tell me straight. Have you guys split up?'

'Ask Matt.'

'Hey, Jodie, I'm really sorry if it's going wrong for you. But I'm just the messenger. Don't bite my head off.'

Jodie made an effort. 'Sorry, Jack, I didn't mean to. I'm a bit grouchy today. Lack of sleep and too much to drink, I guess.'

Jack gave a sympathetic moan. 'I know exactly how you feel.'

I doubt it, Jack. I doubt it very much.

'Sorry I can't help more,' he continued and added hopefully, 'Maybe if you came over, we could drown our sorrows together.'

'No. But thanks anyway. Nice try. So you have no idea where Matt is now?'

'None at all. Honestly, I'd tell you if I did. But I shouldn't worry if I were you. The guy is nuts about you. He'll turn up when he's ready. I expect it was just a mad whim in a drunken moment which he is already regretting, so you mustn't take it seriously. I'm sure he doesn't mean it really.'

Let's start it together, he'd said. *Not torn apart.*

But she had taken no notice. Gone straight on tearing.

'Thanks, Jack.'

'Take care, kid,' he said affectionately.

'And you. Go back to your pit.'

'I swear I'll never ever drink again. Total abstinence from now on.'

'Until the next time, you mean.'

He laughed, but carefully. 'You're cruel.'

'Jack?'

'Mmm?'

She hesitated and he mistook her silence. 'Don't worry, if I hear anything from him, I'll let you know immediately, I promise.'

'Thanks. Sleep well.' She hung up.

She had not been able to bring herself to ask if the blonde from Accounts had also disappeared from the party.

*　　*　　*

She concentrated on the photograph. She swirled the Kodak paper through the dish of developer and the stop bath, and then watched it as it sat out its two minutes in the fixer. The face was now as familiar to her as her own, as intimately known. She found herself talking to it, expressing the words she wanted to say to the flesh and blood version of it. But it was deaf and paid no heed. She ran it through the water wash and then laid it down on the sheet of blotting-paper beside the others.

There were six copies. Okay, so they were fuzzy, but nevertheless the face was her. Unmistakably her. All were identical and each one had the power to set off a buzz-saw in Jodie's head that made her vision as blurred as the photographs themselves. Yet she made herself continue to look at the wide, dilated eyes, the long nose that had at some time been broken and the mouth open in a baring of teeth as the girl jeered obscenely at something out of view. It had taken until the early hours for Jodie to think of searching for the girl among the background crowds on the promenade, but eventually she had found her.

She looked for the person in the face.

But the monster got in the way.

The night was quiet. A few cars brushed through the puddles left behind by the earlier rain but the streets were largely empty, as though the town was taking a rest after the excesses of the night before. A few bottles and cans that had escaped the notice of the day's cleaning crew lay in the horseshoe flowerbed on the promenade and acted as a reminder of the reason for the headaches that each girl bewailed as she arrived at their gathering point. Chloe was the last to join them. She looked as if she had only just climbed out of bed. Her hair stood up in a wild and woolly afro and her black eyes were only half open.

'God, I'm a miserable sinner,' she groaned and drew in a lungful of cigarette smoke, as if to find salvation there. 'When I was a kid my mammy always told me that anyone who stayed in bed all day would burn in hell.'

Pix crowed with laughter and danced round her like a firefly. 'Frigging right too, you lazy bastard.'

Chloe swatted a large paw at her, but Pix dodged it effortlessly.

Jodie wondered what the tiny girl was on tonight. It had her flying high, whatever it was. Or maybe it was just the memory of the fight the night before. Still fizzing in her blood.

Danielle put an arm around Chloe and gave her a hug. 'You'll feel better when we get moving. A few beers will wake you up.' She glanced across at Jodie with an expectant grin. 'Any chance?'

'Don't you lot ever have any money?' Jodie snapped.

'Not after last night,' Chloe moaned and slumped down on to the flowerbed wall. She tugged half-heartedly at a wallflower plant and seemed surprised when it came up in her hand. 'I even drank next week's rent money. But hell, it was worth it. I was so tanked up, I decked a kid proper after the police had gone. Just for the hell of it.'

Jodie sat down next to her. 'You're a nutter, you know that. One of these days you'll get yourself killed. Glassed in a pub or something.'

'Is that what happened to you?' Kit asked. 'Got your face cut up, did you?'

'Not exactly.'

'Naah, she cut herself shaving,' Marianne joked and they all laughed.

Pix was bouncing on her toes. 'Tell us what bastard did it, Jode, and we'll sort them out for you.'

Jodie had the photographs in her pocket. That's all it would take. One word and the girl was dogmeat. One word.

But what would that make her?

One of them. An eye for an eye and a tooth for . . . The temptation swirled like the wine of last night in her stomach and its fumes misted her mind, so that she plunged her hand into her pocket, fingers curled around the six photographs. Twenty-five pounds in five crisp notes sat in the other pocket. A bounty. To the winner the spoils. Using the photograph, they could find her in a matter of hours.

She ached inside she wanted it so badly. The photographs seemed to swell in her hand and her skin could feel the imprint of the face on her palm.

She turned to Pix. 'Thanks for the offer. But I do my own sorting out.'

'Whatever. Just a thought.'

Jodie stood up. 'I don't need those thoughts. Come on, let's go buy that beer.'

'Sounds good to me.'

But then everything would sound good to Pix right now. Whatever it was at home that drove her on to the streets each night, it was drowned in the seductive flow of adrenalin and chemicals that was pumping through her veins. Jodie recalled the scene of the night before, the infectious excitement that raced and raged through the crowd as they bayed for blood, an infection that left no one untouched. No one free from its gut-churning thrill. Herself included.

Suddenly she wanted none of it.

Gang-land bravado was never going to work for her. She had thought it would. That she could make use of it without becoming tainted. But she was wrong. If she stayed, she could not be sure she would not bring out the pictures of the girl in a moment of weakness. Hiding the fear this way was like papering over a crack. It would continue to grow deeper and wider, unseen by passing eyes, until it brought the whole house down.

She pulled the clutch of five pound notes from her pocket and thrust them into Pix's willing hand. 'Here, buy yourselves some joy from me. Thanks for your help.'

Then she turned and walked away, the photographs burning a hole in her pocket.

In the flat, Jodie could not settle. She fiddled in her darkroom, racking up the enlarger to make bigger copies of the face, making it fuzzier and fuzzier until it became an indistinct blur. She wanted it to be as much a blur inside her head, but it stayed pin-sharp, defying all attempts to wipe it from her mind. Or from her nightmares.

She switched off the flat-bed heater under the dish of developer and went into the kitchen where she cooked herself an omelette which she didn't eat. It was just to fill in time. To keep her hands away from again testing the security-chain on the door and her eyes away from the street. She picked up a book, but it was like reading a foreign language. She

drifted around the flat, poking in corners of neglected draw-
ers, uncertain what she was looking for. Until she found it,
that is. Then she knew. At the back of a kitchen cupboard
which was used to give shelter to objects that otherwise had
no home, she came across a pair of table-tennis bats and a
ping-pong ball.

They were Matt's.

Something that was his. She picked up the white ball and held
it lightly in her fingers. It had his initials, MJR, printed in black
pen on its surface, a hangover from the days when he played in a
team. She bounced it on the tiles and it rocketed up to the ceiling
before she could catch it. Its waywardness made her smile, so like
Matt himself with its smooth exterior, its unexpected energy and
a mind of its own. She tucked it inside her pocket, where she
held it tight.

It felt warm and alive in her hand. A part of him.

The doorbell rang downstairs.

Jodie froze.

Matt would have his key. But maybe he was choosing not
to use it.

Hope swooped up as fast as the ping-pong ball had a moment
earlier, but the sound of the door being opened downstairs and
female voices rising from the hallway, followed by light footsteps
on the stairs, snatched it from her grasp.

The girl could have discovered her address. It would not
be hard.

Her throat tightened. A pulse set up a vicious drumbeat in her
ears. She tried to listen for further sounds, but the drumbeat and
a soft swooshing noise in her head, like a curtain being drawn,
obscured all else. Knocking. Behind the curtain noise, dimly, she
could hear knocking. Her legs made no move. She took a deep
breath and forced them to get going. When they reached the
door, she waited for the tightness in her chest to ease its grip
enough to let her speak.

'Who is it?'

She did not recognise her own voice.

'It's me. Anthea. Open the door, will you?'

Jodie undid the bolt, top and bottom, released the security-chain and turned the lock.

'For Christ's sake, Jodie, I've been knocking for ages and it's cold out . . .' She stopped. 'Hell, you don't look too good.'

'I'm fine. Come on in.' She stepped back, allowing Anthea into the flat, and shot the bolts quickly behind her.

Anthea stared at them in surprise, but said nothing. She gave Jodie a hug, sat herself down on the sofa and swung her feet up on to the arm. 'I'm steering clear of swollen ankles,' she explained. 'The curse of pregnancy, I'm told. Morning sickness is bad enough but . . .'

'Anthea, what are you doing here?'

'Visiting.'

'With Mum and Dad?'

'No, they don't know I've come.'

Jodie absorbed that. 'So I assume it's me you've come to see.'

'That's right. With a little sibling advice.' She said it with a smile but her grey eyes held no humour.

Jodie sat down opposite. 'Are you telling me you've driven all this way just to join the queue of people trying to tell me what to do? What was wrong with picking up a telephone?'

'Because I want to see my kid sister's face when I talk. And for her to see mine. It's the only way I'm going to get through to you. Anyway I didn't come by car. I couldn't face all those gung-ho lorries on the motorway, so I took the train.'

Jodie leant back against the cushions, her gaze intent on Anthea and said, 'You know I'm always delighted to see you. So go ahead. Say your piece.'

But Anthea was not ready to be pushed so fast. 'How about a drink first? Something to wash away the grit of the railway tracks.'

'A glass of wine?'

'Good heavens, no. I'm taking this pregnancy seriously. A mug of hot chocolate would soothe the vibrations, don't you think?'

'If you say so.' She stood up and headed for the kitchen.

When she eventually returned with two steaming mugs and

a plate of ginger biscuits, Anthea said, 'I see what Mum means about your hair. A bit drastic.'

'I like it.'

Anthea fluffed up her own dark mane. 'Yours is less trouble to look after, but Henry loves mine this way. Men are real suckers for long hair.'

'Men are suckers for a lot of things.' Like blondes who smile a lot and work in Accounts. 'Talking of men, how is Henry taking everything? Have you told him about the money yet?'

Anthea let loose with a burst of delighted laughter. 'No, I don't have to. I've got it all sorted. Thank God, I can sleep at night now.'

'How did you manage that?'

Anthea held up her left hand. 'See anything?'

The hand was bare. For a moment Jodie did not understand, but then she made the connection. 'No ring.'

'Exactly.'

'So where is the sapphire the size of Wales that Mum told me about? She said you were cock-a-hoop about it.'

'Of course I was. I hocked it immediately for thirty thousand. I got the rest together by selling my gorgeous paintings. They were a real wrench, I can tell you. But at least I'm now out of debt, except for the terrifying mortgage on my flat of course. But I'll shift that when I move in with Henry.'

'But what about the ring? How did you explain its disappearance to him?'

'I told him I'd lost it. It was a bit loose anyway and I made out that it slipped off my finger into the water when we were feeding the ducks on the Serpentine.'

'You conniving bastard.'

'It was easy. Even though he was standing right beside me at the time.'

'And he believed you?'

'Of course.'

'More fool him.'

Anthea laughed. 'I tell you, even I would have believed me. Floods of tears and protestations of misery. Anyway, he's not stupid. He knew he could claim the insurance money and replace the ring, so after the first shock, he wasn't in too much of a panic.

We raised one hell of a fuss searching for it. All pointless, of course, as it was snug as a bug in my pocket. Poor old Henry was mainly concerned that I shouldn't get too upset, for the baby's sake.' She patted her stomach affectionately. 'Nice one, kid.'

Jodie sipped her hot chocolate and stared through the steam at her elder sister. She was every bit as ruthless as the girls on the street. The only difference was that the stakes were higher.

'Anthea, you should be in gaol.'

Her sister chuckled. 'Half the dealers in the City deserve to go to gaol, my sweet innocent, but they've got to catch you first. It gives you one hell of a kick, Jodie. To be right on the edge.'

'*I'll* give you one hell of a kick if you ever do anything like this again.'

'Well, dear sister, I'm glad you think you have the right to tell me what I should or should not do, because that's exactly what I've come to do to you.'

Jodie grimaced. 'Do you really expect me to take any more notice of your words than you do of mine?'

Anthea sat forward, eyes suddenly serious. 'You had damn well better. Unless you want to create more trouble than you bargained for.'

Jodie studied her sister's expression and searched for what was behind it. Whatever it was, it left no room for half measures. Anthea had always been a person of extremes, which was why she had done so well both at school and her job. She committed herself one hundred per cent. So why was she now trying to stop Jodie in her tracks?

'What's going on?' Jodie asked quietly.

'Nothing's going on. I just want you to give up this silly quest of yours. It's ridiculous for you to go on like this, especially when you're starting work again tomorrow. Put the whole business behind you before . . .'

'Before what, Anthea? What do you know that I don't?'

Anthea made a play of giving a convincing laugh. 'Nothing. Don't go turning paranoid on me. It's common sense, that's all. You've got yourself into enough trouble once already, so now is the time to get your act together and move on. For your own sake.' She paused and her eyes scrutinised Jodie's. 'Can't you see that?'

Jodie stood up and moved over to the fire. She knelt down in front of its glowing bars, suddenly chill and in need of warmth. She slipped one hand into her pocket and felt the ball nestling in her palm.

'Who have you been talking to, Anthea?'

'No one. Don't be silly.'

'Matt?'

'No.'

'Dad?'

'No.'

But it came out too fast that time.

'So he's told you that I know what he's up to. Anthea, he's bribing the girl to stay clear of me. Can you believe that?'

'He is only trying to help. Not hurt you.'

'Well he's going about it the wrong way. The only help I need is to be told the girl's name, and *that* he refuses to do.'

'For God's sake, Jodie, don't go over the top. You'll end up splitting the family over this.'

Jodie stared at her. 'Is that what you meant when you said I would be creating more trouble than I bargained for?'

Anthea nodded, but looked away, fixing her gaze on the fire.

'But Dad is not in a position to tell me what to do any more, and he knows it.'

'I am aware of that, Jodie. But this goes deeper than you realise.'

Jodie took a slow breath, then rose to her feet and started to prowl back and forth in front of the fire. 'You bet it goes deeper. Much deeper. You think it's just a silly fixation that I can drop if you come down here and give me a good talking to. Well, you're wrong, Anthea, wrong.'

Jodie tightened her grip on the ball. 'Fear is not like that. It's irrational. You can't argue with it. It sinks its teeth into all sorts of hidden monsters that are lurking in the swamps of our psyche. For me, there was one particularly gruesome creature that this recent attack joined forces with.' She stopped pacing and came to a standstill in front of her sister. 'And I don't intend to "move on" until I have rid myself of them.'

For a moment, neither of them said anything. But the silence united them, rather than divided them. Anthea took a few sips of her drink and said quietly, 'You always kept things to yourself. Even when you were a snotty little kid. If you've got monsters hidden away, you never let on about them. Not even to me. Oh, I know you were a bit wild sometimes and if Dad said white, you said black, but I saw that as normal teenage angst.'

Jodie smiled. 'You were too busy getting yourself to Cambridge to notice.'

'Yes, that's true. But I thought you were just reacting to trying to live up to Dad and his impossible standards.'

'Weren't you ever bullied at school?'

Anthea stared at her, eyes wide with surprise. 'No, I wasn't. Good God, is that what this is about?'

'You were the headmaster's daughter, the same as I was. How come you avoided it and I didn't?'

'That's easy. Don't you remember my best friend all the way through school?'

'Dumptruck Diana. Of course. The biggest girl on the planet.'

'Exactly. No one would dare lay a finger on me, though I did get the occasional bitchy remark, but nothing more. Are you telling me you were victimised because of who Dad was?'

'Call it what you want. Victimised, bullied, decked, flattened, reduced to a screaming jelly. Not that I ever gave the bastards the satisfaction of hearing my screams. They were locked inside.' In her pocket her fingers were twisting the ball round and round, spinning its smooth, soothing surface against her skin.

'Christ, Jodie, I'm sorry. I never knew.'

Jodie shrugged. 'No one did. I found my own way out of it eventually. My own stupid pride did the rest of the damage. Too bloody stubborn to admit I was shit-scared, let alone look that fear in the face. Now, when it's too late, I can see what a dumb fool I was, but back then I was too busy proving that I could hack it.' The image of Holly Dickinson cowering with her kitten rose unwelcome in her mind. Even more unwelcome were the sudden tears she saw in her sister's eyes. She sat down on the sofa beside her and took hold of her hand. 'Hey, lighten up.' She threw in a reassuring smile. 'I'm still in one piece. And making life hard for everyone, just to prove it.'

'I wish I'd known, Jodie. I could have helped.'

'Help me now instead.'

Immediately the grey eyes looked away. 'I can't.'

'Can't or won't?'

Anthea withdrew her hand. 'This is foolishness, Jodie. What will you do to this girl when you find her? Sink to her level, I suppose, and kick the shit out of her.'

'No. No violence. I just need to talk to her.' She ran a hand roughly through her cropped hair. 'She's not a monster, I know that. She's just a vicious gangland girl who takes sadistic pleasure in terrorising others. I have no doubt that she is riddled with problems and monsters of her own. But I don't want to know about them. I want to exorcise my own fear, and to do that I need to confront her. It's that simple.'

'Nothing is ever simple, Jodie.'

'Will you help me?'

'I am not going to be responsible for your being beaten up again. That's final. So please, just be sensible and give up this crazy notion.'

Abruptly Jodie rose to her feet, hurt by her sister's refusal. 'I'm going to bed now. First day of work tomorrow. You're welcome to the spare room if you want it.'

'Thanks,' Anthea sighed. 'What time are you expecting Matt back?'

'Ask him that.'

Anthea looked up, struck by the bleakness of the words, but Jodie left the room before her sister could comment. In the privacy of her own bedroom, she lifted the ball from her pocket and held it, smooth and silent, against her cheek, then laid it gently on Matt's pillow.

23

Anthea was woken by sounds she did not recognise. She opened her eyes and found herself in a room totally unfamiliar. Faces all around her.

And then it came back to her. Jodie.

Oh shit.

Shit.

For God's sake, Jodie, just drop it.

She rolled on to her back and stroked her swelling stomach in slow rhythmic movements to calm herself. Henry said she mustn't get upset. Henry, sweetheart, I promise I'll never get upset again. Damn shame about the sapphire ring, but the forty-thousand-pound millstone has gone. So I'm staying calm. She smiled, blew him a kiss and took to studying the photographs on the walls around her. A touch disturbing, so many strangers' eyes looking at her in bed, but she had to admit some of them were very striking. She had always known Jodie was good, somehow able to make you look at familiar things with fresh eyes, and that's what she had done with a few of these girls. She had caught expressions that could pierce your armour, and body language that said more than any words.

The front door of the flat slammed.

Jodie had gone to work. Anthea thought about the day ahead for her sister and sent up a prayer for her safety.

Oh Jodie, don't do this.

Poor Dad. Going about it all wrong. Doing his utmost to head her off. But his interference was only managing to make her more determined. What a nightmare! And talking of nightmares, that was one mother of a scream Jodie let rip in the night. And no

Matt to comfort the poor kid. Anthea wondered exactly what had brought the curtain down on that partnership. They had seemed so wrapped up in each other, but maybe now, Jodie was too wrapped up in herself. A guy can only take so much.

She continued to stroke her stomach and returned her thoughts to her own guy. Henry Peter Mackintosh. Peter was an appropriate name for him. Her Rock. She was sick to death of the flimsy flotsam she had been floating round with, and was ready to anchor herself to his solid granite. She had it all planned. She would take maternity leave for three months, but if by chance she found she did not fancy returning wholeheartedly to the rat-race, she could stay with Baby playing Earth Mother and just dabble at business from home. Maybe she would devote her time to growing flowers and organic vegetables to create a healing and healthy cosmos for her child.

Who was she kidding?

She chuckled to herself, then placed a kiss on the tip of her finger and transferred it to her stomach. Thank you, Baby, for being there. Henry was ecstatic. He had never had children by either of his previous wives. Bitches the pair of them. And just when he thought his sperm-count was down to a big fat zero, up pops Junior. The fact that it wasn't his sperm that did the trick was something he would never know. Now he thinks he's Mr Sex Superman and can't leave it alone. Anthea imagined him alone in their bed and wondered if he was at it now on his own. He preferred it in the morning. Was altogether better at it after a night's sleep. Well, she'd be back this evening and would make it up to him then. She'd put the leather underwear on and that would get him going.

In no hurry to get up, she snuggled down further, seeking the warmth of the duvet and wishing it had a higher tog-rating, her arms wrapped around her stomach. Just before she drifted into the tunnel of sleep, her mind again threw up the random thought, 'Shame about my ring.'

It was dark by the time her mother dropped her at the car park. The rain was blowing in fits and starts against the windscreen and Anthea wished she had brought an umbrella. She hated the things normally and avoided them like the plague, but when you're carless and pregnant, there are always exceptions that prove the rule.

'It was lovely to see you, darling,' her mother cooed, 'and such a surprise. How sweet of you to come down to wish us all a happy New Year.'

'A bit belated, but I do mean it. For all of you.'

'I know you do and I appreciate the thought.' Her mother leaned over and kissed her. 'And I can't tell you how pleased I am that you've sorted out your financial problems. It's good of your firm to lend you the money. That's a huge weight off my mind.'

Anthea hugged her. 'I'm worth every penny of it.'

'Of course you are. And you make sure you take good care of that grandchild of mine. No smoking, drinking or late nights. And don't work too hard or get too stressed because . . .'

'Mum, I'm a big girl now. I do know what to do. I'm reading all the books and behaving myself perfectly.'

'Good, I'm glad to hear it. And tell Henry to as well.'

'To what? Behave himself perfectly?'

'Yes. You tell him that from me. Not too much you-know-what.'

Anthea laughed. If it had not been so dark, she was certain she would have seen a blush on her mother's cheeks. 'Do you mean sex?' she asked, just to be awkward.

'Yes, I do. You see, love, it's not good for the baby at this stage.'

'Mum, you have to be joking.'

'No, I certainly am not. Just be careful. Promise me.'

Anthea hugged her. 'Okay, I promise we'll be careful.' Perhaps she would skip the leather gear tonight. She started to climb out of the car.

'Anthea, I'm sorry if your father was a bit, well . . . off. He's worrying about things.'

'Don't fret about it, Mum. I understand. Thanks for the lift.'

She pulled up her collar and ran for the steps into the *Westonport Gazette*'s office. As she did so, she noticed Jodie's Mini parked at the far end. Good, that meant she would not have to hang around and should be able to catch the six-forty train. But she could not leave without one last try.

In reception, a crumpled overweight figure with a pencil sticking out of his mouth took one look at her, removed the pencil and said, 'You must be Jodie Buxton's sister.' He smiled and his face grew younger, more effective than any face-lift. 'Welcome to the *Gazette*. I'm Roy Dunmore, the news-editor.'

She shook hands. His was firm and brisk. 'Hello, I'm Anthea Courtney. As you rightly guessed, I am Jodie's sister. I've just come to say goodbye to her before I head back to London.' She gave him a big smile. 'Don't worry, I won't distract her from her work for more than a few moments.'

He opened the door that led to the main offices. 'Feel free, my dear. She's been hard at it all day and deserves a break.' He escorted her along a corridor.

'How did it go? The first day back at work, I mean. I was quite nervous for her.'

'Then you don't know your sister. She's always very profes-sional. If she does have a few personal problems right now, she knows how to leave them at the door.' He shook his grey head, eyes sharp and alert. 'Don't you agree?'

Anthea was careful. 'Of course, that goes without saying. Photography always comes first with her.'

He nodded, satisfied, and turned to a woman who was approaching him with a handful of papers. 'Nice to meet you, Anthea. The photographic department is down there on the left,' he said and replaced the pencil in his mouth. She headed in the direction he had indicated and at the end of the corridor found a door marked *Photographic*. She pushed it open.

Jodie was, as Dunmore said, hard at it. She was bent over, feeding the leader of a film strip into a big brute of a machine with Fuji Minilab advertising its function on the side. Nearer the door, an attractive black girl was sitting at a keyboard and animatedly telling a screen that it did not know its arse from its elbow.

'Hello,' Anthea said.

Jodie swung round in surprise.

Her eyes were as grey as dust. Anthea wondered just how much it had cost her to get herself through the day.

'Anthea, what on earth are you doing here?' She added a smile of welcome, but it didn't fit easily.

'Just came by to say goodbye. I'm pushing off back up to London. Henry is expecting me home tonight.'

'So soon?' Jodie pressed a button on the machine, and remembered her manners. 'Kerry, this is my sister Anthea.'

'That's obvious,' Kerry smiled up at Anthea. 'Not into the shorn-lamb look yourself though, I see.'

'No, damn right I'm not. It changes her, doesn't it? Gave me a shock at first. It must have come as a surprise to you lot here as well.'

'Oh, we're used to that. A lot of things about Jodie come as a surprise.'

'Do you mind not talking about me as if I were not in the room.'

They laughed and Kerry returned to her keyboard.

'How was your day?' Jodie asked, and led the way over to the other side of the room, where she started threading a strip of negatives into a small machine that instantly threw up on a screen a series of pictures of a wall crushed by a fallen tree.

'I spoke to Dad.'

'I don't suppose he came up with any names.'

'No, he didn't. But he said that he wanted you to know that he does not believe the girl you are seeking attends his school. If she did, he says, word would have spread around and he'd have heard something.'

Jodie stopped running the negatives and looked round at her sister. 'Who does he think he's kidding? No way would he, of all people, hear a whisper of what was going on. And anyway, if he says she doesn't go to his school, that just proves he knows who she is.'

'No, Jodie, I really do think you're wrong about that.'

Jodie frowned, picked up a pair of scissors and snipped the sprocket hole on the picture she had chosen. 'Why on earth are you being so negative?' One side of her mouth flicked a small smile and Anthea was not sure if it was meant as a photographer's joke.

'Anyway,' she said breezily, 'Henry is expecting me on the six-forty train, so I can't stay long, but I just wanted to see how you got on today. A bit rough, was it?'

Jodie stayed bent over her machine. 'Not too bad.'

In the silence that followed, Anthea decided there was no point beating about the bush. Her sister was not in the mood for subtle hints. 'Okay, how about this for an idea? I suggest you ask Dunmore for another week off. You honestly look like shit and need a break from everything to do with Westonport. So come up and stay in my flat. I'm at Henry's most of the time, so you wouldn't be crowded or anything. A different place might give you a different perspective.'

To her relief, Jodie nodded. 'Yes, I have thought of that. Leaving here, I mean.' She looked hard at Anthea. 'Did Dad put you up to this?'

'Of course not.'

Jodie smiled, unconvinced. 'But it's no good unless I've first chucked out my demons or I'll just take them with me. So thanks for the offer, but no. I'll stick it out here.'

'Oh hell, Jodie, you can be a stubborn little sod when you want to be.'

Jodie came over and hugged her sister. 'Get your tubby little tummy back where it belongs.' She glanced at her watch. 'Shall I drive you over to the station?'

'That would be great, if you've got the time. It's bucketing down with rain out there.' A few more minutes alone together might help. It was always easier to talk inside the cocoon of a car.

Jodie dug a set of keys out of the bag on her desk. 'Here, go and open up. I'll be through in just a couple of minutes.'

Anthea took them and set off for the car park.

She was feeling tired. Like a lead weight was balanced on her head. She knew it was because of the pregnancy and was frightened she had overdone things a bit, built up too many toxins in her bloodstream. Trauma with both father and sister in one day was more than poor little Junior could be expected to put up with.

'We'll sleep in peace on the train,' she promised as she patted her stomach, and scurried through the rain.

She had unlocked the passenger door and was cursing her sister's penchant for such a low car, when a sharp pain thudded through her kidneys. She gave a low moan and the pain came again. This time she realised it was a blow from behind. She tried to turn, but a strong hand grabbed the back of her neck and thrust her down face-first on to the front seat.

A female voice behind her hissed, 'Get off my back, bitch. This is a warning. Get off or I'll throw you off.'

Then the hand was gone. Anthea twisted her head to one side to enable her to breathe and was promptly sick on the seat.

'Don't look so sulky. You are not moving out of that bed until your blood pressure is down. And don't you even think of sweet-talking the doctor into letting you leave here.' It was Jodie. Sitting on the coverlet, watching her like a hawk, her eyes so full of concern that Anthea felt a fraud.

'But I feel fine. Really I do.'

'That's not what the machine says.'

'What do machines know!'

The hospital bed was unnecessary, Anthea was sure, but they were insisting. She only agreed because of the baby. The nagging ache in her back was not worth this fuss.

'Don't you go getting yourself all worked up over this, Jodie. You're sitting there like butter wouldn't melt in your mouth, but don't think you're fooling me. I know you're furious inside.'

'Aren't you?'

'No, of course I'm not.'

Jodie smiled. 'Good. That means your blood pressure will be coming down.'

'To hell with my blood pressure. The point is that this girl only came to tell you to leave her alone. *Get off my back, bitch*, she said. So steer clear of her, and that will be an end to it. Your involvement is the problem here. Surely now you can see how ludicrous is your refusal to drop this vendetta.'

Jodie picked up her sister's hand and chafed it gently between her own. 'Anthea, I'm so sorry this happened. But you are my sister, my only sister, and the child you are carrying is my niece or nephew, so do you really think I can stand by and see you attacked by . . .'

'Hardly "attacked". More like a couple of medium-sized thumps. I get as much on the Circle Line during rush-hour every morning. Nothing to get cheesed off about. It's quite obvious that it was meant to startle rather than to hurt.'

'You don't end up in hospital because you're startled.'

'Well, okay, but she didn't know I was pregnant, did she?'

Jodie's blue eyes held Anthea's and they were not fooled by her display of equanimity.

'No, she didn't know that. Nor who you were. It's obvious that she mistook you for me, and I blame myself for that. I have been so watchful of danger to myself, but it didn't occur to me that you could be at risk. Just because we look the same. And of course the sadistic bastard doesn't know I've cut my hair.' She squeezed her sister's hand. 'You are almost defending her. How can you act so indifferent?'

Anthea registered the word 'act'.

'Because I have more sense than you, that's why, my silly sister. I have no wish to stir up trouble, which is exactly what you are doing. For Christ's sake, I warned you to leave it alone.'

'I know. I'm sorry.' Jodie looked utterly miserable. 'It's my fault you're in here.'

'So listen to me.'

Suddenly Jodie smiled, but it did not remove the anger from the blue eyes. 'That's enough talk about it. You must relax and rest now.'

'I'm not an invalid.'

'Until your blood pressure is down to normal, that's exactly what you are and don't you forget it. I promised Henry when I rang him that I would make sure you stayed put.' She smiled again and this time it reached her eyes. 'He was desperate to rush down here to mop your fevered brow. But I did what you said and told him to wait until tomorrow. The poor man was quaking with worry, I could hear it in his voice.'

'For the baby?'

Jodie leant forward and kissed her sister. 'No, for you, silly.'

Anthea grinned like a cat with its head in the ice-cream tub. 'Good.'

Jodie reached out and laid a hand on top of the coverlet over her sister's stomach. 'You take good care of Junior. Get some rest now because Mum and Dad will be here soon. A night's sleep will sort you out before Henry arrives in the morning.'

Anthea groaned, shut her eyes and wished she could tell her sister to go and sort out that bloody girl.

24

Jodie's anger was out of control. She could hear it thudding, loud and implacable, in her ears as she ran through the maze of hospital corridors. It tore free the restraints she had clamped over her mind and her tongue at her sister's bedside and unleashed a fireball of fury inside her. Anthea's baby could have died.

Monster.

Mutant.

Murderer.

'You fucking witch,' she cried out.

A passing nurse held out a hand to stop her, but she pushed it aside. Faces came and went, voices lingered, but nothing encroached. She took stairs at speed, raced past the lifts, the main entrance in sight. Her father was standing there. Tall and grey, his expression as unbending as his spine. Beside him her mother was crying into a screwed-up handkerchief. Jodie's heart surged with relief. Now he would tell her. He would name the monster. He could not possibly refuse. Not now.

'Jodie,' her mother sobbed and attached herself to her daughter's arm. 'How is she?'

'Not too bad.' Her eyes fixed on her father's.

'And the baby?' her mother pressed on.

'They say it's okay.'

'Thank God for that. Since you rang, I've been so worried that she would lose it. It's a delicate stage she's at and . . .'

'Dad, tell me her name.'

'Jodie, I have already told you, I don't know who she is.' His eyes looked at her with such a weight of sadness that for a moment the shock of it silenced the roaring in her ears.

'No, Dad, don't.'

'You're upset. Calm down and we can talk properly. I have your interest at heart but you're not thinking straight, so you can't see it.'

'Tell me her name.'

'I don't know it.'

'She has attacked both your daughters and yet still you protect her. What kind of a father are you, for Christ's sake?'

'Stop shouting, Jodie.'

'People are looking,' her mother muttered awkwardly.

'Answer me, Dad. What kind of father are you?'

He frowned and turned away, but only briefly. When he looked back, the flash of anger on his face came as a surprise and the way his hand seized hold of her upper arm. He gave it a sharp shake, exactly as he used to when she was a child.

'Haven't you done enough?' he demanded. 'If it weren't for you and your obsession, this would never have happened. I may not have been the world's perfect parent, but I have worked hard for my family and I love my daughters enough to know what's best for them and to know how to protect them.'

'That's not love. That's control.'

'Jodie, please,' her mother begged. 'Your father is right. Listen to him.'

Jodie knew it was pointless. She shook herself free of them and ran out of the hospital.

The moment she was outside in the car park, the darkness closed in on her. The monster leapt back in her head and she tore at her hair, but was too late to get her fingers round its throat. An engine started up nearby with a snarl. Footsteps to one side made her quicken her pace. She reached the Mini and circled it warily before putting the key in the lock, but as she did so, a female voice behind her made her freeze.

'Do you have change for fifty pence?'

Jodie looked at her blankly.

'For the machine,' the woman explained.

Don't creep up on me, you stupid creature.

'No,' she said and shut herself in her car. She over-revved

the engine and drove for the exit. She was forced to wait for an ambulance to trundle past to the casualty unit and was just about to pull out on to the dark and damp stretch of the main road, when a car's tyres screeched round the corner in the wet. It pulled to a halt in front of her, blocking her path. Headlights bored straight into her skull, blinding her, bleaching out all thought. A door slammed. Knuckles rapped on her window, a voice shouted. Her mind panicked.

She thrust the gear lever into reverse.

Calm, keep calm.

This was her chance. The monster was out of its lair. Its face behind the rain on her window, its voice shouting words she could not hear. Now was the time to confront it.

In the dark?

Alone?

Her fingers undid the lock. With a sudden jerk of her foot, she kicked open the door and heard a grunt as it impacted on the body outside. But it gave her the moment she needed. She was out of the car and facing the dark figure before it had time to recover. Silhouetted against the headlights, it was even taller than she remembered. She dashed the rain from her eyes.

'You bitch,' she screamed. 'You hurt Anthea. You bitch, you BITCH.'

Hands seized her. She struggled, kicked, punched, but the hands would not let her go. Hot breath raked her face. The monster was about to devour her.

And then the voice penetrated. The wall of noise in her head opened up a crack and let in the words. 'It's all right, Jodie. It's me. Stop fighting. You're safe.'

It was not the monster.

She gave a whimper of relief and let the arms hold her tight. It was Matt.

His fingers stroked the taut curve of her hip-bone. Over and over. They had not even got as far as the bedroom but were lying on the rug in front of the fire. Her bare skin felt warm and satisfied, soothed to a state of somnolence that was seeping up into her mind. She could feel her brain-cells shutting down one by one, as if the batteries had been removed. Her head was resting on the cushion of Matt's shoulder, his naked skin as familiar as her own, and she wondered if he could read her thoughts as easily as she could hear the thud of his heart.

'Jodie,' he said firmly.

'Mmm?'

'Time to wake up.'

Was she asleep? Drifting in a dream world where reality could not intrude. Not even monsters could sneak in right now.

'Mmm.' She buried her face in the hollow of his neck and he laughed.

'Ostrich,' he murmured and kissed her hair.

She rolled over on to her back. 'Okay, so what now?'

'Now you talk.'

She didn't want to talk. Talking opened gates that were safer shut. 'I missed you,' was all she said.

He raised himself on one elbow and gazed down at her, grey eyes dark and disturbed. 'I'm sorry, Jodie. Sorry I left. It was all wrong but at the time I thought I had lost you. You had gone so far away. I had hung on and hung on hoping that we could still make something work for us, but that night I believed our relationship meant nothing to you any more.'

'No, Matt, no, I . . .'

'Ssh,' he soothed a finger over her lips. 'When I saw Jack this evening and he said there had been another attack in the car park and I thought it was you, I nearly went out of my mind. How could I have abandoned you to such danger?'

'Matt, we both made mistakes.'

'Not any more, I promise you, my darling. I am going to wring that bloody girl's neck with my own bare hands.'

It was as if a dead weight had suddenly been lifted off her chest. Her lungs expanded freely for the first time in months, the air tasting as sweet as Maltesers. Only now did she realise how lonely she had been since the attack.

'You're amazing, do you know that?'

'Wait till you see me walk on water,' he said and smiled. 'But I was blind, Jodie. I thought that if I gave you any encouragement in this obsession, it would just get worse and eat you up inside.'

'I know, Matt. You did try to help.'

'But nothing worked. You were in your own private hell and there was not a damn thing I could do about it.'

'I admit I'm a head-case.'

'A total nutcase. But I love you and there is not a damn thing I can do about that either.'

The expression in his solemn grey eyes caught at her throat. She lifted his hand and placed a kiss on its palm.

'But Jodie, you were pushing me so far away. I thought it was time for me to leave.'

'Where did you go?' Please God, no blondes.

'To Bournemouth. Over Christmas, John Tarrant had offered me a job on the local rag. I went down there yesterday to accept.'

So no blondes.

But no Matt.

'I see.'

He bent lower and kissed her breast. 'No, you don't see at all, my own sweet nutcase. That was then. This is now. And this,' he kissed her other breast, 'is where I intend to stay.'

She breathed again.

'Now tell me what's going on. Why was Anthea attacked?'

The talking had done it. Just as she had known it would. The gates had opened and the world's hobnail boots were marching in. She sat up.

'The girl mistook her for me. She was getting into my Mini in the car park and it was dark. Matt, she or the baby could have been seriously hurt.' She shivered and nudged nearer the fire.

There was a silence while their minds edged round what might have been.

'But they are both going to be okay, the medicos say,' Jodie continued after a moment. 'Her blood pressure is a bit high, that's all, so they're keeping her in overnight.'

'Thank God for that. But Jodie, it's that sadist of a girl who is the one responsible. Not you.'

Jodie shrugged.

He moved to her side, his bare shoulder almost but not quite touching hers. 'Have you any idea yet who she is?'

Jodie stood up, disappeared into her dark-room and returned

a moment later. She dropped the photograph on his lap, huddled up on the rug again and wrapped her arms around her legs, chin on her knees. It stopped her teeth chattering.

'It's out of focus, but it's her.'

He did not ask how she knew.

'Her name?'

She shook her head.

'Address?'

'No.'

He thought in silence for several minutes. 'Okay, you've got your own pack of bloodhounds, so you use that gang you're so fond of to find her. With this photograph, it shouldn't be a problem.' He turned his head and looked at her. 'But you've considered that already, I assume.'

'Yes. I have. And I came this close.' She held her finger and thumb a hair's breadth apart.

'But?'

'But no. I couldn't.'

He waited for more. She took her time.

'If I asked them to find her for me, I couldn't guarantee they would not put the boot in first. They're a trigger-happy bunch. And even if they did find her and leave her unharmed, or even if they just made enquiries to discover her name, she would hear about it and, being the kind of creature she is, she would come after them. With her own gang in full warpaint.' Jodie rubbed her hands fiercely up and down her shins. 'I couldn't. Matt, I just couldn't.'

'It's okay,' he said gently.

'I know you think they're street-scum. But they're not. These are kids. They've gone off the rails because society has let them down. It's too soft on them. And on their parents.'

'Surely the wild and wicked Jodie Buxton is not advocating zero tolerance.'

She managed a smile of sorts. 'Maybe not that far. But adolescent crime is frightening. It's out of control, Matt. These kids take their hurt and anger out on others and get away with it. Of course they gather into packs. That's their method of survival. They provide the security for each other that their families lack.'

Matt studied her profile, then ran a hand slowly down her slender back, stroking each rib that had been broken. The touch of it eased some of the tension out of her. He said softly, 'You felt safe with them, didn't you?'

She nodded.

'I understand, Jodie. I couldn't protect you out on the street the way they did, and I presume it was with their help that you took this picture.' He flicked the girl in the face with his finger.

'It was because I was with them that I found her, yes.'

He stared rigidly at the photograph in his hand, watching it start to curl in the heat from the fire, and Jodie suddenly realised how angry he was. His soft talk was only skin-deep. She put out a hand and touched his arm, but by the time he turned to her, the anger was hidden. The only trace was a tension around his eyes, a shallow furrow between his brows.

'Okay, Jodie.' He glanced at the clock on his desk. 'It's nearly eight o'clock now. The night is young. Let's track this bastard down.'

The monster roused itself in her head.

'Matt, I want you to know I'm sorry I shut you out before.'

He leaned over and kissed her cheek. 'You can't get rid of me that easily, you should know that by now.'

She gazed at the fire, its glowing bars like a pair of burning lips poised to open up and swallow her. 'I believed that if you knew what was in my head, you wouldn't love me any more. They weren't nice thoughts. Not right for normal people.'

'That just goes to prove how wrong you can be. And anyway, since when have you been normal people?' He smiled and wrapped an arm around her shoulders.

She leant her cheek against his warm skin. 'Matt, I have an idea where we can start.'

The screen went blank. Jodie regarded its dead face with animosity and was just cursing its contrariness when it came back to life. She rewarded it with a smile.

'This is too recent.'

Matt studied the date at the top of the newspaper page that was displayed on screen. It was the third of July, eighteen months ago. He nodded. 'Yes, let's go back further.' His fingers scrolled back the film.

They had spent nearly an hour at it already in the newspaper offices. Jodie was beginning to wonder if her mother had made a mistake. *Two years ago*, she had said, *maybe a bit more*. To be on the safe side, they had started by checking the *Gazette*'s pages from as far back as two and a half years earlier, day by day for a year, over three hundred editions of them. Nothing. No mention of this particular house-fire.

Matt threaded another spool of microfilm through the gate and a new front page was thrown up on the screen. This time the date said three years ago. They started again. Surely her mother couldn't be *that* wrong. Jodie frowned and concentrated on the screen. Fires came and went, but not the one they were searching for. No Sheila Richards in widow's weeds. No hostile glare to camera. What was concealed behind those eyes? They had recognised the photograph of the girl, of that Jodie was certain, but what more did she know? The hunt through the *Gazette*'s archives was a stab in the dark.

The dark. It wound itself through her mind like the film through the viewing machine. It hung all around her at the deserted desks, its shadows skimming and shifting towards . . .

Stop it.

She crushed a hand against her forehead.

Stop.

The darkness cleared. An idea slid smoothly into its place.

The librarian's filing system was known to be a law unto herself. It was down in the basement. Matt punched the security code-number into the keypad and they opened the door into a long narrow room that smelt of dust and paper, and which contained a daunting array of metal shelving, all neatly stacked with files of cuttings and photographs that the *Gazette* had run. The problem was, where to start.

The box files were red, blue or black, but if there was some kind of colour coding, its significance was elusive. Starting at opposite ends, they cruised one row and met in the middle.

'Alphabetical,' Matt declared and headed for the section under 'F'.

They both spotted it at once. A box file, appropriately red, perched between a blue one labelled FESTIVALS and a black one labelled FLOODS. FIRES was printed in block capitals on its spine. Matt lifted it down and flicked open its lid. It was divided into two; one half stories, the other half photographs.

'Here,' Matt said and handed her the bundle of photographs. 'I'll scan through the cuttings. It's bound to be here.'

But it wasn't. They went through them a second time but it did not alter the fact that it was not there. Jodie came across her own picture of the science-block inferno and she lingered for a moment, but it kicked a dull thud of pain into life at the base of her skull, so she turned its face over. The date was written in neat handwriting on the back of each photograph, but that did not help them.

'It was a fire, for Christ's sake,' Matt exclaimed. 'So why isn't it here?'

Jodie dumped her bundle back in the file. 'Okay, so let's think of alternatives.' She tapped the side of her head, as if to speed up its activity. 'How about DEATHS?'

'Or SUICIDES.'

'ARSON.'

'ALCOHOL.'

They tried them all. As well as ACCIDENTS and SMALL BUSINESSES, in the hope of some reference to the jewellery business.

Zilch.

At the end of forty minutes they were no further forward.

'It's back to page-by-page scanning on the film records, I'm afraid,' Matt said. 'Let's get a coffee and start again upstairs. Don't look so downhearted. We will find it. A story like that must have been covered by the *Gazette*.'

'But where?'

'Your mother obviously got the date all wrong. We will just go back even further.'

Jodie sighed and looked once more along the shelves. 'It's here somewhere, damn it.'

She walked impatiently along one of the rows to the far end

and was about to turn back along the next, when she passed half a dozen cardboared boxes stacked against the wall. She had vaguely noticed them before and paid them scant attention. But now she was desperate. She went over and examined them more closely. On the side of each one was scrawled, 'Miscellaneous'.

'Matt,' she called.

'Anything?'

'Maybe.'

She opened the first box.

It was in the third box, Matt found it. In an envelope marked FATALITIES OF FIRES. There were twelve photographs in it. One was of a man's face, loose-lipped with large unpleasant eyes and a drinker's veined nose. On the back of the picture was written 'George Richards, 12 May 1994'. Nearly four years ago.

Within minutes they were upstairs and had the story on screen.

FATAL FIRE

Last night fire tragically claimed the life
of local jeweller, George Richards, at his
home in Stanwell Road, Westonport. Fire
crews were called out at 11.45pm but were
unable to save Mr Richards, who had been
asleep in a downstairs room. First reports
indicate that this was where the fire
started. Considerable damage was done to
the rest of the house. Mr Richards leaves
a widow and two children.

Jodie was disappointed. It added little new. All that work for nothing. She pushed back her chair and glared round the vacant desks, as if the absent reporters had let her down.

'Now where?'

But Matt was not listening. He was continuing to scroll through the microfilm.

'It's no good, Matt. We've wasted enough time here.' The emptiness of the building was getting to her.

He glanced over his shoulder, took in the expression on her face and nodded. 'Two minutes, that's all.'

'What are you hunting for?'

'Didn't your mother say the fire was caused by Richards setting fire to the alcohol on his clothes? Probably with a cigarette.'

'Yes, she did.'

'How did she know?'

'Of course. The inquest report.'

'That's what I'm looking for.'

It did not take long. A small article was tucked away at the bottom of an inside page, detailing the coroner's comments. Jodie's mother had been right. High levels of alcohol in his blood, whisky over his clothes and chair, ignited by a cigarette or by the lighter found at his side. Verdict of accidental death.

'Well, that proves your mother's memory was correct. Mrs Richards might have told her about it two years ago, but it actually happened some time earlier. But none of this exactly helps us, does it?'

He glanced round again at Jodie. Her gaze was fixed on the screen, her blue eyes wide with shock. Her hand was clasped to her mouth. It was shaking.

Matt looked back at the screen. Beside the coroner's report was a small photograph of a dreary woman and her two daughters. It was captioned, 'Mrs Sheila Richards leaves the inquest with her daughters Emma (11yrs) and Sandra (14yrs).' One was fair. The other was dark, with a long aggressive jaw and eyes that were too old for her.

'It's her, isn't it?'

'Yes,' Jodie said quietly. 'It's her.'

25

They were sitting in the car. The street was deserted. Rain blurred the windscreen, making their isolation complete. It was eleven o'clock. Darkness had taken full possession of Stanwell Road, as even the streetlamp at the edge of the patch of grass had given up the struggle and yielded the swings to oblivion.

'Jodie, are you sure you want to do this?'

'I'm sure.'

'Is it wise?'

'Who wants to be wise?'

'There's no reason you can't stay here. I could speak to her alone.'

'No.'

He nodded. 'I thought you would say that.'

She turned to him. His face was obscured in the shadows, so she put her hand across and touched his arm. 'Matt, you don't have to get further involved in this.'

'You're not trying to deprive me of the pleasure of wringing the bloody slut's neck, are you?'

'As if.'

'Good. That's settled.'

She held on to his arm a moment longer, then let it go and released her seatbelt. Her fingers found the door-handle. 'Okay, let's do it.'

She thought the words sounded fine, so was surprised when Matt asked, 'Is it always this bad? Getting out of the car.'

She gave a faint shrug, the movement invisible in the dark, and opened the door. The rain swept over her in a damp blanket, but she welcomed its chill touch fretting against her cheeks. Her blood was heating up. She could feel it in her veins, simmering like milk before it boils over. Matt was at her side before she realised she was standing immobile on the pavement.

The house was in darkness. No light in any window. It loomed grim and silent in front of them. Matt knocked on the door.

They took it in turns for the next ten minutes. The knocker grew warm in their hands and the noise of it triggered a light to come on next door and across the road. But nothing more. Eventually Matt retreated to the roadside, picked up a couple of stones and tossed them both at an upstairs window. One bounced off the wall harmlessly but the other found its target. A loud crack announced success. A light snapped on, a face peered blindly down through the damaged window and the sound of feet soon scurried on the stairs. The skylight above the door was suddenly flooded with light, casting its bright rectangle into the gloom outside, and a voice called out from behind the door, 'Bloody vandals, what the frigging hell do you think you're doing?'

Jodie hardly recognised it as Sheila Richards', it was so full of animation. Only the hostility was familiar.

'Mrs Richards,' she responded curtly, 'it's Jodie Buxton here. I want to speak to you. And to your daughter, Sandra.'

'Go to hell. It's too late at night for talking. Anyway, Sandra doesn't live here no more.'

Jodie and Matt exchanged glances at that unexpected snippet of information.

'Mrs Richards,' Matt said gruffly, 'I am Detective Sergeant Russell and I require your elder daughter's present address. Now please open this door.'

There was a pause. Her voice dropped to a whine. 'I don't know where she's living now. One of you broke my window. I'll . . .'

'The door, Mrs Richards. Unless you want me to call in the CID with their lock-busters.'

The sound of bolts. An angry muttering. Then the door opened a crack. Matt instantly put his shoulder to it and barged past into the hall. No doors slamming in faces this time. Jodie followed more warily, checking doorways for hidden figures. Too late, Sheila Richards realised her mistake.

'Get out of my house, you bastards,' she screamed. 'I'll call the police and have you charged with unlawful . . .'

'Go ahead,' Jodie said. 'There's the phone.'

'Get out of here.'

'I have told you why I've come.'

'You're here to make trouble.' The woman's angular frame was wrapped inside a threadbare towelling dressing-gown that had once been pink. Her eyes were spitting fury. Her breath smelt of beer. Maybe that was the source of her animation. 'Bugger off.' Her hand flashed out and slapped Jodie across the face.

Jodie's head rocked back and by the time she had blinked, Matt had the woman pinned against the wall.

'Count yourself lucky I'm not tearing your scrawny limbs apart for that and tossing them to the buzzards,' he snarled.

The woman's eyes went blank. A stone wall. No fear. A routine she had been through before. Her mouth hung loose, revealing no front teeth in her top or bottom jaw. Jodie wondered who had knocked them out. Her husband? Her daughter?

'Leave her, Matt.'

He tightened his grip. 'I want an answer first.' The vein in his neck was pulsing. Jodie saw the woman look at it.

'Don't make life hard for yourself, Mrs Richards. We don't want to hurt you.'

'Like hell we don't,' Matt growled.

'Your daughter attacked my sister tonight. It was meant for me. My boyfriend here does not take kindly to that.'

'Damn right, I don't.'

The dead eyes stared at him.

'The police are not yet involved,' Jodie continued. 'But if I don't receive some cooperation from you, I intend to call them immediately.'

The woman shifted her gaze. 'You've got no proof, or you'd have called them already.'

Jodie gave her a smile. 'You don't understand, do you? Sergeant Dawson is just waiting for the slightest excuse to pin something on your daughters. He will be in here like a shot with a search warrant.'

A flicker of fear.

What was it? Drugs? Stolen goods? Under Emma's mattress or in her wardrobe?

'Let go of me, you bugger,' she spat out at Matt.

He was still holding her shoulders. He lowered his face close to hers. 'Do you want to argue about this?'

'Mrs Richards, he's very angry. Let's get this over with quickly.' Jodie stepped nearer, but was careful to offer no threat. 'Tell me her address and we'll leave you in peace.' She managed another smile. 'I have no wish to cause trouble for you or Emma.'

'Trouble! That's all you've ever been to my family.'

'Don't you even think of slagging her off,' Matt said fiercely. 'Your daughter is the one who causes all the trouble. She should be locked up and the key thrown away. If you had any decency in you, you wouldn't be defending the slut. You'd be . . .'

'Call him off,' the woman said suddenly. 'Get him off me.'

'Matt.'

'No. She's not getting away with it. Not until I . . .'

'Matt, leave her,' Jodie said sharply. She put a hand out, took the woman's arm and drew her from Matt's grasp. 'There, you're okay. Now, if you want to stay that way and to keep clear of the police, tell me Sandra's address.' She said it gently.

The woman sagged, as though her bones had melted. Her dressing-gown was all that was holding her together. She sat down on the stairs. Jodie sat down beside her and waited.

'I don't have no address, just a phone number.'

'That will do.'

The woman shook her head. 'She'll kill me if I give it to you.'

'I'll kill you if you don't,' Matt snarled.

'Matt, stop it.' She felt the woman's body lean fractionally against her, seeking protection. 'Mrs Richards, what I suggest is this. You ring your daughter now. Tell her I'm here making life difficult for you but that you have refused to give me her number and that I have agreed to leave on condition that she meets me in half an hour in the school yard where she watched the fight on New Year's Eve. Just Sandra and myself alone, no one else.'

The woman turned her face and looked at Jodie. The eyes were scornful. 'You're a fool.'

'Just tell her. And make sure she knows it was my sister she attacked tonight.'

'It's your funeral,' the woman shrugged. She stood up and

walked over to where the telephone sat on a dusty three-legged table. She turned her back on her unwanted visitors, so they could neither see the buttons she pressed nor hear the whispered conversation.

Jodie and Matt waited in silence.

The receiver was replaced. 'She says yes. In the yard in half an hour. She said to tell you to bring a bag with you, because you'll need it to pick up the pieces. I've done what you wanted, now get out, the pair of you.'

They left her standing at the bottom of the stairs, a woman who had forgotten how to do anything but survive.

Outside, the darkness came as a relief. The moment the door closed behind them, Matt said, 'You were right. It worked.'

'The good-cop-bad-cop routine. It always does in films.' Jodie tucked an arm around his waist. 'You were scary.'

'When she slapped you, I would have happily yanked her head off. But where do you stop? When you start, where do you stop?'

'After slaying the monster. That's where.'

Jodie stood alone in the centre of the school playground. The rain had eased to a half-hearted drizzle that was slowly soaking through her clothes. Her teeth were chattering but she chose not to question whether it was from cold or fear. She had been standing there in the pitch dark for nearly an hour.

Damn the girl to hell. The Spanish Inquisition had nothing on her. Where did she learn such exquisite torture?

Her ears were tuned acutely to every sound. In her pocket lay the pencil torch her grandfather had given her that day in the flat. *I don't like to think of those girls laughing at you*, he had said. But not for much longer. She focused on the school's front wall, its long black shadow deeper than the darkness around it, her eyes well adjusted to the night's secrets. The patter of the rain kept her nerves jumping.

But when it came, she almost missed it. A faint scrabbling.

They flowed over the wall like rats scenting blood. Dark flutters of movement that set sick dread clawing at her stomach.

'No guts to come alone, I see,' Jodie said to the figure that approached her across the yard. Others shifted and strutted behind.

'Don't get smart with me, you fuck-head. You didn't really think I'd be that dumb, did you?'

'No. I didn't.'

She could see her now, wrapped in a duffle-coat with hood up against the rain. Tall and broad-shouldered like a swimmer. The shark's eyes just visible in the gloom.

'That kicking I gave you must have scrambled your frigging brains,' the girl said with a sneer. 'Got some kind of death wish, have you? Because I don't like midnight meetings with fuckheads.'

'But you came.'

The girl swaggered closer. 'Sure I came. To tell you this. Don't bugger around with my family. You stay away from them, you hear me?'

'I hear you. You stay away from mine.'

The girl gave a wide, unfriendly smile. 'How was I to know you'd cut your hair? She looked like you. And was getting into your car, the stupid bitch.'

'You're the stupid bitch. She's pregnant and could lose the child. I swear to God I'll have you up for manslaughter if she does.'

The shark's eyes blinked, but that was all. Behind her the rustle of movement tightened, so that Jodie could make out the figures quite distinctly. Five of them. All clad in black. With a jolt she recognised the heavy, slower one and the elusive dancer who had spat in her face. The feel of the spittle slithering down her cheek had left a scar as real as the one on her cheekbone. And Emma. She was there this time, the lower half of her face buried in a scarf. But it was unmistakably her, sheltering in her big sister's shadow.

'Okay, I'm here. So what? You've got ten seconds to say what you got me out on a shitty night like this for.'

'To prove to myself that creatures like you really do exist. That you're not just something I scraped off the bottom of my shoe.'

The girl's fist was pushed in her face. 'You're asking for this down your throat.'

'Thump her.'

'Go on, do it.'

'Put the boot in.'

The voices swirled around her. It was happening again. In the dark and the rain.

'No, this time I am prepared. Not even you are dumb enough to make a mistake like that, Sandra.' Using the girl's name had a striking effect. The monster in her head shrank. Not much, but enough. She said it again. 'Not even you, Sandra.'

'Get stuffed. I do what I like.'

'But now it's different. This time I know exactly who you are. I know your name. Sandra Richards.' She gestured to the smaller sister. 'And Emma Richards. I know her address and the police would have no trouble finding yours. So don't threaten me. It's all bluff. You and I both know it.'

For a second, she thought she had gone too far. The girl's face twisted in a savage growl that she turned on the murmuring figures behind her. 'Shut your traps,' she hissed.

But she was on the defensive.

The monster shrank further.

'Don't kid yourself, you stupid bitch. You got no chance. We'll all have alibis. Your word against ours.' She grinned wolfishly. 'So start running.'

'Your mother could testify. She knows I am here with you.'

'My mother does what I say. She'll give me and Em our alibi. Happy families at home, all cosy in front of the TV. So don't get your frigging hopes up.' She laughed.

It was that monstrous sound that did it. It roared through Jodie's head.

'Doesn't your mother get sick of lying for you, Sandra? Sick to death.'

'What the fuck are you trying to say?'

'To death. About death. What's the difference?'

'Shut that trap of yours or I'll shut it for you.'

'Like you did your father's?'

A shriek rose from the darkness behind the girl. It was Emma Richards. Her sister ignored it. She pushed her face so near that Jodie could see the raindrops on her skin like sweat. There was fear in the shark's eyes. Fear and fury.

'Say your prayers, you bloody little shit.'

The dark shapes closed in. Their eagerness was so rank, she could smell it. The girl reached out and seized her shoulder, as if to pull her into the monster's gaping maw.

She knocked the hand away. 'You killed him, didn't you? You waited until he was too drunk to know what was going on, then poured his own whisky over him and set light to it. It had to be you. Your mother was too frightened and your sister too young.'

'Shut up, bitch.'

'What was he doing? Using his fists to beat up on you all? Or was it sex he wanted?'

'You're dead meat.'

Jodie snatched the torch from her pocket and flicked its beam into the girl's eyes, blinding her for a split second. 'Nothing excuses what you're doing to others now. Do you hear me? NOTHING. You just add to the pain.'

The hand came at her once more. The shadowy figures fanned out. No words left. And that was when Jodie shouted. A wild and warlike release of the rage that was in her. It stopped them in their tracks. It was the signal. By the time the wolf pack had gathered itself again to attack, they were no longer alone in the schoolyard. From out of the deepest shadows by the front wall emerged Matt, and in his hand he held a dog leash.

At the end of the leash strutted Goliath.

Black and brutish with hackles raised, her grandfather's dog was blocking their retreat. Jodie turned the torch like a spotlight on the dog's snarling muzzle and sleek muscles just to enforce the point, but briefly. She did not want to rob him of his night vision.

The effect was instant. Words became irrelevant. The group of girls disintegrated into shrieks as they huddled together and retreated, wolves suddenly transformed into sheep.

Matt herded them against the far wall. 'You left it bloody late, Jodie. I was about to set Goliath loose and damn the consequences, if you had not shouted just then.'

The dog could smell the fear. He was straining to get at the cowering pack. The wait and the tension had been too much for the animal and his taut nerves were quivering at fever pitch.

He was up on his toes, fangs exposed and a low snarl like a death-rattle in his throat.

'Okay, you load of street-scum,' Matt shouted above the row, 'you get the message. You lay a finger on Jodie Buxton ever again and I promise you this dog will be let loose on you. Wherever you run, wherever you hide, he'll track you down and none of your pathetic insults or pleading will cut any ice with him. He'll tear your throats out. Got that?'

No answer.

'Got that?' Matt repeated. He allowed the dog a step forward.

'Yes,' came the collective cry.

'Yes, yes, we've got that.'

But Sandra Richards was ignoring the dog. She was staring at Jodie with undiluted venom. 'You fucking whore, you planned this,' she said in a low voice. 'You kept asking for me to come and see you, just so that you could set this animal on me.'

Jodie nodded. 'Now you're getting the picture. He is my nuclear deterrent. My guarantee of peace. You can't threaten or frighten him. I wanted to speak to you because I was stupid enough to believe there must be a human being inside you somewhere.' She turned her back on the girl. 'But I was wrong. There isn't.'

The rain was falling harder now, its moisture cold on her face. But not as cold as her sense of failure.

Matt was angry. He was striding back and forth in front of them, the dog maintaining its hostile growl. 'Which one of you kicked her ribs in? Which one of you cut her cheek open? You revel in putting people through misery, don't you, but let's see what you're like at taking it? Maybe if you really learnt what it's like to be on the receiving end, you would think twice before you lay into someone again.'

They didn't argue or plead. Just stood there clinging to each other, minds numbed and tongues silenced by fear.

'And don't bother with the cops,' he told them. 'We'll have alibis far more convincing than you come up with. The difference is the police will believe ours, whereas they automatically assume you scum are lying.'

'What are you going to do to us?' a voice whined. It was the dancer, well hidden behind a larger girl.

'They're not going to do anything,' Sandra Richards said fiercely. 'They haven't got the guts. No one is going to release a vicious dog like that on us.'

Instantly Matt loosened the leash and the Dobermann leapt forward, its teeth closing on the edge of the jacket of the slowest girl. There was a scream and a loud tearing of materials as she threw herself backwards and pressed flat against the wall, trying to climb inside the bricks.

'Don't count on it,' Matt warned.

'What's the matter with you?' Sandra Richards taunted him. 'Shagged your brains out, has she? You and her are full of shit, like all your kind. You'd never risk it.'

'I am warning you.'

She laughed.

Matt turned to Jodie. 'Hold Goliath.' He handed the lead to her and started to take off his jacket. 'I don't need the dog,' he said quietly to Sandra Richards.

'Fuck you, you wouldn't hit a girl.' She laughed again, nervously this time.

'Try me.'

Suddenly she was off and running. Disappearing into the rain-sodden darkness before anyone had time to move. A roar of encouragement issued from her wolf-pack.

'Go for it, Sandy.'

'Leave 'em cold.'

'Bugger their threats.'

Matt took off after her.

'No, Matt,' Jodie shouted. 'Stop running.'

Puzzled, he turned. Just in time to see her bend down and very deliberately release the lead from the Dobermann's collar.

'No, Jodie, don't. He'll . . .'

It was too late. The dog flashed past him. It caught the girl as if she were standing still, leapt on her back and together they collapsed in a heap to the wet ground. The screaming and snarling drowned out the shrieks of alarm from the others as they crowded forward. Matt reached the writhing bodies first and seized the dog's collar, but it was Jodie's voice beside him that called out, 'Goliath. Release.'

Instantly, the Dobermann backed off. But he stood only inches away, wolf-eyed and stiff legged, snarling his resentment. A chunk of dark cloth hung from his jaws. Sandra Richards was curled up in a terrified ball, hands clutching the back of her neck, moaning and whimpering like a puppy that has been stepped on.

The gang giggled.

Jodie knelt down and immediately smelt urine. The girl put up no resistance. The duffle-coat's hood was torn into jagged holes but beneath it was the protection of a thick woollen scarf. When Jodie pulled it away, there was no more than a trickle of blood underneath. Goliath had found only a mouthful of material on which to vent his fury.

'She's okay. Shaken, that's all.'

But the blood was on Jodie's hand, as warm and viscous as her own.

She slipped the dog's lead back on. 'I warned her.' She stroked Goliath's back to calm the quivering muscles.

'She knew the risks,' Matt said.

'Like I did.'

He looked down at her, still kneeling beside the girl. 'When you chased her down that alley?'

'Yes. I was like her then. Had something to prove. We both made the wrong choice.'

Goliath's growl alerted them to a sudden movement, as the gang of girls abandoned their leader and scuttled over the wall. The rain gusted after them, wiping out all trace.

'So much for loyalty,' Matt commented in disgust.

'Loyalty has to be earned. She was the one who was jumping ship first, leaving them to sink or swim on their own. Even her sister meant nothing to her. Look at her now, Matt.'

The girl was immobile, huddled in a foetal heap, eyes fixed on the Dobermann's jaws. Matt prodded her with his foot.

Slowly she began to uncurl, but as she sat up, the whimpering started again, soft sobbing sounds that flowed from her mouth as readily as obscenities had earlier. Jodie watched her.

Where was the monster now? Where was its foul breath that had misted the paths of her mind like fog on a motorway?

It was lying dead on the ground. Along with the fear. Shrivelled to no more than skin and bones. Slain by the night's reality. And where it had been, there was a huge empty space in her head. Jodie took a deep breath, sat back on her heels and turned her face and hands up to the night sky, seeking the cleansing rain on her skin to wash away the dirt and the blood.

'On your feet.' Matt pulled the girl upright.

Shock still blanked out her eyes, but some pretence of swagger was returning to her limbs. She shook herself free of him and edged further away from the dog.

'You bastards,' she said, but it was little more than a whisper. 'He could have killed me. Leave me alone.'

'We will leave you alone,' Matt said, 'on one condition. That you leave us alone. That means us, our families and our friends. Do you understand?'

A moan. 'I've wet my pants, you . . .'

'He said do you understand?' Jodie demanded.

'Yes.'

'Because if *anything* happens to any of us, anything at all, I will hold you personally responsible. And Goliath here,' she touched the dog's head, 'has companions who would be only too happy to help out.'

Jodie thought of the black-and-white Tess, who would be more likely to lick Sandra Richards to death.

'You're crazy,' the girl muttered. 'Fucking maniacs. That dog should be . . .'

'Shut up,' Jodie snapped. 'Shut up and get out of here.' She turned her back on her.

The girl needed no second bidding. She walked awkwardly and unsteadily the few yards to the wall and scrambled to the top of it, but instead of dropping down on the far side, she sat herself astride it and turned to face her tormentors. A Humpty Dumpty who had not quite been put back together again. The cracks showed in the tremor in her voice.

'You think you've won, don't you?'

'It's not a question of winning,' Jodie said.

'That's where you're wrong, you stupid . . .'

Matt leapt forward to within an arm's reach of her. 'One word out of place. That's all.'

She dropped her eyes away from him. 'Okay, okay, keep

your filthy hands off.' She swung round to Jodie. 'Ask your frigging father why he was paying me money. Go on, ask him.'

'What?'

'Ask him.'

'I know the answer already. He paid you to stay away from me.'

'Like fuck he did.'

Jodie peered through the damp gloom at the girl perched above her. 'So tell me why did he pay you?'

Sandra Richards eyed Matt and the dog nervously, and then Jodie again. 'You made me look a fool,' she spat. 'Like trash in front of my mates. Well, I'm telling you, you're the fool. Because now your fucking father is in deep shit.'

'My father has nothing to do with this.'

'Get real! He's the cause of this crap. He's the one who started that fire in the first place.'

She was lying. She had to be lying. No way would her father damage his precious school. He would rather set light to himself. Matt and the girl were looking at her, waiting for a reaction, the rain blurring their faces.

'Sandra, you are a thieving, foul-mouthed liar. We know it, your mother knows it, and sure as hell the police know it. You are just another no-hope kid making up crazy stories because of a grudge against a headmaster, so don't think for even one second that anyone will believe you.'

'But it's true.' Her voice was sullen.

'Why on earth would he burn down the building he had just built and was so proud of? It does not make sense.'

'How the fuck should I know? But if it's not true, why is he still paying me to keep my trap shut?'

Jodie reached out and locked a hand round the girl's ankle. 'I advise you to remember what I said just now. If *anything* goes wrong for my family, and that includes my father, you are the one I will blame. You will be dogmeat. Any payments end right here and now. And while I think of it, that goes for Holly Dickinson as well. I want you and your sister to make real certain that nobody touches her again. Got that straight?'

The girl snatched her leg away to the safety of the top of the wall. 'You bitch,' she said miserably and dropped down on the other side. Her fleeing footsteps echoed on the pavement like erratic heartbeats in the rain.

26

The house lay in darkness. Jodie pressed the bell again and this time a light flicked on upstairs, but it was some while before her father's voice called out from behind the door, 'Who is it?' It was wary and unwelcoming, but at one o'clock in the morning, who could blame him?

I blame him.

'It's me. Jodie.'

The door swung open. 'Good God, girl, what are you doing here at this hour? Look at you, you're drenched.'

She ducked in out of the rain and realised she was frozen.

'Come on in the kitchen and we'll find you a towel.'

'No. I haven't come for a towel.'

He stopped fussing. 'So why have you come? What is it that is so urgent it could not wait until a reasonable hour in the morning?'

He looked old. The skin round his eyes was puffy from sleep and the V of his chest revealed by the dressing-gown was mottled and hairless. In his nightwear, he seemed vulnerable. She had come alone. This was something neither Matt nor Goliath could help her with.

'I have spoken to Sandra Richards.'

He did not move, yet something in him seemed to back away from her. 'I see. So are you satisfied at last?'

'No.'

He nodded. 'I thought that would be the case.' He turned and led the way into his study, as if its four walls represented a haven of orderliness that could counteract the fact that his daughter was out of control. Jodie followed and looked round the room. It was rigidly neat. Its shelves were full of tomes arranged in alphabetical order, the objects on the desk in careful alignment, the overhead lighting harsh and revealing. No clutter and nothing personal. Jodie recalled as a child being awed by this room, like in a church, nervous of any summons to its hallowed silence.

'I want an explanation.'

She said the words calmly, the way she did when she was seven and had asked him why it was that men got to rule the world. Even then the calmness had been to hide the shock of the discovery.

'An explanation.' He sat down at his desk and she took the chair opposite. 'What is it you want me to explain?'

'Why you have been paying Sandra Richards to keep quiet. Why you set fire to the science block.'

'Is that what she told you?'

'Yes.'

'And you believe her?'

'Give me a reason why I shouldn't.'

He looked at her for a long time, then dropped his gaze and rested it on the clock on his desk. Its electronic face gave him no grief. 'I could deny it and say she is a liar and a thief. But I won't.'

'So it is true?'

He nodded, but did not look at her.

'Why, Dad?' She wanted him to deny it, to glare at her with offended dignity and climb up on the high-horse of his self-righteousness. 'Why on earth would you do something like that? It doesn't make sense for you to risk a lifetime's career and the school you've devoted your life to. Tell me why you did it.'

Slowly he lowered his face into his hands, his shoulders shrunken, his back bent. 'Because I was a fool,' he murmured.

Jodie hid the shock. She said nothing. Just put out a hand and lightly touched his wrist. His skin felt dry and cold, like dead leaves whose veins no longer carried any life.

He made no comment.

She stood up, suddenly finding his silence unbearable. 'Dad, what's going on? I have a right to know. I'm caught bang in the middle of it, yet you won't tell me what it's about. For some reason that I can't understand, you were involved in the fire and have allowed this girl to blackmail you. So what she claims must be true, that you were responsible for it.' She started to pace the room, as her thoughts raced ahead of her. 'And that means you weren't trying to protect me from her at all. The exact reverse in fact.' She shook her head in disbelief. 'You were keeping her safe from me. You were afraid I would find out the truth from her about your own guilty secret.' She came to a halt in front of his desk and leaned over it. 'That's true, isn't it?'

For a moment, he did not move, then, with the stiffness of an old man, he leaned back in his chair and stared up at her. His eyes were bleak. 'Yes, it's true.'

'Why, Dad? Why did you do such a thing? I don't understand what you could gain by burning the school. And where were the moral standards you've thrust down my throat all my life? It would seem that you believe in one rule for yourself and another for everyone else. Why this insane about-turn?'

Her father's breathing was laboured.

'Because of me.'

It was Anthea. Her voice came from behind Jodie. She was standing in the doorway. A silk oyster-pink nightdress clung to her figure, emphasising the full curve of her stomach, and her dark hair fell loosely around her shoulders, giving no hint in its smooth waves of any rushed departure from a pillow. Groomed and in control even at night. Jodie wondered how long she had been listening there.

'I thought you were in hospital.'

'No, I discharged myself. I was sick of being treated like a dead thing, so came home with Mum and Dad.'

Her father made a gesture of dismissal. 'Go back to bed, Anthea.'

'No, Dad.' She smiled sadly. 'She might as well know the truth.'

Jodie looked from one to the other and realisation slid into place. 'It was one of your wild schemes, Anthea, wasn't it? To make money. The insurance, is that what you were after?'

'I did it for the school's sake,' Anthea insisted. 'For Dad.'

'I should have guessed.'

Anthea shrugged, walked into the room and perched herself on the edge of her father's desk. 'It was a simple plan. There should have been no problems. A small fire as a distraction, the computers stolen while all eyes were on the fire, and hey presto, brand new equipment for the media suite, courtesy of Mr Prudential. An easy scam that hurt no one but got Dad the computers he needed. If you want something in this world, there's no point hanging round waiting for someone to give it to you. You've got to go get it.'

Jodie turned to her father. 'And you went along with this?'

'No, of course he didn't.'

'I did in a way,' her father contradicted her in a low voice. 'I had bemoaned to Anthea the fact that I had a magnificent new science block but no money left to equip the computer technology department the way it should be. Your sister, with her usual flair for the devious, came up with this insurance swindle.'

Anthea tried a laugh, but failed dismally. 'Dad naturally gave it the big "No" at first. But I went ahead anyway. I set it up. Then what should have been a small fire got out of hand and suddenly it was *Towering Inferno* over again. A bloody disaster. But,' she gave a smile, more successful than the laugh, 'the school did get a roomful of new computers out of it.'

'And Sandra Richards. Where did she come from?'

'Oh, for God's sake, Jodie,' Anthea said impatiently, 'can't you ever forget about her? She's nothing. A shitty little nobody I pulled out of a gutter and paid to do the dirty work. That's all. If you hadn't chased after her that night in the car park, none of this would have happened. No beatings, no blackmail. It was only because she was frightened of you sniffing around and of your connection with the newspaper that she threatened us with the police.'

'Anthea,' her father said sharply, 'the blame is not Jodie's. It's ours.' He stood up and corrected himself tiredly. 'The sin is mine.'

'You knew,' Jodie said, barely above a whisper. 'You knew all this, while I was going through hell.'

'Yes, I knew. I knew I was the cause of my own daughter's suffering. Not Sandra Richards.'

'Why didn't you tell me? You could have explained everything.'

'How could I? You didn't see yourself lying in that hospital bed. I could not tell you I was responsible for putting you there.' He glanced across at his elder daughter. 'Anyway, Anthea had put herself in the firing-line for me, and I couldn't be sure what that journalist boyfriend of yours would do about it, if he found out. I could not risk the police.' He ran a weary hand across his face. 'I was greedy; greedy for my school. You have no idea what a constant struggle it is to find sufficient funding for everything.'

'That's no excuse.'

'Don't you think I know that?'

Their eyes held.

'Jodie, I'm sorry. You'll never know how deeply. Earlier tonight you asked me what kind of father am I. The answer is a selfish one.' He shook his head in despair and his grey eyes looked out at her from a world that had crumbled around him. The sight of his feet of clay was ugly. 'You might like to know I have tendered my resignation to the board of governors. I am taking early retirement at the end of this school year.'

Anthea stared at him aghast.

Jodie walked over to his side. 'It's finished now. For both of us. I told Sandra Richards there will be no more blackmail.'

She put her arms around him, the way she should have done on the night of the fire when maybe they could still have helped each other. After a moment's stiffness, he held her close.

'Stop at the station.'

Matt looked across at Jodie, surprised by the sudden instruction. She knew she had been quiet all morning, but that was because there was room in her head for thoughts now. Great open spaces where she could walk without looking over her shoulder. They had been covering a story at the local zoo and he was driving them back to the *Gazette*'s office to get the job ready for the newsdesk before midday.

'Stop,' she repeated.

Matt swung a left and found a gap among the taxis camped like a wagon-train outside the station. 'What now? Not more drama.' After a close look at her face, he added gently, 'Wasn't last night enough for you?'

'Enough for a lifetime.'

'Then what are we doing here?'

Jodie picked up his hand and tucked it between her knees. 'There's something I want to discuss.' She took a deep breath. 'Anthea has offered me a job in London. Henry can pull a few strings, she said. He wants me to come up to town tomorrow to have a chat with a few people. I'm here to book my tickets.'

Matt sat very still. 'You didn't mention this last night.'

'No.'

A small silence settled like ice in the car.

'It's a great opportunity, Jodie. I'm sure you'll knock them dead. If that's what you want.'

'I'm a photographer, for Christ's sake. Of course it's what I want.'

'End of discussion then.'

He took back his hand and pressed the button of her seat-belt. It jumped back, releasing her.

'Thanks, Matt. For everything.' She leaned over and kissed his cheek, then slipped out of the car. Before she walked towards the ticket office, she bent down, gave him a parting smile through the window and was gone.

Matt watched the wind chase a stray plastic bag along the gutter and wrap it round a lamppost, as if trying to throttle it. His own hands closed around the steering-wheel with similar intention. It was not until ten minutes later that she emerged and ducked back inside the car, blue eyes bright and hair ruffled into life by the wind. A freewheeling energy came off her like sparks.

'Tickets,' she announced and dropped them in his lap.

Matt picked them up and examined their mute faces. He turned his head slowly to look at her.

'These aren't to London.'

'No.'

'They're for Bournemouth.'

'That's right.'

'You've bought two returns.'

'I thought it was time to find out if Bournemouth needs a damn good photographer.'

He grinned at her. 'They'll be fools if they don't.' His eyes studied hers. 'Are you sure that this is what you want?'

She put a hand out and rested it on his thigh. 'Yes, I'm sure. More than sure. I don't want handouts from Anthea's guilty conscience, thank you. I'm going to get there myself, doing it my own way. Bournemouth sounds like a good place to start. Whatever the town, people don't change. It's just the way you look at them that changes.' She smiled at him, as if she had never even heard of agoraphobia, and lifted her camera to her eye.